PAYBACK

PAYBACK

KRISTEN SIMMONS

TOR
TEEN

A TOM DOHERTY ASSOCIATES BOOK
NEW YORK

PAYBACK

Copyright © 2021 by Kristen Simmons

A Tor Teen Book
Published by Tom Doherty Associates
120 Broadway
New York, NY 10271

www.tor-forge.com

Tor® is a registered trademark of Macmillan Publishing Group, LLC.

The Library of Congress Cataloging-in-Publication Data is available upon request.

ISBN 978-1-250-17587-8 (hardcover)
ISBN 978-1-250-17635-6 (ebook)

Our books may be purchased in bulk for promotional, educational, or business use.
Please contact your local bookseller or the Macmillan Corporate and Premium
Sales Department at 1-800-221-7945, extension 5442, or by email
at MacmillanSpecialMarkets@macmillan.com.

First Edition: February 2021

Printed in the United States of America

0 9 8 7 6 5 4 3 2 1

For Melissa Frain, who has made me a better writer with every !!!, eye roll, and deleted comma.

Sean, Kiran, Colin, Ross, Henry, and yes, even Andrew, love you, and so do I.

Thank you for all of it.

PAYBACK

CHAPTER 1

'm not feeling it."

Henry Kowalski, the hustler with a heart of gold, rakes his blond hair to one side—a sign I've come to recognize as a nervous tic—as I track two men hurrying through the dark across the parking lot of the NightStar Canning warehouse. They knock on a rusted door marked "Employees Only," and after a quick exchange with a big, burly bouncer, disappear inside, just like the dozen others that came before.

"You've got this," I tell Henry, pulling him behind the corrugated metal wall of NightStar's smoke shack, a free-standing structure twenty yards from the back entrance. "Just follow my lead."

He shifts, the leather jacket he got for tonight creaking against my shoulder. It's faded at the stress points. I know this, because he pointed it out no less than six times. It's supposed to make him look tough.

Now he just needs to act that way.

"No, I know," he says, smoothing down the wild waves of my dark, chin-length hair and absently straightening the collar of my coat. "But what if instead of me being your cousin, I'm a young entrepreneur who's gotten rich off developing this app—"

"No."

"Just listen. It connects athletes with personalized eating tips and hot new workout attire trends—"

"*No.*"

"And I'm looking to blow my tidal wave of cash in a seedy establishment with sweaty men who like to wrestle." He wiggles his eyebrows, and leans closer to whisper, "I've even got a name. Dolph Müller. Good, right?"

A bitter December wind rattles the roof of the smoke shack.

I step closer. Take his warm hands. Try to smile so it doesn't look like I'm about to kill him. I've timed our entrance so we aren't here too early—don't want to draw unnecessary suspicion—but Henry's change of heart is threatening to put us behind schedule. "What if Dolph doesn't speak English and lets me do all the talking?"

He pouts. "You don't like it."

"I like the strong but silent angle more."

He lifts the collar of his jacket, giving me his best tough guy pose, and waits for me to change my mind.

I don't.

With a sigh of resignation, he heads toward the warehouse, and my hesitance evaporates with the confidence in Henry's stride. Soon, we're standing in front of the rusted door, my fist poised under the faded "Employees Only" sign.

I give Henry one last look. His green eyes find mine. For a moment, the weight of this mission presses against my chest. Every day that Dr. O is still playing puppet master at Vale Hall is another day that we're in danger. Charlotte and Sam are depending on us. Margot and all the students before her that Dr. O has erased from existence need this to work.

Caleb needs this to work.

Henry nods.

It's go time.

I knock. The door pulls inward, and a man the size of a school bus hulks in the yellow ring of light above. He takes one look at our faces, ten years younger than the last guys he let in, scoffs, and begins to shut us out.

"Wait!" I cram my foot in the jamb, the rubber sole of my Chucks blocking the exit. "We've got money."

Slowly, the door swings back open. My ears tune in to the raised voices somewhere down the dark hallway behind him.

"What do you want?" The school bus has a cross tattooed on his neck, and a lump of chewing tobacco in the pocket of his cheek. For a moment, I'm back in Devon Park, standing outside Pete's apartment, waiting for his bouncer, Eddie, to let me in.

I imagine they're pulling the same drug-selling routine in prison, thanks to a narcotics bust I kindly set up on their behalf.

"I want to bet on a fight," I tell the school bus.

"Don't know what you're talking about."

The door starts to close again. My worn-out Chuck stays locked between us.

"Girl," he says, clearly annoyed, "you don't move that foot, this door's going to take it off."

Before he can act on that promise, I pull a fold of cash from my coat pocket and wave it through the crack.

Now I've got his attention.

The door opens wide again, and the man's gaze moves from the money to Henry, who wilts under his hard stare. So much for the confident young entrepreneur.

"My dad's out of town," I say with a guilty smile. "He left my cousin and me some pizza money."

The bus's brows flatten. "That's a lot of pizza."

I force a laugh when he doesn't step aside. "So what's the cover? Twenty?"

We both know there's not a door charge, but if a little green is what he needs to let us in, so be it.

"A hundred. Apiece." He smirks at Henry's leather jacket, the zipper of which Henry is nervously jerking up and down.

My face paints a portrait of disgust.

"That's extortion," says Henry, before catching himself. "And I should know. Because I'm kind of a businessman—"

I flatten a hand on his chest to stop him.

"Fifty apiece," I tell the bus. He wants to play? Fine. We'll play.

"Sixty," he counters, and I can see in his hard eyes he's not budging. "And the jacket's mine. It'll look good on my nephew."

He tilts his chin at Henry, whose hand stalls on his zipper midway up his chest.

"*My* jacket?" Henry asks weakly.

"Deal," I say, tugging it off Henry's back. He resists for only a moment, then gives in.

"It's vintage, so you'll want to be—"

He makes a sound like he's dying when the bus snatches it out of his hands. I drag Henry down the hall before he can make a scene.

"That was my lucky coat," Henry laments, looking over his shoulder.

"We all have to make sacrifices, Dolph."

"Got to keep your coat," he mutters.

With the bouncer behind us, my pulse quickens, bringing a grim smile to my lips. I know I shouldn't enjoy this as much as I do—too much hangs in the balance—but running game feels right in a way few other things do. Maybe I'm an adrenaline junkie.

Maybe I was born to be a con.

The linoleum beneath our feet is yellowed and warped around the corners. When we reach a metal staircase, our gazes follow the noise downstairs.

In the center of the room below, two men, already shirtless and bloodied, face off with bare knuckles. One has a tattoo across his back of a coiled rattlesnake. The other is a head taller, with a forehead the size of a three-car garage. Their makeshift ring is marked by orange traffic cones and rope, and behind the rows of jeering fans, cardboard boxes marked with NightStar's logo have been shoved against a conveyer belt.

Snake Tattoo strikes, and a spray of crimson erupts from Forehead's nose.

"I'm positive there are at least five health code violations happening right now," Henry says, wincing.

My chin lifts toward the opposite side of the catwalk, where a group of guys hover near the railing. Two of them are muscle, meant only to guard the bookie—a short man dressed in black, sucking on the end of a toothpick. The rest are pointing at the fight below.

On the fringe, a guy in a red baseball cap chews his thumbnail.

"Hello, James," I say under my breath.

James Rolo—at least that's the name he gives the bookie when he places his bets—has been here three times in the last year. In between, he's made a killing at the Brick Barrel in Amelia, and the Tulane Auto Parts Factory in Sycamore Township—big street-fighting venues on the south side.

I know this, because I've been following him since we bumped into each other—something I made certain didn't look deliberate—on the train two weeks ago.

James always wins. It was just a matter of time before someone figured out how.

Below, the fighter with the snake tattoo is pummeling Forehead into the dirty cement. It's a knockout match. No fouls. No refs. The fans on the catwalk are cheering, fists in the air. They've got big money riding on this. Last I heard, the minimum bet was five large.

"Ready?" I ask.

Time's ticking. I can feel the rush in my blood, urging us to hurry.

"I was born ready," Henry says, then gives a small fist pump. "I've always wanted to say that."

We make our way around the far side of the catwalk, pushing through the small clusters of people watching the fight below. As we approach James, I feel an old swagger take hold. My hips sway. My mouth curves into a grin.

A few feet away from James, we stop, and I lean over the railing.

"You're right," I shout to Henry over the noise. "You can see better over here!"

The comment, purely for James's benefit, isn't a lie. From this side, a smear of blood on Forehead's jaw is visible. The crack and slap of skin on skin echoes off the floor.

I pull back, and do a double take when James's gaze darts away. "Oh, hey!" I slide toward him. "We met on the train a couple weeks ago, right?"

He crosses his arms over his chest, recognition lighting his eyes even while suspicion pinches his features. "What are you doing here?"

His gaze slides over my fitted jeans, my sharp gray coat, and the clean lines of my wavy hair, hanging just below my chin thanks to Charlotte's latest inspiration.

He's making judgments—maybe he thinks I'm too young to be here. Maybe he thinks I'm rich and naive.

He has no idea who I am.

"Same as you, I guess." I give him my most reassuring smile. "Who've you got tonight?"

His eyes dart back to the ring, and he frowns. "McCann."

That must be Forehead, who is now weaving from side to side like he just failed a Breathalyzer. My eyes land on the other fighter, dodging skillfully to avoid McCann's wild right hook. He's in his twenties. Older than the picture in the file I stole from Dr. O's safe.

"Ooh." I make the *too bad* face. "Got a lot riding on him?"

"More than I'd like, given the way it's going."

Probably something like ten grand, which is what he bet on the last two fights. Not an outrageous bet in a place like this, but enough to pull a solid purse if the underdog can actually win.

Slowly, Henry makes his way to the other side of James.

James notices.

"I've got the other guy," I say quickly, bringing the focus back to me.

"Ramos," says James as a cheer erupts across the catwalk for the fighter with the snake tattoo.

"Looks like I'm not the only one." I look down at Ramos. His cheeks are flushed, one eye half closed from an old injury that hasn't quite healed. There's another bruise on his side, a purple oval on his ribs he guards with his right elbow.

I don't know much about fighting, but it's easy to see Ramos knows what he's doing. McCann's angry, his jaw flexed and his eyes wild, but Ramos is focused. His fists are up and ready. He's light on his feet. This clearly isn't his first rodeo.

James pulls on the brim of his hat. "You watch a lot of fighting?"

"My uncle was a Red Gloves champ in high school."

His brows lift in recognition. Red Gloves is a big deal on the south side. Their gyms are always open to kids who need somewhere safe to go, and their fighters always beat the soft, north-end kids. My ex-boyfriend Marcus was all about it until he started selling drugs for Pete.

"I did Red Gloves for a while," says James.

I know. He was wearing an old Red Gloves shirt when we met on the train.

"Really?" I say.

James nods.

Below us, Ramos swings hard, but somehow manages to miss McCann's jaw and stumbles forward.

"Oh!" Henry slaps a hand on James's chest. "Did you see that?"

We're all watching intently now as McCann throws an upper-cut to Ramos's jaw, sending him flying backward into a conveyer belt. McCann takes that opportunity to rush him, raining down punches on the ribs Ramos isn't fast enough to protect.

My pulse kicks up a notch.

"No!" I shout as Ramos falls to one knee.

Henry's gaze heats the side of my face.

I thought we had more time.

One hit ends it, and Ramos crashes to the floor.

The crowd goes crazy. Everyone's shouting for him to get up. People are cursing McCann, who's barely standing himself. Henry's jumping up and down, his arm around James's shoulder. If I didn't know better, I'd say he actually likes fighting.

"Lucky call," I tell James through clenched teeth.

"Very lucky." James's smile is giddy, his eyes bright. He opens his mouth to say more, but behind him, Henry catches my eye and nods.

Time to move.

"See you next time," I say quickly, shoving back from the railing. Adrenaline spikes in my veins as Henry and I push through the crowd toward the stairs.

"We're going to miss him," Henry says beside me.

"No, we're not."

In the ring below, McCann has raised both arms and is strut-ting across the floor. Ramos is back up, rushing away through the NightStar machines. I don't blame him; he was favored six to one to win. He's probably trying to get out before the mob tears him apart for screwing up their bets.

"Go out the front!" I shout. "I'll cut him off before he reaches the highway!"

"On it!"

Henry veers left down the hall where we entered. I hit the stairs at a run, sweat dewing on my hairline as I jump down the last three steps. A hulking machine throws shadows over the cement floor before me. Boxes with NightStar's logo are stacked on wooden pallets lining my path. The fighter is nowhere to be seen. Panic squeezes my temples. I can't come this close and fail.

A dim red exit sign across the floor pulls my attention, and when I squint I see the door below it softly closing.

I sprint toward it, ducking between machines, ripping back the door to find myself beneath a bright security light. The loading docks and employee parking lot stretch to the right. A row of dumpsters to my left lead to the front of the building, and the highway beyond.

Movement draws my attention that way. In the shadows, a man in a thick gray flannel jogs awkwardly away, one hand gripping his ribs. He's not moving fast, and it's easy enough to catch him.

"Ramos!" I call. He doesn't stop, though he must hear me. "Ramos, hold up!"

When he still doesn't slow, I use his real name.

"Rafael Fuentes."

I don't know how he moves so fast. He's injured; he should be slower. And yet before I can dodge out of the way, he's got me pinned against the side of a dumpster, one fist pulled back, ready to strike.

My heart hammers against my ribs.

"Who are you?" His thick brows are flat, his stare hard and unforgiving. Up close, even in the low light, the bruises on his face are more apparent, and make him even scarier.

"A friend," I say quickly.

"I don't think so." His grip on my shoulder tightens. My hands wrap around his forearm, finding solid muscle.

"I can be. I can help you."

The corner of his cracked lip twitches.

"You're one of his." The word warps with disgust.

His. As if I'm owned by someone else.

"I go to Vale Hall," I admit. "I know what happened to you and I know how to make it right, but I need your help."

Rafael exhales in a hard breath. His fist drops. He releases my shirt.

I tip forward, the knot in my stomach unclenching.

Footsteps clatter off the ground, heading in our direction. I catch a glimpse of Henry's golden hair.

Somehow, he's gotten his lucky jacket back, and under the beam of the yellow security light, he does look tough.

"He's with me," I say as Rafael's shoulders bunch at the new threat.

"And I'm very dangerous if provoked," Henry adds. "I recently had a very ugly breakup, and I'm not entirely stable." The leather coat creaks as he raises his fists in a fighting stance.

"How'd you find me?" Rafael demands. He sounds so much older than twenty-three, but that's what the file I stole from Dr. O's office says.

"We knew you were a boxer from your student records," Henry says, approaching slowly. "When we couldn't track you down, we started looking into illegal fights."

"Figured you had to make your money somewhere," I say.

"There are a dozen underground matches a week in this city." Rafael wheezes as he grips his side again. Henry lowers his fists, exhaling his relief that there won't be a confrontation. "None of them ask for names or records. There's no paper trail."

"We didn't need one," Henry says, pride rushing his words. "Brynn pretended to be a waitress at this bar in White Bank. She met the bookie there, and they got to talking—"

"He was complaining about a guy who'd won fifty grand at a fight in Amelia betting *against* the favorite," I say, seeing a flash of recognition in Rafael's eyes. "It was almost like he knew when the fighter would finally lose."

"Or like he'd been tipped off," says Henry. "What's that called? Throwing a fight?"

"A guy could make a decent payout placing bets for a boxer who planned on taking the fall," I say.

Rafael's getting nervous; the panic is welling in his eyes. "You followed Rolo to me."

James flashes through my mind, the brim of his red hat pulled low over his eyes. He didn't suspect me at all when I struck up a conversation with him on the train from his job at a Sycamore supermarket.

"It wasn't easy," I say. "We had to put a tracer on his phone. Like you said, there are a dozen matches a week in this city."

It's amazing what you can order online. Sam found the paper-thin device at a concerned parenting blog. Once we had it in hand, it was just a matter of planting it on Rolo's phone so we could follow him to his next fight.

Enter Henry.

"I took it off his phone tonight," Henry assures Rafael, as if this is our mark's biggest concern. "He'll never be able to trace it back to you."

"Keep it down." Rafael takes a step back. His teeth flash as he searches the dark behind Henry.

I close the gap, feeling Rafael's fear ripple between us. "You win until the odds are in your favor, then you throw the fight." I can't help but smirk. "Only a con can take the fall so convincingly. Anyone else might make the move look deliberate. Like they were fixing the game."

Rafael's expression is a mixture of annoyance and pride. "What do you want from me?"

"We're getting the band back together," I say. "Everyone Dr. O has erased from their life. He's been winning a long time. Now *we're* going to throw the fight. Show him he can't make all his problems disappear."

Rafael holds my gaze for a long moment, his shoulders heaving with each pained breath. My gaze moves from bruise to bruise across his face, and I can't help the pity that storms through me. What has he had to do to survive, anonymously, these last six years? How deep do his wounds go?

He turns toward the freeway, and for a moment I think he's going to walk away and pretend he never saw us. Then his head falls forward, and his chest caves in, as if the weight on his back is too much to bear.

"I was supposed to have a full ride to Arizona State on a boxing scholarship," he says. "They were already looking at me for the Olympics."

He turns back toward us, his back drawing straight. "Dr. O took everything from me. You want to cut him down? Count me in."

I smile and glance at Henry, who's already reaching to shake Rafael's hand.

One more Raven has joined the flock.

CHAPTER 2

Two bus transfers and one hour later, we reach the Sycamore train yard.

We don't have much time. In exactly forty-six minutes, Henry and I will need to drive home from the movie theater where we left the car and our traceable cell phones. It's not easy getting away from Vale Hall without alerting our security staff or Dr. O to what we're doing, and we can't chance getting caught in a lie.

My pace quickens. After two weeks away from what Margot Patel—founder of our resistance operation—has claimed as home base, I'm eager to share our latest victory and get a face-to-face update on everyone's progress.

Plus, it's been nine days since I saw Caleb at the bowling alley where he works.

Not that I'm counting.

"You have to cover your tracks when we meet here," Henry is telling Rafael behind me. "It's top secret, so you should switch up your train routes to make sure no one's following you."

"If this is a setup, both of you are going down with me," Rafael says bluntly.

Henry winces. "Noted. And thank you for the fair warning."

"It's not a setup." I don't blame him for the threat. He has cause for suspicion. He was cut out of Vale Hall without even his own identity. Left to survive on his own with nothing.

As we approach the train cars, I feel the weight of his wariness, even if I know better. Being here reminds me of the first time I crossed this lot, tailing Caleb's shadow to a recruitment rally I had no idea was set up in my honor. It was the first but not the last time I would be conned.

The gravel crunches beneath my feet as we pick our way over the last set of tracks, lit only by my phone's dim flashlight. Ahead, the abandoned trains are lined up in rows, tagged by old graffiti and empty apart from spiders, rodents, and old wooden shipping crates. I count three rows down, then cut in at a rusted caboose, nerves prickling up my spine as we pass the dark freighters and approach the railcar marked by a white spray-painted wolf.

Henry knocks on the closed door three times.

"The password is *blue butterfly*," he says, tone serious.

The door cracks, and inside, a metal bolt slides loose.

"For the last time, Henry, there's no password." The door rolls back to reveal a girl in a puffy blue coat and jeans, her long dark hair braided over one shoulder. She holds a lantern in one hand up to reveal her mile-long lashes and a narrowed gaze.

Margot Patel, the burned, ex–Vale Hall con artist, is a far cry from Myra Fenrir, the bright-eyed waitress at the restaurant where we met. Even now, in the light of the lantern, I can see the intensity in her gaze, the way she measures threat in everyone who crosses her path.

"Rafael, this is Margot," I say. "I think you'll find you two have a lot in common."

Margot flinches, and digs her hands into the pockets of her coat. "Did Dr. O kick you out and hire a hit man to murder your boyfriend Jimmy too?"

Rafael's brows arch. "Nah. He told me if I talked, they'd find my kid brother at the bottom of a lake."

My eyes round. Beside me, Henry whispers, "Yikes."

"Margot," she says with a grim smile.

"Raf."

Behind Margot, two people have risen from the foldout chairs, and my heart gives a hard throb when Caleb Matsuki appears beside her.

I soak in his charcoal hoodie and jeans. His shaggy black hair.

His eyes meet mine through the thick frames of his glasses. *You okay?* they seem to ask. My chin dips in answer.

"Raf?" From the ledge, Renee Gibson gapes at him, her eyes growing glassy. She's a couple years younger than he is, and thin as a rail, with coiled black hair. We didn't realize until Caleb brought her in last week from a shelter in southern Michigan that she and Raf might know each other. I thought she might help us find him, but even the mention of running a con had her hands shaking.

"Renee?" Rafael climbs into the car, searching for any threats hidden in its corners before giving her a quick hug. "What happened?"

"Long story." She scowls, then shakes her head impatiently. "I looked for you for a while."

"I was hard to find."

"Me, too." She gives a breathy laugh.

I grab the edge to follow Raf inside, but am held back by a wave of unsteadiness. When Henry and I leave tonight, we'll return to a mansion with a private education, a cook, and our own giant plush beds. Those inside the car have been barely hanging on since their expulsions.

Even though we're on the same side, the divide between us feels like a valley.

I should have brought food. Gotten out money at the ATM. Something. But we don't have time. We're on the clock, and need to get back before the others get suspicious about how long we've been out.

Henry clearly doesn't feel the same guilt, because he jumps into the car and throws his arms around Caleb.

"Nice coat," Caleb says.

"I *know*," Henry answers. "It was almost stolen tonight, but I rescued it."

They don't do the awkward pat-on-the-back, half hug. They embrace like brothers, and watching them loosens the knot in the center of my chest that was tied the night Caleb got kicked out.

As Henry launches into a play-by-play of tonight's events, complete with sound effects, Caleb crouches, and extends his hand in my direction. He only glances my way, still focused on Henry's story. The move is so casual, so second nature, that it feels wrong not to accept.

Our fingertips brush. My palm slides against his. His grip

tightens, and as he pulls me into the railcar, my stomach does a little flip-flop, like we've driven over a bump in the road too fast.

He lets go as soon as I'm up, and my sudden rush is halted as he slides the heavy wooden door closed behind me. It shuts out the breeze, but not the cold, leaving the air thin, and smelling like rust.

The railcar has been swept clean. It's lit by half a dozen windup lanterns. A construction spool serves as a table on one side of the space, topped by a police scanner, a deck of UNO, and some boxes of crackers and cereal. Positioned around it are crates and foldout chairs, and two sleeping bags and nasty egg-crate foam mats lean against the far wall.

Henry's now running in slow motion, glancing back as if someone's chasing him. Leave it to him to make our mission sound like an action movie.

"So did you find Penny?" I interrupt.

"Kind of." Caleb sighs.

"She's scared, and I don't blame her," Margot says, breaking from her conversation with Renee and Raf. They're standing in front of the far wall, where Caleb has pinned the pictures of the expelled students from the files I stole from Dr. O, along with any notes of their whereabouts. Strung across the top of the collage are cutout snowflakes Henry insisted on putting up last visit. If this train car had an outlet, I'm sure he'd hang twinkle lights too.

Margot reaches for a picture of a petit blonde in a Vale Hall polo and tears it down.

"What happened?" asks Henry.

"I found her yesterday at a halfway house in Dayton." Caleb folds his arms over his chest, and I'm struck by the clean tips of his fingers. He used to have ink stains on his left hand from all the architecture drawings he would do, but those have faded away.

The knot yanks tight again in my chest.

"Strung out on Wednesday pills," Margot adds with a bitter smile. She pulls down the card beneath the photo that lists Penny's hobbies and potential places she might have gone after Dr. O sent her away.

I know more than I should about Wednesday pills. Not just

because our school director is an owner of Wednesday Pharmaceuticals, but because the pills my mom's ex-boyfriend Pete stole and sold on the street were all marked by that tiny *W*.

"You didn't bring her back?" Henry asks. "If she needs help . . ."

"She ran," Caleb said, and it's evident in his rough tone he's taking this failure personally. "I tried to talk to her. She didn't want anything to do with us or Dr. O."

A solemn silence falls over the group—for this girl none of us knew.

For this girl any one of us could have been.

"There were eight other files," Henry says, rallying hope "With Renee and Raf, that leaves six people still out there to find."

Caleb scowls. "Will, Jackson, and Sierra are all locked up. I matched their pictures on an inmate database this morning."

Their images come to light in my mind. Will and Jackson, brothers with lanky builds and desperate lights in their eyes. Sierra, who could have been a prom queen, an attribute I'm sure Dr. O recognized when he sent her out to gather blackmail on his marks. Three more people, just like me, who ended up in jail because of our director.

"Okay, this is bad," says Henry.

He's right.

"There's still three files left." I swallow, my throat dry. "If we find and bring them in, we'll have eleven of us—Raf, Renee, Caleb and Margot, me, Charlotte, Henry, and Sam."

It feels like a lot, and not nearly enough. Are eleven stories condemning enough to threaten Dr. O's carefully laid reputation?

"Sounds like ten too many."

I bristle at Margot's tone. She's been edgier these last few weeks, more desperate than ever to shut down Dr. O. I don't blame her—she lost someone important to her, and hasn't exactly been living in luxury since—but it catches me off guard. When we worked together at The Loft, I thought of us as friends.

At least, as close of friends as two people who are lying to each other about their identities can be.

"We'll make a stronger case together," I say carefully. Caleb's eyes flash to mine, and my cheeks heat.

"The bigger the party, the bigger the mess," Margot says. "This should have been quick. One person on the inside needed to take him out. That was it."

She looks at me.

My skin prickles.

Taking down Dr. O was Margot's idea, I get that. She started this, and when Caleb refused to compromise our safety, she chose me to end it. But there are other ways to destroy a person besides *taking him out*. There are still students at Vale Hall we can't forget. And there are people out there like Caleb—like *her*—who need our help.

I won't turn my back on them.

"What *is* the plan?" Raf asks. "What are we going to do—go to the cops together? They'll never buy this story."

I shiver at the idea of it. When I was a kid, a cop came to my school. He smiled, and handed out badges, and called himself a community helper. But he wasn't like the other cops I'd seen in our neighborhood. When they drove by the mini mart, they didn't smile and shake hands. They slowed their cruisers, and waited for those on the corners to break up their conversations and rush home. They patrolled Devon Park like a prison yard, and when I saw them, I knew to keep my head down and my hands out of my pockets so they'd know I wasn't hiding anything inside.

The thought of going to them now makes me wary.

"No cops." Margot tosses Penny's picture on the table, facedown. "Dr. O has ties with the police. He has connections all over Sikawa through his charity programs and politicking. Who knows who he's got on the hook through one of his students' blackmail."

I cringe. I was one of the students doing Dr. O's bidding just a few months ago.

"We're going to do to him what he does to his marks," I say. "Use what we know against him. Threaten to expose him if he doesn't give us back everything he promised—identities, futures, all of it. Then we're going to tell him to get as far away from the city as possible."

"Expose him? You mean go public. Talk to the press." Raf's skeptical gaze turns my way. He's not happy I roped him into this, and I get it. You can't knock out a prizefighter without a strong punch.

"Yes," I say. "Dr. O thinks he's untouchable with all his secrets but we've got secrets too, and he can't make us all disappear."

Caleb's watching me intently now, the corner of his lips tipped in the smallest of smiles.

He's not at Vale Hall anymore, and even if getting him kicked out wasn't my intent, that's on me. I promised to fix this, and I'm doing it. Not just for him, for all of us.

"What happens to the school?" Renee asks. "If Dr. O has to leave, you know he's burning Vale Hall to the ground on his way out the door."

"The board will take over," Caleb says. "If anything happens to the director, the school's maintenance falls to a board of directors. They're mostly ex-students. They'll be invested in keeping our affairs private."

"And their own affairs private too," I add. Dr. O doesn't just provide room, board, and an excellent education. He provides scholarships, and contacts in the field of your choice. He sets up kids like us, who don't come from much, with a real future.

It's a lot to lose.

"Can you imagine if Damien left *Kings of Rochester*?" Henry gasps. "Right after his mom's cousin betrayed them with that diamond thief last season? That would be *awful*."

"Who?" asks Raf.

"Damien *Fontego*," Caleb and I both say at the same time, then smile. As famous as Damien may be, I will always think of him as the guy who showed up to my recruitment rally and kissed my hand. "He's currently the board's president," Caleb adds.

"More importantly, he's an Emmy Award–winning actor," says Henry, looking personally offended. "Shooting on location in Baltimore, although I heard on *Pop Store* that he's being heavily recruited for the new *Mutant X* reboot." He cups one hand over the side of his mouth and stage whispers, "There's supposed to be a shower scene with Davis Reynolds."

"I've heard of Fontego," says Raf. "I didn't know he was an alum."

"I didn't know the school had a board," adds Renee.

Neither did I until Sam told me about it a few weeks ago. *More of a looks-good-on-paper appointment,* he told me. It was necessary to have a board to be considered a legitimate private school, but they clearly didn't have much oversight of the day-to-day activities.

Raf scratches his chin, brows drawn together. "What's to stop Dr. O from saying we lied? There's no record some of us even exist, much less went to his school. For all any reporter knows, we're just a bunch of scammers targeting some old rich guy."

"It's risky," Renee agrees. "He can turn this around in a heartbeat. I've seen him do it."

She's right, and her doubt is a needle through my confidence. Dr. O is dangerous, but what better option do we have? Even if we wanted to, we can't go to the cops. I'm sure he has legal connections that will keep him out of jail. The best option we have is to beat him at his own game—blackmail. To talk about what Vale Hall truly is, and the conning he's made us do to earn our places there.

"He can't stop all of us. Not with what we know," I tell her. "He needs to be afraid of us for once."

"We're being careful," Caleb says. "Renee's right, if he calls our bluff—if we go to the press and there's an investigation—none of us will get our identities back. All the people who went through the program will be under a microscope."

"That's best case," says Margot. "Worst case, he uses his connections to retaliate and we all end up in a ditch somewhere like Jimmy." Her voice cracks, and she tilts her head back, as if blinking at the ceiling will stop the tears. "He needs to pay for this. He's literally getting away with murder."

I glance at Caleb, his expression grim as he crosses to her and pulls her against one side. He's just being a good friend, but I can't help the spike in my pulse as I see the way she fits against his side. How she turns her face to his shoulder and leans into him like it's the most natural thing in the world.

And it was. Before Caleb was my boyfriend, he was hers.

"We're going to stop him before he hurts anyone else," Caleb says.

"We need more people," Henry says. "Current students, like

Brynn and me, and Sam and Charlotte. We're enrolled in the program. He can't say we're trying to scam him; we have too much to lose."

"Who else would risk getting kicked out?" Caleb's hand covers Margot's now on his chest, but he's looking at me.

I focus on Henry. "Joel would do the right thing."

"If we can convince Paz," Henry adds.

He's right. They're a package deal these days, and Paz knows she's got a good deal at Vale Hall. Still, Joel was friends with Caleb, and took it hard when he was expelled.

"Most of the others are too scared to go against Dr. O," I say. They're not wrong. I once thought of him as a vigilante, masked in a private school director's suit. Now I wonder if he's the villain, who will do anything to make the world match his vision, even if it means stepping on his own students to rise to the very top.

"Or they're scared Belk or Ms. Maddox will turn them in," Henry adds.

I nod, picturing the brick-set security guard and Vale Hall's silent, elderly housekeeper, who has a penchant for eavesdropping. Both of them are as loyal to Dr. O as lapdogs.

The thought reminds me that we'd better wrap this up soon. The last thing Henry and I need is either of them spying on us.

"Imagine if either of them came out against Dr. O," Margot says quietly. "Maddox alone has enough secrets to destroy him. She's been there from the start."

"Good luck with that," I say. I've run enough cons to know when a mark is a dead end, and neither Maddox or Belk is budging.

"What about June?" Henry asks, bringing to mind our newest sophomore, decked out in goth clothes. "She's all about sticking it to the man."

"June Park," Caleb says, turning to me. "She's new. How well do you know her?"

Not well. She's only been at Vale Hall since Caleb left. Dr. O had him vetting her before she was accepted into the program.

She seems all right, but every time I look at her, I think of Caleb, and steer the other way.

"I'll check it out," I tell him.

He nods, dark eyes filling with caution, like they do every time I offer to help. "In the meantime, I've got a lead."

"Who?" I ask.

"Dylan Prescott."

Dylan is the oldest of the expelled students in the files. He's twenty-six now, and no one's been able to find any information on him since we started.

"He goes by a different name now," says Caleb. "Charlie Mc-Ginnis. He was picked up by local police in Mason two nights ago and released on bail."

Caleb listens to the police scanners and checks the listing of arrests daily—that's how he knew some of the others we were looking for are locked up. A con on their own with nothing to lose is bound to brush up against the system at some point.

Lucky Dylan got out before the cops could look deeper into his past, or lack thereof.

"What did he do?" asks Henry.

"He was caught racing on Highway Sixty-two," says Caleb. "It's an initiation run for the Wolves."

A chill crawls down my spine as again, my eyes find Caleb. We have history with the Wolves of Hellsgate. Caleb's assigned mark at Vale Hall was the mayor's daughter, Camille, and after he reported her mom's secret meetings with the motorcycle club to Dr. O, Camille retaliated by turning Caleb in to the Wolves.

The only reason we're still standing here is because we managed to divert their attention to my mom's train wreck of an ex, Pete.

Caleb points at the bright-eyed ginger on the wall beside us. He can't be more than fifteen in the picture, and I can hardly imagine him in a leather cut on a motorcycle. "Dylan—or Charlie, I mean—is patching in to the Mason charter two days from now. The after party's at a diner owned by one of the members. It's a good entry point."

"The Wolves are bad news," I say.

"I thought this was a no-student-left-behind operation," Raf scoffs.

I bristle at his words. "I'm just saying it's dangerous."

Henry puffs out his chest. "It's a good thing danger is my middle—"

"No," says Caleb, reaching for his shoulder. "You and Brynn have been gone a lot. I've got this one."

He's right—there's only so many excuses we can make for disappearing from school—but that doesn't mean I like what he's proposing. "Someone might recognize you."

"My only contact with the Wolves is in jail," Caleb says, his grim look adding, *thanks to us.*

"I'll go with him," says Margot.

Every eye turns in her direction. She may want to bring Dr. O down, but she hasn't exactly been a big supporter of pulling in other students to help with the operation.

"What?" she says, tilting her head at me. "Someone's got to have his back."

Heat shoots up my collar. Margot might be a better con than any of us, but I'm not ready to stake Caleb's life on it. If he's recognized, they won't just beat him up like last time. He'll be lucky to die quickly.

I'm trying to catch his eye when Henry elbows me in the side.

"If we don't go soon, I'm going to turn into a princess."

"I'm not sure that's how Cinderella works, Henry," I say, but he's right. It's late, and we're cutting it close. The only reason we got permission to go to a late movie on a Sunday night was because we told Shrew it was a documentary on foreign relations—something that might help us in class as we begin our Model United Nations activity.

"We need to get back to school," I say, guilt burrowing through me again as Renee sends me a narrowed glance.

"Enjoy my bed," Margot says, reminding me that before her expulsion, my room was hers.

I'm sure I'll sleep like a baby now.

Caleb starts to follow us to the door when she stops him with a hand on his biceps.

"Can I crash at your place again?"

Again?

Caleb's eyes dart to mine. "Sure. Of course."

It's nothing. He's just looking out for her. He'd do the same for anyone.

I'm 98 percent sure.

"Bye," Henry tells Caleb with another hug, and in the dull glow of the lantern, I can see the bruises beneath his eyes from the nightmares he refuses to tell me about.

The nightmares only Caleb could fix.

"Be careful," Caleb tells him. "I mean it, okay?"

I want to hug Caleb too, but I hesitate before stepping into his arms. We've barely touched since our breakup, and even though I know there's still something between us, we haven't said the words.

We have bigger things to worry about.

I tell myself that a lot.

"See you later," he says. Maybe it's just me, but it looks like he wants to say more.

Walking away feels like tearing off a Band-Aid, and as Henry and I hurry out of the maze of train cars to the swells of gravel and tracks, I look back over my shoulder.

"Someone needs to keep an eye on Margot," Henry says, nervously finger-combing his hair as he glances back over his shoulder.

I know he's not talking about her staying with Caleb, but it feels that way when a thread of jealousy weaves through my rib cage.

"Agreed," I say, realizing that Caleb might be the only one who can.

CHAPTER 3

I wake to an elbow in my face and the indentation of M&M's pressed into the back of my arm. Before I can form a coherent thought, Charlotte Murphy sits up, her wild, orange hair sticking out on one side.

"Wake up. Tell me everything."

She was sleeping when I got in last night. My head's still cloudy, but I vaguely recall scooping up the M&M's she'd spilled on the sheets and curling up in the corner of the mattress. The girl spreads out like a starfish.

"Ten minutes." I roll over.

She rolls onto me.

"I passed out reading *The Awakening* for English. They should call it *The Asleepening*. Anyway, you were supposed to get me up when you got in." Her back is smashing me down into the mattress. When I open my mouth to gasp, I inhale a mouthful of her hair.

"Gross. Get off." I swipe the hair away and try to dislodge her, but she's stuck like glue.

"Did you find Rafael?"

She says the name in a whisper, but it still triggers an alarm in my brain. Now I'm wide awake.

"Yes. Yes, okay?"

She slides off my side, and pulls up the covers over our heads. We're in a tent now, pinpricks of early morning light siphoning through the holes in the fabric.

I turn on my side to face her.

"He's in. It was a little dicey for a second, but we pulled it off."

"Good."

I'm not sure if she's talking about Raf or the M&M she spots and pops into her mouth. I make a face, and she gives me a look that says not to judge.

"Details," she demands, grabbing the bag and spilling it, on purpose, between us.

As we eat a breakfast of champions, I tell her about the fight, and Henry's smooth grab of the magnetic phone tracker. How Raf ran after he lost, and his wariness going to what Caleb now has me calling *resistance headquarters*.

"How is Caleb?" she asks, as if reading my mind. She rolls on her back, lifting her knees so the blanket stays tented overhead. She's got a tiny baby bump these days, but it's hard to tell unless you're looking.

She's banking on that with the staff at Vale Hall, who haven't seemed to catch on to her growing obsession with baggy clothes. It's a good thing it's sweatshirt season.

"He seems all right," I tell her, shaking away the thought of Margot spending the night.

They're just friends.

Who used to date.

I remember, with a pinch to my side, that this used to be her room—this bed was where she used to sleep. Maybe she even shared it with Caleb.

Isn't that a lovely thought.

"I wish he was here," Charlotte says, fingertips walking across her belly. "I wish we were all together."

"Me, too."

My throat grows tight with the reminder of how little time we have left together. After the semester is over, when Charlotte and her boyfriend, Sam Harris, take off to see their families for the holidays, they won't be coming back. They'll disappear, change their names, and have their baby far away from where Dr. O can find them. We say we're going to find a way to see each other again, but I'm not sure how.

An image forms in my mind of the four of us in caps and gowns, but quickly slides out of focus. No image of graduation is right without Caleb.

"It's going to be okay," I tell her, too hopefully.

Sometimes I think it would be better if she just left now. Grab as much as she can, and find a safe place to hide. But if she runs with the secrets she has, what's to stop Dr. O from sending someone after her?

I won't let him hurt her.

"It's going to be okay," I tell her again, more firmly.

My phone rings.

I jolt up, reaching over her to grab it off my nightstand. The time on the corner says it's just after seven, and Henry's goofy smile is lighting up the screen.

Fear clutches my chest. We see each other every morning before class. He wouldn't call unless there was a problem.

"Henry? What is it?"

"Brynn. Hey! Good morning. How are you? Look, I think you should come downstairs and have breakfast. Like, now would be great. Sound good? Good."

"Um . . ." I'm already scrambling out of bed, grabbing my jeans off the floor. "What happened?"

"Great waffles down here," he says quickly. "Don't want you to miss out. Okay, bye!"

He hangs up.

Charlotte's out of bed, face pale. She's spilled the M&M's again in her rush.

"Is he okay?"

"I don't know. He says we need to go downstairs. Now."

Without another word, she launches herself toward the door and runs into her room. I switch shirts to a clean sweater, and meet her in the hall between our doors. She's pulled on Sam's NYU sweatshirt over her pajama pants. It's big enough to cover what she's hiding underneath.

We race past the other doors, most of them closed, toward the spiral staircase that leads to the kitchen. Cold whispers over the back of my neck, despite the heat in my blood. I see Caleb behind my closed lids, holding a box of his possessions as he's kicked out of Vale Hall. Is someone else leaving? Has the staff figured out what we're doing?

There are a dozen things that could go wrong on any given day.

But when we reach the bottom floor, there's no trouble. Ms. Maddox, the housekeeper, is making waffles in the kitchen, and Min Belk, our PE teacher/security guard, is standing at the counter, giving Charlotte and me a cold, appraising look as he fastens a tie around his blunt ponytail.

My gaze darts away. Since I left my job hostessing at The Loft three months ago, I've avoided him as much as possible. I don't know for a fact that he was behind Matthew Sterling's intern supervisor, Mark Stitz, getting jumped, but it was a rare coincidence if not. Belk was scoping out Mark pretty hard after I told Dr. O that Mark may have had knowledge of Jimmy's disappearance. That night, Mark ended up in the hospital.

Across the kitchen, in the living room, a crowd of students has gathered around the television, between the enormous Christmas tree Ms. Maddox put up last week, draped with gold ribbon and glass ornaments, and the menorah over the fireplace. Henry and Sam stand in the back, their arms crossed and backs curtain rod straight. It looks like they're watching a speech, or a press conference.

"What's going on?" I ask, sliding up beside Henry. The shadows are deeper beneath his eyes this morning, and I can't help wondering if he had another rough night sleeping.

Sam is focused on the television, but slides an arm protectively over Charlotte's shoulders.

"Breaking news," he says with a tight grimace. "Look who's back on the job."

On the screen, a woman stands behind a podium in a crowded room. I don't have to read the caption beneath to recognize her.

Mayor Erica Santos.

". . . relieved my name has been cleared from the recent accusations," she's saying, "but I always knew justice would prevail—that Sikawa City's hardworking police force would come to the truth." She holds a fist in front of her chest, her expression determined, her dark eyes focused. She's as clean cut as any ad I've seen of Matthew Sterling. Her hair is perfect. Her blue suit modest and professional.

"I have always maintained that I was innocent throughout this investigation. That I was threatened by the Wolves of Hellsgate Motorcycle Club to turn a blind eye as they brought violence and drugs into our great city. I did what I had to, what any mother would do, to protect her child. But I refused to compromise the safety of our great city."

"Isn't that sweet." At the front of the group, Geri Allen twists a silver necklace around her finger. It's not even eight, but her makeup is on point, and her black sweater dress clings to every curve.

The sight of her puts me on edge. Not just because she's Geri, but because her father is the hit man Dr. O hired to kill Margot's boyfriend.

Mayor Santos reaches to the side, and a pretty girl about my age in black pants and a white flowered top steps beside her. My throat tightens.

"Oh, wow," says Henry.

"Camille Santos," Sam mutters.

Charlotte grabs my hand.

Camille Santos is the mayor's daughter.

And Caleb's mark.

The only reason the accusations about her mother meeting with the Wolves were made public was because Caleb brought them to light. He befriended Camille. Went into her home. Caught her mother in the act.

Dr. O used that information to blackmail the mayor and start an investigation that should have led to her dismissal. It was an effort to clean up the city, to get rid of the corrupt officials that were tearing it apart.

But now the investigation is over, and somehow the mayor has been cleared of the charges.

It doesn't make sense.

The mayor pulls her daughter close. "Now that the truth is finally out, and the people behind these threats and accusations have been properly punished, my family can return to their lives, and I can return to working hard for our citizens."

"Oh, great," says Henry.

"I see now, more than ever, we need to crack down on the crime tearing this city apart."

I'm not the only one tensing at her words. Cracking down on crime means more police presence. Not in the posh north side neighborhoods like where Vale Hall is, but definitely in places like Devon Park, where I grew up, and White Bank, where Caleb's family lives. It's something that's going to make the mayor's loaded donors feel safe—like the dangers of the world only exist outside their gated communities—but that will leave people in less fortunate neighborhoods very uneasy.

We don't need more cops with arrest quotas and itchy trigger fingers. We need better houses and community centers so kids like me aren't out running scams because they can't afford to put food on their tables.

Just weeks ago, one of our own senators was arrested for the murder of an innocent woman. Matthew Sterling told us he would fight for families. That he believed in the safety of our children." She looks directly at the camera, and my stomach bottoms out. "Matthew Sterling lied."

Charlotte's hand squeezes mine harder. In front of us, Paz tosses her long brown hair over her shoulder, reminding me of how she and Joel might be useful allies—a package deal. "That's all you, girl."

I try to smile, but my mouth is frozen.

The others know I was involved with bringing Matthew Sterling to justice, but they don't know the real truth. That the senator is in jail because Henry planted evidence—Susan Griffin's phone—at his house, and that Matthew Sterling is actually innocent.

Only a few of us know who actually killed Susan Griffin.

The thought of it, even now, makes my stomach clench.

"Glad she's finally catching on."

Charlotte and I jerk apart. Behind us stands Grayson Sterling, wearing a black Vale Hall T-shirt and jeans. His dark hair is combed back and wet, like he just got out of the shower. His lips tilt in a bitter smile.

The same smile he wore the night he told us he'd run Susan off the road not as an accident, but because Dr. O told him to.

Henry stiffens beside me. His hands ball into fists. I link my arm around his elbow.

"Easy," I whisper.

"His father's in jail because of me." Henry's voice quivers.

I feel his anger. Grayson fooled us both, and now Matthew Sterling and Caleb are paying the price.

"We need more strong-willed warriors in this town," Mayor Santos goes on. "People who will stand up for what's right. People who really believe in family, and supporting our children. Matthew Sterling has been dismissed from the U.S. Senate, and I am delighted that the state legislature has appointed my recommendation for interim senator to fill his position."

A slick and bitter dread fills my chest as a man in a navy suit takes his position on the other side of the mayor. He lifts his chin, gaze scanning the room with a determined kind of hope, a confidence that says, *Trust me. Believe in me.*

"What's he doing there?" Henry asks.

"What do you think?" Geri says flatly.

Mayor Santos beams. "I would like to introduce you to a person with *real* family values, who knows how to put children first because he does it every day in the school he runs. Our interim U.S. senator, Dr. David Odin."

CHAPTER 4

Whoa!" Paz is the first one to speak. "Did you know? Did anyone know?" She elbows the broad-shouldered boy beside her hard enough to make him grunt.

"I had no idea," says her boyfriend, Joel. He looks back at us, brow furrowed.

"It makes sense," Geri says, but she's obviously shaken. Her finger is so twisted in the silver necklace, the tip is turning purple. "He's always going on about making the world a better place, isn't he? Now he can really do it."

The reporter is giving details about Dr. O now—showing a picture of him in front of Vale Hall, and talking about his long-standing reputation as a community philanthropist. He'll be sworn in on New Year's Eve, and will begin work in January.

I don't know what to say.

Charlotte, Henry, Sam—we're all gaping at the TV. Even Grayson doesn't seem to know what to say. His gaze is flat, like he can't even see the screen at all.

A tentative hope lifts my chest. If Dr. O is becoming a senator, does that mean he's leaving the school? The board could take over for him—maybe they could reinstate Margot, Caleb, and the others.

But Dr. O would never let that happen. He can't allow people he's erased back into his school. They're a liability. They know too much.

What's he planning to do with those of us still here? Use us to spy on other politicians? Blackmail us to keep his secrets?

Three weeks until New Year's Eve, when Dr. O is sworn in. We have to stop him before he takes this game to the next level.

"Well, good for him," says Bea, pulling absently on one of the silver dangly earrings I haven't seen her wear before. "We should throw a party to celebrate, right, Charlotte? That reporter said there's a ceremony on New Year's Eve. That's enough time, isn't it?"

My jaw clenches. I may be consumed with bringing Dr. O down, but there are others who still worship the ground he walks on—who don't know about Susan, and Grayson, and what happened to Jimmy Balder.

"Uh." Charlotte, normally the first in line for party planning, blinks.

"Maybe you should plan the next event, Bea." Sam squeezes Charlotte's shoulder. "Our finals this semester are brutal. I'm not sure there will be time to put together a party."

He gives her a knowing look. One that says they have other things to plan, like an escape.

My stomach sinks.

"Right," says Charlotte with a tight smile. "Someone's got to pick up the torch, right?"

Bea clasps her hands and bounces on the balls of her feet.

"Hello? Am I not standing here?" Geri shoves in front of Bea. "I'll do it. You can address the invitations, Bea."

Bea deflates. "Fine."

"I'll help you, Bea," Paz says, a little too eagerly. The worry on Joel's face as they all walk away reminds me of Henry's suggestion at the train yard last night. Joel might have his concerns about Dr. O, but he's not rocking the love boat.

Not yet, anyway.

As the others move toward the kitchen for breakfast, our circle closes. Charlotte's shoulder aligns with mine. Henry and I are already connected. Sam closes the gap.

"What is this?" Charlotte mutters.

"I didn't even know he wanted to be a senator," says Henry.

"We're screwed," Sam says. "If we thought he had power before, we were wrong."

He's right. A U.S. senator votes on legislation that changes the country. If he can make people disappear as an ordinary citizen, what will he be able to do with the law on his side?

I need to call Caleb. I keep a burner phone in my room, hidden in the back of my closet for emergencies. I've never used it before, but now feels like the time.

Our rebellion just got fast-tracked.

Charlotte's cringing. "It had to have been planned from the beginning. He probably wanted Sterling arrested just so he could slip into this role."

"That's what they're doing." Henry glances at me, worry drawing his brows together. "We knew he and Grayson were in on something together. It had to be this."

I nod, but it doesn't sit right. Dr. O was genuinely shocked when he learned the phone had been planted on the senator. He'd wanted to blackmail Matthew Sterling, not take his place.

Sam runs a hand over his jaw. "First, he uses Caleb's intel with the mayor to spark an investigation on corruption, then he alleviates the pressure by offering her an out. He makes her problem with the Wolves go away so she can vouch for him for senator. It's brilliant, if you think about it."

"It's diabolical," says Henry.

"Diabolical? You aren't talking about me again, are you?"

I turn to find Grayson striding over, a waffle in one hand like a giant chip. Any wariness from the announcement is gone now, shrouded by the playboy mask he wears so well.

I don't know how much he heard, but we need to be diligent. Grayson has secrets, the kind he's willing to send his innocent father to jail to hide.

"You forgot a plate," I say, motioning to the waffle.

He takes a bite.

Henry looks offended. "How can you eat that without syrup?"

Grayson chuckles under his breath.

"Hungry?" Sam asks Charlotte, his hard gaze staying on Grayson.

"Starved," she says flatly.

Grayson smiles as they leave, amused at being the obvious reason for their departure.

I plant my feet and cross my arms over my chest. "Pretty wild that Dr. O's filling your dad's position."

He tilts his head. "Is it?"

I look for some sign that this has affected him, that he cares that his father is in prison and will be tried for a murder he didn't commit. But I find no remorse. No fear. Nothing.

"How long have you two been planning this?" Henry asks, unable to hide the betrayal in his voice. It's always there when he has to talk directly to Grayson.

It's often there when he just looks at him.

"Awhile." Grayson takes another bite, avoiding Henry's gaze completely. "More important question: how was the movie last night?"

A muscle in his throat ticks. He may think he's as smooth as a politician, but I know a deliberate topic change when I hear one. We're hedging in on something he doesn't want to discuss.

"Fine, I guess." A dozen unwanted memories claw at my control. Him hitting a security guard at Riverfest. The fear in his eyes when he told me violence runs in his family. His fist in my shirt the night he kissed me in the pit.

I believed every bit of his act.

Part of me still does.

"What'd you see?" he asks.

"*Oceans Between Us,*" I tell him, at the same time Henry blurts, "I-don't-remember-I-was-too-busy-making-out-with-my-new-boyfriend."

Grayson's gaze shifts to him.

A flush rises up Henry's neck. He focuses on what must be the most interesting button in the world on the bottom of his shirt.

I wonder just how many times he's practiced that line in his head.

"Wow," Grayson says. "And here I thought you were still hung up on me."

A few of the others are listening now. Alice. Beth. I catch sight of Geri on the outskirts of the group, smirking in my direction.

"He was never hung up on you," I say.

"Jealous, princess?" Grayson asks. "Maybe next time we can double date."

I glare at him as Beth and Alice snicker. "You wish."

"Why do you do that?" Henry asks.

Grayson's head tilts. "Do what?"

"Pretend like nothing matters. Like you don't care about anyone or anything." Henry's voice is firm now, unwavering. He doesn't seem to care that Bea and Paz have joined Geri's crew of eavesdroppers.

My hand slides from his arm.

Grayson stares at him. His mouth opens as if he's going to deflect the accusation with some witty comeback, but nothing comes out except a weak laugh.

"Oh, man," says Geri, loud enough for everyone to hear. "You really do have it bad for him."

Henry's gaze shoots to Geri, stepping out of the group and into our business. "No, I don't."

"Clearly." Geri's smile is filled with challenge. "I'd bet twenty bucks Grayson's name is circled in hearts in your diary."

Great. Geri stirring up drama is exactly what we all need.

"I don't . . . even have a diary," Henry stammers.

"Come on. Let's go get breakfast," I say. If this becomes a contest of who hides their feelings best, Henry will lose every time.

Geri ignores me, her attention now 100 percent on Grayson. "And I'd bet another twenty Grayson here has developed some kinky fetish collecting Henry's socks or old bottles of hair gel."

"His boxers actually," Grayson says, making the red in Henry's face spill down his neck. The others are gawking now, but Geri's speech has given Grayson a chance to recover, and he actually seems to be enjoying the attention.

"Let's go." I try to pull Henry away, but he shakes me off.

"No, please stay," Geri says with a sigh. "The tension between the two of you is making it hard for the rest of us to study, so if you could just kiss and get it over with, that would be great."

"Kiss?" Henry sputters. "*Him*? Are you serious?"

"You didn't seem to mind before," Grayson offers.

"I knew it," I hear Beth whisper.

"Stop," I tell Grayson. "Henry. Breakfast. Geri, go be you somewhere else."

"Suit yourselves," she says. "But when the sparks burn this place to the ground, don't say I didn't advocate for a peaceful resolution." She glares at me as if this is my fault, then, with a little hair flip, she strides off to class.

"Was that fun for you?" I growl at Grayson as Henry storms off to the kitchen. Geri sticking her nose where it doesn't belong is expected, but beyond the sport of it, I don't know what Grayson could possibly get out of humiliating his classmates. He's old pals with Dr. O, which means he's the top of the food chain here. He knows we can't fight back.

"Come on. We were just playing around."

As I try to pass him to chase down my friend, his fist closes around my arm. He leans close.

"You should play around a little too," he whispers. "People are starting to notice."

The room around me slows. Quiets. Fear pulses in my eardrums, echoing the cannon fire of my heart.

"Hands to yourself, Sterling," comes a low voice behind us.

Grayson's fist slowly unfurls from my arm, but his icy imprint remains on my skin, chilling me to the bone.

Hugh Moore is standing in the threshold of the living room, looking menacing with his hard gaze and crisp, black suit.

I exhale, remembering I have a front to maintain. Moore may work for Dr. O, but he's got our backs. He's one of the few people I trust here—not just because we're from the same rough neighborhood, but because he's been there when I've needed him. Hard-browed, and annoyed, and steady.

"Yes, sir." Grayson salutes with his half-eaten waffle.

"Get a plate, this isn't a zoo," our head of security warns. He's been watching Grayson closely these last few months—there's hardly a day I see Grayson where Moore isn't somewhere close by.

Maybe it's taking a toll on him, or maybe he's sick, but as Moore moves closer, the bruises beneath his eyes become more apparent, and there's a fine layer of scruff on his jaw, as if he hasn't shaved.

Grayson looks at his hand in surprise. "I knew I forgot something."

Without another word, he joins the others in the kitchen, leaving me unsteady in his wake.

People are starting to notice.

Was that a warning or a threat? If he's caught on that we're sneaking out to the tracks, he could tell Dr. O or Belk. My mind flashes to my mom, currently at her cush job as a receptionist at Wednesday Pharmaceuticals. What will the director do to her if I step out of line? Where will she go if the apartment set up through her work is suddenly taken away?

She's in danger, and so are Caleb, Margot, and the others.

So are *we*. Henry and I could be expelled. We could be the next ones to disappear.

Cold fear brushes against my raw nerves. I haven't been careful enough. I need to be ready for anything.

"Good morning," Moore says stiffly, watching Grayson strike up a conversation with Geri. "Ms. Shrewsbury wants to see you. She's in the gym."

I cringe at the mention of our Senior Studies teacher. I've finally caught up with Vale Hall's curriculum so that I can graduate on time. What could she want?

People are starting to notice.

"Okay," I tell Moore, giving him another once-over. He doesn't look good, but this isn't the time or place to ask about it. With a nod, I head toward the pool outside, and the gym beyond it.

Threat or not, Grayson's right. I need to act normal, and that means carrying on even when the world around me is spinning out of control.

CHAPTER 5

The Shrew is preparing for our schoolwide Model United Nations activity when I enter the gym. She's positioned small tables and chairs around the glass walls, and moved a podium into the center of the floor.

"You wanted to see me?" I ask.

The birdlike woman squints in my direction, batting at a stray silver curl with one of the small country flags in her hands.

"Yes. Come here, Brynn. We have something we need to discuss."

My stomach churns as I walk toward her. Has she noticed my absences? Is that what Grayson meant? I've been careful. Diligent in my efforts to keep what happens at the train yard a secret.

"Okay." I stop just out of arm's reach. It's not like the old lady's going to wrestle me into a submission hold, but I'm ready to bolt anyway.

"What are your plans?"

Sweat breaks out on my hairline. "Sorry?"

"Your plans," she repeats, as if she expects me just to spell it out. "Where do you see this going?"

I take a slow step back, sweat dampening my hairline. "See what going?"

"*This,* Brynn. Don't play the fool, I am well aware what that brain is capable of."

I swallow.

"College," the Shrew says, exasperated. "You've heard of it, I'm sure."

College. My plans for the future. Obviously that's what we're here to discuss.

"Oh, right. I haven't really figured that out yet." *I've been too busy plotting against your boss.*

"Well, when, exactly, were you planning on doing so?" she asks. "You're up to speed on your coursework. You'll be taking the advanced placement exams in the spring. Your SAT scores aren't stellar, but they'll be enough with Dr. Odin's recommendation."

Urgency drips into my veins. Once, getting out of Devon Park was all I wanted, all I could think about. Now I have bigger problems—friends who are depending on me to fight for them. A future that's relying on our plan to outsmart the smartest con I've ever met.

My problems are here, and I can't leave until they're fixed.

"I was thinking maybe NYU?" I throw out the first university I can think of—the one Sam got early admission to before I ever came to Vale Hall.

"Why?"

"Because . . ."

Shrew's head tilts. "What do you want to do, Brynn? Who do you want to *become?*"

I don't know.

Heat rises in my cheeks. I have a plan to get through today. A plan to gather Vale Hall's expelled students and for us to take our stories public so we can bring down Dr. O. A plan to call Caleb as soon as I get a free minute to run upstairs and grab the burner phone. But I have no idea what I want to do after that.

I'm not particularly good at anything but conning.

Shrew moves closer and rests her flag-clad hands on my shoulders. I stiffen, unsure if she's going to try to shake me. She isn't particularly soft when it comes to delivering bad news.

That's kind of why I like her. She doesn't pretend things are fine when they're not.

She doesn't lie.

"It's time to start thinking about these things," she says, in a way that makes me want to forget about resistance headquarters and focus on that original plan that drove me to Vale Hall in the first place: getting out of this messed-up city.

"I will help you get anywhere you want," she tells me. "But you have to give me a direction. Do you like the literature we've read? The environmental studies section we did? Anything related to history or business? I know you've done well in Mr. Moore's Vocational Development class. I don't love the idea of you going that direction, but maybe something in acting? Geri's lining up college visits already. Theater is always an option."

I didn't know Geri was doing this, and knowing she's got the jump on me makes my jaw tighten like I've just eaten something sour. But it also reminds me of another actor that went through this school. Damien Fontego.

Will he side with us when Dr. O leaves the school?

I can't think about college while the director still has the power. While he's leveling up to the U.S. Senate, and Caleb and Margot are on the streets, and any of us might be cut loose or offed by a hit man.

"Think about it," Shrew tells me. "We're going to revisit this soon. I want you to think of three interests before then."

"Okay," I say. And then, because it seems like she does actually care, I add, "Thanks."

A rare glimmer lights her eyes. "Don't make me regret believing in you."

I try to make a quick exit, but between the news and our little run-in with Grayson, it's already time for class. Sam and Henry are the first to arrive, Grayson following with a smirking Geri beside him. The sight of them makes me uneasy. That's an alliance I wouldn't trust if the world depended on it.

Normally we're separated by year, but because of the UN activity, all twenty-nine students are present today. The crowd is a good distraction for me to sneak out and warn Caleb about Dr. O's new play, but as I walk by Paz and Joel, I run straight into Min Belk.

He's my least favorite of the two security guards, and not just because he gave me a B in last summer's ballroom dancing section of PE. He's as loyal as a bloodhound, and anything he sees or hears is delivered straight to the director.

"Going somewhere?" he asks.

I jolt back. "I . . . um . . . forgot to brush my teeth."

"Ew," says Paz over one shoulder.

"I was in a hurry," I tell her. Which is true, but now that I've brought that fact to light I'm extremely aware of my own dragon breath and cover my mouth with one hand.

"Here." Behind Belk stands the newest addition to our student body. June is taller than me by several inches, and is wearing black boots, black jeans, a black corset over a black long-sleeved tee, and enough black eyeliner to rival Cleopatra.

She fishes a box of mints out of her backpack and tosses them to me.

Belk smiles.

"Thanks," I mutter.

"Here to serve," she tells me, reminding me of how we first met at a restaurant when she was a pocket-picking waitress, and I was running game on Matthew Sterling's staff.

"That guy's a ray of sunshine." She motions toward Belk, now moving tables where Shrew points. "His vocational development class is about as much fun as a kick to the face."

Over the past month, Vale Hall has implemented its conning curriculum, though with several notable changes. The first is that Min Belk has taken over for Moore, a fact which none of us is particularly delighted by. The second is that all materials and readings relate to sales, and marketing yourself, and other perfectly legitimate career advice, even if the underlying point is that we'll use this knowledge to do exactly what Dr. O wants.

I glance across the room to Grayson again. Though he comes to the other classes, he never attends Vocational Development. I guess that's because he's already mastered the skills. He conned me from the start.

"Yesterday Belk told me I'd stand out less on a job if I changed my makeup," June says, dabbing a finger at the corner of her dark painted lips. "It's a shame he was so distracted by the way I looked." She lifts her wrist and pulls up her sleeve, flashing Belk's bulky silver watch she undoubtedly lifted without his knowledge.

I grin, thinking of the meeting last night at the train yard. Maybe June would be a good asset to the resistance.

"Watch yourself around him," I say.

Her gaze holds mine for a moment, then darts away. "Watching myself around all of you, but thanks."

She saunters off toward Joel, then glares at him until he gives her his seat.

Charlotte hurries in, toting my messenger bag over one shoulder. She's already put my UN research binder inside, and when I reach for it, I find a protein bar too.

"What was that all about with you-know-who?" she whispers, pulling me toward one of the seats at the table marked "Australia."

I glance around her to where Grayson, Geri, Alice, and Beth have clustered at another table. They're all laughing as he waves the blue and white flag in the air.

It feels wrong. The first time I saw him he was a loner, barely acknowledging those he'd invited to a party at his own house. Now I can't tell if that was the real Grayson, or this is.

"Nothing," I tell her, straightening the red, white, and blue Australian flag we pulled out of Shrew's UN box last week. "He was just trying to embarrass Henry."

"He's such a jerk."

"I can think of better descriptors." Sam joins us, Henry at his side.

"I want to attack Switzerland," Henry announces. The fierce determination on his face sets off a new alarm in my brain.

My gaze flicks to Grayson, who's now tucking the Swiss flag behind Geri's ear.

Henry's fists clench around his laptop.

"That's aggressive," says Charlotte. "But I'm in. Do we have nuclear bombs?"

"No one attacks Switzerland," Sam tells us. "Switzerland is neutral."

"Switzerland is definitely not neutral," I say. With Grayson and Geri on board, I'd be surprised if this entire Model UN didn't end in the third world war.

"We'll take them down," Sam assures us. "Just wait until we get to communications technology in industrial development or the growing demands of sustainable energy." He laughs.

Henry and I stare blankly at him.

"I love it when you talk dirty," Charlotte says.

Sam winks at her, making her giggle.

"What did Shrew want this morning?" He lowers his voice, focusing the conversation my way.

I'm about to tell them about the whole what-do-you-want-to-be-when-you-grow-up inquisition when I catch a glimpse of the NYU emblem on the sweatshirt Charlotte's wearing. Sam's going to be an engineer; he once told me he's known since he was seven. Charlotte's always wanted to go to law school. She wants to help kids like her, and prosecute those who try to hurt them. Even Henry announced a few months ago that he wants to be a social worker. If he gets his master's in it, he can even be a therapist.

Maybe plans have been changed due to the baby, and our precarious situation with Dr. O and Grayson, but at least they had plans. I can't see anything beyond right now.

Nerves crackle just beneath my collarbones.

"Nothing," I say. "She had a question about my physics quiz."

Charlotte frowns.

"Good morning, Ravens. Welcome back to the prep stage of Vale Hall's Model UN," Shrew announces, more pep in her voice than should be legal for anyone talking about diplomacy. "Let's get to work on those research binders. We need facts. History. Treaties, conventions, and resolutions. It's our last day for exploration. Opening statements start tomorrow morning—that's when stuff gets real, as you kids like to say." Joel gives her a fist bump as she walks by. "Remember, the country awarded the highest marks will be the next proud caretakers of our favorite mascot."

"So I'll just keep Petal in my room then?" Geri asks sweetly.

Vale Hall's prized silver, spray-painted piggy bank has traded hands many times over my months at Vale Hall, but has been residing in Geri's room for the last two months since Henry handed her over. He couldn't stand keeping her after his ballroom dancing victory with Grayson.

With Petal on the line, everyone is quick to get to work. Voices rise as people open their laptops and begin searching for useful research for the coming days. I've just taken out my binder when Ms. Maddox, our nosy housekeeper, enters the room, pushing a fancy silver cart topped with mugs of what looks like steaming coffee.

Shrew approaches her, and after reading a note on the tray, snorts and motions for Ms. Maddox to pass out the drinks.

"Students, it seems that Switzerland has already chosen to begin negotiations with a peace offering. Swiss hot chocolate, to help you conduct your research."

At Switzerland's table, Alice and Beth exchange a high five as Geri smiles victoriously down at her binder. Grayson leans back in his chair, fingers woven behind his head, but when he grins our way, there's a strain around the corners of his eyes that doesn't match his team's delight.

If I didn't know better, I'd say this was an actual apology.

"Why is he torturing me?" Henry groans. "He knows I love hot chocolate!"

Irritation heats the back of my neck as Grayson raises a mug in our direction. Whatever flash of worry I thought I saw is gone now, and all that remains is a smug look of satisfaction.

"Sam," I say, "we have to destroy Switzerland."

I DON'T HAVE another free, unmonitored moment until after lunch, when I fake a trip to the bathroom to duck into my room and grab the burner phone. I haven't called Caleb on it before; we said it was only for emergencies.

Dr. O has rigged the game to become a U.S. senator, and is using Caleb's old mark to do it. This feels like an emergency to me.

I quietly lock the door behind me. Ms. Maddox is downstairs prepping dinner, and Belk is teaching the underclassmen PE. Moore is taking someone to a job in the city, but I'm not worried about him. It's the other two who are always listening.

My palms are damp as I reach for my copy of *A Tale of Two Cities* on my bookshelf beside the desk. It looks like any of the other books Shrew has assigned since I've been here, nothing anyone should notice if they happened to snoop around. As I open the cover I take a few seconds to flip through the drawings Caleb did last summer. Pictures of buildings he's seen and wants to see. Pictures of me that morph over the pages into graceful towers and fountains.

A knot ties in my throat.

I flip to the back of the book, where I've cut out a block of pages and hidden the small black phone inside. It takes only a moment to turn on.

No messages. No missed calls. I check every night before bed—that was our agreement. Caleb leaves his phone on—no one cares if he's carrying a burner—but if I get caught, I'm in trouble.

I need to hurry. If Shrew doesn't notice I'm gone soon, one of my classmates will.

My fingers dial the numbers I've repeated in my head a hundred times.

It rings once. Twice.

"Answer," I mutter.

Caleb picks up before it can ring a third time.

"Hello?" He's out of breath.

"Hey, it's me."

"Brynn."

The way he says my name makes my throat tighten, even as my pulse slows. There's not an hour that passes I'm not scared something bad might be happening to him, and hearing his voice, even under these circumstances, is a relief.

"What happened?" he asks. "Are you all right? Where are you?"

"Here," I whisper, hurrying into the closet. I know the doors aren't soundproof, but I slide them closed anyway. "At school. I'm fine." My arm sweeps to form a gap in my hanging clothes and I sink to the floor, back against the wall.

"Henry? Charlotte and Sam?"

"They're fine. Did you see the news?"

He blows out a breath. "Yeah. I saw."

I can picture him raking a hand through his black hair.

"Can you believe it?" I whisper. "Do you think this was his plan when he sent you in with Camille?"

"I don't know." His voice sags with regret. Caleb may be good at conning, but his moral compass points truer than the rest of ours. He always felt bad about hurting the mayor's daughter, even after she sent the Wolves after him.

Caleb's moving. I can hear the click of a door, and then the rush of traffic outside. "If I didn't know him better, I'd say Dr. O was improvising. You said he was surprised when Sterling was arrested, right?"

"Yes." I remember right after the cops took him to jail. Dr. O called me into his office, demanding I tell him if I had anything to do with it.

Henry and Grayson were off the hook. The director might have suspected their involvement afterward, but he never questioned Henry, and as far as I know he didn't talk to Grayson either.

"All he ever told me was that he wanted Mayor Santos out of the picture. He said she was corrupt. Once I saw her meeting the Wolves, I figured he was right." A siren on his end grows louder, then fades. "Now I'm wondering if he set those meetings up. For all we know, Sterling's Senate seat might always have been the endgame, and he just played us all to make it happen."

Caleb's right—this doesn't sound like improvisation at all. It sounds like deliberate scheming.

"You all have to be careful," Caleb says. "He had a ton of free-dom as the director, but people will be watching him once he takes the Senate seat. If any of you step out of line—"

"We're done, I know."

We're both quiet a moment, imagining what that looks like.

"How are you?" I ask him, my voice thin.

"Okay. Not bad. I mean, considering." He gives a rough laugh. "Actually, I had some good luck."

"Yeah?"

"I went to pay rent this morning and Joe said not to worry about it—until *summer*."

I picture the old man who owns the bowling alley where Caleb lives and works. He's crotchety on a good day. I wouldn't exactly take him for the charity type.

"He's letting you work it off?"

"No, he's still paying me. He said he had more leagues sign up than usual, and I should save my money."

I don't buy it.

"You don't think he's lying, do you? No one knows where you are?"

"If they did, I doubt they'd be paying my rent."

Fair point. But it still doesn't feel right.

"Maybe you should move, just in case. We have an assignment for conning class—how to get something for free without stealing it. I can say I'm practicing tomorrow. We can look for a new apartment."

Grayson's words whisper in the back of my head. *People are starting to notice.*

It doesn't matter. If Caleb's in trouble, I'll be there.

"I'm all right," he says softly. "Thanks, though."

I bite the inside of my cheek.

"I was actually going to call you," he adds. "Margot's . . . not feeling great."

My chest clenches. "Is she okay?"

"Yeah," he says. "It's just . . . cold at HQ. She needs a place to crash."

Headquarters. I imagine the drafty train car at the abandoned lot. It's a step up from Margot's last apartment—a shared studio next to the bus depot she was afraid to go home to.

"Right." I know Caleb will look out for her, but something about his tone has me waiting for the other shoe to drop.

"She's not going to make it to the Wolves rally in Mason tomorrow night."

The plan to make contact with Dylan Prescott, aka Charlie McGinnis, flashes through my head.

"Hold on," I say, reading between the lines. "That doesn't mean you're going alone, right?"

"It's not going to be a big deal," he assures me. "It's not a closed party—there'll be lots of people there who aren't members. I'll wait until Dylan's alone, and—"

"Nope." I'm shaking my head. "Not a chance, Matsuki. You may not remember last time you crossed paths with the Wolves, but I do. Probably because I didn't have a concussion."

I shiver, recalling too easily the night he called me down to the pit. His face and ribs were a mess of bruises and cuts. His lip was sliced and swollen. His glasses were in pieces.

This might be a different charter, the man responsible for Caleb's attack might be in jail, but I'd just as soon chew off my own foot than let Caleb go alone.

"You and Henry were just out. Sam's got his hands full, and none of us want Charlotte risking more than she has to."

"What about Raf?" I ask. Renee isn't ready; she's still too scared.

"Have you seen the guy? He's a ticking time bomb."

He's right. Forget the bruises and injuries, Raf looks like he's waiting for another fight. Bringing him to a motorcycle gang's party isn't a smart idea.

This is why we need more allies, like Henry said.

"What's wrong with Margot? How do you know she won't be ready by tomorrow night?"

"She won't be," says Caleb, in a firm, protective way that puts me even more on edge.

"Then it's me." I push myself up off the wall. "I'm going with you."

"Not a chance, Hilder."

I can hear the cocky smile in his voice.

"We can't miss this window," I say. "Once Dylan's patched in, he'll be a Wolf. Who knows when we'll be able to get close to him again?"

"I told you, I've got—"

"I told you, I'm going with you."

He's quiet. If I didn't hear the traffic in the background, I'd think he'd hung up.

"Since you're clearly not taking no for an answer, why not? Let's go to a Wolves party. It'll be fun."

Now I smirk. "Or we'll die."

"Or we'll die."

I need to get downstairs. We've been on the phone too long.

"I should go," I say, just as he says, "See you tomorrow?"

"Yes," I say, and then laugh, because he says "Right" at the same time.

I don't want to hang up.

I don't think he does either.

"Brynn?"

His quiet tone pulls at me. "Yeah?"

"You can call me when there's not trouble," he says. "If you just want to talk, I mean."

My skin warms.

"Okay."

"Be safe," he says.

I tell him goodbye. Then I tuck the phone into the book, hide the book on my shelf, and start planning how to use our Vocational Development assignment as a cover so I can leave Vale Hall tomorrow night.

CHAPTER 6

Tuesday morning is consumed by a study session for our English final, opening statements in our Model UN, and the fallout of Grayson's smooth promise to work diligently with the representative from Australia—*Henry*—to provide anything our country might possibly desire.

In response, Henry shuts off all trade and negotiations with Switzerland, spurring a tidal wave of whispered speculations of what is really going on between the two "countries." He then spends the remainder of the session angrily drafting messages to all the participating nations that Australia and Switzerland have never been involved in negotiations of any kind, and that taking further bribes of hot chocolate will be considered criminal and punishable by the UN human rights committee.

Team Switzerland finds this very amusing.

Dr. O remains unseen through the morning, and by the afternoon it's apparent Belk isn't coming back from driving him around. I ask Moore for permission to go Christmas shopping so I can work on my conning class assignment, and since I don't have my license yet, I need Charlotte to join me.

He reluctantly agrees, but only if we take Henry, whose sudden Eeyore attitude is upsetting the balance of the house.

Cons and killers Moore can take, but Henry on an off day is too much.

Not that I mind. Since our night on the roof when Grayson confessed he'd driven Susan off the road at Dr. O's command, Henry and I have become unbreakable friends. I'd trust him with my secrets and my life. But it's less suspicious if both of us aren't always out together.

By five the three of us are in the Jeep, and after a short detour to pick up Caleb at a train station in Uptown, we're heading north toward Mason.

"You look beautiful, Charlotte," Caleb says, sliding into the back seat across from me. I figured shotgun was the least I could offer Henry after this morning's Grayson drama.

"I can't button my pants anymore," says Charlotte. "And all I want is cake and barbeque chips."

"Ugh, same," grumbles Henry.

Caleb raises a brow my way, but I shake my head, telling him not to ask.

"Where's Sam?" asks Caleb.

"Holding down the home front." Charlotte's voice is light, but I catch a glimpse of her worried brows in the rearview mirror, and know she wishes he were here.

Caleb shrugs out of his hooded sweatshirt, revealing the black long-sleeved thermal underneath that hugs every line of his chest and arms. The bottom of the shirt has come up a little over his belt to reveal a strip of copper skin, and the indentation of his abs has me mesmerized.

Until he looks over and catches me, and then I fix my stare on the back of Henry's seat.

"Sam's a great guy," says Henry, combing his hair over his forehead with an impatient hand. "Really thoughtful. Caring. He probably hasn't even tried to kill anyone today! You have great taste in guys, Charlotte."

"Sure do," says Charlotte with a weak laugh. "Music?"

"Music," says Henry.

Charlotte turns on the radio, and soon pop music is blaring from the front seat.

Caleb slides down, leaning my way.

"Why does it feel like we're driving on eggshells?" he whispers.

I lean his way, and our shoulders bump.

"Things are a little tense at school right now," I say quietly. "Geri's putting together a big party for Dr. O's swearing-in ceremony. She reserved a ballroom at the Rosalind," I tell him, picturing the historic pink hotel in Uptown. "She's inviting everyone. Politicians. Law enforcement. Big donors."

Recognition flashes in Caleb's eyes. The Rosalind was where I first learned what had happened to Susan Griffin, and said good-bye to Marcus, my old boyfriend.

The last I heard from him, he was thinking of trying out for the baseball team at his new high school in Baltimore. He was even kind of excited about it.

"Also, Charlotte's growing a human and Henry's declared war on Switzerland."

"He what?"

I smirk. "Doesn't matter. They've just got a lot on their minds."

"What's on your mind?" he asks.

His question catches me off guard. I inhale, breathing in his spicy scent.

"Aside from how we're going to recruit a Wolf? You know, the usual. Staying alive. Cramming for finals. Figuring out what I want to be when I grow up."

His shoulder shifts against mine, but he doesn't pull away, and soon we're propped up against each other, watching the gray sky darken over the highway between the two front seats.

"What's the verdict?" he asks, shoving a pretend microphone in my face. "How are *you* going to save the world, Brynn Hilder?"

And just like that, the old Caleb and Brynn are back.

"I have a three-step plan," I say into his fist. "First, plant lots of trees. We all could use a little more oxygen."

He smiles.

"Second, equal access to Rice Krispies treats. I'm talking big, gooey ones. Any time of day."

"Remarkable. Your third step, Ms. Hilder?"

"Thank you for asking, Mr. Matsuki. Third, I'm going to build a colony on Jupiter. So much attention wasted on Mars and the moon. Let's think bigger."

"What about that giant red tornado in the eye that's bigger than Earth?"

"What about it? We didn't get this far playing it safe, did we?"

He's grinning as he drops his hand. "I guess not."

Quiet settles between us.

"Are you leaving town?" he asks. "You always wanted to get out of this place."

I pick at my thumbnail.

Caleb's right. I always did want to get out of Sikawa City. But now when I think about it, all I can see are the problems I need to fix before I go.

"I'm kind of living in the moment," I say, giving my reality—that I can't imagine what the future looks like until we bring down Dr. O—a nice spin.

"Me too," he says.

I glance over at him. "What about med school? Or the architecture thing?"

He shrugs, the brush of his arm against mine sending warm shivers down to my fingertips. "Is there a college program for hustling bank managers? Because it turns out I'm pretty good at that."

My brows rise in question.

He frowns. "Dad's hospital bills are piling up. He had a trust set aside for college for me and my brothers—not a lot, but enough to get us through a few more months. Turns out the bank needed his signature to switch the account."

I imagine Caleb walking into the bank. Using his father's name. Tricking the manager to get access to that money.

I'd be impressed if I didn't feel so bad about it.

"Trying to take one day at a time," he says.

He has his identity back—I gave it to him when I stole his records from Dr. O's safe—but if he tries to go to school or applies for his GED, there's a chance Belk or Dr. O will find out and come after him. He can't take that risk.

He can't move forward until Dr. O is under control.

"It's a stand-up thing you're doing for your family," I say, my whole body warming. "Your dad would be proud of you."

I picture Mr. Matsuki, lying still in that bed at the rehab center, breathing and eating because of a bunch of tubes, unable to even open his eyes.

"I wish I could talk to him," Caleb says, then clears his throat.

My heart clenches.

"What do you think he'd say?"

Caleb's mouth quirks at the corner. "Take care of your mom and brothers. Get good grades. Quit worrying about me."

"I'd like to have met him."

I regret the words as soon as they're out of my mouth. I have met him. It's not like his father's dead, he's just not conscious.

"I'm sorry, I didn't mean—"

"It's okay," Caleb says. "You'd like him. He told the worst jokes. And he was really smart. Family always came first. Loyalty was a big deal to him."

Family. Loyalty. Sounds a lot like Caleb.

The back of his knuckles brush mine. Then he straightens his hand, and links his pinky finger around mine.

I hold my breath as warmth cascades through my veins.

"He loved this city. He loved trying to make it better. He made me want to make it better too."

I think of all the buildings in Uptown Caleb knows by name. The love of architecture his father gifted him. We used to think we could save this city by working for Dr. O, but now we know the only way to do that is by removing him from the picture. He's more dangerous than I ever thought possible. I can see it now that I'm not desperate for the home, the food, the *chances*, he'd once dangled in front of me.

If he becomes senator, he will do anything to cover his tracks. Margot knows this too well. I refuse to let Caleb, or my mom, be another problem the director needs to make disappear.

"When this is all done, we'll figure out your next step," Caleb says. "I'll help you look at colleges. We'll put together a three-step plan: College. Future. The world."

A huge sigh rushes out of me.

He smiles.

I smile, even after his finger slips out of mine.

As Charlotte and Henry dance to the music, Caleb and I fall into easy conversation. He tells me his mom is working long hours cleaning, but still makes the trip to his dad's rehab hospital every night. His brothers are trying to help out as much as they can.

Christopher's in a comics phase and is obsessed with the new Hulk. Jonathan is teaching himself how to skateboard, but sucks at it and falls every five feet.

"He's doing it for a girl, I think," Caleb tells me. "Some freshman down the street."

"An older woman," I say, wiggling my brows. Jonathan's in eighth grade. "I thought he was saving himself for me."

"Nope, that was his big brother," Caleb says with a smile.

An hour later, we reach Mason.

Charlotte parks in the back of the lot for a designer brand outlet mall right outside the small town. The shops are decorated with white and red lights, and around every door and overhang are twists of green garland. As we step out of the Jeep, the breath fogs in front of our faces. I hug my coat closer, watching Caleb pull on his hoodie again.

"You should take my jacket. It's good luck." Henry's already sliding out of the worn sleeves. It's clear he's anxious about our mission.

"That's all right," says Caleb, pulling a gray knit hat out of his pocket to shove over his head. The black tips of his hair stick out around his ears and at the base of his neck. "It's not that bad."

His nose and cheeks are pink, but the coat, vintage as it may be, will stick out in a diner filled with black leather cuts. Caleb's dark hoodie is much less conspicuous.

Henry bites his thumbnail. "You sure you don't want some backup?"

"We got this," I tell him. "Keep your eye on Charlotte. Make sure she gets me something good for Christmas. No weird clothes."

"Die in your jeans and Converse shoes, see if I care," Charlotte mutters. But she hugs me anyway. "Don't mess around."

"Never," I tell her. "Back in an hour." I slip my school-issued phone, which security tracks the whereabouts of, in Charlotte's purse.

With that, Caleb and I turn away from the mall and begin walking at a brisk pace down the sloping sidewalk toward the cluster of fast-food restaurants at the corner. Past them, three-quarters of a mile down the road, is a dive called the Greasy Spoon, where, according to Caleb's intel, the Wolves are holding their after party.

I can see it in the distance, lit by neon lights, and surrounded by dark farmland on either side of the road. Not a lot of cover if we have to make a quick exit.

We need to make sure we won't.

"All right," Caleb says. "Once we find Dylan, I'll make contact. You'll watch my back but keep a distance." Caleb's contacts in the motorcycle club may be in jail, but we're still not taking any chances of his being recognized.

"It should be me," I say, walking faster. It's freezing out, and the cold is needling through my jeans. "Sam's mom is in jail with a bunch of old ladies from this chapter. He called her this morning to see if she had any tips, and she told him lots of single girls go to these parties. They all want to hook up with the new member or something."

If it's true, it's as good an angle as any to get close to Dylan.

Beside me, Caleb has stopped.

"I'm not really going to do it," I say.

We walk again.

"I'll be close," Caleb says gruffly.

"I'll put up my hair in a ponytail if I need backup."

He nods.

"I sleep on the floor," he says.

"What?"

He clears his throat.

"When Margot spends the night. I sleep on the floor. I thought you should know."

A tense, electric anticipation slings between us.

"Okay," I say.

"Okay," he says.

His brows are furrowed, and I can't help thinking he's remembering our past—how things ended at Vale Hall, how I kissed Grayson when we were apart.

"How is she doing?" I ask.

My stomach grows tight as his scowl deepens.

"Angry."

Henry's words from the train yard whisper from my memory: *Someone needs to keep an eye on Margot.*

I get it. If I'd lost someone the way she lost Jimmy, I don't know what I'd do. Still, this is the girl who cheated on Caleb with her mark. Who only pretended to be my friend in order to turn me against Dr. O. We're allies now, but that doesn't mean I'm not keeping a careful distance.

"Because I won't slip strychnine into Dr. O's coffee?" I ask, trying to contain my resentment. Just because I want to find the others doesn't mean I don't want to bring Dr. O down.

He shakes his head. "Because it's easier than being sad."

His words seep through my skin. Maybe anger is easier, but it's also riskier. She's been operating solo so long, she's forgotten she has others depending on her. That she has people on her side. I didn't understand that until I came to Vale Hall.

It's strange that Dr. O was the one to teach me about loyalty.

We can hear the music from the Greasy Spoon now, the wail of country rock and the laughter above it. A shiver crawls over my skin as a sickle moon slides out from behind the clouds, making the frostbitten fields on either side of the road glow a pale silver. Ahead, just before the diner, a weathered barn presses up against the road. It's tilted, like it might tip over in a strong wind. You can see straight through the breezeway in the middle.

"Well, if we are going to die, this is a good place to do it," I mutter.

He blows out a tight breath. "Ready?"

"One second." I pull out my phone from my coat pocket. In the mirrored reflection, I trace my lips with a cherry-red lipstick, pressing them together to spread the color. Then I tug the zipper of my coat halfway down to reveal the low-cut, black, long-sleeved top I have on underneath.

"Do I look all right?" I say, tucking the phone and lipstick into my back pocket.

Caleb's wide-eyed stare moves over my face, my neck, and even though I haven't changed clothes, all the way down my legs.

"I'll take that as a yes."

He blows out a tense breath. "I was getting there."

The parking lot of the Greasy Spoon is gravel, and packed with motorcycles and cars. People are spilling out the doors, gathered in groups to smoke out front, or look at each other's bikes. We aren't the only ones without the leather cut and howling-wolf patch on our backs, and there's enough movement that no one seems to notice as we head up the front steps and through the heavy wooden door.

Inside the music is blaring. It's hot, and the floor is littered with peanut shells. A half dozen booths line the front walls, all of them filled with everyone from kids to grandparents, and every table is full of girls in tight jeans and crop tops. Most of the guys in the black cuts have gathered at the bar at the back of the restaurant, where a deafening cheer echoes off the low ceiling. They're doing shots, and I'm guessing it's for one of the two guys sitting on tables set directly on the bar.

I focus on Dylan—Charlie, as people will know him here—on the right. He's aged since the picture in his file, and even with the scraggly red beard his cheekbones look more severe. Still, he's smiling, his black T-shirt and cut lit up by the glowing neon lights at his back.

I turn to tell Caleb we're on, but he's already disappeared.

Lifting my chin, I make my way toward the bar, but a blonde with thigh-high black boots snags my arm. She smells like vanilla and has clearly spent a long time edging her perfectly frosted eyeshadow.

"Nice try, honey."

My brows lift in confusion.

She grins and leans closer. "Get in line."

Her chin jerks to the right, and I see what she means. There's a line of girls leading up to the bar, seven women ranging in age from somewhere close to my seventeen to the woman in front of Boots, who must be at least eighty.

"What is this?" I ask.

"It's the receiving line," she tells me, crossing her arms over her well-endowed chest. I make special note of her long, white nails, which look like they could do some damage in a fight.

"Winner takes all, girls," says the old woman in front of her. "And tonight, I'm feeling lucky."

Boots laughs wickedly. "Our new boys get their choice of the house. One night, and one night only." She leans toward the old lady. "Charlie's mine, you old cat."

They can't be serious.

But everything about this, from the line to the men on the countertop, tells me they are.

"Fine with me," says the old woman. "I got my sights set on the ugly one. Women always underestimate the ugly ones, but they know what they're doing, you feel me?"

"I feel you," says Boots.

They cackle.

Sam's mom was right with her lead—there are a ton of ladies here for the new recruits. But I can't help being disgusted by the idea of all these women lining up for a new recruit to choose them.

My eyes lift to the bar, where a girl in her early twenties is hoisted between the two new members. The old woman wasn't kidding about ugly. The other new guy is short, muscled, and has a face like a potato that's been left too long in the pantry. As I watch, the girl leans toward him and kisses him passionately.

The entire restaurant cheers.

The girl stands with a whoop, and turns to Charlie, lowering to take his face in both her hands. By the time she's done with him, he nearly falls out of his chair.

Then she bows, holds out her arms, and lets the crowd of Wolves help her to the floor.

"You playing, honey?" taunts Boots, her ice-shadowed eyes hard with competition.

"I wouldn't be here if I wasn't," I say.

The line moves forward.

Heat rushes up my neck. I don't know where Caleb is in the room, but I can feel him watching.

I push him to the back of my mind. It's time to tame a Wolf.

CHAPTER 7

'll say this much. That old lady's got game.

The Wolves call her Mama. It takes four of them to hoist her onto the bar, and once she's there, she picks up her denim skirt and shows a little leg for the crowd. Cheers erupt around her, and nerves aside, I'm grinning.

After she shimmies around the other recruit—Baxter—she plants a chaste kiss on his cheek and follows it up with a light slap.

"You take care of Mama, she's gonna take care of you," she tells him, and howls fill the bar. They're joking, I think. From the way Baxter's bowing down before her, I'd say she's a top dog around here.

She sits on Charlie's lap and kisses his forehead. "You piss Mama off, you're gonna be in a world of hurt."

She's kind of sweet, actually.

The other Wolves help Mama down at the end of the bar, then Boots is up, and she's going in for the kill. The other recruit—Baxter—gets lipstick smeared from his nose to his chin. When she moves to kiss Charlie, she grabs his hands, giving another view of her long, deadly nails, and slides them down her back to her butt.

The girls behind me in line cross their arms and shout that her time is up.

And then it's my turn.

Nerves flare in my chest. I smirk like I've got this, but I can't stop wondering where Caleb is, and if he's about to watch me kiss another guy.

Two guys lift me onto the bar, their hands under my elbows. The polished wood is slippery beneath my Chucks, and the lights overhead are too close, and hot. I feel like an actress on the stage.

I am.

I need to get Charlie alone. I need to make sure he picks me.

Taking a cue from Mama, I saunter toward Baxter, the swing in my hips earning a howl from the crowd. The new Wolf smells like beer and cigar smoke, but I keep my smile strong.

I lean in like I'm going to kiss him, then back away at the last minute and wag my finger.

"Sorry," I say. "You want a kiss, you're going to have to pick me first."

His scruffy face goes cherry red.

"That's not the way this works," he complains.

I give him a sexy shrug, my jacket falling down over my shoulder. The audience has all eyes on me now. I've changed the rules, and everyone wants to see what I do next.

With one leg, I part Charlie's knees, and slide between his thighs, my back to the others. The buzz is filling my veins now, my pulse pumping fast as I place my hands on Charlie's chest and lower my lips to his jaw.

For one fraction of a second, I let myself pretend it's Caleb.

That we're on this stage in front of everyone.

That it's his thighs flexing around mine.

My lips hover over Charlie's skin, and make a path to his ear as he blows out a hard breath.

"I want to talk about Vale Hall, Dylan," I whisper. "It won't take long."

He tenses as I pull back.

His eyes lock on mine. His mouth is flat, the corners pinched in anger.

Have I played this wrong? Should I have kissed him and taken my chances?

"Smile," I tell him, hoping he can't sense my hesitance.

He blinks, then his lips tilt in a murderous grin.

My blood runs cold. This was a mistake. We don't have an ally here.

Dylan is Charlie now, and Charlie is a Wolf.

I spin back, but before I can climb off the bar, Charlie catches my wrist. His hands are cool, his grip firm. He stands and pulls me back against his chest.

The Wolves below us clap and cheer as Charlie's hand slides

across my belly, locking me against him. I grab his opposite wrist, now holding my shoulders against his chest, but there's no getting out of his embrace.

The urge to wrestle free rises inside me, but the harder I squirm, the tighter Charlie's grasp becomes. My eyes dart around the room in search of Caleb, but I can't see him. There are too many people. The lights just overhead are too bright, casting a yellow glow over every black cut.

"I found my winner!" he calls out, and the entire bar roars. All except the girls who waited to kiss him. At least six of them are glaring in my direction.

"Your turn," Charlie whispers in my ear.

This is still my game. I've got this.

I smile.

But I'm coiled tight, and ready to spring.

Charlie helps me down from the bar, careful not to let go of my wrist as my feet touch the floor. He slides in front of me as I'm jostled by the tightly packed group and takes both my wrists in his hands. I try to lift my arms—if I can put my hair in a ponytail maybe Caleb will see and be close enough to help if this goes wrong—but Charlie's grip is unfaltering, and I'm shorter than most of the guys around me. Caleb couldn't see me even if he was looking.

Charlie carves a path past the bathroom, where a line of people cheer us on to the office at the end of the hall.

"Wait," I tell him. "Hold on a second."

But he shoves me inside, and a guy behind us with a long, wispy goatee slams the door with a smile.

For a moment there's only darkness. I blink rapidly, trying to adjust my eyes. My hands are outstretched before me, ready for anything. My heart is beating a mile a minute.

The lights switch on, and I blink again, now squinting against the bright bulb over Charlie's head.

"What is this?" I ask between clenched teeth. "Kind of old for seven minutes in heaven, don't you think?"

My gaze darts around the room. A desk piled high with papers and an old computer sits against the far wall. A utility shelf stands behind me, packed with toilet paper, towels, and cleaning supplies. The air is cool in here, and smells strongly of bleach.

"You have thirty seconds to tell me what you're doing here," he drawls. The anger is back in his eyes. I can feel it hum between us, a guitar string plucked too hard.

"You can drop the threats," I tell him. "I just want to talk."

"Twenty-five seconds," he says. "Then I'm telling the boys out there you're one of the Outsiders' girls, and they sent you to send a message."

"I don't even know what that means."

"We all got enemies. I've got a good feeling you're one of mine." He pulls a knife off his belt and opens the thick silver blade. My throat closes down to the width of a straw, and my hip bumps the desk hard as I back away. But Charlie doesn't come at me. He presses the tip of the knife against his forearm until a bead of crimson rises from his skin.

He's out of his mind.

I see what he means as the blood begins to drop around his forearm. He's going to tell the others I'm from a rival gang, and that I came here and attacked him.

I get how that would go poorly for me.

"Okay, stop," I tell him, hands up in surrender. "My name is Brynn. I'm not here to hurt you."

The knife moves a quarter inch, drawing more blood.

"Sure seems like you are," he says calmly.

"All right. Look, I know who you are because I stole a file from Dr. O's safe. I know what he does to people who break his rules. I'm here because a group of us are trying to stop him."

Charlie lifts the blade from his skin.

"Stop him, huh?" The knife points toward me, and causes my breath to catch. "Because from my end, it sure seems like he's tying up loose ends."

"Wh-what do you mean?"

Charlie takes a step closer.

Behind him, there's a thump against the door. Voices are raised, but it's impossible to make out what's being said—the noise in the restaurant is too high.

Charlie's blue eyes flash pure ice.

"Jack Hauser was a friend of mine. Odin cut him loose a year before me. They found him two weeks ago under the Caraway Bridge with a needle in his arm. Overdose, they called it. But I don't think so."

Charlie moves closer.

I'm going to scream for help. That's what I need to do, but there's not enough air in this room to breathe.

"Sonya Hallsburg found me two years ago. She was a freshman my senior year. Got cut loose for telling her dad. They found him in the Sikawa River. You know where they found her last Tuesday?"

I swallow.

"Locked in a freezer at the restaurant where she cleaned. Seems like one crazy accident to me."

I shake my head, trying to grasp onto Charlie's words. Students we've been looking for are dead. Is he right? Is Dr. O getting rid of his liabilities before he becomes senator?

If so, Caleb and his family are in more danger than we all thought. Margot, Raf, and Renee need to find a safe place and hide, *now*.

But we need them to stop Dr. O.

"So tell me again. Why are you here? Whose team are you on?"

"Yours," I tell him. "I swear. We're going to get him back for everything he's done. Enough of us stand together, he can't make us disappear. You wouldn't have to be Charlie anymore—you could get your life back."

Dark thoughts swirl inside me. They say that Margot is right. That blackmailing Dr. O and banishing him from Vale Hall won't be enough. We need to stop him before he hurts anyone else.

Charlie laughs. The knife drops an inch, but I breathe no easier.

"This is my life," he says. "Those boys out there are my brothers. I've got a new plan now. I've got someone looking out for me for real." His voice pitches, the first break in his cool, detached tone. In that instant, I see a flash of the kid he was at Vale Hall. I see the hunger he must have had when Dr. O promised him a future, and gave him a room at the residence.

I see the betrayal he's locked inside for the nine years since he's been expelled.

Charlie's voice hardens. "I don't know what you've got going on, and I don't care. Odin and his soldiers aren't screwing this up for me, you understand?"

He moves closer, and cold fear slices through me. I don't know what his intent is. All I know is that knife is still out, and we're alone, and that spells bad news in my book.

"Please." I'm not above begging now. "I'm not working for him. Not right now. If he finds out I'm here, I'm dead. My friends aren't safe. My mom's in trouble—he's got her working for his pharmacy company now."

Recognition makes his jaw twitch. "His pharmacy company. *His.*" Charlie's upper lip draws back in a snarl. "My mark was the heir of the Wednesday Pharmaceuticals fortune, did you know that?"

I didn't. The files don't give any specific information on anyone's job, just their academic records and identities.

"He was a decent guy. Kind of nerdy, but all right. I had to convince him to convince his dad to make Dr. O a shareholder at Wednesday. You know what happened once he did?"

I'm afraid to say yes.

"My mark's dad disappeared. Left a note saying he couldn't hack it anymore. Took off on his wife and his kid like *that.*" Charlie snaps with his other hand. "You know who was the majority shareholder of Wednesday afterwards? Who got all that medicine money?"

Dr. O.

A chill rakes through me.

Charlie knows enough to put Dr. O away for life. Part of me still clings to the hope he can be turned, but the anger inside him is solid. I can't direct it.

Charlie takes another slow step toward me. "And when I objected, when I told him to give that money to his son, I got dragged out by the scruff of my neck by Min Belk." He shakes his head. "That guy. He's worse than Dr. O, you know. He does whatever his master wants. No questions. *Ten seconds,* he told me. *You've got ten seconds to run, then you're next."* He laughs suddenly. "What I wouldn't give to get my hands on that guy."

My throat is too dry to swallow.

"What?" he asks. "Too much truth, sweetheart? You know what they say. *Vincit omnia veritas."*

Vale Hall's motto. *Truth conquers all.*

"You could bury Dr. O with that story."

"You think I don't know that?" Charlie's mouth twitches, conflict warring inside him. "I know how he trains his students. I was there, remember? You think you can walk in here and pretend to be on my side—"

Survival takes hold. Charlie thinks I'm here for Dr. O—that everything I've said is a lie. He's not about to end up like Jack or Sonya, and I'm not either.

I grab the desk chair, swiveling it between us. I'm ready to shove it toward him, but before I do, there's a hurried knock on the door, and someone is pushing inside.

Charlie drops the knife, hiding it from sight against the front of his thigh, but doesn't take his eyes off me.

Behind him, in the threshold, Baxter appears. His cheeks are ruddy, and his unibrow is pinched in the middle.

"We got trouble outside," he says. "Think it's the Outsiders."

That's the second time since I've been in this room that the Outsiders have been brought up. They must be a rival gang. Looks like Charlie's traded in one enemy for another.

Then Baxter is gone.

"This isn't over," Charlie warns me. He chases Baxter out the door, into the hall that's now bursting with movement. I catch a flash of their Wolf patch on the back of a cut before the door's slammed shut.

Cold splashes down my back. My mind races through what kind of "trouble" might be waiting outside—what these Outsiders might be capable of.

I rush toward the door, hand gripping the cool, bronze handle. It turns, but won't open. Something's blocking my exit from the outside.

I bang on the wood with my fist. "Hey!" I shout. "Open up!"

I can hear shouting now, and the roar of a motorcycle engine. "Hey!"

The door jostles, and then shoves inward, knocking me back a step. My fists are up in a flash, ready to fight, ready to defend. My gaze locks on the black sweatshirt and jeans. On the messy, raven hair and thick, black-framed glasses.

Caleb.

My arms fall.

His hand cups my cheek, warm and steady. "You all right?"

I nod.

Relief slashes through his wild, brown eyes as he takes my hand. "Good," he says. "Because it's time to go."

CHAPTER 8

Caleb leads me down the now-empty hall toward the diner's seating area, where people crowd against the front window, watching the orange flames of a bonfire streak into the night sky. Outside, there's a loud hiss, then a shout, and a small explosion draws a chorus of shrieks as those closest to the glass duck into booths.

Caleb wrenches me to the left, into a door marked "Employees Only." We stumble beneath the bright lights, past the metal ovens and the utility refrigerator, narrowly missing a cook in a stained apron and hairnet as we sprint toward the back door. I don't care about Charlie or the two dead students now; all I know is that we need to get out of here.

Cold night air slaps against my damp face and neck as Caleb shoves through the exit. I swallow hard, trying to shake off the trapped feeling of that office, but the black sky presses down on me, and I can't run fast enough.

Ahead, the broken asphalt gives way to high weeds, and a patch of dirt before the creepy, tilted barn. In the distance, the road dips, and the bright lights of the fast-food restaurants come into sight.

Beyond that is the mall's parking lot.

Caleb avoids the turn that leads us back to the road and plows straight through the weeds toward the barn. Long cattails whip my legs as we pass. Gravel crunches beneath our steps, barely louder than our labored breaths. A quick glance back at the Greasy Spoon reveals a plume of thick, gray smoke rising into the air, and on the road, two motorcycles tear into the night, heading toward the mall.

"Look around the back! He couldn't have gotten far!"

A male's voice makes me stumble and crash into Caleb's shoulder. I've righted myself in an instant, and we fly into the barn's open breezeway, then slam to a halt beside a sliding wooden stall door.

"Shh." Caleb's finger touches his lips as the sound of footsteps reaches us. We flatten against the door as they grow closer. I hold my breath. There's at least two people heading our way, and it doesn't take a genius to realize they're after whoever started that fire.

"Looks like someone went this way," says another male voice, this one older, deeper.

"Can't believe they torched Bull's bike."

"Probably some kind of initiation. No patched Outsider would pull a stunt like that and run."

My gaze finds Caleb's. He gives a one-shouldered shrug—enough to tell me he's behind the fire—then pulls the phone I gave him out of his pocket. His fingers hover over the screen.

I cover his hand with mine and shake my head. If we send a message to Charlotte and Henry now, they'll come here, and if they come here, the Wolves will turn on them.

I tilt my head toward the barn's exit, thirty feet away.

"We run, they'll follow," he breathes.

The Wolves will chase us down. I don't want to find out what happens if they catch us.

We're going to have to hide. I glance through the rusted metal rungs of the stall door, but the inside is packed with old rolls of barbwire and moldy hay. We can't fit in there, and if we chance crossing the breezeway to the opposite side of the barn, the Wolves outside will see us.

"Coat," Caleb says suddenly, shoving the phone back into his pocket. "Take it off."

Confused, I watch him toe off one of his shoes and toss it a few feet away. He yanks the knit cap out of his hoodie pocket and stuffs it onto my head, then starts to remove his sweatshirt.

"They're looking for me," he says. *"Alone."*

I get it then. If they're looking for one guy, they won't expect to find two of us, *together*.

The footsteps are coming closer. The voices have silenced now. Maybe they've heard us inside. They're probably trying to sneak up on us.

I shuck my jacket like it's on fire and toss it in the dirt. It's freezing out, and the thin fabric of my long-sleeved shirt feels like tissue paper.

We listen. The footsteps have stopped.

The Wolves are right outside.

I fist Caleb's thermal and pull him close. He hesitates only a moment, then smashes into me, sandwiching my body between his warmth and the cold, wooden door. I cup the back of his neck, pulling his head down to my throat. His jaw skims mine. I hike my leg up his hip and his hand grips my thigh. His breath on my neck sends shivers over my skin.

My body turns to fire.

Something scuffs against the barn door, just beyond us, in the shadows.

They're here.

I force a hard breath, and giggle.

Then sigh. Loudly. Like we're doing a lot more than just posing.

Caleb goes stone still.

I grip his hair, feeling the silky strands slide between my fingers, and when my shirt comes up a little, his cold belt buckle skims my stomach. I don't fake the gasp that slips from my lips.

Caleb's breath catches.

"Malcolm, get a load of this."

Caleb jerks back, as if in surprise, and throws a hand in front of his face to block the flashlight beaming our way. Like a gentleman, he quickly blocks any view of me.

"Kind of busy here," he calls. "How about a little privacy?"

"My bad," says one of the guys. "Come on, they need a little *privacy*."

The older voice—Malcolm—chuckles. "Nothing like a patching in to get the blood flowing."

Their footsteps fade as they jog away.

Caleb doesn't move. I don't either. For one frozen moment, we hold on to each other, my fists in his shirt, his knee pressed between my legs. His ragged breath warms my lips. His palm, now on my ribs, slides down my waist like he's moving through water.

His eyes lower to my mouth.

My fingers spread on his chest. His heart pounds against my hand.

The air feels electric. Every part of me sizzles like I'm a live wire.

"You're shivering." His Adam's apple bobs as he swallows. "I'll get your coat."

He doesn't back away.

My chest rises with each breath.

He's close enough to kiss.

"Caleb?"

Gravity's changed course. It's not pushing me down, it's pulling us closer. We fit like this. We belong like this.

Another motorcycle engine growls in the night, breaking the spell. Caleb blinks, and slowly pulls away. My back arches toward him, my body unwilling to let air fill the space between us.

"We should go." My voice sounds far away, like I'm whispering down a tunnel.

My muscles are slow, but find momentum as I snatch my jacket off the ground. He pulls his shoe back on and rights his sweatshirt. His idea worked. It looks like we were doing a lot more than pretending.

"We should stick to the fields," I say. "Stay off the road."

"Agreed."

We move at a brisk walk, keeping far away from the street as we follow the hill toward the bright fast-food signs. He keeps close enough that our arms keep brushing, but doesn't look at me.

I know he's thinking, and I know when Caleb's got something on his mind it's best to give him space to work it out, but I can't stand the silence when my thoughts are so loud.

"Did we get him?" Caleb asks.

I blink, and see the tip of Charlie's knife, pressing into his forearm.

"No." My steps slow. "He's too far gone. He said two of the others—Sonya and Jack—are dead. Dr. O killed them. He thought I was there to kill him, I think."

Caleb's hand winds behind his neck.

"Did he hurt you?"

"No."

He must hear the drop in my voice, because he glances over. The moonlight puts a glare on his glasses, hiding the emotion in his eyes.

"No," I say more assertively, and on my next breath, my tense conversation with Charlie returns, and disappointment spirals through me. "He could have destroyed Dr. O with what he knows. If he'd joined us—if we'd have even hinted of taking his story to the press—we could have ended this."

When a cloud of steam rises from Caleb's lips, I pass his hat back to him, but he waves it off and pulls up his hood.

"It's not your fault," he says. "If you couldn't turn him, no one could."

I twist the hat in my hands. Maybe I really was our best bet, or maybe Margot could have done better, worked him like she worked me. We'll never know now.

"I couldn't see you," Caleb says, voice tight. "I couldn't get past the guy at the door."

I imagine Caleb trying to smooth-talk his way in, then pushing by when he wasn't allowed through. If he caused a fight, he would have been outnumbered.

"So you lit a bike on fire?" I laugh. I can't help it.

Soon, he's laughing too.

"I almost burned the whole place down," he admits.

It isn't a declaration of love or anything, but it hits me hard. I put on his hat and pull it low over my ears, catching the clean scent of his shampoo.

"I shouldn't have let myself get shut in that office," I say.

"I'd love it if you tried to avoid that in the future."

I smirk.

We've reached the fast-food restaurants now, and are skirting around the shadowed lot that surrounds them. I'm about to suggest calling Charlotte and Henry for a pickup when I see the two black motorcycles parked in front of one of the restaurant's doors. Their owners must be inside somewhere.

We've made it out; we can't get caught now.

Hurrying through the shadows, we slide down into a storm ditch, then climb up the other side. The faraway rumble from the freeway reaches my ears, but I can't make out the roar of any motorcycle engines.

Heaviness descends. Charlie's lost. If his story about Sonya and Jack is true, Dr. O is even more dangerous than I thought.

Charlie could have changed the game. If we'd threatened to take what he knew public, Dr. O would have been gone by morning.

Or he might have lashed out against us, like a dog backed into a corner.

Jimmy Balder is dead. Sonya and Jack, too. According to Charlie, his mark's dad and Sonya's dad went with them.

We are fighting a losing battle against a power-hungry sociopath. Against a *senator*.

Caleb and I walk faster, finally reaching the edge of the mall's parking lot. The Jeep comes into view, another black car pulling in beside it. White flecks of salt shine on its gleaming base, and though it could be any one of a thousand black cars in this city, my stomach bottoms out at the sight of it.

The car's engine goes quiet. The driver's side door opens.

Min Belk steps out.

I grab Caleb's sleeve and pull him behind a hedge, strung up with twinkling lights.

"What's he doing here?" Caleb asks as we crouch in the shadows.

"I don't know." My stomach ties in knots. Did something happen back at Vale Hall? Why would Belk drive over an hour to find us?

As we watch, Belk circles the Jeep, peering in the tinted back windows. He pulls his cell out of his pocket, then raises it to his ear.

There's nothing in the Jeep. It's a shared car so no one keeps anything in it. What did he see that caused him to make the call?

And who is he trying to reach? Dr. O? Someone worse?

I think of Charlie's story—how Belk gave him ten seconds to run.

Caleb mutters a curse under his breath then rips the burner phone out of his back pocket. He dials Charlotte's number, but it rings twice and goes to voicemail.

"She's talking to someone," he says.

Maybe Belk.

Maybe he's trying to lure her outside. The parking lot's practically deserted. He could hurt her, or throw her in the back of his car, and no one would see.

Caleb starts to dial Henry's number, but stops.

At the mall, two people appear between the fake Christmas trees marking a side entrance. Henry hurries toward the car, adjusting the paper shopping bags over his arms. Charlotte's beside him, her phone pressed to her ear.

One guess who she's talking to.

"They're walking into a trap." I rise, unable to hold still any longer. "We have to warn them!"

Caleb grabs my hand as I reach for my phone, his expression torn. "They're in Belk's line of sight. If he sees them take a call, then run, he'll know something's up."

I hate that he's right. I hate that we can't do anything.

It doesn't matter. Across the lot, Henry's stopped. He and Charlotte are both staring at the car. At Belk, leaning casually against the Jeep.

Henry and Charlotte glance at each other, then continue forward, tentatively.

Panic explodes in my chest. Charlie's story is still ringing in my ears. "I'm going over there," I say.

Caleb stops me. "I'll go."

But Caleb's not supposed to be here, and if there is a chance that Belk's followed us for some other reason, his presence will be trouble for all of us.

Caleb knows this. He hates it—I can see the frustration in every taut line of his face.

"It'll be fine." I force a breath. I'm strung too tight. I let Charlie get to me. Belk's had a ton of chances to hurt us, and he hasn't. Why wait until now?

Because Dr. O is going to be a senator now.

Because Dr. O's tying up his loose ends.

Because someone found out what we've been doing.

It doesn't matter. Charlotte and Henry aren't facing him alone.

"Got my back?" I ask.

"Always."

I look at Caleb one more time, and the resolve in his eyes gives me a burst of strength. I shove the fear down, and put on my game face.

Hands in the pockets of my coat, I stride toward the car. There isn't time to go through the mall and exit from one of the shops, letting me act as if I were browsing the whole time. I don't want to let Charlotte and Henry out of my sight, and this way Caleb will be able to watch me.

I feel his gaze on my back and square my shoulders.

Henry sees me first. With frantic eyes, he tilts his chin toward Belk, as if I don't notice the broad, ponytailed man in the long black coat just in front of him. Belk must pick up on Henry's not-so-subtle warning, because he turns quickly.

"Oh, there you are!" Charlotte says. "We were just going to call you." When Belk turns she purposefully smooths her hair, which makes me touch my own, and realize I'm still wearing Caleb's hat.

I fight the urge to take it off. Maybe Belk will think it's mine. Hopefully.

"Where were you?" he asks, eyes narrowing.

"I told you—she was at one of the jewelry stores doing her Vocational Development assignment. We split up so we wouldn't run out of time." Henry circles around Belk, shopping bags jostling as he stands beside me.

Belk juts a thumb behind him. "Mall is that way."

Henry links his arm in mine. The flex of his biceps against my hand tells me I'm not alone, but his siding with me at all makes us look suspicious.

It's Belk, I tell myself. My PE teacher. The security guard I see every day at Vale Hall.

I know this, but I can't shake Charlie's words, and I can't help feeling like Belk *wants* me to be afraid.

"I got hungry." I mirror Belk's move, jabbing a thumb behind me in the direction of the fast-food restaurants—in the direction of Caleb, hidden behind the bushes. "Grabbed a taco."

Belk lowers his arm. "You forgot your phone."

Which he knows, because he's been tracking us.

Wariness coils in my muscles.

"I know," I say, layering annoyance into my tone. "I realized once I got down there I put it in Charlotte's purse when we were trying on clothes earlier."

In the distance, I can hear the growl of motorcycles, and my hands clench into fists.

Charlotte, brows lifted in surprise, opens her purse and searches inside. "I forgot about that! Sorry! Oh, here it is." She gives the phone a little shake and passes it to me.

Belk exhales with a flare of his nostrils.

"What are you doing here?" I ask, glancing around to make sure no one's followed us from the Greasy Spoon. "Did something happen?"

"Should something have?"

"That's cryptic," says Charlotte. "Clearly you didn't drive all this way just to say hi."

Belk gives a half smile.

"Things are changing. The director was concerned when he'd heard you drove all this way alone."

"Why?" asks Henry. "We've come here before."

"Because he's a senator," I say, and look to Belk. "At least, he will be on New Year's when he's sworn in. Is that what you mean?"

The white parking lot lights bring out the shadows beneath Belk's eyes. "Security's going to be a little tighter from now on. No more excursions without adult supervision."

He's right—things are changing, *quickly*. If we can't even supposedly leave alone for homework he assigns, how are we supposed to meet Caleb and the others at HQ?

"What about work?" Charlotte asks. "Are you going to be holding our hands on a job?"

"If that's what it takes to keep everyone safe." Belk smiles as he adds, "It would be very bad for the director if anyone was doing things they shouldn't be."

The threat hangs among us in the icy air.

Henry lifts the bags. "Well, I was just doing my homework."

"You were successful by the looks of it." Belk looks directly at me. "How did you fare?"

I swallow.

"You did complete the homework, didn't you?" He takes a step closer, and I automatically move back, like the wrong end of a magnet. "I know I wouldn't grab a taco after driving all this way unless I'd finished what I came to do."

"Well, obviously," says Henry.

My jaw clenches.

The motorcycles are coming closer. I can hear them on the road just beyond the parking lot. We need to find Caleb and get inside the car, or head back to the mall.

"You got those earrings, right?" Henry asks me.

I hope he gets the hint to shut up by the look on my face, because I can't exactly say it out loud.

His eyes dip to my waist. To my *pockets*.

I slide my hand into my coat pocket and find a small, velvety box inside. He must have stashed it there when he came to stand beside me.

"Yeah," I say. "Of course I finished my homework first. Picked up something for my mom." I open the box, and find two gold tear drops with red stones nestled inside. They aren't Mom's style at all, but that doesn't matter. "She's going to die when she sees them."

"That would be a real shame." Belk laughs, like this is some kind of joke.

My blood turns to ice water. My hand, holding the earrings, lowers.

The threat is clear. He might as well have just come out and said it: *If you step out of line, your mom's going to suffer.*

I need to get her away from here—from that job she took at Wednesday Pharmaceuticals, and the apartment the staff there so nicely found for her. She needs to run far away from Dr. O and everyone who works for him, including me.

But if she does, Dr. O will know I've told her the truth about what we do at Vale Hall. About what some of us are doing outside it.

He'll make her disappear too.

"Well, everything looks all right here to me," says Belk. "If you're ready to head home, I'll follow. Otherwise, I could do some holiday shopping myself."

"We're done," says Charlotte.

Silently, we head toward the Jeep, parked in front of Belk's car.

He waits for us to get in before sliding into his own front seat. Only once I'm sure he's inside and the door is shut do I glance back for Caleb.

I don't see him.

Instead, I see a gray haze of smoke in the distance, and two motorcycles racing down the road back to the Greasy Spoon.

With Belk following us, we can't go back for Caleb. We'll have to leave him here, and hope he navigates the Wolves prowling the streets and finds a way back to his apartment at the bowling alley on his own.

My breath comes faster, and soon Henry's hand is gripping my shoulder from the back seat.

He shows me a message on his phone from a blocked number.
Go.

"He'll be fine," Henry mutters, but I'm not sure if he's saying it for me, or himself.

"I'm more worried about us," says Charlotte quietly, turning the key in the ignition. "Don't tell me Dr. O sent Belk because he just realized we were gone."

"What do you mean?" asks Henry.

"She means someone ratted on us," I say.

Someone at the house knew this wasn't just a shopping trip and tipped Belk off. Someone who's been watching us closely—who's playing for Dr. O's team.

Someone like Grayson Sterling.

People are starting to notice.

Henry's hand slips from my shoulder. "Of course they did."

Even now, after Grayson's joined Team Geri to mess with him, Henry looks dejected, and it makes me even more furious with the senator's son.

"Be safe," I whisper, knowing Caleb can't hear me, but hoping he knows I mean it all the same.

CHAPTER 9

I call Mom first thing in the morning, and when I'm sure every-thing is fine, I hang up to find Sam waiting on the stairs, wearing the worst reindeer sweater I've ever seen with a pair of gray pants. He looks like he's been picking at the pine garland on the bannis-ter for quite a while; there's a small pile of green needles on the step beside him.

When he sees me, he pounces.

"Hey," he says as I come up beside him. "Did he get home all right? Henry told me what happened."

He, of course, is Caleb. Even though Sam deliberately left out his name, I cringe at his volume. Someone here sold us out last night. I have a pretty good idea who, but I'm not willing to chance anyone else overhearing our discussion.

"Everything's good," I say.

Sam waits for me to explain as we start down the stairs, and when I don't, he glances around to make sure no one's following.

"And?"

"And nothing." I rub my eyes, exhaustion thinning my patience.

Caleb called me after he convinced a woman to buy him a bus ticket so he could get to his sick sister. We stayed on the phone through the bus transfer, to the SCTA station, all the way until he got home.

That was two hours ago.

A creak in the stairs has us both bracing, and when I glance over my shoulder, I see Henry marching down, looking uncharacteris-tically disheveled in snowflake pajama pants and a wrinkled white undershirt under his lucky jacket.

"Hi. How's it going? Good? Great."

I stare after him as he brushes past. "What was . . ."

Sam is scowling. "I thought you'd know. He's been up since dawn on some kind of secret mission."

"What mission?" We agreed last night on the car ride home to keep a low profile for a couple days. "I know nothing about a mission."

At the bottom of the stairs, Henry bumps into June, still in all black but with a flare of bright pink lipstick. She bares her teeth at him as he hurries away.

"On it," says Sam, taking off after Henry. June glares at him on the way by, too.

She folds her arms over her chest as I come down. "I don't know how you manage the people around here. Everyone's so dramatic."

Henry and Sam have already disappeared into the kitchen.

"Is that a bad thing?"

"Not if you love drama."

When I step to the floor, she's a full three inches taller than me. Still, she's younger, and when her eyes dart to the side, I feel her insecurity. June's still new here, and I haven't seen her hanging out with anyone. I've assumed that's out of choice, but maybe I had that wrong.

"I don't." My head is pounding. We lost Charlie last night, and Penny two days before. People are dying, and it will only get worse as Dr. O moves into his new position.

Maybe Margot was right—this needed to be done quickly and quietly. She wanted me because she believed that I, over anyone else, could get to him on the inside. But every time I considered it, I saw what Dr. O did to Caleb and to her, and it seemed an impossible task to accomplish alone.

I've been telling myself we're stronger together, but what if I'm wrong? What if more people really do just mean a bigger mess?

June's brows hike up beneath her straight, black bangs.

"Sorry," I say. "I didn't sleep well last night."

"Me either." June hesitates, gripping the strap of her bag. "Kind of hard getting used to the beds at this place."

"I know," I say. "They're really soft."

"And the food is really good."

"Way too good."

She cracks a smile. "And it's so annoying that people are always cleaning up after you and doing your dishes and stuff."

"The worst, right?"

Her smile widens. I almost smile back, but then I remember that June is here because Caleb's not. That Caleb recruited her as his last job for Dr. O before I accidentally got him expelled. I'm treating her the way Geri treated me when I first moved into Margot's old room.

None of this is her fault, but it makes it hard to relax, all the same.

"You get used to it," I say, because even though we're joking, we're not. Even the good things are overwhelming when you come from so little.

"Maybe." She straightens as Geri and Alice come down the stairs behind her. Maybe she thinks she's hiding her reaction, but it's clear to me as she quickly steps out of their way that they've gotten under her skin.

"You should eat lunch with us today," I tell her. "We can talk about the UN project."

And I can feel out your loyalties to Dr. O and this program.

"Okay." She looks to the floor. "Whatever."

Now I do smile. If I were Henry, I'd close this deal with a hug, but I don't because I'm not ridiculous.

Which reminds me of what Sam said—that Henry is on some special mission this morning. I'm just about to head into the kitchen to search for him when the door to Dr. O's office creaks open, and two men step out beneath the two black marble ravens on their high white pedestals.

Dr. O is wearing a cream-colored sweater and slacks. The other man, thicker through the arms and shoulders, is in a navy suit with shiny shoes. At the sight of him, I jolt sideways, into June.

Geri's father.

The man Dr. O ordered to kill Jimmy Balder.

"Time to lay off the mouthwash," June mutters as I quickly right myself.

What is he doing here? An alarm screams in my head. I have to warn someone. Geri's father is a hit man. His meeting with Dr. O in private cannot possibly mean anything good.

"Good morning, Brynn. June." Dr. O's warm smile seems genuine, but I know better. His gaze lifts behind me. "Grayson."

I turn sharply to find Grayson around the turn at the bottom of the stairs, scowling. His eyes move from Geri's dad, to Dr. O, then to me, before he paints on a tight smile. "Good morning."

He recognizes Geri's father, but whether that's from Family Day, when he came to Vale Hall, or another time, I don't know.

"Hey, Dr. O," June mumbles, as Grayson stalks away.

I can't find my voice to give a response. Just the sight of the director with this man has a cold fear churning in my gut.

These two men are responsible for people's deaths.

I need to call Caleb. He needs to warn Margot and the others.

"Thanks for meeting me," Geri's father says. "I can't wait to see the colleges fighting over my little girl."

"And they will," assures Dr. O. "Geri is an incredible talent."

I swear he looks at me as he says this.

Geri is talented. She was working with, and reporting on, my mom for weeks at Gridiron Sports Bar and I had no idea.

"I'll say goodbye to her before I head out," Geri's father says.

He shakes Dr. O's hand, then passes by June and me on his way to the kitchen.

My pulse is beating a mile a minute. The whole house feels like a sauna.

What were they just talking about? Was it really Geri, or someone else?

"Brynn, do you have a minute?" Dr. O asks, eyes twinkling.

No. Not for you. Not after what you've done.

I trusted you.

The pressure increases beneath my ribs.

I trusted you.

That's the worst part of it all. He chose me. He told me I was special, and that he needed my help.

And I believed every word.

But he is the bad guy he told me we were fighting. And facing him now, I feel bad too, for every part in his master scheme that he made me play.

"Brynn?"

I have to act normal. I have to pretend everything's fine.

My body moves in slow motion as I leave June's side and walk beneath the marble ravens into Dr. O's office. I've been here many times, but now, crossing by the stone tablet bearing the words *Vincit Omnia Veritas,* I'm terrified.

"How are you?" he asks, and when I face him, my jaw clenches. Behind him is the large portrait of the thin woman in the white dress. Susan Griffin.

The sister he told Grayson to run off the road.

"Fine," I manage.

"Good. I'm sorry I've been absent lately. I've had quite a bit going on behind the scenes."

"I guess so."

His smile falters the tiniest bit. "You of all people know how complicated these last few months have been."

If blackmailing mayors and making people disappear isn't complicated, I don't know what is.

"Congrats." I try to smile. "I didn't know you wanted to be senator."

"When opportunity presents itself, you have to strike."

Was Charlie in the way of opportunity? I want to ask. *What about Caleb, and Margot, and Jimmy Balder? What about me?*

He moves to his couch in front of the fireplace, and motions for me to sit.

Reluctantly, I move in that direction. I take a seat on the couch opposite him, hands spread on the maroon velvet beside my thighs. His office has been decorated like the rest of the house, with white candles and red holly wreathes. Sprigs of spruce are neatly tied in ribbons over the fireplace. The whole room smells like pine.

A few months ago, I would have been enchanted by it. The mansion has been transformed into something out of a story. But now it feels like pretty wrapping on a ticking bomb.

"We can make changes this way, Brynn. Real changes. Not like before."

"We?"

He slides to the edge of the couch, leaning toward me. There's a light in his eyes I haven't seen there before. It's a lot like the look Grayson gets before he punches someone.

"It's important that you keep what we do here confidential. Now more than ever."

"Right."

"I need to hear you say you understand that."

"I understand."

"You know what's at stake if word of our work gets out."

"I do." It starts with Caleb and my mom, and ends with a roof over my head and my still-beating heart.

He claps his hands against his knees. "Wonderful. You have questions, I'm sure, about the future. Let's hear them."

Is he serious? He's actually going to pretend he cares after all he's done?

"Is this real?" I ask before I can stop myself.

He inhales slowly. "How so?"

"Are you really going to be a senator? Or is this just a front so you can do something else?" There's anger in my tone, and I hate it, because it means he'll know he's gotten to me. It means he'll know I care, and if I care, I can be hurt.

"Brynn, we are all pretending to be something else. Some of us own that. Some of us don't. It's a choice you have to make for yourself."

I get it. He's pretending to be a school director, when really he's a sociopath.

Dr. O sighs, and rests his elbows on his knees. "You're concerned for your future. About the promises I made you and your fellow students."

My jaw clenches.

"This school is my family," he says. "I would not let my family come to harm. I'd protect it against anyone who tried to hurt us."

I silently scoff. He's like the loving parent who hits their kid for "their own good."

But Dr. O is immune to my doubt. He continues to smile reassuringly, and it's in that moment I realize that he doesn't know that *I* know that he ordered his own sister's death.

Grayson told Henry and me that he ran Susan off the road because Dr. O told him to, but he never mentioned that he told us to the director—Dr. O would have acknowledged it otherwise. He wouldn't sit in front of me and play the family card if he suspected I knew he'd ordered his own sister's murder.

Which could mean it didn't happen, and Grayson lied by trying to deflect the blame for what he did. Or that Grayson is hiding things from Dr. O.

People are starting to notice.

Grayson's warning works a chill straight to my bones. The stupid game he and Geri started yesterday about Henry liking him has distracted the entire school. People are now wondering what exactly happened between them, and are dazzled by Grayson's charm as he makes his declarations from Switzerland to Australia.

But no one's wondering why Grayson is here anymore, not even after his father's arrest for covering up the death of a woman he ran off the road.

Is Grayson being his arrogant, entitled self? Or is he playing at something?

"That's a promise my own father couldn't make," Dr. O says, glancing over his shoulder to where Susan stares across the room, forever trapped in time and paint.

"Your father the congressman," I remember, a chill creeping up my spine. Another person from his gene pool in charge of laws and lives.

"Yes," says Dr. O. "A man of many secrets."

I guess Dr. O had to learn somewhere.

"You and I are similar in that way, Brynn. I, too, was raised by my mother. I grew up just south of the city, in an apartment no bigger than this office."

"I thought this was your family's home," I say.

His smile is thin. "It was *his* family's home. Susan grew up here. Her mother was his wife."

My brow arches. "And your mom?"

"Was forgotten." His chin drops. He weaves his fingers over his lap. "My father came around to see us from time to time. He'd bring money. Food, sometimes, if we were fortunate. But he was never there when we needed him. In fact," he chuckles dryly, "once, when she was sick, I came to this house to get help. He had me escorted off the property. Left down the street. It was mostly farmland then."

"That's cold." What more does he expect me to say? *Sorry, I understand why you hire hit men now.*

"*Cold* was raising my mother's hopes that he loved her, only to return to his wife and daughter in this house." There's a bite to his voice now. "*Cold* was handing her a gun the night she said she'd rather die than be without him."

My eyes widen. I don't want to imagine a younger Dr. O finding his mother dead, but I do, and the pity is as sure as it is unwelcome.

"You can see why I was reluctant for my sister to end up in a relationship with another married politician," he growls, and I look again to the portrait, and imagine her standing beside Matthew Sterling, Grayson's dad.

"How old were you?" I find myself asking.

"Fifteen," he says. "Old enough to inform him that my mere existence was enough to destroy his career." He inhales. "My father resigned shortly after that. He and Susan's mother were found not long after in an abandoned car in Michigan. Apparently, he'd made some bad deals with the Irish mob over the years."

Wariness climbs up my spine. I don't know if this story is real. Even if it is, I don't want to know this about him. It doesn't make what he's done okay.

"I'm sorry to burden you with this. I wasn't thinking. I just . . . I suppose I trust you, that's all. And I want you to know that your trust in me is not ill-placed."

I tuck my hands beneath my thighs so he doesn't see them shaking.

His eyes meet mine. "You don't need to worry about your future, Brynn. You'll be taken care of, as promised. Soon enough, the time may come when I'll call on my old students for special jobs. Wouldn't that be exciting?"

I imagine myself pulling cons for a senator. Sneaking in and out of political offices. Dealing with other people just as powerful as he is. Once, I would have jumped at that opportunity—the higher the risk, the greater the payout. But now, I dread what he might ask.

"Yes." I brighten my smile.

"I'll have to shift my responsibilities as I transition into the Senate role, of course," he continues. "I will miss Vale Hall very much."

"You won't be director anymore?" If Dr. O's gone, we could be safe. We could find a way to make the others safe. To bring them back.

"It's a conflict of interest, I'm afraid," Dr. O says. "But don't worry. I plan on keeping a very close eye on the school. I do have a personal connection to this place, after all. I wouldn't want to see my students lose their focus in my absence."

"Who's going to take your place?" My thoughts shift to the Vale Hall board of directors we were counting on to take over in his absence.

"I've given my recommendation to the board. We should know soon what they decide." He stands, making it clear I'll be getting no more insight into the situation. "I'm glad to see you. I hear you're thinking about colleges. That's wonderful."

I rise, and start walking toward the door when he holds out a hand.

"I don't know what I want to do yet," I say, because it seems like the safest answer.

"There's still time," he says reassuringly. As if we're just any student and school director talking about the future. "Can I offer you some advice?"

No. "Sure."

"Think about who you are. What makes you *you*. And if that's not the person you want to be, use the next few years as a vehicle to get you there."

I give a stiff shrug. "What happened to *you're fine just the way you are?*"

I'm trying to lighten the conversation, but the words fall flat.

Dr. O chuckles. "Then I suppose you, like me, have found your place in this world."

He holds open the door for me to step out, and I do, taking my first full breath in minutes.

But through the slim window beside the door, I see Geri's father make a turn around the fountain in his red sports car, and feel like I've just stepped off the edge of a very steep cliff.

CHAPTER 10

Geri's father was at Vale Hall to talk about Geri's upcoming college visits. At least, that's what Geri thinks.

Or rather, what she tells me.

She knows what her father does, and she keeps her nose out of his business. The less she knows, the better. If she interferes with her father's jobs for Dr. O, that puts her dad in jeopardy, and he only works for Dr. O because he wants to give her the best shot at making something of herself.

But I can't help thinking something bad is about to happen.

And I can't help wondering if Grayson is worried too. At breakfast, he lets his cereal go soggy before pouring it down the drain. During our calculus exam review, he stares blankly at the wrong textbook. I want to ask him what he knows, but I can't be sure it won't go straight back to Dr. O.

I tell Charlotte, Henry, and Sam about our visitor. I call Caleb, and he promises to go to headquarters at the train yard and spread the word to Margot, Renee, and Raf. I look for Moore, hoping that he has some clue as to why Geri's dad was talking to the director, but he's gone, driving Dr. O to political strategizing meetings with the mayor.

It's like waiting for the other shoe to drop, when that shoe is wired with explosives.

I'm unable to think about anything else until Model UN that afternoon, when I realize as June stalks in, avoiding my gaze, that I blew her off at lunch.

"I'm sorry about earlier," I tell her before the session starts. Shrew's already announced that it's going to be a doozy—we're teaming up to strategize a resolution to world hunger, which is hard to get in the right frame of mind for with the holiday music piped in through the overhead speakers. "I had to do some stuff before class."

"I'm not crying about it," June says, chomping on her gum. "Do whatever you want."

I hurt her, and I wish I hadn't.

"Maybe tomorrow?" I offer, overhearing Geri, across the room, singing the harmony to "Deck the Halls."

"Are you even going to be here?"

My back straightens. "Why wouldn't I be here?"

"I don't know." She prods gently at her thick mascara with one fingertip. "Aren't you and your pals part of some secret club?"

My heartbeat slows, each single beat pounding in my ears.

People are starting to notice.

My eyes lift across the gym, to where Grayson has just joined Switzerland's table. He's watching me, too. His gaze is narrowed and unflinching.

"Of course not," I say.

"That's what I'd say if I were in some secret club too," she says.

I can't tell if she wants to be a part of the group or doesn't. Either way, she's paying attention to what we're doing, and that can't be good.

Unless we can trust her.

We need more allies at school, people not loyal to Dr. O. June doesn't appear to be spreading anyone's business, even though she's clearly observing from a distance. If she's looking for friends, we might be able to turn her before Dr. O gets his hooks in too deep.

We need to move fast. He'll be a senator in two weeks. And if Charlie was right, the director is already tying up his loose ends.

"Let's talk tonight," I tell her, leaning close. "There's something I want to ask you about."

Her eyes light up.

"What's this? China and Australia conspiring before the start of session?" Grayson, striding over from his table, flashes his son-of-a-senator grin, but his gaze stays hard on mine. "Pretty sure that's not fair."

"It's about as fair as a Swiss hot chocolate delivery," says June.

She's one of the few people here unimpressed by Grayson, which happens to be a prerequisite of our rebellion.

"But everyone likes hot chocolate," he says. "And no one likes secrets."

I'm reminded again of what he didn't tell Dr. O, and that worried look on his face this morning when he saw Geri's dad.

"Good thing I've got nothing to hide, then," I say. "How about you, Grayson?"

The air cools between us.

"I'm an open book," he says. "Ask me anything you like."

A strange look passes over his face—challenge, I realize. As if he wants me to ask him something, and he's ready to answer.

I square my shoulders. I do have questions, but I'm not asking them here, with half the student body filing into the gym. Even if I did confront him on what he knows about Geri's dad, or even the true nature of his relationship with Dr. O, I couldn't be sure he was telling me the truth.

"Oh, good!" Henry strides toward us, cutting across the gym floor. He's wrangling a messenger bag over his shoulder like it's alive—the strap pulls at the collar of his undershirt as he struggles to reach inside.

"Henry?" I move to intercept. Whatever Henry's planning here can't be good. Just the sight of Grayson has him unhinged.

"I got you something, *Switzerland*," says Henry.

"Is it a thank you for the hot chocolate?" Grayson asks. His voice is amused, but his eyes are anxious. He's been caught off guard, and he doesn't like it.

Henry pulls a silver, spray-painted piggy bank from his bag and holds it in front of Grayson's face. He's drawn a lot of attention now; almost everyone is staring in our direction.

"Since you're so intent on winning everything, here you go. Take Petal. We don't want her." Henry shoves the coveted platinum pig into Grayson's chest.

"Hold up," Geri says, marching toward us in her platform heels. "Did you go in my room?"

Henry winces. This must be the secret mission Sam mentioned.

Grayson's smug grin has faded.

"No one picked a winner yet, Australia," calls Joel, but no one's listening.

"I know what you did last night," Henry tells Grayson, jabbing a finger into his shoulder.

"Drama," sings June. "I told you."

"Henry, I need your help over at our table." I yank on Henry's arm. This is not a conversation I want everyone overhearing.

"I know you told Belk we were messing around, but we were just doing homework."

Grayson folds his arms over his chest as Geri grabs Petal out of Henry's hand. He doesn't even seem to notice.

"Okay," says Grayson.

"This isn't a game," Henry continues, his cheeks flaring red. "I'm a real person. We're all real people. The things you do affect others."

"What about the things you do?" Grayson counters. "What about the games all of you play?" He's speaking quietly, but the entire room is watching.

Henry blinks rapidly.

"Grayson, stop." I might as well be a gnat. He doesn't even register I'm there.

"What did I do to make you hate me?" Henry asks quietly, as if realizing Grayson's true feelings for the first time.

It's that simple with Henry. He doesn't see people using others as pawns, even in our line of work, because he wouldn't.

I'm ready for another snappy Grayson comment, but it doesn't come. Instead, he deflates like a balloon, chest caving inward, head tipping forward. He stares at the ground at Henry's feet.

"I don't hate you." His voice is a bruised whisper.

"What's going on over here?"

I jerk at the sound of Moore's voice, hard with anger, as he strides over to where the crowd has gathered. His gray suit is wrinkled today, but his glare is cold and steady.

"Get to your seats," he orders. "Henry, what's the problem?"

But Henry isn't moving. He's watching Grayson, who now appears to have run out of batteries and stalled completely.

"Nothing," says Geri. "We were just discussing Petal." She holds the pig up.

June's gaze glances off mine. She purposefully turns her chair away from the crowd, as if to say she was never a part of it, and hunches over her team's research binder.

"Henry," Moore says more pointedly. "Is Grayson bothering you?"

Grayson gives a small snort, then finally lifts his head.

"We were just messing around, weren't we, Henry?"

"I didn't ask you," snaps Moore.

Lightning zings down my spine. If there was one thing I learned from living with my mom's ex, Pete, it was how to read when someone was on the verge of losing their control. I like Moore. I trust Moore. But right now, he's about to crack.

Around us, the song has switched to "Jingle Bells." The cheerful melody sets my teeth on edge.

Geri backs slowly away with a long *"Okay."*

I should do the same, but I force myself to stay. Not just for Henry, but for Moore. Something's wrong with him. He can't be sick, like I thought before. He's become edgier since Grayson's arrival. That cool, calm demeanor is slipping. He's no longer the man who picked me up from Devon Park to deliver me to Vale Hall.

"We're fine," says Henry, but he doesn't sound very convincing.

Moore's gaze zeroes in on Grayson. "I thought I made it clear to you that if you so much as looked wrong at a single student in this school, you would answer to me."

My eyes widen. Moore threatened Grayson? Moore told Henry and me to keep our distance from the senator's son, but he never mentioned that he'd told Grayson the same.

Grayson's strength returns at Moore's words. His shoulders roll back. A smirk lifts his mouth just as a dangerous gleam brightens his blue eyes.

I've come to learn that this look from Grayson is very bad.

"You don't have to worry," he says, smooth and untouchable again. "Henry and I had a disagreement, but we worked it out. He put me in my place, didn't you, Henry?"

Grayson lifts his arm and drops it over Henry's shoulders.

Henry doesn't even have time to respond. Moore is on him like a shot. He shoves Grayson and Henry apart, and pins Grayson against the glass wall of the gym.

My heart leaps into my throat. This isn't right. Even if Grayson is nothing more than another of Dr. O's henchmen, he's still a student. Moore can't hurt him.

My hands are fisted in the back of Moore's suit. His hands remain on Grayson's chest. He's knocked two chairs over in the attack, but doesn't seem to notice.

Grayson doesn't fight back. He stares at Moore with hate in his eyes, but his arms stay limp at his sides.

"Moore!" I pull harder, hearing stitches pop in his jacket.

Henry's jumped between them too, and is trying to pull Moore's grip free.

"What is this? Grayson? Mr. Moore!" From behind comes Shrew's shrill voice, pumping a new fear into me.

"You have to stop," I hiss at Moore. "Moore!"

He releases Grayson at once, and his quick glance in my direction says he's shocked to find me standing there. In horror, he looks at Grayson, then jerks back two full steps.

"Take your seats," he says unevenly. "It's time for class."

He turns and strides past Charlotte and Sam out the gym doors. I glance at Henry, finding equal confusion on his face, and then tear after our security guard.

Moore doesn't head back to the house. He cuts a straight line across the lawn toward the entrance to the garden. I look over my shoulder, but no one's following us, so I pick up my pace, intercepting him right at the bench near the garden entrance.

"What was that?" I demand.

"Get out of here," he growls.

"No. You just attacked a student! You could be fired!"

"I could be." He paces in a tight circle, rubbing his forehead. I've never seen him so unnerved. I've never seen anything get to him.

I throw myself in front of him, but he only diverts his course and keeps pacing. "*I could be?* That's it? You leave, and I'm . . . we're . . ."

Alone.

If Moore is fired, we're alone here with Dr. O. Henry, Charlotte,

Sam, and I are at the mercy of Ms. Maddox's spying, and Belk's threats. Even the other students who don't see what the director is doing need Moore here. He's the only adult we can really trust.

Moore has stopped, and is staring at Barry Buddha, the fat-bellied gold statue on its marble column that someone's dressed up in a Santa hat. How many times have I wished for Barry's help when I've been in trouble? Now Moore's staring at his jolly smile with the same desperate intent.

"I can't do it with him here," he says.

My brows crinkle. I move slowly closer.

"Who? Grayson?" I ask, even though I'm not entirely sure he's talking to me.

"I promised to protect them. But every time I look at him, I think about what he did . . ."

"Who did you promise? Dr. O?" Is he talking about his job?

He clasps his hands together, bringing them to his forehead, as if praying.

Everything inside me begins to quake. Moore can't leave. He can't fall apart. He's the rock here. I didn't realize how much I depended on that until this moment.

Everything I've been doing has been a risk, but I always thought, deep down, I'd be okay because Moore would be there. He'd have my back.

I never thought he'd be struggling too.

"I'm sorry." His voice is a broken whisper.

I don't know if he's talking to me, or someone else.

I don't know what to do.

We need each other.

If I were Henry or Charlotte, I'd hug him. If I were Sam, I'd explain how logically this doesn't make sense—his job is to protect the students, despite our line of work.

If I were Caleb, I wouldn't say anything. I'd listen. Then I'd tell him we'll figure it out.

But I'm not my friends. I'm me. I come from the hard side of the wrong end of town. I fight for everything I need. I don't give up, ever.

And that's why I like Moore. Because he came from the same place. Because he fights too, and he doesn't need a hug to tell him I care.

So I straighten my back, and tell him the same thing he told me three months ago when I was falling apart.

"That's enough. You're Hugh Moore from Devon Park. You don't do this."

His hands fall slowly to his sides.

"If you've got a problem, fix it. But do it fast, because there's another twenty-eight students at this school besides Grayson Sterling, and we need you."

Moore's chin lifts.

He nods once, his eyes still on Barry.

"Good," I say, and leave him to gather his thoughts.

CHAPTER 11

We lie low for the next few days. Breakfasts are uneventful. Evenings are quiet with everyone studying for exams. The Model UN is strictly by the books. There are no more hot chocolate deliveries, or pledges of support from Switzerland to Australia. Grayson doesn't even turn his chair in our direction, but I catch him staring at Henry when he thinks no one else is looking, and the hurt in his eyes worries me.

June joins our group for lunch, and instantly fits in. She tells us Geri's had it out for her since June got the part of Lysistrata in their drama elective, and that ever since, Geri and her friends have been stealing all the blueberry bagels at breakfast, which is the worst, because that's the only kind she likes.

Henry pledges to replace them with raisin bagels when they aren't looking.

My afternoons are consumed with physics, precalculus, and music theory, which now involves chords, aka tons of notes all put together at the same time. Finals are next week, right before Christmas and Dr. O's swearing in-ceremony on New Year's Eve, so after dinner it's down to the pit for homework.

We pretend like everything's normal. We eat copious amounts of Ms. Maddox's Christmas cookies while pretending she isn't listening to our conversations as she cleans up after us. We stream the cheesiest holiday movies we can find. Charlotte studies like crazy, blaming her recent weight gain on impending internship stress. Sam makes daily trips to the public library, where he claims to focus better as he works on their escape plan. Henry and Grayson find a way to act cordial when they're in the same room. Even Moore is back to his usual cool and collected self. But it feels like we're tiptoeing around land mines. Every hour we draw closer to

Dr. O's swearing-in is another we're all in danger. Our friends are out there, vigilant but unprotected. Charlie's probably the safest among them, and he's surrounded himself with Wolves.

Anytime I'm not focused on a task, my mind drifts to dark places. If Dr. O can use his resources to hunt us down, and get rid of our marks and those who stand in his way, what good will us blackmailing him do?

It won't matter what we know, he isn't afraid of us.

But short of making *him* disappear, I don't know what to do. If he stays, we're in danger. If he becomes senator—which he will in less than two weeks if we don't stop him—he'll have even more power. If he goes to prison, he'll find a way to punish us— we'll all end up there with him, or dead, like the others Charlie mentioned.

He's rigged the game. To beat him, we have to be better than him, and even all together, I don't know that we are.

Friday, just before lunch, I go up to my room to change my books and check the burner phone when I find a message lighting up the screen.

It's Caleb's number.

911. Meet @ bridge.

My stomach plummets. He's in trouble. Geri's dad's gotten to him, or someone else, maybe even the Wolves. I need to find him.

Meet @ bridge. The intentional vagueness is for both of our protection—in case someone else finds the phone, they won't be able to find him. But I know exactly where he means.

The bridge over the Sikawa River, beside the Rosalind, where I went last summer when I'd gotten mad at Henry for planting a bunch of Pete's pills on Grayson. Caleb found me there, and we walked along the waterfront, pointing out buildings and interesting architecture.

It's where we first kissed.

I call his number. He doesn't pick up.

"Come on," I mutter, trying again.

There is no voicemail.

My heart pumps faster.

"Pick up!" The message was sent two hours ago. There are a million things that could have happened to him in the last two hours.

Tucking the phone into my pocket, I grab my bag and race down the stairs, already thinking of an excuse. *Sam's right,* I'll say. *I need to study at the public library this afternoon. Quieter there. I'll get more done.*

That spot on the river is near the outdoor mall in Uptown. It's a straight shot on the train, I just need to get past Belk and his *no unsupervised outings* rule and find a ride to the station.

Being able to drive would really come in handy right now.

The other students are spread across the dining room, living room, and kitchen eating lunch. The room smells like reheated enchiladas and melted cheese, and through the chatter cuts the measured cadence of Joel's drumsticks against the hearth across the hall.

Charlotte—my go-to driver—isn't here.

"Brynn," comes a stoic voice beside me. "You all right?"

I turn sharply to find Grayson standing a full punch-length away, wearing a soft black sweater and beige pants, and looking every bit the priviledged son of a senator. We haven't spoken since Moore threw him against the wall in the gym.

"Do you care?" I ask.

He shoves his hands in his pockets. "Maybe. I'm full of surprises."

That, at least, he's right about.

"I need to find Charlotte. Have you seen her?"

"She left to take Sam to the library ten minutes ago." He sighs. "They got some special permission from Shrew to research their final history essays so Belk would let them go."

My head tilts back. I glare at the glass chandelier overhead, irritated that I missed her until I remember where she was actually going.

The ultrasound.

Charlotte was going to a free clinic on the south side today to find out if she's having a boy or a girl.

My heart gives a hard lurch. We talked about it on the ride

home from the mall. I asked if she wanted me to go with her. She said I needed to keep a low profile after the whole Wolves thing.

I need to find another way to the SCTA station.

"Who else can drive?" I wonder aloud.

"Hi." He holds out a hand. "I'm Grayson. Have we met?"

A cold laugh escapes my lips. "Yeah, I'm not getting in the car with you."

Even if Grayson didn't run Susan Griffin off the road at Dr. O's bidding, I don't trust him. I'm not leading him anywhere near Caleb.

"Where are you going?"

"I . . ." If I tell him I was going to the library to study like Sam, it will look suspicious that I didn't go with him and Charlotte. "I need to pick up a congratulations gift for Dr. O."

Grayson's smile comes with a sigh.

"I bet you do."

"What?" I say. "Becoming senator is a big deal."

"Really? I had no idea."

He's still smiling, but the lines beneath his eyes have pinched. I wonder if he's talked to his mom and sister at all since the arrest. I wonder if they know that Grayson's the reason Matthew Sterling is in jail.

"You should run it by the queen," he says, then motions to Geri, who's currently gathering the others to meet in the pit for the party planning committee.

I groan aloud. It will be very obvious if I miss Geri's meeting. She already sent two calendar reminders about it, and made certain we knew that duties would be assigned.

But Caleb is in trouble.

"Why are you standing there?" Geri calls over, her voice as sugar-sweet as her bubblegum-pink dress. "We're meeting in the pit in five."

"I have to go out for a while," I tell her.

She strides over, murder in her eyes. "No, you don't."

"Yes, I do."

"Did you think I wouldn't notice that the entire senior class is ditching my meeting?" Never has pink lipstick looked so venomous.

"Hi," says Grayson, holding out a hand. "I'm Grayson, also a senior. Have we met?"

She ignores him.

"You're not getting out of this," she tells me.

"Just assign me something. I'll blow up balloons."

"Balloons?" she scoffs. "*Balloons?* What kind of party do you think this is? He's not celebrating his fourth birthday, Brynn, he's being elected senator."

I step up to her, no longer intimidated by the Geri wrath. I'm not sure why's she's chosen this particular ax to grind—she's got her own reasons to watch herself with Dr. O—but I'm not going to let her steamroller me.

"Technically," I tell her, "he isn't going to be elected. He's going to be appointed. There's a difference."

"Well, this is a very exciting game of Who Knows the Director Best," says Grayson. "When do you get into your silk pajamas and have a pillow fight?"

Geri and I both glare at him. He lifts his hands in surrender.

"Boarding school should be renamed *boring* school." He shrugs. "Anyway, yes, Brynn, include me on the plaque. *G-R-A-Y-S-O-N*. Don't use an *E,* for god's sake. I hate it when people do that. Do I owe you money?"

"What plaque?" asks Geri, crossing her arms.

"The plaque for Dr. O," says Grayson, before I can decipher what he's talking about. "Brynn's going to pick up a big thank-you plaque from all of us for the party in two weeks. Is it just the senior class, or the whole school?"

His eyes gleam as he looks at me.

"The . . . whole school," I say. "There won't be personal names. Just a general message from all of us."

A scowl pulls at Geri's mouth. She knows I'm not leaving for a plaque, but she knows better than to call me out on it now.

I hope.

"I'll assign you to gifts, then," she says. "That was a decent idea, I guess."

"Now's where you kiss and make up," says Grayson. "No? What are the benefits of coming here again?"

"I'd better go," I say. "The shop closes at five, and it's across town."

Before either of them can make this weirder, I cut toward the back door, hoping to find Moore in the gym and convince him to take me all the way to the mall in Uptown. But as I walk away, I glance over my shoulder at Grayson.

He didn't have to bail me out with Geri back there. I'm not sure why he did, and it leaves me off balance. I can't figure out what he's doing. He warned me that people were noticing I was leaving, then joined with Geri to humiliate Henry, maybe to divert attention off himself. He asks if I'm all right, then gives me an out when I need it.

Favors don't come for free, so what does he want from me?

Moore isn't in the gym, and when I return to the house, I find Belk in the kitchen making a sandwich. I don't want to ask him for help, but time is ticking, and I need to get to Caleb. If he takes me to the train station, he won't know where I go. I can turn off my phone and pretend the battery died, making my trip untraceable.

"Hey Belk?" I say, trying not to show the nerves bursting inside me. No wonder Grayson asked if I was all right. I'm practically twitching.

"Yes?" He doesn't look up from his sandwich fixings.

"I need a ride to the SCTA station. I have to go pick up a gift for Dr. O for the party next week."

"Which store?"

I hesitate. If I tell him where I need to go, he'll take me. I'll never be able to get to Caleb.

If he's still there.

Belk looks up. "I think I mentioned that security is tightening down. No more free days in the city. We can go to whatever store you need when I'm done with lunch."

There's challenge in his tone, and I don't have a good answer to counter it. If I try to get a pass from Shrew, it might make Belk look closer at Charlotte and Sam, and I don't want to divert any extra attention their way today. Charlie's words whisper in my mind: *That bastard Belk told me I had ten seconds to run, then I was next.*

"Where are you going?" Moore strides in from the foyer, lifting his sunglasses to the top of his head. He's still wearing his wool coat; he must have just gotten in from somewhere.

"I need to go pick up a gift for Dr. O." I meet his gaze, hoping he can see my urgency. "Are you busy?"

"I just said—" Belk starts.

"Sure," says Moore. "You need to practice driving anyway."

A look passes between our security guards, a wordless confrontation that makes my skin prickle. Moore gestures toward the door.

"Let's go."

I practically run to the garage.

TEN MINUTES LATER, we're on the highway to Uptown in one of Vale Hall's sleek black town cars. Moore wasn't kidding. I'm driving, and he's sitting bolt upright in the passenger seat as if a meteor might crash through the windshield at any moment.

"Sixty-five," he says, pointing to the speedometer.

"I am." But I'm not. When I look down I'm crossing eighty. I lift my foot off the gas.

"Check your mirrors."

"I just did."

"Check them again. You need to be aware of where everyone is all the time."

I am—almost. Charlotte and Sam are at the doctor. Grayson, Henry, and the rest of our classmates are at the party meeting with Geri. Belk is lurking somewhere, and Dr. O was in his office when we left.

But I don't know for certain that Caleb is still at the bridge, and I don't know what Geri's dad is up to.

I force a deep breath.

Moore didn't ask any details about the gift I'm supposedly picking up. Maybe because he trusts me. Probably because he doesn't want to know. Either way, we're not mentioning what happened with Grayson at the house, or in the garden after, either.

The car in front of me is winning the slowest-driver-ever contest, so I turn on my turn signal, check my mirrors, and merge into the fast lane.

"Good," Moore grunts.

"Maybe I can get my license soon."

"You changed lanes without killing anyone. Let's not go crazy."

"You wouldn't have to go everywhere with me, then," I say. "Think of all the freedom you'd have."

"No one's going anywhere alone for the foreseeable future," he says, reminding me of Belk's warning that security was getting tighter. Caleb's message might have distracted me from the swearing-in ceremony, and the loose ends Charlie said Dr. O was tying up, but they're still festering in the back of my mind.

Now if I'm expelled, any license I might get goes up in smoke. And if Dr. O decides I'm a loose end, it won't matter anyway.

I glance over to Moore, shades pulled down over his eyes, jaw tight. One hand is gripping the handle above the passenger side window. The other is pressed firmly against his own thigh.

It occurs to me that Moore might also have a deal with Dr. O. Some blackmail arrangement, where if he speaks a word of what happens outside of the inner circle, he too gets disappeared. I can only imagine the kinds of secrets he must carry, having been here as long as he has. Each one makes him more of a liability.

Can Moore really talk to anyone outside of Vale Hall? Does he have any friends or family, or is it just us? He certainly isn't dating Shrew or Belk or Ms. Maddox. I've seen the underclassmen teachers, and they aren't in his league either.

"Do you have a someone?" I ask.

"A what?"

"A someone. A girlfriend. A boyfriend. Like a favorite stuffed animal, but alive."

His heel begins to tap. "Not that it's any of your business, but no."

"Is it because of this? Dr. O and Vale Hall and everything?"

He's quiet a moment. "There are few people who understand what we do."

"Who you can trust, you mean."

His chin dips. "That too."

I sag a little in my seat, my own problems feeling lighter, but my bones like lead. Even if Caleb and I were back together, it's not like anyone could know.

"Have you ever been in love?" It's a soft question, and too personal, even considering what I just asked. I wish I would have kept my mouth shut.

"Yes."

My brows lift in his direction.

"Eyes on the road," he snaps.

I face forward.

"And?" I say.

"And what?"

"What happened?"

He shifts in his seat. "It ended badly."

"Because you screwed it up, or because of the job?"

He grunts. "Both." His heel stops tapping. "I never should have been with her in the first place."

I wonder if Margot thought the same thing when she was falling for Jimmy. If Charlotte ever thinks that about Sam now that they're plotting their secret escape. If Henry will ever have more than the student body to choose from. Even Damien Fontego hasn't been linked to anyone, and he's out of Vale Hall.

"Do you regret it?" I ask.

"No."

Pity sloshes through me as I picture him taking this faceless woman out to dinner. Calling her. Smiling.

I wonder if Dr. O made her disappear too.

I'm too afraid to ask.

"The right person unlocks the best and worst in you," he says, staring out the side window. "They show you who you really are. Only a coward regrets that."

I think of Caleb, standing outside the door of my room my first night at Vale Hall, asking if I'm hungry. His hand under mine as we played the piano in the pit. The first time he took me to meet his family.

I have never been so happy, so scared, or so angry with anyone in my entire life. He has seen me run cons with expert precision. He's seen me struggle with classes and making friends and missing home.

I can't lose him. Not to Dr. O, or Geri's dad, or Belk, or anyone tied to this twisted school.

I press harder on the gas, edging just above the speed limit.

I have to find him.

CHAPTER 12

After our bonding moment, I feel bad giving Moore the slip as soon as we get to the outdoor mall in Uptown. Really, he should be better at tailing—he's security at a school for con artists—but it's as easy as, "Oh, I want to try on that sweater," at a posh boutique, then sneaking out the employee exit and turning off my phone.

Five minutes after we park, I'm at the river.

The spot where Caleb and I kissed isn't far; it takes me less than five minutes to run there. It's near the McCray Bridge, and under the balcony of the ballroom at the Rosalind Hotel, now draped in holly garland, where Caleb stood when we took down Pete and the Sikawa branch of the Wolves.

In two weeks, it's where Geri is throwing Dr. O's celebration.

The walkway is practically empty on account of the cold and the afternoon timing. I don't see Caleb as I approach, and with each step a crushing kind of dread presses through me.

I got the meeting place wrong. I'm too late.

Something's happened.

The bridge's shadow overtakes me, and soon I'm under the rusty beams, the sound of the water lapping against the shore magnified by the metal around me. My fingers weave together as a frigid breeze shoots up my coat sleeves and around my collar, but my chill isn't from the cold.

Three hours have passed since Caleb sent that text.

Three hours, and he could be anywhere.

"Brynn?"

I turn, and Caleb's standing behind me.

A hard punch of relief shoves the breath from my lungs. He's here. He's all right. He's wearing his black hoodie and jeans, and every part of him seems to be intact.

I throw myself at him, my arms around his neck, my feet stepping all over his. He loses balance and we nearly fall, but I don't let go.

"I'm sorry I took so long." My words fly out.

His arms come around me, squeezing tight. I'm shaking. I can barely catch my breath.

"I had to take a walk. My feet were going numb." He lowers his chin to my shoulder and then turns, and his cold nose brushes my neck, sending shivers across every nerve. "I'm glad you knew where to come. I wanted to call, but my battery died."

I squeeze my eyes closed, holding on to him for one more second before I realize I don't even know why he sent the text, or what's happened. I just hugged him, like we do this all the time. Like we're an *us* again.

Slowly, I unwind my hands from the back of his neck, and take a step back.

"Sorry," I say, cheeks warm. "Too much time with Henry."

"Or maybe just the right amount of time with Henry."

I smile, taking this to mean the hug went over well. "Maybe."

Caleb smiles, and my heart feels too big for my chest.

"What happened?" I ask. "Is it Margot? Is everyone all right?"

His eyes widen, as if he's just realized he hasn't told me. When he speaks, his voice is quiet, and rough.

"It's my dad."

Every muscle in my body wrenches tight. It's like I'm on a train that just slammed on the breaks and switched to reverse.

I picture his father, laid out in a bed in the rehab hospital. I see the tubes in his mouth, and the delicate pieces of tape holding his eyes closed, and the protruding bones of his arms.

He will never get better. That's what Caleb told me the first time I saw him.

For as long as I've known him, he's been waiting for his dad to die.

I hurt for him—a sudden, merciless punch to the chest.

"Caleb," I whisper. "I'm so sorry."

"No," he says. "You don't understand. Brynn, he woke up."

It takes a moment for this to sink in.

"He . . . woke up?"

Caleb's nodding now, his eyes glassy. In a rush, he tells me it happened last night when his mom and brothers were leaving. It was all a big mess, his dad choking on the vent and Christopher running to get the nurse because they thought he was having a heart attack. Jonathan called Caleb, but he didn't get the message until early this morning. When he heard, he went straight there.

"He can't talk yet, but he squeezed my hand, and he looked at me. Straight at me. He remembers, I know it."

Caleb's arms move in quick circles as he talks, the words growing louder, like he's just taking a shot of adrenaline to the heart. I can feel his excitement. I'm gaping at him, ready to jump up in the air and shout.

"He's going to need therapy, and more specialists. Maybe more surgery. I think a lot of his muscles have atrophied." He shakes his head. "I don't even care. We'll figure it out, you know?"

He looks at me as he says this, like I'm part of the *we*, and I lift another inch taller.

"We will," I say.

"Mom sent me back to go to class so Dad can rest. I almost blew it and told her I got expelled."

My brows pinch together. Caleb still hasn't told his mom or brothers where he is. He's using his family's trust to pay the medical bills, and letting his mom think Dr. O's still writing them off.

If we don't get him back to Vale Hall, she'll have to find out, sooner or later.

We can deal with that at another time. Right now his dad is awake, and that is the only thing that matters.

"I thought he was gone. Jonathan was crying in the message. I thought . . ." Caleb looks at me, his shoulders rising with each breath. Fear rolls off him in waves, combating the relief, stealing his voice, challenging the happiness in his eyes. "You were the first person I wanted to tell."

Then he takes my face in his hands and kisses me.

A gasp of surprise locks in my throat just as joy explodes inside my chest. Sirens, fireworks, a full-on marching band with baton dancers and acrobats throwing candy. It's like Mardi Gras has found a new home city between my ribs and spine.

But outside, I am frozen in shock.

He jolts back. His mouth makes a small o. I can still feel the pressure of his lips on mine, and his hands on my jaw, and his fingers, weaving through my hair. Now that I've regained the use of my body, I'm cursing myself for not kissing him back.

"I . . ." He exhales hard, looking more panicked then I've ever seen him. "That was not what I meant to do. I mean, it is what I wanted to do—what I've been wanting to do for a while—but not—"

"How dare you," I say.

His jaw shuts with a snap. He nods, maybe in agreement.

"I wasn't even ready."

He stops nodding. His eyes lock on mine for confirmation, brows hiked above the black plastic rims of his glasses.

A laugh bubbles up my throat as I reach for his sweatshirt and pull him down to me. He's smiling, and so am I. We're in a bubble, separated from the world, immune to the cold. His knuckles skim my cheek, and I lean into his touch. My arms fit beneath his, my hands splayed over his shoulder blades.

Our smiles fade.

His lips brush mine, side to side, and warmth rises from the deepest part of me, flushing my skin. He moves closer, his feet bumping mine, his hips to my hips. His gaze is dark and safe, his long black lashes magnified through the lenses of his glasses.

He kisses my bottom lip, feather soft.

My breath comes faster.

He kisses my cheek.

I grip the back of his shirt.

His mouth finds mine, and he's watching as my eyes drift closed. There is nothing but the feel of him then. The gentle parting of his lips. The softness, and the taste of our kiss.

Does he feel this? He has to. This isn't just a kiss. This is everything. This is *finally*.

He pulls back the slightest bit. "Was that better?"

I nod, because all the words have fled from my mind.

It's then that I catch movement over his left shoulder. Someone's coming down the path, moving quickly, dressed sharply in black. He doesn't slow as he sees us; in fact, he seems to walk faster.

My stomach twists.

There's no use hiding now.

"We're busted," I say.

Caleb follows my gaze over his shoulder, then turns, taking both my hands in his. He leans in my direction, his eyes on Moore.

"How much does he know?"

"He thinks I'm trying on sweaters."

Caleb considers this with a scowl. "Not too late to make a run for it."

"It's all right," I tell him. "I trust him."

Caleb glances at me, then lifts his chin again. "Then I trust him too."

"That doesn't mean he won't drown us both in the river."

Caleb's hand squeezes mine. "Still not too late to make a run for it."

But it is, because Moore's within striking distance now, and that vein on his neck that bulges when he's angry is about to burst.

He stops.

We wait.

"So this is a thing again," he says.

"Hi, Moore," says Caleb.

"Don't 'Hi, Moore,' me," he barks. He spins away, then, after a moment, turns back. He waves a hand at Caleb. "You need a haircut."

"He looks all right to me," I say, a little giddy that Moore hasn't decided to drown us after all.

"I didn't ask you," he snaps. He looks again at Caleb, then shakes his head and sighs. "Well, come on."

Moore turns without another word, and strides down the Riverwalk, toward the mall.

Caleb and I glance at each other, confused.

"He's not going to kill me, is he?" Caleb asks.

"I don't think so."

"Come *on*," Moore shouts over his shoulder.

We come on.

MOORE BUYS US a late lunch at a sandwich shop. He tells Caleb he can get whatever he wants, and I feel a slash of guilt when he orders an extra-large with everything on it, and three bags of chips for later. I wonder when the last time was that he had a solid meal he didn't take from the bowling alley snack shop.

Moore doesn't ask Caleb any specific questions about his life, and Caleb doesn't give any unnecessary details. Instead, Moore asks if Caleb has enough money, if he's got a coat, and if he's talked to anyone about his "current situation."

"Just Brynn," Caleb says. He doesn't mention Henry, Charlotte, or Sam, or any of the other expelled students.

Moore takes out his wallet and peels free a hundred dollars.

"I don't want it," Caleb says.

"Then the busboy's about to get a very nice tip," Moore responds as he stands.

Caleb takes the money, but he doesn't look at me when he tucks it in his pocket.

"I'll give you a ride to your apartment," Moore tells him, winding his maroon scarf around his neck. "We need to make a stop on the way."

Again, he walks away without further explanation.

"How does he know where I live?" Caleb asks quietly as we both slide out of the booth and gather our trash.

"I don't know." I want to reassure him that it's all right—that I trust Moore—but we've all been careful to keep Caleb's apartment a secret, especially now that Dr. O's upped his game. If Moore knows where Caleb lives, who else does?

We follow him outside, and then to the garage where I parked the car. This time, Moore drives. He heads to the freeway, and Caleb and I share a confused look when he takes the on-ramp that leads north, the opposite direction from Caleb's apartment.

This must be the stop Moore mentioned, but it's certainly not on the way.

Beside me, Caleb's frown etches deep lines into his face. He keeps glancing nervously out the window. Does he think Moore's taking us somewhere to get rid of us like Geri's dad did with Jimmy and Margot?

I reach for Caleb's hand and give it a squeeze.

He smiles weakly in return.

The trip is faster than expected, and soon we're turning in to a lot filled with cars in front of a blunt stone building. I read the letters over the entrance.

"DMV?"

Is this what I think it is?

I bite the inside of my cheek, squeezing Caleb's hand hard enough to break his fingers.

Moore parks the car and turns around in the front seat.

"If you're going to sneak out to see your boyfriend, you can go ahead and leave me out of it."

He gets out of the car. I can't help it, I squeal. The lines between Caleb's brows relax and he laughs.

Moore knocks on the window. "You have to pass the test first."

Right. There's a test. He gave me the study booklet a few weeks ago. I read it all in one night, even though he said I wouldn't be ready to test until the spring. It was mostly stuff he'd already taught me—stopping at a red light before you turn right, and using your turn signal to change lanes.

I'm getting my license today.

I practically drag Caleb out of the car and run to the DMV. Inside, there are about a million people in line, but I don't mind the wait. Caleb quizzes me with a practice test in one of the bins hanging from the wall, and Moore sits in the waiting area, looking grumpy.

When we get to the front, he joins us and signs the paperwork indicating that I've completed driver's education classes through Vale Hall. I take the test into a quiet room, where ten other people are working through their own tests, and then hand it back to a woman who couldn't be less interested in my upcoming life change.

I'm getting my license.

When she sees I've missed only three questions, she takes me for an eye exam, which I pass, and then grabs a clipboard. We head out to the parking lot, where I show her that the brake lights on Moore's car work, and the mirrors are all in place. Then I wave goodbye to Moore and Caleb, and take her for a drive around the block.

That's when the nerves kick in.

I go two miles under the speed limit, then three over. I stop too quickly at a stop sign and have to pull up. I try to summon the confidence I use when I pull cons, but that doesn't matter here. This lady doesn't care if I'm confident, she cares if I can drive.

By the time we get back, I'm sweating, and I feel like I might vomit. Dr. O might hold my actual life in his hands, but it feels like the DMV lady does too, and when she takes notes on her clipboard, it's all I can do not to scream, *Did I pass?*

"Watch out, Sikawa," she says flatly when she's done. "Another teenage driver is on the road."

I bolt out of the car to run to Moore and Caleb, still standing on the front steps of the DMV, but forget the keys in the ignition so I have to turn back. Once I've got them, I try to walk calmly across the lot, but I'm practically flying. When they see me, I raise my hands in a victorious V. Caleb pumps his fist.

Even Moore smirks.

My driver's license picture is terrible. I didn't have time to put on makeup when I left the house, and the cold has tinted my nose and cheeks a little too rosy.

I don't care. I have a license.

For the first time in weeks, I wish my mom could see me. I want to call her, but she's at work—answering phones for Wednesday Pharmaceuticals, the company Dr. O owns. The reminder threatens to swamp me, but I refuse to let it.

For this moment, everything is all right.

"Do you want some celebration doughnuts?" I ask the guys. "What's the farthest doughnut shop you can think of? I'll drive there. You know why?"

"Because you have your license?" Caleb pushes up his glasses with his index finger, and everything inside me warms and pulls tight. I can't help it. Those glasses are my kryptonite.

"I was going to say because I love doughnuts, but you know what, Caleb? You're absolutely right. I do!"

"Is this going to continue very long?" Moore asks.

"Just until Dr. O decides to erase my identity."

Caleb chuckles weakly. Moore gives me a stern look.

I smile my widest smile. "Too soon?"

"Stop talking." Moore sighs.

His phone rings, and he pulls back to answer it. Caleb, thankfully, isn't upset by my comment, and reaches for my hand. As his fingers intertwine with mine, warmth slides up my arm, tingling beneath my collarbones.

"Congratulations," he says.

I wonder if Caleb will kiss me again. Does he care that Moore's here?

Are we "a thing" again, like Moore said?

I want to be.

But even now, I can feel reality pressing against the edges of my high. How much does a stupid driver's license matter when your identity doesn't even exist? When *you* don't even exist? Caleb did this once too. He had his own driver's license, and school ID, and a dozen other records and forms of identification, and now they're nothing but paper. He was wiped clear of any database that will let him graduate, open a bank account, or apply to college or for a real job.

And suddenly I'm so angry I could kick something.

How dare Dr. O give him a future, just to take it away? And now, Caleb's dad will need more care—and more money—than ever. How is Caleb supposed to make that happen passing out shoes and selling popcorn at a bowling alley?

"What is it?" he asks, watching me in that way he does, like he's trying to solve a puzzle.

"Nothing." I grasp on to the elation I felt only moments ago, but it's already slipping away. "I just wish this was real."

His brows pinch together. "It is."

For now. But I want more than right now. I want to drive us to the doughnut shop next week, next month. A year from now. It seems impossible to hope for anything more than these minutes we have together.

"We need to leave," Moore says, breezing by us. He snags the keys from my hand. "*Now*. Get in the car."

Caleb and I share a wary glance and jog after him. As soon as we're in and the doors are closed, he tears out of the lot, careening down side streets toward the west side of town. I hold on to the armrest, trying to buckle my seat belt as he swings around a turn and guns it down a two-lane street lined by shops and old oak trees.

"I guess we're not modeling safe driving anymore," I say.

Caleb leans forward, looking out the windshield. "This is Bakerstown. What are we doing here?"

Something tells me this isn't where Moore thinks Caleb lives. He's driving too fast, and honks as we swerve around a blue van.

"Moore, what's going on?" I ask.

Moore's squeezing the wheel tight enough to break it. Urgency rises in my chest, filling me with a cold, slippery fear.

"Moore," I shout, just as he swerves across the lane into the lot of an old, run-down apartment complex. He barely pulls between the white lines before he slams the car into park.

"Stay here," he says.

I look to Caleb, who gives a small shake of his head, as if to say, *Don't argue.*

We watch Moore rip out of the car, slam the door, and run toward the apartment building. He takes the concrete stairs to the second floor, then disappears around a corner.

"We're going," I say.

Caleb's already got his hand on the door. "Yep."

We're quieter in our departure, but still quick. I don't know this area of town, and I have no idea who might possibly be here that's got Moore so upset. Either way, something's seriously wrong, and I'm not about to hide in the car and wait for that danger to come to us.

Caleb and I slow to a walk at the top of the stairs, our warm breath misting in front of our faces. The sun is already falling behind the horizon, and the clouds overhead are low and dark.

A few crunched beer cans litter the scuffed cement walkway. An ashtray full of half-smoked cigarettes is spilling over outside someone's door. As we near the corner, Caleb stops and glances around the peeling beige paint of the building's edge.

"See anything?" I ask.

He shakes his head.

My heart pumps harder as we follow the walkway around the bend. Three doors face out on this stretch. The first is number 6, and has a pitiful Christmas wreath around the peephole. The second, number 7, has a "Beware of Dog" sign taped to the wood.

Number 8 is cracked open.

After exchanging a quick glance, we sneak toward it, but just as we're passing number 6, a crash comes from down the way, inside apartment 8. Caleb stops short, but I shove past him. If Moore's in trouble, he might need our help. He has my back, I have his.

But as I reach the door and push inside, I don't know what to make of the scene before me. Moore's standing over a table that's tipped onto its side, his shoulders rising with each heavy breath. Behind him, on the floor, a body lies still, socked feet turned out at an awkward angle.

Moore's stare lifts to mine, and his jaw flexes.

"Get out," he growls, angrier than when he threw Grayson into the wall.

"Who is that?" My voice is shaking.

Caleb is right behind me, his hands gripping my arms.

"Get *out*," Moore repeats. "Go back to the car. You can't be here."

"Raf?" Caleb pushes past me. Moore intercepts him before he reaches the person on the floor.

Legs like lead, I push myself past the overturned table, into the tiny kitchenette. Moore is too busy holding Caleb to stop me, and as I get closer to the man stretched out on the ground, I take in the faded jeans, ripped at one knee, and the twisted, long-sleeve T-shirt, pulled tight across muscular shoulders.

It *is* Raf.

His jaw is hanging slack. His eyes are open and unseeing.

"Did you . . ." I clap my hands to my mouth, staring at Moore. I'm not sure if I'm going to scream or throw up.

He shakes his head.

My vision blurs, hot tears filling my eyes. Moore is talking, and maybe Caleb is too. I don't hear them. I blink, and it looks like Raf is surrounded by stars. Tiny white stars. But that's not right.

I lean closer, and see there are pills on the ground beside his open hand. A fistful of them, spilled across the warped linoleum. One of them is close enough to pick up, and maybe it's gravity pushing me down, or just fear, but as soon as it's between my fingers, my stomach gives a hard twist.

A small *W* is pressed into the white, chalky circle of the pill.

"Look at me."

Moore's crouched in front of me, his hand cupped firmly beneath my chin. I look at him but my gaze can't stick.

Raf is dead.

Raf overdosed on Wednesday pills. On Dr. O's pills.

Why would he do that? I just saw him last week. He was going to help us. He was going to take Dr. O down.

"Brynn, look at me." Moore is calm now. "You're going to stand up, turn around, and walk to the car."

"I don't . . ."

"Stand up," he says.

I do. Caleb is beside me, his face pale. He's still staring at Raf, lying on the floor.

"We need to leave," Moore tells us. "The police are going to come and take care of this."

"This?" Caleb looks at him, horrified. "What happened? How did you know he—"

Moore turns us so that we're facing the door and he's the one looking at the body. "I paid the landlord to contact me if anything suspicious started going on."

"Why would you do that? How did you even know he was here?"

"Because it is my job to look out for the students of Vale Hall," he says.

I promised to protect them.

He's keeping track of where the students go when they're expelled, that must have been how he knew where Caleb lived.

"Raf wouldn't have done this," Caleb says. "I just talked to him yesterday. He sounded fine. He and Renee—"

Moore's chin snaps to Caleb. "Renee Gibson?"

Caleb nods.

"Do you know where she is?" Moore asks, the urgency in his tone scraping across my nerves.

Caleb shakes his head. "She was staying here with him."

The apartment is only one room. Moore does a quick once-over, but no one's here.

"He did this, didn't he?" I ask, tears finally breaking free from my eyes. "Dr. O killed Raf. He's tying up loose ends, just like Charlie said." I picture Geri's father, standing in the threshold of Dr. O's office. I picture him here, catching Raf by surprise. Hitting him, or choking him, or covering his face with a pillow, then spreading pills on the ground to make it look like an overdose.

If it had come to a fair fight, Raf would have stood a chance. He was a prizewinning fighter. He should have gone to the Olympics.

"Charlie who?" asks Moore.

I close my eyes, but I still see Raf on the floor. "Dylan Prescott. He goes by Charlie now."

Moore doesn't deny that Dr. O's behind it, which frightens me even more.

"If the landlord saw someone here, we need to tell the police. He could ID who did this." Caleb's voice is shaking.

"No," says Moore. "We need to get out of here."

"We're just going to leave him like this?" Caleb asks. "He's one of us. He *was* one of us."

My stomach churns. Bile climbs up the back of my throat, hot and poisonous.

"We were never here," Moore says, and it's clear in his tone that this is the final word.

I glance down to the table, turned on its side. He sets it upright carefully, then looks one more time at Raf.

"I'm sorry, kid," he mutters. Then he ushers us to the car.

CHAPTER 13

We drive for five minutes in silence before Moore pulls over in the parking lot of an ice-cream parlor. I've managed not to throw up yet, but the giant pictures of fudge sundaes in the windows threaten to push me over the edge.

Once, in Devon Park, there was a fight outside Jay's Mini Mart. One guy stabbed the other, and by the time the cops had come he'd bled out on the sidewalk. I was heading home from school when I saw the body. It was surrounded by people, some crying, some pushing and shoving, some trying to help. A whole group to witness what had happened.

This is different.

Raf was alone. He'd been alone since Dr. O expelled him, and he'd died alone, a lie covering up what had really happened. Would the police even investigate? Or would they write him off as another junkie who died holding the pills he loved too much?

"He has a brother," I say, remembering what he told us that night at the train yard. Dr. O had threatened to drown his brother in the lake if Raf ever talked.

"His brother thinks he's dead," Moore answers flatly. "Rafael hasn't seen him in seven years."

Because of Dr. O.

All of this is because of Dr. O.

Caleb is staring out the window. "Am I next?"

His voice is too calm. Inside, I am raging, barely able to stay in this car, in this *skin*, but Caleb is somewhere far away.

I grip his hand, but it is loose in my hot, shaking fist.

"No. That's not going to happen." But I don't know why I say this after what we just saw. Raf is dead. Charlie mentioned others too. Margot knows Jimmy was killed by Geri's dad, because she almost died too.

Caleb needs to run.

Moore turns in his seat. "Do you have anything I need to know about at your apartment?"

My stomach twists painfully.

Caleb is still staring out the window. "No."

"No phones. No records. No old ID's," Moore rattles off.

"A few books from school. I moved my pictures—"

"Don't tell me," Moore interrupts.

Caleb's chin drops to his chest. "My dad woke up."

"I know." Moore's turned toward the front of the car again, staring ahead at the restaurant as if hoping it has the answers we need. "The security guard at the hospital and I have an arrangement. Your dad will be fine there for now. No one who isn't authorized will have visitation."

It is my job to look out for the students of Vale Hall.

"You paid for Caleb's apartment," I realize. Caleb thought the owner was just cutting him a break until spring, but no one's that nice.

Caleb's chin jerks up, as he looks to Moore for confirmation.

Moore doesn't respond.

"What about my mom and brothers?" Caleb hand has begun squeezing mine, a gradual pressure that's now threatening to crack my knuckles.

"Where can they go?" Moore asks.

Caleb gives a weak laugh, and I know what he must be thinking. He doesn't have any other family here. His dad's parents live in Japan. His mom's mother and sisters live in California.

She's not leaving for the West Coast with his dad just waking up.

"My mom thinks I'm still in school," Caleb says.

Moore scratches a hand down his jaw.

It seemed less dangerous for her to know the truth about Caleb's situation before, but how will he move his family without telling them what's really happened? His mom will wonder why he didn't say anything. She'll want to know why he hasn't reenrolled in public school, and what this means for his father's health care, which Dr. O was covering as long as Caleb went to Vale Hall.

The more they know, the more danger they're in.

Panic is swelling inside my chest—for Caleb, for his mom, Maiko, and Christopher and Jonathan. I have to do something, but what? My mom has an apartment, and if I asked, I'm sure she would let them crash there for a little while, but Dr. O would find out. I'm sure he's watching her. She works for Wednesday Pharmaceuticals, the company that made the drugs now on the floor beside Raf's still body, because Dr. O wants her to work there. Because he knows that's how he can control me.

Rage charges like lightning through my veins, giving way to more fear.

I cannot let Dr. O hurt my mom, or Caleb, or his family.

But my delay has cost Raf his life.

Margot was right. We waited too long. We should have found a way to get rid of Dr. O without gathering the old students. I thought we could all help each other, but Dr. O made another move while we hesitated, and another one of us is dead.

"I have a house," Moore says finally. "Your family can stay there until we figure out something else."

"Dr. O doesn't know about it?" I ask. That seems unlikely.

Moore shakes his head. "It was my aunt's. We'd lost touch. She willed it to me when she died."

I remember him mentioning an aunt before—she taught him how to run scams outside the bingo hall.

"It's in Devon Park," I say.

Moore grunts, which I take as a yes.

"How do I convince my mom to move there?" Caleb asks. "If she senses I'm lying, or something's off, she could call the school. She could show up, if she wanted. She knows where it is."

The car falls silent as we each try to piece together how to make this work, fast, while giving Caleb's family as little information as possible.

"We need to evict her," I say.

Caleb presses his thumbs to his temples.

"It doesn't have to be real," I say. "Or permanent. Just for a little while. Until we can figure out something else."

I close my eyes, willing the pieces of this plan to come into place. "If someone she thinks works for the city comes to the house and kicks her out, she'll listen to them, right?"

"She pays rent on time," Caleb says. "If we post an eviction notice, she'll know it's a scam and call the cops."

There has to be another way to get her out of the house. There are empty houses in Devon Park all the time. People get arrested and don't come back, or move because they can't make rent. Of course, most of those places are infested with rats and who knows what else . . .

"Termites," I say, releasing Caleb's hand to scoot forward in my seat. "We tell her she has termites. They have to spray termite poison in the house and she can't be there for a couple weeks. By then we can think of something else."

Caleb's gaze finds mine for the first time since we left Raf's apartment. Drive flickers in his eyes and gives me a small burst of hope.

"Who can we convince to tell her? Not you or me. She'd recognize Moore."

He's right. We don't want to pay some random person off the street; who knows who they will tell? "What about Henry? He can pull it off."

"Mom would recognize him from Family Day," Caleb says. Neither of us wants to pull Charlotte into this, which reminds me that she's probably done with her appointment by now.

She knows if she's having a boy or a girl. Somehow, that makes her situation feel a hundred times more real, and I'm more afraid for her than ever.

"Sam," Moore says in the front seat.

Yes. Maiko wouldn't recognize Sam, because he's always at Bennington Max Penitentiary visiting his mom on Family Days.

Caleb's already yanking his phone out of his pocket. He texts Sam a series of numbers—a code to call him back from an unmonitored phone—and less than a minute later, his cell rings.

Moore fixes a pointed stare at Caleb, pausing him from answering. "You trust him?"

Caleb nods. The phone rings again.

"You're absolutely sure?"

I glance at Caleb, finding a furrowed line between his brows, and know why Moore's asking this question.

Raf was fine before he reconnected with us. He was living on earnings of illegal fights and didn't have any connection to his family, but he was alive. Dr. O may be tying up loose ends, but he had help finding Raf, and there are only a few people who knew how to reach him.

Renee, and who knows where she is now? Margot. Charlotte. Sam. Henry.

Caleb, and me.

Did one of us let something slip about Raf in front of the wrong person? Did Belk or Geri's dad follow Henry or me when we were scouting out that fight, or following the guy placing Raf's bets?

Could his death be our fault?

People are starting to notice, Grayson told me. *Warned* me. And then steered Geri off my path so I could meet Caleb.

The phone is still ringing. Caleb's gaze meets mine, and with a quick shake of his head, he's made his decision.

If you can't trust your friends, you can't trust anyone.

"Hey," he says. "I need a favor. How quickly can you get to White Bank?"

VALE HALL IS quiet by the time we get back. Dinner is long since over, and most everyone has retreated to the pit to study for finals or play Road Rules, or gone upstairs to bed. I paint a smile on my face just like Moore told me to and show off my new driver's license, but all I can think about is Raf, and Caleb, and the look on Maiko's face from our hidden spot across the street when Sam knocked on her door and told her she and the boys needed to leave that night.

He'd made an official letter from the library before he'd met us. The city had found evidence of termites, and were going to tent the house with the overnight crew to begin spraying poison in the morning. He played the part perfectly, adding enough details to banish her doubts.

For tonight, at least, they're hidden.

But as I show Paz and Bea my new driver's license, they're unimpressed. Paz has some new phone she traded her Vale Hall model in for—something I'm pretty sure is against the rules—and everyone is flocking around her to see the fancy camera functions and pose for pictures. I can't help but think back on Grayson's warning and wonder what's being said behind my back.

And who might be talking to Dr. O.

The weight of it all presses down on me as I climb the stairs. I wish there was a way to shrug off this blanket of suspicion. To crawl into bed and forget what we saw sprawled across that dirty kitchen floor. But the image is still there, clinging to the edges of every thought with its sharp, pale claws.

Raf is dead.

Raf is dead after I recruited him to fight against Dr. O.

What if I'm the reason he's gone now?

Panic swells in my chest with every breath. What if I'm being watched right now? What if Dr. O knows that I was with Caleb today, and he's the next spread across the floor of Moore's house in Devon Park, a bottle of Wednesday pills spilled out around his lifeless hand?

People are starting to notice.

I shouldn't have come back to Vale Hall. I should have gone to get Mom. Called Charlotte and told her to round up Henry and Sam, and as many of the others as will come with us. We all need to run.

But for how long? If we run, Dr. O will find us eventually.

Act normal, Moore told me before we came inside. *If you act normal, Odin won't have reason to threaten you.*

But he already has. Maybe we weren't supposed to find Raf, but his cold body on the floor was a warning all the same.

I feel like I'm balancing on the edge of a knife.

As I pass June's cracked door, I hear a muttered curse and pause. I'm revved too high, my heart pounding, and when she lets loose a stream of profanities, I shove inside her room without a second thought.

"June? Are you . . . *oh*."

I'm greeted by a familiar sight, a gut punch of memories I'd rather not have. Her room mirrors mine in its L shape, and the desk, bookshelf, and bed are all in the same places. But the comforter is pulled back to reveal soaking wet sheets, and her clothes—the black ones she favors anyway—are all cut into fringe across the floor. The standing mirror beside the bathroom door is decorated with the word *FREAK* in lipstick graffiti. The wall on my left boasts a sprawling *Vincit Omnia Veritas* in bubblegum pink.

Truth conquers all.

Pretty sure Geri was wearing the same color this morning.

"Great, right?" June says, her voice more flustered than I've ever heard it. "Guess someone didn't like my decorations and thought they could do better."

I glance to her nightstand, where small, plastic bones hang from a miniature charred Christmas tree. It's festive. Kind of.

"They did the same to my room after I moved in." I think of Geri, of how much I hated her before I learned she was working for Dr. O. We've never been best friends, but I thought we'd evolved, at least a little.

I was wrong. Geri will always be Geri.

June's eyes flick to me, just long enough for me to see the gloss of tears.

"It's ridiculous." She snags a shredded pair of black jeans off the floor and chucks it in the trash can beside her desk. "And frankly, unoriginal. Do they think this is going to hurt my feelings? Like no one's ever called me a freak before?"

Her back is to me, but I can see her swipe at her eyes with the back of her hand.

Anger heats my blood, and I'm grateful for it. I need to feel something, anything, other than the crushing despair right outside this room.

"You're not a freak," I say.

"Of course I am," she snaps back. "I don't belong out there. I clearly don't belong in here. I don't even know what those stupid words mean." She motions to the school motto on the wall behind me.

"Truth conquers all," I tell her.

She snorts, and then looks at the word *freak* again, and I wish the anger had stayed longer because now there's only regret, punctuating the cool air.

"It's just stupid hazing," I say, but I remember when it happened to me, and it didn't feel stupid. It felt personal. Another sign that I wasn't good enough to be here.

I head to June's bathroom, anxious for something to do with my hands, selfishly grateful to get out of my own head for one single moment. "Lucky for you, I'm a pro at taking lipstick off walls. Did Ms. Maddox give you some makeup remover?"

"Under the sink," June mutters.

I find the box of disposable cloths and am on my way back to her when I catch movement outside the window near her bed. A boy in a gray coat and jeans walks down the stone path through the yard toward the gardens. Even from here I can make out his dark hair and purposeful stride.

Grayson.

My skin tightens as he stops before the entrance to sit on one of the park benches. I don't know what I expect will happen. It's not like he's going to meet with Dr. O and kill someone in the yard. He's just sitting there.

He looks . . . lonely.

Anger burns within me. For the punch of pity I feel watching him. For the fact that I can't figure out what he's playing at. Because he killed a woman on Dr. O's orders.

Because even now I want to believe there must have been a reason, something that pushed him off that ledge.

The realization comes with a hard exhale. I want to believe he's being blackmailed like the rest of us. That he didn't want to hurt Susan, and that the guilt of what he's done to his father is why he's alone now, staring at nothing.

As much as I try to hate him, I can't.

"There he is," says June, coming up beside me. Her arms are crossed over her chest, and her fingers make white marks in her biceps as she squeezes them. "Holding down the bench again."

"What do you mean?"

Her shoulder lifts in a jerky shrug. "He's always there. That's his special spot or something."

My brows knit together. "What's he doing?"

"I don't know." She waves her hand at the window. "Communing with nature. Meditating. Making mental lists of stupid pickup lines. Sometimes he's on the phone."

"With who?"

"I can't exactly hear him from here."

I shake off her patronizing tone. "How often does he do this?"

June sighs. She seems relieved the spotlight is off her. "Every day."

My gaze lifts beyond him, beyond the garden, through the naked tree branches to a house at the back of the property. It's a miniature version of Vale Hall, an echo of twisting spires and wide windows, normally hidden from view by the outcropping of woods at the back of the property.

It's where Dr. O lives.

Has Grayson been in that house? Though it's well known where Dr. O sleeps, no student I've ever heard of has been into the lion's den.

I can only imagine what he's hiding in there.

"You notice a lot about other people," I say to June.

Her cheeks grow pink. "It's a special superpower of mine. Noticing mundane details."

She's joking, but maybe she shouldn't be. Someone who notices details about other people can come in very helpful.

"What else have you noticed?"

She takes the box of makeup cloths and returns to the wall, scowling up at the pink school motto. "About who?"

I take a cloth and begin scrubbing at the pink corner of the *V*. "Anyone."

"Well. Henry's obviously hung up on the benchwarmer outside."

Unfortunately, I think she's right.

"Paz is wasting Joel's time. She's got a thing for Bea."

"She does?" I picture Joel and Paz tangled up in the living room, where I caught them one night after curfew. The image was unfortunately seared into my mind. I hadn't noticed if she was interested in Bea.

"What else?"

"Charlotte's packing it on these days."

I freeze. Force myself to keep moving.

"I think she looks good," I say.

"Uh huh," says June. "Don't worry. I'm not telling."

She knows Charlotte's pregnant. Maybe it was stupid to hope no one would notice her sudden change from fitted clothes to sweatshirts and yoga pants, but we did. Still, I can't bring myself to confirm it, especially with that intrigued tilt to June's smirk.

"Nothing to tell," I say. "What about me?"

"What about you?" she says, her smirk melting. Her stare holds on the wall.

"I know you've got something on me if you've collected all this info on everyone else."

Research, we would have called it in conning class. *Know your mark. Know their habits. Become what they need.*

She gives me a side-eye. "You sure you want to hear this?"

I smile to lighten the mood, but my stomach clenches. "Absolutely."

"Okay." She tosses the rag on the floor and grabs another. "You leave a lot."

"We went out the other night to do our assignment for Belk."

"You must have a lot more assignments than I do."

I frown.

"Is it a guy?" she asks, a little aggressively, as if she's been waiting a long time to find out.

"I wish," I tell her, the lie slipping easily from my lips.

"Is it a girl?" She lifts a brow in my direction. "I remember that girl you brought to the restaurant the first time I saw you. You were with a bunch of people, and that loser who bought me a new pair of boots."

It takes me a second to remember what she's talking about. The first night I saw June wasn't here, but at a Mexican restaurant in

Uptown, near the club where Dr. O had planted me to find out about Jimmy Balder. The loser she's referring to is definitely Mark Stitz, Sterling's intern supervisor and misogynistic jerk. June lifted his wallet and gave herself a nice tip—apparently a pair of boots—before I managed to get it back.

The girl must have been Margot. We were friends—kind of—back then.

I almost say her name, but catch myself. "Myra? You remember her?"

June's cheeks turn as pink as the lipstick on the walls. "She was . . . memorable."

"Oh, I see." I give a small laugh, and it's genuine. I can picture Margot with June. They have similar views on authority. It wouldn't surprise me to see either of their faces in a police lineup for arson.

Despite my current state of Trust No One, I'm starting to get a very good feeling about June joining the cause.

"What do you think about Dr. O?" I ask, trying to be nonchalant.

"Does that mean you aren't telling me what you're doing when you leave campus?"

I grin.

"I think he's dangerous," she says.

"Why?"

"Because people with money and power always are."

I swallow, thinking again of Raf, of his socked feet, and the gash on his head, and his wide-open eyes.

"Your turn," she says, and now it's me avoiding her gaze. "I told you what I know, so what do you do when you're not here?"

Focus.

Don't think about Raf. Push it down.

I try to focus on Dr. O instead. Conjure his face in my mind.

We have to make him pay. We have to make him *suffer.*

I should tell June to come with me and see what I'm up to. She's saying the right things, and with her natural intuition and attention to detail she could be valuable. But that wariness from earlier is back. I can't take any chances.

"Do people talk about that?" I ask, throat making an audible dry click as I try to swallow. "Me leaving?"

"Some."

"Who?"

"Who do you think?" Her voice has dropped to an angry growl. "Same star student who just painted my walls with lipstick."

"Geri?" My teeth automatically clench together over her name.

"The one and only."

"What is she saying?"

"I don't know," June says. "You're up to something. The usual paranoia."

That seems pretty mild for Geri, actually, but it still burns under my skin. She's worked for Dr. O before, spying on my mom without my knowledge. Is she spying for him again?

I am so sick of her games.

I am so tired of walking on eggshells.

"She's done messing with you," I say, tossing down my rag. I know I need to play this smart, but the heat is pushing against my collar, and I'm tired of living in fear of Geri Allen.

That, at least, is one thing I can control.

Geri's room is just across the hall, and I knock twice while pushing inside.

"Hello, privacy?" She sits up in bed, wearing silk polka dot pajamas and twin French braids. In her hands is a book with a half-naked pirate on the cover.

"Leave June alone," I tell her, crossing my arms. I can feel June behind me in the hall, lurking out of sight.

"I don't know what you're talking about," she says, feigning annoyance. "And even if I did, who says I take orders from you?"

"I mean it. Stop messing with June, and stop spying on me." My eyes land on Petal the Platinum Pig, who has returned to her nightstand, and my fury wrenches tighter as I remember Henry's botched mission to deter Grayson. "If you don't stay out of my business . . ."

I trail off, unsure what I'm going to do. All I know is my fists are clenched, and my blood is rushing too quickly through my veins, and I am sick and tired of being scared.

She sits on the side of the bed, her cheeks flaming. Slowly, she rises, and then walks toward me. When her pace doesn't slow, I brace for a confrontation, but she passes me and slams the door in June's face.

"You can't just—" I start, reaching for the door, but Geri blocks my path.

"You'll what?" Geri says quietly. "You'll tell Dr. O and he'll kick me out like Caleb?"

My hand falls.

"I won't be kicked out," she says. "Unlike you, I remember what exactly is at stake here. I stay on the right side, and—"

"And your dad takes care of the rest."

Her sharp intake of breath is like gunfire in my ears. I'm glad June is outside now. She doesn't need to hear any of this.

"You know I don't know anything about that," Geri says evenly.

I know, because when she begged him to stay away from Caleb after Sterling's arrest, he told her never to talk to him about work again.

It was the only way he could keep her safe.

I shouldn't have brought him up. I shouldn't even be talking about this with her. It's too much of a risk. If she's the one spying on me for Dr. O, I do not want to make her mad.

But right now, I don't care. Because her father may have killed someone today. One of us. I don't know how to stop him, and neither does she.

I focus behind her, on the foot of her bed where, beside the book with the pirate, sit a half dozen brochures for different colleges. Remembering what Shrew said about her looking at acting programs just fans the fire.

She wants to be an actress, while people around her—students, just like her—are dying.

My furious thoughts grind to a sudden stop.

She wants to be an actress. She's looking at college. She probably needs to talk to people in the industry as well—real, working actors.

Like Damien Fontego.

I picture him as I last saw him—on *Kings of Rochester* when we were all watching the finale last month in the pit. He's famous. An Emmy winner. A notable alum. We've been counting on him as a board member to manage the school if we could banish Dr. O with our blackmail, but maybe he could do more for us.

Dr. O wants power, and people who want power are afraid, more than anything, of losing it. Damien may not be a politician, but he's got a lot of social sway. His threat could carry the weight we need to scare the director.

If Damien goes to the press, the whole world will listen.

I know what I need to do, but it's a risk.

I lift my gaze to Geri's. "I'll take you to Margot."

Geri's face pales. She is staring at me like I've just sprouted antlers and a forked tongue.

After Sterling was arrested, I told Geri that her father had let Margot go free the night she and Jimmy disappeared. Geri begged me to take her to Margot, but Margot refused. Something about Geri being dead to her.

I don't blame Margot. If my best friend's dad killed my boyfriend, I'd be pretty pissed too.

"Where is she?"

I know Geri's been watching when I leave and wondering where I go. June's caught on to it, but I doubt she knows why Geri's so interested in my whereabouts.

"What have you told Dr. O about me?"

Her lips draw back in a wince, and I almost, for a flash, feel bad for using Margot against her.

"Contrary to popular belief, not all I do is sit around and think of you."

I shrug, and head back toward the door.

"Stop." Her hands are wringing together. "I don't tell him anything."

"Someone is." Someone who knew about Raf, and that we had found him.

The room tilts as the hole punched by his murder carves deeper into my chest.

"In case you haven't noticed, teams are forming. The director's got all of us in his pocket, and not everyone's so keen to jump out. Even we have rules, Brynn, and breaking them has consequences."

I pause.

"Dr. O wants to know who he can trust and who he can't," she says.

"And does he trust you?"

"I make certain of it." Her gaze holds mine. "And if you're smart, you will too."

This isn't a game to Geri. All her twisted school spirit and party planning are for the purpose of hiding under the radar. She once told me her dad had a record, and if she didn't do what Dr. O wanted, he would use the information he had to send her father to prison.

Geri's afraid, and if I know anything about running a con, it's that fear is a powerful motivator.

"I want to see her," Geri says.

"I want you to take me to Baltimore."

"What?" Her brows draw sharply together. "Why?"

"You want to act, right? Let's go see Damien Fontego. He's shooting on location there." At least, according to Henry's *Pop Store* research.

"How do you . . ." She transfers her weight from foot to foot, the very mention of it making her nervous. "Why do you want to see him?"

"Maybe I want to be an actress too."

She folds her arms over her chest. "What is this about?"

The floor creaks in the hallway. We both look in that direction, but the sound beyond the closed door stops.

To my surprise, Geri lifts a finger to her lips, telling me to be quiet, or watch what I say.

"I'm glad you finally came around," she says loudly. "I told you that you'd be good at acting."

Why do I get the feeling she just turned the tables on me?

"When?" she asks quietly.

"As soon as possible."

She laughs.

I don't.

"I'll work on it." She lowers her voice. "Now tell me where Margot is." She bites the corner of her lip. I wonder how exactly she thinks a visit with her ex–best friend will go. *Hi, sorry my dad tried to kill you. We're good, right?*

I don't know how I'm going to get Margot to agree to this.

"After Baltimore," I say.

As I leave the room, I nearly collide with June, who is leaning against the outside of the door. She spins quickly away, but it's obvious she was eavesdropping.

"How'd that go?" she asks, her face flushed from getting caught.

"She won't bother you again."

June nods. She heads back to her room, but stops in the threshold.

"Who's Margot?"

A cold stone sinks in my gut. Geri and I were quiet, but obviously June caught some of the conversation. Even though I was just considering telling her everything, something now stops me from pushing forward.

I don't trust Geri, but she's predictable. When it comes down to it, she's always out for number one. But I don't know about June. What does she get out of her little observations? What does she do with that information?

I don't know who to trust anymore, and after Raf, I have to be more careful than ever what I say.

"An old student," I say. "Someone else Geri used to bully."

I stride by June, my stomach in knots, looking into her room one last time to see the faint pink echo of our school motto shadowed on the wall.

Vincit omnia veritas.

Truth does conquer all. I just wish I knew which version to trust.

CHAPTER 14

That night I dream of the apartment in Bakerstown.

Dread is thick in my blood as I run up the concrete stairs and around the corner. It permeates the air with the smell of rotten leaves, and crawls across my skin like the wispy legs of spiders.

I know what I'm going to see, but I barrel toward the cracked door anyway, unable to stop my running feet. The door flings open before me, as if pushed by a burst of wind. Raf's apartment is dark—black-hole dark—and I can feel the void pulling on my clothes, my hair, my bones.

I don't want to go inside.

I don't want to see.

But it doesn't matter what I want. He's there, lying on the floor on a gleaming pile of white pills. His socks are dirty on the bottom. His jeans are scuffed.

Closer I step, a scream trapped in my throat. Closer, and closer, until I'm standing right over Raf.

But it isn't Raf.

It's Caleb.

It's the Caleb who was caught by the Wolves, and called me down to the pit to patch him up. There are bruises on his face, and a cut on his lip. His eyes are open and his glasses are shattered pieces of plastic and glass but it doesn't matter because his stare is so vacant, so cold, I know he's gone.

I wake with a start, sweat hot on my neck and chest. My heart pounds against my ribs. With shaking hands, I kick off the comforter knotted around my legs, and reach underneath my pillow. The cards he once wrote me spread and bend beneath my frantic hand, but I'm not looking for them.

My fingers close around the burner phone. I kept it close tonight, just in case.

With the press of a button, the screen lights up. It's 3:23 in the morning. So much could have happened in these hours Caleb and I have been apart.

I dial the number, my heart in my throat. It seems to take a lifetime to ring, but when it does, he answers immediately.

"Brynn?"

At the sound of his voice, my breath comes out in a shudder. Tears burn my eyes. I hug my knees against my chest and grip the phone like it's the only thing keeping us both alive.

"Brynn, what is it? What's going on?"

I don't trust my own voice to answer. It's too unsteady. *I'm* too unsteady.

"Are you okay?" he asks. "Where are you? I'm coming."

"No," I manage.

He's quiet a moment. "What happened?"

I press my hand to my throat, willing it to open.

"Nothing," I choke. "Bad dream."

He blows out a tense sigh.

My jaws grip together, refusing to let the sob building in my chest break free.

"Want to talk about it?" he asks.

I don't want to talk about it. I don't want to think about it. I want everything to go back to normal.

I don't know what normal is anymore.

"He's dead," I say.

He makes a small grunt, as if in pain. "I know."

"I can still see him."

"Me, too."

"You can't get hurt."

"Hey." His voice is softer now. "I'm not hurt. I'm fine."

"Where are you?"

"With my mom and brothers. I told them I'd feel better if I knew where they were staying. They think Dr. O's on board."

Which means he's safe, at least for a little while.

I nod, as if he can see me. The next breath comes a tiny bit easier.

"Brynn, I'm okay," he says in that same gentle tone.

"I wish you were here."

He would be if I hadn't gotten him kicked out. I know he doesn't blame me, but that doesn't mean it isn't my fault, and knowing it makes all of this a million times worse.

I feel raw, scratched open. The old me never would have showed this side of myself. The old me would have been strong, and kept my shield up. But I can't with Caleb. I can't, and I don't want to.

The right person unlocks the best and worst in you. They show you who you really are.

I am scared.

I'm scared Raf's death is my fault.

I'm scared Caleb is next.

"That's funny," he says quietly, "I was just wishing you were here."

Quiet stretches between us. My face is wet, my throat raw. The ache in my chest has slowed to a bruising punch.

I hear him shift on the couch, or maybe a bed. "We could eat leftover noodles and watch TV."

I blow out a tight breath.

"What's on?"

A beat passes. "Infomercials . . . nineties' sitcoms . . . and *Kung Fu.*"

"Definitely *Kung Fu.*"

"Excellent choice."

My forehead rests against my knee. I picture us sitting on a couch, side by side. The reflection of the show in his glasses. The weight of the plate on my lap.

"The noodles are good," I say.

"I'll let Mom know."

"Is she awake?"

"No. Everyone's asleep."

"Just us," I say.

"Just us."

I imagine the dark house. The way we put our plates down and settle against the couch. My back to his chest, his arms around my waist. I can feel the rise and fall of his chest as my fingers weave through his.

I'm not crying anymore, and I dry my face with the pulled-down sleeve of my nightshirt.

I remember listening to him play piano once. How the quiet, simple melody sunk into my skin, into my blood, and then with each rising note began to swell, filling me up until my skin was tight and my bones felt like they might break with the overwhelming beauty of it all.

That's what Caleb is to me. A symphony. A quiet song that slips inside, and fills all the cracks, softens all the edges, and then builds until all the things I'm feeling can't possibly be contained.

"Can I stay with you?" I ask, as if I'm really there.

"All night," he says.

I'm stronger now, and able to talk to him about the dream and my run-in with June and Geri. I tell him Charlotte's having a girl—before I came to my room, I went to hers, and she was so excited I couldn't tell her about Raf. After I left, I packed a go bag with all the things she'll need—clothes, and cash I had in my wallet, and extra toiletries from the supply closet. Just in case.

"It feels more real now," Caleb says.

"It does." I don't just mean with Charlotte and the baby, I mean with him and me.

We talk a little longer about Moore's little run-down house in Devon Park, and Caleb's mom and brothers and dad. And then we start to yawn, and long stretches of silence start to overtake the conversation.

"Don't go." It's the last thing I remember telling him.

"I'm not going anywhere," he promises, but maybe I'm already dreaming.

I WAKE WITH a start to my door shoving inward and a self-righteous pixie standing in the doorway, hands on her hips.

"What the—"

"Oh, sorry," she says. "I thought we don't knock. That's our special thing."

I jerk the comforter up my chest, hiding the burner cell and Caleb's notecards beneath it.

"I locked the door."

"Really? You think that matters at a place like this?"

Fair point.

As Geri moves closer, I tighten the blanket around my chest and blink away my bleary fatigue. The clock on the nightstand says it's just after eight, and even though the reason she's here must be important, part of me can't help mourning a lazy Saturday wake-up.

Then I remember Caleb, and I fight the urge to grab the phone and check for messages. The battery's probably dead by now. I don't even remember hanging up.

"What do you want?" I snap as she tucks the hairpin she used on the door back into her updo.

"Oh, Brynn." She sits on the bed beside me, crossing her legs and her arms, her back curtain-rod straight. I glare at her black pencil skirt and gray leggings, and the corded sweater that hugs her chest and arms. She's already wearing lipstick. "I've had a very busy morning."

My brows arch.

"When you want something done, you ask Geri," she says, a little proudly. "Turns out my father isn't the only fixer in the family."

Everything inside me lurches forward, like I'm in a car that just slammed on the brakes.

"Talk," I prompt.

"I arranged an on-location visit to Damien's set. He's seeing us tomorrow afternoon."

Today is Saturday. Two weeks exactly to Dr. O's swearing-in on New Year's. Will Damien be able to help us this quickly? If he's willing to turn on Dr. O, we can blackmail the director by the end of the week.

"How'd you do it?"

"I asked the director," she says, and I experience another lurch, this one even less pleasant. "He likes me, remember? I play nice."

"Great. What did you say?"

"I told him I'm interested in University of Maryland's theater program, and I was looking at a campus visit when I heard a rumor that Damien was filming there. Pout the lips, bat the eyes, and presto. He made the call."

Dr. O has Damien on speed dial. That can't be a good thing.

"We leave tomorrow morning," she says. "Our flight's at eight-thirty. Campus tour is at one. Damien's fitting us in at five before a night shoot. We're staying at the Four Seasons, and flying back early Monday morning before finals."

I scowl.

"What?" Her jeweled flat, which has been slapping against her heel each time she flexes her toes, stops. "That not good enough for you?"

"It just seems, I don't know . . . kind of easy."

She balks. "Oh, I'm sorry. Did you think you could do better?"

"No," I say quickly, unable to shake my wariness. "Belk followed us to the mall the other night. It feels odd that Dr. O would let us go out of state alone without a chaperone."

Geri actually flicks her hair.

"I've got it covered."

"I'm actually scared right now."

Her grin is as sharp as her claws. "I told Dr. O you've been act-ing a little funny, and he asked me to keep an eye on you."

"What?" I jerk up sharply, catching the comforter just before it reveals the burner phone by my hip.

"Relax," she says. "It was nothing he didn't already suspect."

I cringe, wondering again who's talking behind my back—June? Grayson? For all I know, Geri really is using this time to report to Dr. O any extra information.

I've got to make sure to keep the upper hand—keep Margot dangling in front of Geri like a carrot on a stick.

Her foot has stopped again. She's staring at my far wall as if she might be able to knock it down with the intentness of her stare.

"Dr. O doesn't seem to have anything on you," Geri says quietly, which seems unnecessarily kind for her. "But he's suspicious."

I think of Raf again, and all the others Dr. O may have harmed. His suspicion should make me back off, but it only makes me push harder. We have to stop him. Soon.

"And I can make him more suspicious or less suspicious, depending on what you tell me," she adds.

There she is. *Geri Allen, ladies and gentlemen.*

"Guess you better make sure we don't have any trouble in Baltimore, then," I tell her.

Her lips press together. "Monday morning I want everything you have on Margot."

We actually shake on it, and as soon as Geri leaves the room I plug in the burner and text Caleb the new development.

CHAPTER 15

The rest of the day is a flurry of activity. Shrew, excited by my sudden new interest in college, lays out a plan for what I should be looking for once I get to campus tomorrow. While Sam visits his mom in prison, Charlotte helps me pack, throwing in way too many outfits for a two-day trip. Then she and Henry set up an all-day screening of Damien Fontego's show, *Kings of Rochester*, in the pit while we try, in vain, to study for finals.

We are never alone long enough to go into details about the real purpose of my mission to Baltimore. Every time I turn around June is lurking. She tells us *Kings of Rochester* is pretentious, but she never leaves, and even after dinner I find her in my room, gossiping about the other students and waiting for me to return the favor.

It's probably harmless, but I can't commit to trusting her after what happened with Raf. She hears too much.

I hardly sleep that night. Caleb's with his family. He texts me to say that everything is all right, but I hate each hour that passes after without word.

When I lie in bed, a dozen faces swirl through my mind. Raf and Renee. Margot, hiding since she received news about what happened in Bakerstown. Charlie and the Wolves. June. Paz and Bea and Joel. Geri and her father. Henry and Grayson. Moore, with his broken heart.

I think of Mom, and the picture she sent earlier in the day of the Christmas tree she's put up in her new apartment. It's real, so much better than the skimpy plastic one we had when she was with Pete.

Devon Park feels a million miles away now. The slums where I was raised don't seem so dark and scary anymore. At least there, we knew who we were and who we were dealing with. Danger wasn't disguised by the glimmering mantle of wealth. If someone meant to hurt you, you knew it, you didn't have to wonder and wait.

And after checking the burner for the hundredth time, I find my fingers typing a message, not to Mom or Caleb, but to an old friend I haven't seen in what feels like a long time.

He doesn't answer, and I don't expect him to. But somehow, as soon as I press *send*, I'm able to fall asleep.

THE TRIP TO the airport is my first drive not accompanied by an adult, and I make Geri leave an hour before we have to just in case we hit traffic. We park in an overnight lot, and after navigating through the security checkpoint, I follow Geri to our gate. I've never been on an airplane before, and despite the seriousness of the task that lies ahead, I'm thrilled by all of it. The giant jets on the runway outside the floor-to-ceiling windows. The people running to catch their next flight. The neon light display in the long hall where we ride a moving sidewalk. The sushi bar in the middle of our terminal.

I can't stop looking at everything.

Geri can't stop rolling her eyes, but every once in a while, I catch her smirking.

When they call our boarding group, I grab my messenger bag and stand in line. I've seen how this goes in movies, but I still feel a flutter of nerves tingling between my ribs as I approach the gate agent and show her my ticket.

"Thank you, Ms. Hilder," she says curtly, and then I'm following Geri down the jet bridge, my Chucks squeaking against the floor, my hands pulling down my black Vale Hall sweatshirt with the silver Raven in the center.

We take our final steps into the plane, and then a flight attendant in a blue suit says good morning and returns my smile, which is burning my cheeks because it's so big.

"You sit there," Geri says, like I'm a child. I give her the face that says as much, but I'm secretly grateful to have a window view. I stuff my bag beneath the seat as she takes out a book and a sleep mask and tucks them into the pouch on the back of the seat in front of us.

"Excuse me, do you mind switching seats so I can sit by my girlfriend?"

I turn at neck-breaking speed to face the source of the voice, now standing in the aisle beside the seat next to Geri's.

Even as I soak in the face I have committed to memory a thousand times, even as he smiles and that shimmer of heat flushes my skin, I still can't believe what I'm seeing.

My girlfriend?

"Are you kidding me?" Geri cranks her glare in my direction. "You wanted a trip to Baltimore to hang out with *him?*"

Reality catches up with me in a hard lurch, and before I can stop it, I'm gaping like a fish, unable to explain why Caleb is here because I honestly didn't consider it a possibility.

"Sure," the woman at the end of our row says reluctantly, giving us a strange look before rising. Caleb directs her a few rows back, and her expression lightens as she notices the handsome man in the business suit whom she'll be sitting beside.

Caleb sets his backpack on the seat she just vacated. He's gotten his hair cut. I liked it shaggy, but this is good too. More than good, actually. The top is long enough to run my fingers through. The sides are short, and I have the sudden desire to know what it feels like against my cheek.

"Do you mind if I sit by Brynn?" he asks Geri, as if this is a perfectly normal request made by any other student who magically appeared on the airplane.

Muttering under her breath, she slides out, and he takes the center seat.

He grins at me, and even if this is a terrible idea he's managed to somehow execute, I feel the corners of my mouth tilting up.

He's here. Raf is gone and I have no idea how we're going to turn Damien, but *he's here.*

I'm not alone.

"Anytime anyone would like to offer an explanation, that would be great," says Geri through her teeth.

Fear threatens to break through my haze. "What are you doing here?"

He shouldn't be here.

Geri could report him to Dr. O at any minute. Someone could be waiting in Baltimore for us. His family would be left on their own.

He must sense my unease, because his hand turns over on his thigh in offering. I place mine in it without hesitation, grounded by the warm strength of his fingers curling over my knuckles.

"We're in this together, right?" he asks, again, just for me.

My throat goes tight, but I nod.

"A friend is keeping an eye out on the house," he adds.

He must mean Moore—clearly he doesn't want Geri hearing this. Maybe that's for the best.

He squeezes my hand and turns to our classmate. "I missed you, Geri. Thought this would be a good chance to catch up."

"First? Doubtful," she hisses. "Second, how did you even get on a plane? Last I checked you didn't exist anymore."

She lowers her voice at the end as a flight attendant passes by, miming for us to buckle up.

I try to, but the ends of the seat belt don't exactly look like they belong together. One is a hollow metal square, the other looks like a deck of cards.

"I got a new ID yesterday." He slips out his wallet and passes me a small, laminated state ID bearing the name Sam Harris. The address is somewhere in Amelia—maybe the house Sam grew up in—but the picture is Caleb's smiling face.

While I'm inspecting it, Caleb reaches to my waist. Wordlessly, he presses the metal end of the seat belt into the buckle, then pulls the strap snugly across my hips.

I blink, dragging my focus away from the slide of his hand over my stomach. "How . . ."

"He borrowed Moore's machine."

Moore has the ability to make ID's—he created new ones whenever we needed them for a job. And since Sam Harris technically is a real person, Caleb wouldn't have been flagged using his identity.

"We bought the ticket yesterday at the library. I wanted to tell you, but I wasn't entirely sure it would work."

Sam was supposed to be at the prison visiting his mom. I didn't think he'd be with Caleb at the library orchestrating a plane trip to Baltimore to help me.

A wrinkle forms between my brows. I glance at Geri, and then back to Caleb.

"You're sharing an awful lot," I tell him.

He passes Geri her end of the seat belt, which had slid between their seats. "She's not going to say anything."

"What makes you so sure?" Geri asks. "*She* might not want to be caught associating with a Vale Hall *reject*."

Caleb sighs. "Because if you talk to Dr. O, Belk, or anyone else, Margot's going to send an anonymous note to Dr. O announcing that she's alive, and that you and she are scheming against him."

Geri sinks in her seat, jaw clenched.

"I want to see her."

"After this trip." Caleb turns back to me. "That was the deal, right?"

My smile is back and at full wattage. "It sure was."

"I hate both of you," says Geri.

It really is a terrible loss.

We're distracted by the ding of a bell, and the flight attendant gives a series of announcements about wearing your seat belt, and where the lavatories are, and how oxygen masks will be dropping from the ceiling if we "lose altitude."

"Does that mean crash?" I say, a little too loudly.

Caleb pats my leg. "Statistically you're more likely to be eaten by an alligator."

"Also something I'd like to avoid." I think I might be shouting. I don't mean to, but the engine is really loud.

But then the plane is pulling back from the gate, and we're heading toward the runway, and I'm forced back into my seat as we pick up speed.

This is happening. I'm flying out of Sikawa City for the first time in my life.

"Ow." Caleb chuckles.

I glance over, and his fingertips have turned white from the force of my grip. He's smiling, though, and I'm smiling, and then I feel it, the sudden shift as the front of the plane rises and lifts off the ground.

I must make some kind of riding-a-roller-coaster sound, because the next sound I register is his laughter. I can't look over, though; the runway is shrinking into a tiny strip of gray, far behind us. The cars on the highway look like ants on a mission, and the houses make swirling neighborhood patterns like designs etched in the sand.

Up we go. Up and up and up, until I'm sure we're going to poke a hole straight into the sky. As the plane evens off, the houses become pinpricks. Baseball fields and parks become thumbprints, and the river turns into a silver ribbon, shimmering in the sun.

It's incredible.

From here, the city is beautiful. The ugliness is untouchable, too far away to see. All of our problems have become microscopic, and what's left of them inside me slides out of knotted muscles into the scattered clouds below.

I turn to Caleb, desperate to see if he feels it too, but he's not looking out the window. He's staring at me, a quiet, secret kind of smile playing on his lips.

"Hi." I'm not sure if I say the word out loud, or if it's only a breath.

"Hi," he whispers back.

I lean closer, releasing his hand to crumple his sweatshirt in my grasp. The small blast of air from the nozzle above moves his hair the slightest bit, and the greedy urge takes over to touch that too. Then, even that isn't enough. His hair, the frames of his glasses. My fingertip trails a line down his nose and around his jaw and over his slightly parted lips.

A soft, golden light warms me, fills me. Nothing can hurt us up here. We belong to the sky. We don't even exist to those below.

I lean closer, and my nose brushes his. Our lips touch, and explore, and draw open. It's easy kissing him. It's the rightest thing in the world. I close my eyes, and imagine us somewhere else, alone, and when I open them he's staring back in understanding.

Geri makes a little huff and turns away, focusing entirely on the book in her hand. She reminds me where we are, and that the things I want have to wait.

So I rest my head on Caleb's shoulder, finding the perfect place in the crook of his neck. He presses kisses against my hair and forehead, and then we watch our hands weave and unweave and weave again, all across the sky.

OUR PLANE LANDS at the Baltimore airport two hours later. It's sunny outside, and a white blanket of fresh snow covers the rooftops of the buildings we pass in our taxi. The roads are wet and shiny, and not even the traffic on our way into the city can stifle my thrill.

It's like Sikawa, but not. The skyscrapers still stab through the clouds, smashed so closely together it's like they're weeds, competing for the sun. People rush by, huddled in their big coats. Car horns and distant sirens fill the air.

"I sent Belk a message that we're here and heading to the hotel," Geri says sourly. "Just us girls, obviously."

"Thanks," I tell her, impervious to her bad mood.

Caleb let me sit by the window, but he leans close, peering out over my shoulder. I am equally as aware of the strange new sights flashing around us as I am of his hand on my thigh.

"Look," he says, pointing through the jungle of brick and metal to a white stone fortress bracketed by columns. "That's the Peabody Library. It's supposed to be amazing inside. Five balconies. A huge glass skylight. They call it the Cathedral of Books."

"Which is useful to anyone . . . because . . ." Geri examines her nails on the far side of the seat.

I grin at Caleb. "I love that you know that."

My cheeks heat. I didn't mean to say *love*. Did he catch it?

Maybe it's okay that he did.

"It's from the 1870s," he adds, wiggling his eyebrows.

"Gross," says Geri. "Get a room."

Caleb leans closer, his nose brushing the shell of my ear and sending a hot jolt straight to my belly.

"There's a building on Light Street that's classic art deco," he whispers, his breath moving my hair. "I read it was built in the 1920s."

"Wow," I manage.

"Vomit," says Geri.

I curl my fingers around Caleb's, watching the way his gaze dips down to where we touch. We're far away from home, and no one cares that we're holding hands—no one but Geri, and she can't do anything about it—and suddenly I want to see that art deco building. I want to kiss him inside it, in front of all the people walking by. I want to walk down the street with my hand in his, and go out to dinner, and see a movie, and be us.

The us we are supposed to be. The us that isn't worried about Dr. O.

We reach the hotel, a huge tower of blue-green glass right on the winter-gray water of the Inner Harbor. The lobby is like something out of a dream, even after living in Vale Hall's mansion. Sandy marble floors, so glossy I can see my own reflection. Chandeliers of glass baubles and twisting silver. An enormous vase of white flowers cascades over the edges of a table in front of reception.

"Whoa," I say.

Caleb smirks. "A definite step up from the bowling alley."

"I'm sure they'll have a nice couch for you to sleep on," Geri mutters, then crosses to reception.

Heat sears up my neck. Even if Caleb sleeps on a pullout sofa, we'll be spending the night in the same room. The last time—the only time—that's ever happened was after the Wolves got ahold of him and he was beaten and zonked out on Pete's illegal pain pills.

I suddenly hope that couch is big, and that Geri's a very heavy sleeper.

I hang back with Caleb, unsure what to say to the man behind the counter. It's better for Caleb not to make himself too noticeable anyway, but soon Geri's heading back, looking even crabbier than before.

"The room's not ready," she says. "And we need to get to campus for the visit soon. I guess we're just going to have to get ready in the spa."

"Sounds awful," I say, mimicking her superior tone. "Don't they have anything nicer?"

Caleb snorts.

Geri marches off without another word, and after cringing at Caleb, I jog after her.

The spa turns out to be bigger than a house, with cedar lockers, steam showers, and the heady scent of lavender. I didn't really expect to change before going to campus, but since Charlotte managed to pack approximately forty-seven outfits, I decide it can't hurt anything.

I pull on a fresh pair of jeans, these a little more formfitting than the ones I was wearing this morning, and a soft red sweater that hugs my hips. This isn't just a visit to a movie set, it's a business meeting. I need to appear mature, thoughtful enough to gain Damien's trust. My hair is still holding the same gentle waves from the morning, so I let it be, and trace black eyeliner and mascara around my eyes. As I paint the cherry gloss over my lips, I wonder if Caleb will notice the subtle change.

I still can't believe he's here.

I manage to finish before Geri, who's decided to flatiron her hair for the second time today and put on knee-high black boots with her tights and knit dress. With a belt fastened around the small pinch of her waist she looks like a vengeful pixie. Maybe it's this place—this whole city—but before I can think it through, I tell her she looks really nice.

"I know," she says, clearly not needing my input.

We repack and leave the spa, finding Caleb near the doors of the lobby. He's changed too, into a light blue button-down shirt that contrasts with the black bomber coat Henry got him earlier this fall. His dark jeans skim the lean muscles of his legs, meeting his shoes, the same as mine, and before I catch myself, I'm walking faster, the pull of attraction like a magnet seeking its match.

His eyes grow wide as we approach, but he's not looking at Geri. It's like the lights have gone dark, and there's a spotlight shining on me alone.

"That's a . . ." He swallows. "Red sweater. Your sweater is very red."

So are the corners of his jaw.

"I definitely think you're college ready," I tell him. He covers his face with his hands and groans.

We leave our bags with the concierge and take another taxi to a place called College Park. Caleb's hand stays in mine the entire ride, his thumb making slow, tantalizing circles over my knuckles. We drive under an archway bearing the words *University of*

Maryland, and pass by old, redbrick buildings, and crisscrossing concrete paths. Students not much older than we are carry backpacks or satchels, some listening to music, some laughing with their friends. We're dropped off in front of the library. It's not quite as glorious as the Peabody downtown, but it's still monstrous, and for a glancing moment, I can see myself going to school here.

I have to survive high school first.

As the taxi pulls away, we walk toward a group of students and parents gathered on the stone steps beneath the spindly, gray branches of a naked tree. A youngish-looking guy in a Santa hat is holding up a sign that says "Campus Tour" while he talks to a girl and her mom, and as we head toward them, a new kind of wanting burns inside me.

I've never been on a college campus before. Not even Sikawa's local community college. This is so different from anything I could have expected, even from movies. It's like its own city inside a city. A completely separate world.

And as I'm walking toward the tour guide, my heart a buoy bouncing in my chest, I hear the two words that send me crashing down to earth.

"Bloody Brynn!"

spin toward the voice, an old, remembered anxiety clawing to the surface of my skin, but it dissipates in seconds as the boy I've known my entire life leaps off a stair to our left and strides toward us.

"Marcus?"

This guy looks like he could be Marcus's twin brother. His face is the same—his buzzed fade and bright blue eyes I would recognize across the universe. But his smile is wider, and his jeans actually fit, and when he lifts his arms to give me a hug I can see the hint of an actual belt sticking out beneath the bottom of his gray wool coat.

"You weren't lying!" I'm crushed in his embrace before Caleb can grab my hand to pull me back.

"When I got your message, I thought this might be a trick," he says. "No way Bloody Brynn's coming to see me. But here you are! And damn, you look good, girl."

He steps back to size me up, chin resting on the check mark made by his thumb and index finger, and I can't help it. I laugh.

"I didn't think you got the message," I say, remembering the text I sent before I fell asleep last night. My eyes dart to Caleb, who looks at Marcus like he might start throwing punches.

It occurs to me that the last time these two saw each other Marcus had just outed me to Grayson—my mark—and Caleb had sped across town to save me.

It wasn't a particularly friendly meeting.

"Um, Caleb, you remember Marcus," I say, motioning awkwardly between them.

"This is the guy." Marcus points at him, amused, and part of me withers and dies.

"I hope so," says Caleb stiffly. He holds out a tentative hand, which Marcus grabs, only for the sake of pulling him into a hug.

The difference in Marcus hits me again. He's happy. There aren't bruises beneath his eyes from sleepless nights, or taut lines around his mouth from stress. He isn't trying to act hard or assert his place.

He's just *Marcus*.

I smile so wide my jaw feels like it might break.

"And who is this?" Marcus practically pushes Caleb aside when he notices Geri, arms crossed, hip cocked, and lips pulled in a tight frown.

"This is Geri," I say. "We go to school together."

"Geri." Marcus tries on the name, a wicked grin tilting his lips. "I didn't know there were any angels named Geri."

"Are you kidding me?" I'm not sure who she's more annoyed with—Marcus, Caleb, or me. She spins toward the tour guide and stomps away.

"Watch yourself," I say. "She's got claws."

He winks at me. "All my favorite people do."

I snort, but I can't help feeling bad. Geri's a pain on her best days, a viable danger on her worst, but I've been a third wheel before, and it's not fun.

"Welcome, visiting students!" calls our Santa tour guide, and when he runs through our names to see if everyone's arrived, I raise my hand. The group takes off, and with a tilt of my head, Marcus, Caleb, and I follow. I can see Geri just ahead, scribbling something in a journal she's taken out of her purse.

Either she's writing me a hate note, or she's really taking this seriously.

"So you're going to college, huh?" Marcus slings an arm over my shoulder, the way he used to do when we were home, before everything fell apart.

My gaze flicks to Caleb, who is scowling on my other side, hands in his pockets.

"Probably," I say, and realizing I owe Caleb an explanation, I say, "I sent Marcus a message before we left. I didn't think he got it."

"My aunt takes our phones after dinner," he says. "Lucky she didn't see all the nasty things you wrote."

My head cranes in Marcus's direction, but he only squeezes me tighter and blows out a tense breath.

"Marcus, I miss you. Marcus, I want you back. I'm coming to Baltimore to get that—"

I shove him hard enough he nearly falls, but rights himself in a burst of laughter.

"I didn't say any of those things," I tell Caleb, whose scowl is deepening with each passing second.

"Yet." Marcus is still laughing. "But I'm keeping the hope alive."

"I don't blame you." Caleb shakes off his tension with a shrug. "Some people are worth waiting for."

We both glance at him.

"Not that I advise you doing that," Caleb tells Marcus. "I'd rather you move on, if it's all the same."

Marcus smirks, and then cracks up. He juts a thumb in Caleb's direction. "He's all right."

"Yeah," I say, blushing.

Caleb tilts his head toward the group, now stopped in front of a massive brick building. "I'm going to see how Geri's doing."

"Put in a good word for me!" Marcus calls as Caleb walks away, then he hugs me again. After a moment, I hug him back, giving in to the familiar steel of his arms and the new spicy cologne he's wearing.

"It's good to see you," he says. "It's like being home, without the worst of it."

He's right about that.

The group moves on, and I fall into step beside him, smiling again at how good he looks.

"Your aunt takes your phone after dinner, huh?" I ask.

He grins. "She says conversations after dark lead to bad decisions."

"Oh, wow." I laugh. "You like living there?"

"It's all right." He says this like I would say the Four Seasons is all right, and that makes me even happier. "I'm retaking junior classes. Got a B-plus on my French test last week."

"You're taking French?" I don't even know who I'm talking to.

"Oui," he says. *"Je m'appelle Marcus. Où se trouvent les toilettes?"*

My mouth drops open.

"That's pretty much all I know."

As the group moves on he tells me about his aunt, who's strict but nice, and his cousins, who are trying to talk him into going out for track in the spring. He has a curfew—which is negotiable for special occasions as long as he checks in. His mom is doing well, and is planning to move out to Baltimore by February so they can live together.

"Guess we both got out after all," I say, but the words are hollow. I may have moved to the north side, but I'm still playing chess with a monster.

"I don't know," he says thoughtfully. "Baltimore's got its own Devon Parks."

I narrow my gaze his way. He's pulled his life together, he doesn't need to slide back into old habits.

"Relax," he says. "I'm just saying, Devon Park's a place. You give it hate, you give it power. I didn't realize that until I left."

"And this place?"

"Well," he says. "I'm trying to give this place something else."

"That's deep." I don't know if I'm more awed or shocked at his sudden depth and transparency, but I like it, all the same.

"I go to school now, remember?"

"*Oui.*"

He smirks, and this time when his arm goes over my shoulders, I wrap mine around his waist.

"So this guy—*Caleb*. He decent? Or am I going to have to teach him some manners?"

I shake my head. We both know I can take care of myself on that front.

Caleb's with the group up ahead. His eyes hold to the top of the buildings, even while everyone else is watching the tour guide. He's probably calculating the slope of the roofs, or trying to date the architecture. It makes me think of what Marcus said, about what happens when you give part of yourself, something other than hate, to a place. Maybe this entire college sprang from one architect's good intentions.

"More than decent," I say.

"You trust him?"

"Yes."

There's no hesitation in my answer, and the word rings through me like a declaration. Love belongs to the heart, but trust is in the bones. Where we come from, that's more important.

As we reach the student union, I start catching snippets of what the tour guide is saying. This is for show, I'm not really interested in theater—at least, I don't think—but it is kind of exciting to hear about dining options and dorm life. They even offer classes dissecting zombie movies and comic book superheroes.

But every time I find myself getting excited, I check the time on my phone.

We need to meet Damien at five, at some location outside the city. As helpful as Geri's been to make this trip happen, and as bad as I feel for her with the boys tacking on, I don't want her there when Caleb and I talk to Damien. She needs to have deniability should someone question her about what happened.

As we cut through a field to the music building, I make my way to Geri's side. She's scribbled pages of notes in her journal, and has taken a dozen or more pictures of the buildings we've passed.

"So. You think you want to go here?" I ask. Behind us, Marcus and Caleb have struck up a conversation. I'm pleased to see Marcus smiling as he talks, and Caleb tilting forward and clutching his side in laughter.

"Are you honestly trying to make small talk?"

I push my hands into the pockets of my coat. "I'm sorry. I didn't plan for it to turn out like this."

"You mean with all your boys chasing you from city to city? I'm sure."

Okay, I deserve that.

"I didn't expect either of them to come."

She turns on me, cheeks tinged pink. "But they did. Just like they always do."

I frown and pull up the collar of my coat. It's still sunny, but the wind has taken on a bitter chill, and the cold from the cement paths is sneaking through the fabric of my shoes.

"I don't know what you're talking about," I say.

"Please." She stuffs her phone into her bag. "Caleb? Marcus?

Grayson? Not to mention Henry and Charlotte and Sam and everyone else you manage to charm."

Irritation gets the better of me. "Charm? What are you . . ."

She hurries after the group, and I speed up to stay beside her. "You do nothing and people adore you. Meanwhile I'm over here working every angle I've got, and I'm barely surviving the Vale Hall war zone. Do I want to go here? Yes. Graduation can't come soon enough."

She sounds like me just months ago in Devon Park.

"Hold on," I say. "People don't *adore* me."

"Sure they don't." Her words are sharp and cold.

"I'm not . . . I mean, I don't think—"

"Save it," she says. "I don't need you making me feel better. I know what people think about me. My own best friend hates me, and what's worse, I wasn't even sure she was actually alive until you told me."

She shrinks in on herself at the mention of Margot, and I can't help pitying her. She's right, I do have friends, but it hasn't always been that way. In Devon Park, I was a nothing. Worse than nothing. It was only once I got to Vale Hall that my life changed. For a while, I actually thought I could be myself.

But that's been Geri's problem. I see that now, looking at her perfect makeup and her pristine hair. Her notepad of facts about a place far away she might be able to fit in.

She wears a shield. One created by her father's job, and Dr. O's secret projects, and her failed attempt to con Grayson. Now that it's slipped aside, I see the real her. The girl who keeps people at a distance. The girl who is alone.

She's been awful to me. But I haven't been particularly kind to her either.

"I'm sorry," I tell her.

She is so small without her self-righteous anger holding her up.

"I was kind of looking forward to a girls' trip," she says quietly. "It's stupid. Don't even say it."

I wince, picturing what it could have been like if we were close. How we could have explored this city together. Taken our own notes and compared them at one of the little coffee shops on campus.

I bet Geri hasn't had a real friend since Margot got kicked out. If anyone has a reason to fight Dr. O, it's her.

If there was anyone at school we could really use on our side— who had an ear with the director, and a hit man father—it's her.

"Geri." My brows scrunch. I blow out a tense breath, unable to believe what I'm about to do. "We're talking to Damien about blackmailing Dr. O to get him out of the school."

I wait for her response, but she only stares ahead, motionless, as if she hasn't heard me.

I know she has.

"He's dangerous," I say quickly. "What happened to Caleb and Margot has happened to others. People are dying—"

"I'm in."

I blink. I wasn't sure what I expected. Laughter? Her immediately picking up the phone to report my insubordination to Dr. O? At least a lecture on why this is a stupid idea.

"You're in?" I manage.

"He sent my dad after my best friend," she says quietly, her lip trembling the slightest bit. "And my dad couldn't say no, because if he did, Dr. O would have made me disappear."

I shiver.

"I can't live like this anymore." Her hard glare meets mine. "If you're taking down Dr. O, I want in."

I look for some sign that she's playing me. That this is one of her wretched games. But I don't see it. I can't feel the breath of uncertainty down my spine telling me not to trust her.

Her words feel honest, the intent behind them solid.

My chin dips in a slow nod. Once again, I've underestimated Geri.

"All right," I say.

"What's the plan?"

"The truth. We tell Damien everything we know that Dr. O's done." About Margot and Jimmy. Caleb. *Raf.* "A group of us are going to threaten to take it all public unless Dr. O leaves town."

She tucks her chin into her coat collar. "And if Damien's in Dr. O's pocket?"

"We run."

"We'll be on a closed set with security."

"Then we'll run *fast*."

I don't mean to make light of it, but once we expose our plan to Damien, we won't have many options. He could call Dr. O and tell him what we've done—that Caleb's involved. All of our families could be targeted before we even leave the state.

My fingers close around the phone in my pocket. Henry knows our plan and is awaiting my call. If things go south, he'll meet us at headquarters. He'll alert Moore, who's still looking for Renee, to move my mom and Caleb's family. Charlotte's go bag is ready. She and Sam will disappear on their own.

I won't get to say goodbye.

It doesn't matter. They'll be safe. That's all that's important.

"Okay," Geri says.

"Okay?"

"I said I was in, what else do you want?"

I smirk.

She bites the corner of her lip. "So your friend, Marcus. He lives here?"

I glance up, finding Marcus through the crowd, kicking a pine cone toward Caleb as if they're playing soccer. "He does now. We grew up together. We used to go out."

Her cheeks flush. "Oh. Well."

Her words hang between us.

"You think Marcus is cute," I say with a grin.

"I do not."

"Admit it," I tell her. "This is what friends do. They talk about things."

"We're not friends."

"Come on," I say. "People find me charming. They *adore* me."

She rolls her eyes. "You're ridiculous and so is he. It makes sense that you were together."

"We're not together anymore," I sing.

With a nasty look, she's off, and though I let her go, I can't stop grinning.

This day has been full of unexpected surprises.

CHAPTER 17

Kings of Rochester, the Emmy-winning drama about two art thieves trying to take down a gangster, is shot outside Baltimore, at an abandoned electric plant on the Chesapeake Bay. The main site is comprised of six stories of crumbling red brick and smashed-out windows, and the gravel lot out front is filled with parked trailers and temporary sheds.

"I can't believe you know Damien Fontego!" Marcus howls from behind us as we search for the set's entrance in the chain-link fence.

It wasn't my plan to bring him, but after the tour Geri and I discovered that he and Caleb had been bonding over the show in our absence, and Geri invited him to come.

Caleb was skeptical of putting more people at risk, especially after I'd told him that Geri was in on our plan. But she made a good point that Marcus would be less noticed if there were two guys with us. *More people, more distraction*, she'd said, quoting a lesson from conning class.

Secretly, I think she just wanted to keep Marcus around.

"I can't believe you watch *Kings of Rochester*," I say, my toes curling in my Chucks against the cold. We could have called a car, but Marcus insisted it wasn't a far walk from the commuter train. Now it's not the nerves pushing me faster, but the subzero chill in the air.

"Who doesn't watch *Kings of Rochester*?" Geri scoffs.

"Yeah, Bloody Brynn," Marcus mimics her tone. "Who doesn't watch *Kings of Rochester*?"

I groan. This is exactly what I need. More people on Team Geri.

"What's that about anyway?" She makes a face. *"Bloody Brynn."*

"It's what they call her in Devon Park," says Marcus.

"Unfortunately," I mutter, digging my hands in my coat pockets.

Caleb's gaze seeks mine, worry pinching his brows. He knows how much I hate this nickname.

"Why?" asks Geri.

"Because freshman year we had this speaker—you remember him, Brynn? That guy that owned the noodle place."

"How could I forget?"

"Okay," says Caleb. "Maybe we should—"

But Marcus is already talking. "He's doing this speech, all twitchy and cranked up on something, and he starts checking Brynn out."

"He *what*?" Geri looks to me for confirmation.

I glance over my shoulder at Marcus. There was no checking out that I recall.

"Yeah," says Marcus. "So he starts heading toward her, and she's staring him down like if he tries anything, he's dead, and he's so messed up he trips himself and crashes into her, trying to get a handful of something, you know what I mean?"

He's gracious enough to show us with his hands.

"What did you do?" asks Geri, horrified.

"She cracked him in the nose." Marcus's shoulders are bouncing in laughter now. "With her *forehead*."

Geri's staring at me in wonder.

"That's not . . ." I'm baffled as Geri lifts her hand to give me a high five.

"Blood everywhere," says Marcus. "All over the guy. All over her. People called her Bloody Brynn after that, and no one—not junkies, not even gangsters—messed with her."

I blink, unsure what to say. He seems to have reworked key points of the story—specifically, the part where the guy tripped on the mic cord and randomly cracked his nose on my face. But Geri's looking at me like I just won a street fight, and Marcus is nodding his head like I'm some force to be reckoned with, and it makes the other stuff, the snide whispers and name-calling, seem not quite as awful.

Caleb squeezes my hand.

"What can I say?" I tell them, still baffled. "I'm kind of a badass."

Marcus winks at me, and I wonder if he knows he's embellishing or if he's changing the story for my sake, but as we find the gate, a patchwork of chain-link fence marked by "Private Property" signs, I realize it doesn't matter. The past twists in the favor of the teller. Sometimes, that's for the best.

A security guard greets us as we approach, and I give him my name, which he echoes into a walkie-talkie. After a garbled response, we're allowed in.

"Friends of Fontego, huh?" The guard's forearms are as thick as my thighs. He's wearing a slim leather coat despite the cold, and peeks down at us over the rims of his sunglasses.

"That's right," says Marcus. "Best friends."

"We go to the same school he graduated from," I add, giving Marcus a side-eyed glare.

"Does he know you've been expelled?" Geri asks Caleb as the guard locks the gate behind us.

Caleb pulls down the brim of his baseball cap and hunches in his coat. "I'm not sure."

I reach for his hand, gripping his fingers as they thread through mine. Anticipation is wearing a hole through my chest.

This has to work. Damien's the key. If we can convince him Dr. O is unstable and a danger to the students, we might be able to save the school and our own lives before Dr. O takes the Senate seat on New Year's Eve.

"Remember, if anyone at school asks, Caleb was never here," I tell Geri.

"Remember, I want to see Margot as soon as we get back," she answers quietly, flushing as Marcus reaches for her hand to help her over a mud puddle.

The guard leads us toward a beige trailer on the opposite end of the lot. There's a star on the door and a sign beneath that says "Ben Dwyer." Nerves shiver in my belly as I recognize Damien's name on the show.

"This is awesome," says Marcus. Even Caleb smiles.

This is going to work.

"That's where they filmed the shootout in the season finale," the guard says, pointing toward the entrance to the brick warehouse. "Down there in the river was where Ben saved Julie in season two."

"For the kiss heard round the world." Geri clutches my elbow.

She's making a soft, high-pitched squeal I'm pretty sure only dogs and rodents can hear.

"You're worse than Henry." I have to bite my lip to keep from grinning.

"You've got thirty minutes before he needs to go to makeup," the guard says. "He tried to get you a pass for shooting, but it's a closed set today. He and Julie . . . you know. Reunite." The guard blushes.

"They get back together?" Geri shrieks. I've never seen her fangirl like this before. Any other time I'd be recording it for proof later.

"I didn't say anything," says the guard, holding his hands up in surrender. He steps up the wobbly stairs to the door and knocks twice. "Damien, I got your friends here."

"Just a minute!" comes a muffled voice through the door.

Geri blows out an unsteady breath. I give Caleb a huge smile.

"Oh, boy," he mutters, but there's amusement in his eyes.

The door opens inward, and Damien Fontego stands in the threshold in only jeans, hanging low on his waist, while he scrubs a towel over his glistening, wet hair.

He looks like an underwear model. In fact, I'm pretty sure he *is* an underwear model.

"Hey there." A dimple digs into Damien's smooth cheek as he beams down at us. "Sorry. I just got out of the shower. Have to grab my workouts when I can."

"Of course you do," Caleb says.

"Wow," says Geri.

"Damn!" Marcus points. "You're him! Ben Dwyer, in real life!"

There is no averting my eyes from Damien's very well formed pecs.

"In real life," says Damien. "I'm glad you guys could stop by."

Geri climbs the stairs first, and he gives her a kiss on the cheek and a hug. I follow, and when I ask if he remembers me, he pulls me close and says, "How could I forget?"

"Okay," says Caleb, behind me. "Put your shirt on already."

Damien laughs, and while they hug he whispers something I can't make out in Caleb's ear. Caleb glances up at me, his jaw a little pink, and says, "Yeah. That's her."

I want to ask him what that was about, but Marcus bowls into the trailer and starts peppering Damien with questions about his workout regimen and how he got his six-pack abs.

The trailer is smaller than I expected, even after seeing it from the outside. There are no mirrored walls or bouquets of flowers. Instead, there's an unmade twin-size bed in the back, and a treadmill crammed in beside it. The main area is open, with five sets of free weights on a rack next to a small fridge and a sink. On the fold-out table beside the door is a platter of fruits and vegetables, a blender, and a foil container marked *quinoa salad*. Beside it is an open binder holding what looks suspiciously like a script.

I fight the urge to glance over it for spoilers.

"Want something to eat?" Damien asks. "I've got . . . health food?" He laughs. "Sorry. No good stuff until we're done shooting this season."

"I'll eat," says Marcus, reaching for the salad container. "Quinoa's a complete protein *and* a grain."

"Who *are* you?" I ask.

He gives me a toothy grin.

"So you're all interested in acting, huh?" Damien grabs a T-shirt from the small closet beside the bed and pulls it on. "Stage or film?"

"Stage," says Geri.

"Nice," says Marcus.

She blushes.

"Actually," Caleb says. "There's something else we need to talk to you about."

A wary look passes over Damien's face. "Yeah?"

"Maybe Marcus should step outside for a minute," Caleb suggests.

Marcus, now digging into the salad, makes a face. "Man. I thought we were friends."

I don't like it, but Caleb is right. "Just a few minutes, Marcus. This . . . isn't something you want to know. Trust me on that."

Seeming to grasp the seriousness of the situation, Marcus sets down the salad. He gives me a pinched look, then nods. "I'll be outside if you need me."

My stomach lurches as the door claps shut behind him.

"It's about Dr. O." Caleb rubs his hands together, and I can feel his anxiety stretching across the space between us.

"What about him?" Damien's voice is grim as he crosses his arms over his chest.

"He's done some terrible things," I say. "Things we can't ignore anymore."

Damien glances out the small window, as if expecting someone might be listening. "Look, if you're coming to me because I'm on the Vale Hall board, you should know my position is mostly honorary. Complaints about the school need to go to security."

"I've gotten kicked out," Caleb says.

Damien's arms drop to his sides. "You're kidding."

Caleb shakes his head.

"What'd you do?"

"Nothing," I say. "And it isn't about what he did, anyway. It's about what Dr. O is doing."

Damien groans. "No. *No*, you can't do this. You shouldn't be here." He looks to Caleb. "I'm sorry, but I can't get mixed up in this. He'll ruin me."

"That's the point," pipes in Geri. "He *will* ruin you. Aren't you tired of that? Always worrying that if you step out of line he'll take all this away?"

I glance over at her, impressed. Inviting her was a good idea after all.

"That's the deal we signed," Damien says, more firmly now. "We do his work, we keep our mouths shut, he gives us anything we want."

"And he takes it away whenever *he* wants." I step closer. "We need to stop him, Damien. We need your help doing it."

"My help?" Damien collapses in a chair. "And what if I refuse?"

"Then more people will die," I say.

"Die?" He caves forward, forehead in his hands. "You need to go. I'm sorry. I'll tell Dr. O the visit was fine. I'll say I never saw you, Caleb. But you need to go."

"What do you mean you'll tell Dr. O?" Geri's voice hitches.

"When he called yesterday he alluded to some trouble back at school. He wanted a full report of what we talked about. I didn't think much of it at the time—"

"He knows what we're doing." Geri closes her eyes.

People are starting to notice. Grayson's words echo back to me, fraying my patience.

"I won't say anything," Damien says again.

"You're next." At my words, Damien's head jerks up. His jaw tightens as his eyes narrow.

"Are you threatening me?"

"No," I say simply. "Dr. O is."

Caleb gives me a nervous glance.

I step closer to Damien. "Maybe not today. Maybe not tomorrow. But one day you're going to walk into this trailer, and there's going to be someone waiting for you. He'll tell you that you messed up—maybe you slipped in an interview, or said too much about Vale Hall to a friend. If you're lucky, he'll give you an option. You can swallow a bottle of Wednesday pills, or take a drive with him outside of town. Either way you'll know what he means." I take the seat beside Damien, my fingers numb, my whole body cold. "That you could have stopped him, but you were too late."

Damien stares down at his script with unfocused eyes. "He wouldn't . . . he's not—"

"Rafael Fuentes was expelled six years ago. We found him dead in his apartment with a bottle of pills the day before yesterday," Caleb says. "Renee Gibson was living with him, but we haven't heard from her. Moore's looking, but . . ." He shakes his head.

Geri makes a small, pained noise, then covers her mouth with one hand.

There was a time I wouldn't have cared how that made her feel—her dad may be responsible, after all—but things are different now. I squeeze her shoulder. "Dylan Prescott has joined the Wolves of Hellsgate. He was cut loose too, after his mark's dad named Dr. O majority shareholder of Wednesday Pharmaceuticals then disappeared. Two of his classmates were murdered in the last month."

"Stop," Damien says weakly.

"My mom and my brothers are hiding in a safe house," Caleb

says. "Margot Patel's been living on the street since Dr. O killed her mark."

"My dad is only working for him to keep me alive," Geri says quietly.

"Dr. O gave my mom a job with Wednesday. He moved her into an apartment where he can keep tabs on her." I lean in. "Dr. O's ramping up before he takes the Senate seat. He's getting rid of anyone who might cause him trouble."

"*Stop.*" Damien rises so fast his chair flips backward. "Enough, all right?"

I stand, hands balled into fists. "If you think you're immune to this because you're rich and famous, you're wrong."

"I'm not rich and famous!"

Damien's voice slaps off the tight walls. He staggers away from the table, hands clasped behind his neck.

"I'm not rich anyway. At least, not by Hollywood standards."

"Cry me a river," mutters Geri.

Damien crumbles. "Look, I know what he's like, okay? I left Vale Hall with nothing but a tip on an audition in New York. Everything I have, I earned."

"With some substantial backing," Caleb says.

"That's what I'm trying to say," says Damien. "That backing isn't there. He tells you he's sending you to college, that you'll meet some big director, whatever. But it's a myth. After graduation, I got a reminder of all the illegal things I'd done for him, and how he could send me to prison in a heartbeat." He turns to face us, defeat heavy in his stare. "It could be game over for me just for telling you that."

Silence stretches across the gaps between us. I can't fully process what Damien's saying. No scholarships? No connections? I came to Vale Hall to get out. I did his favors because it came with that reward. But if isn't there . . . if we've all been doing this for nothing . . .

"It's a con?" Caleb finally asks.

Damien nods.

"This is a joke, right?" Geri asks, her voice a little higher. "I'm going to college. I'm getting a theater major. Four years of intensive stage and dance work, voice coaching on the side, and then I'm going to Broadway."

"Hope you've got the pipes," says Damien.

"No," I say, pressing the heels of my hands against my temples. "Someone would have come forward. We would have heard this is a scam!"

"Would *you* come forward?" Damien asks. "You don't know the kinds of things I've done for that guy. We're talking serious prison time."

"I don't understand," Caleb says. "The house. The stuff we all get. My dad's medical care was managed by him for *three years*."

"You sure?" asks Damien. "You write checks from a fake account and it takes a long time before someone catches on. I should know."

Caleb pales.

"Look, I don't know all the answers," Damien says. "All I can say is that he shells out enough to hook you, then, once he's got enough to bury you, you're dropped."

I feel as if the air has grown heavier. It fills my lungs like liquid lead.

"But he has the money," I say. "He owns Wednesday."

"That's not the point, is it?" Beside me, Caleb is gripping the edge of the counter. "He doesn't want to share his money. He's scamming us."

"And keeping the cash for himself," says Geri, and Damien's grim look is confirmation. "I thought . . . even with all the trouble . . . I thought it would pay off in the end."

I know what she means.

The reality of this is infuriating, but somehow so terrible none of us can move.

"It's okay." I swallow. "This is good, actually. We tell the others at school they're doing this for nothing. They'll be upset. Dr. O can't keep this up if we all turn against him!"

"Believe me," says Damien. "If he didn't already have enough to ruin each of you, you wouldn't be there in the first place."

His words cut deep. If we rally the other students we put them in more danger.

"Still," I say. "They need to know. They can make the choice to stand up to him or not once they know the truth."

Caleb nods. "Agreed."

"I can't believe this," says Geri. "My dad will be furious when he finds out."

A dark part of me hopes she tells him, and that he is. I'd like to see what Dr. O does then.

"You know what? Screw this." Damien presses his fist against the wall to his left. When he looks up, there's a fire in his eyes I've only seen on *Kings of Rochester*, when Ben Dwyer's back is against the wall. "Let's do it. I'm in. What's the plan?"

My relief expels in a cold rush of breath, dispelling the disappointment clouding my mind just seconds before. "Tell him you're going to call a press conference and make a statement about what he's done if he doesn't disappear."

"The school will be closed within the month," he says.

"I thought operations would fall on the school board," Caleb says.

Damien scowls. "The executive board staff. Which is me, Tim Loki—"

"Who's that?" I interrupt.

"An alum, I guess. An entrepreneur. Guy's as rich as they come. He's got a half dozen companies overseas, I think."

Great. Another mogul to contend with.

"And," says Damien, "some woman named Susan Griffin I'd never even heard of until that senator got arrested for her murder."

Matthew Sterling. My gaze flicks to Caleb, whose face is now ashen.

Dr. O's backup plan for Vale Hall includes some businessman Damien's never seen, Susan Griffin, who's dead, and Damien, who was too busy acting to pay attention.

The worst part is, I'm not even surprised.

"All right," says Caleb, trying to rally. "So if Dr. O's sister is out, the school falls to you and Tim, right?"

"If the director leaves suddenly. Dies, or gets deathly ill, or something." Damien drums his fingers over his opposite biceps. "That's not the case here. Dr. O's nominated Min Belk to take over when he leaves. He and Tim have already signed off on it."

I've given my recommendation to the board. We should know soon what they decide.

Of course Dr. O put Belk in charge. Belk does whatever the director says. It's as good as keeping the position himself.

"Did you sign off?" Caleb asks.

"Not yet," says Damien grimly. "I've been busy shooting. But it won't do any good if I abstain. It's a split vote with only two active executive board members. The tiebreaker would go to Dr. O."

"Maybe we can find Tim," I say. "Get him to change his mind."

"Good luck," says Damien. "I think he lives out of the country. Dr. O mentioned that once."

I close my eyes, trying to clear my mind. Even without our scholarships, we still have the present to worry about. Vale Hall can't disband—we need our identities, we need to *graduate* so we have a chance of making it once we walk away empty-handed. We don't want Belk taking over—just thinking of it reminds me of what Dylan said about Belk giving him ten seconds to run. But without Dr. O calling the shots, Belk should be easy enough to knock down.

"We'll figure that out later," I say. "Right now we need to stop Dr. O. We've got thirteen days left before he becomes senator."

He can do an enormous amount of damage in that time.

"A press conference," Damien mutters, then extends a hand in my direction. "Why not? I'll call my publicist to set it up."

My throat knots as I shake his hand. "We'll talk to the other students."

"I'll go have lunch with my dad," says Geri, her face still pale as a ghost. "We're past overdue for a father-daughter chat."

This is it.

We've done it. Setbacks aside, we've recruited Damien Fontego, a world-famous actor, to stand with us against Dr. O. I want to scream at the top of my lungs so loud the director hears me and trembles. *You can't hurt us anymore.*

All I manage is a whispered "Thank you."

"Stay alive," he answers grimly.

A knock on the door and a call from outside signify it's time for Damien to get to hair and makeup. After we exchange numbers and a brief goodbye, we're back outside with Marcus, being led toward the chain-link gate at the front of the set.

A rush fills my veins, making it hard not to run straight back home and finish this, but it's dampened by the sight of Geri walking ahead alone. I'm sure she's thinking of all the things we said inside, and how much her dad has to do with it. Maybe even how she's going to tell him about college. I remember the way he looked leaving Dr. O's office the other day. Happy. *Proud.*

I'm about to go after her when Marcus catches my arm. When it's clear he wants a word, Caleb goes ahead to talk to Geri.

"Everything all right?" Marcus asks.

I nod. "It will be."

Now that we've got Damien, it feels like the dominos have been tipped and are falling forward, one by one.

He frowns. "Then why do I feel like it's my turn to get you out of town?"

A hairline crack mars the surface of my hope. Every good con knows when to keep at it, and when to cut and run. I pushed Marcus out of Devon Park because he's trampled that line. Now I can't help wondering if I have too.

It doesn't matter. I'm not leaving Dr. O to tear apart more of my friends' lives.

I link my arm in Marcus's. "There was trouble, but Damien's going to help us fix it."

"You're sure?"

I blink, and see Dr. O's face when we tell him he's done. The fury melting away into panic as the truth strikes home. I see him packing up the few items he can, and running out the front door of Vale Hall.

But as much as I try, I can't see past that moment.

"I'm sure," I say.

CHAPTER 18

Marcus agrees to take us back to the hotel, and soon I find my-self standing on a crowded train, watching him teach Geri dance moves to the music coming from his cell phone. She hasn't wanted to talk about her father, but seems all too happy with the present distraction.

Caleb's side rocks against mine as we round a turn, and his hand settles beneath my coat on my hip. His eyes stayed glued to the small screen of his burner phone, though, his brows scrunched.

"What are you looking at?" I ask.

"I'm trying to find Tim Loki," says Caleb. "It's strange. There's nothing public on him."

I glance down at the screen with a frown. "You sure? Didn't Damien say he owned a lot of companies?"

"Yes. Overseas," says Caleb. "Maybe he uses a different name."

"Maybe he's been disappeared."

Caleb snorts. "Couldn't be much use to Dr. O, then." He closes his phone. "I'll have Sam look at it when we get back." His chin tips to Geri and Marcus. "They're getting along."

So are we, I think. Who'd have thought Geri and I would ever end up on the same side?

Everyone will be as soon as they hear they aren't getting the deals Dr. O promised.

Any fury is overrun by a growing anticipation. Tomorrow, we're going home. I'm going to convince the others at school to join us, and together, we're going to end this.

I'm sure of it now. He can't touch all of us together. Once they know his promises are lies, they'll rise against him. We'll tell him if he harms another one of us, Damien will take everything he's done straight to the press. The entire world will know how he's blackmailed politicians and students, murdered Raf, and ordered the death of his own sister.

Dr. O will be scared, and even if banishment is better than he deserves, he'll be gone before the end of the week.

"This is us," Caleb says as the train shudders to a stop.

We smash through the door with the rest of the crowd, and I'm pinched with regret as Marcus lifts me off the ground in a giant hug.

"Don't go," he wails, loud enough that people nearby throw shady looks our way. "We can go get tacos, or sneak into the Orioles' stadium, or throw ice cubes at the skaters at Inner Harbor."

I'm about to tell him we can't—things will move fast with Dr. O once we get back and we need to prepare—but Geri speaks first.

"Okay."

Marcus sets me down, and we all turn to Geri, whose fingers are so twisted in the strap of her purse the tips are turning white. Her gaze bounces between Marcus and me, cheeks redder by the second.

"I mean, if they're tired, I could stay out. If you wanted."

Marcus slides beside Geri, and when his arm reaches around her shoulders, she giggles.

It's a sound I'm not accustomed to her making.

I glance at Caleb. As much as I trust Marcus, leaving Geri alone with a guy she barely knows feels like a very not-friend thing to do.

"I guess we can hang out a little longer," I say slowly.

"No." Geri's instant rebuttal has my chin jutting forward. "You look exhausted. You really should get a good night's sleep."

Caleb smirks.

I meet Geri's gaze. "You're sure about this."

"I'm sure. I'll call you if I need anything, but I have a feeling you'll have your hands full." She lifts a meaningful brow from Caleb to me, and I realize that her going with Marcus means that Caleb and I will have the hotel room to ourselves.

Now it's my turn to blush.

Geri lifts her hand and wiggles her finger in a wave. "Have fun."

And then she and Marcus hop on the next train, and are whisked away into the city.

THE FOUR SEASONS is four blocks from the station. It's frigidly cold, and we could duck into one of the restaurants lining the street to grab dinner, but hunger and frostbite are the last things on my mind.

Caleb slows as we approach the drugstore on the corner. "Do you think something might happen back at the hotel?"

Images of Geri's dad and Belk and even Dr. O waiting to ambush us rise in my mind, distracting me from the invisible hook dragging me toward the hotel.

"Security seems all right, but we can see if they can put the room under a different name, or switch rooms, just in case. I can call Geri—"

"That's not exactly what I meant." His mouth is still hidden beneath the collar of his coat, but his eyes are smiling.

So he is thinking about our hotel room.

"Oh." I bite the corner of my lip. "Definitely?"

He laughs. "Then we definitely need to make a stop."

A sense of finality settles over us, the same way it did just before we went to the Wolves to clear his name and turn them against Pete. With it comes a reckless rush of bravery, a tingle at the base of my neck. The bite of the air seems harsher. The lights, brighter. It feels like the last night of the world.

"Okay."

We walk to the corner and step through the automatic doors into a brightly lit drugstore. Fake Christmas tree boughs are weighed down by too much red tinsel. Plug-in menorahs are on a two-for-one special. There's an awkward moment where we both pretend to look through an endcap of shampoo, then he takes my hand and leads me to an aisle where giant boxes of feminine hygiene give way to tiny boxes of condoms.

He scowls at the different types. There is every size imaginable— from small to wishful thinking. There are colors and different materials, ribbed and plain.

I rock onto the balls of my feet, acutely aware of the woman buying tampons down the row.

"Sorry," Caleb says, scratching the back of his neck as his gaze tracks down each row. "There's . . . um . . . quite a selection."

I glance sideways at him, wondering if he's nervous too, or if he's never bought them before. He probably wouldn't need to—they're free at Vale Hall. He could have gone into the supply closet and grabbed them by the handful before sneaking into Margot's room—now *my* room.

I push the image aside. It doesn't matter. It's not like Marcus and I weren't together.

"I think normal is good for me," I say, very helpfully.

He grabs a box. We make our way to the line, which we stand in for approximately five years before a clerk asks if we'd like to add a donation to charity—she'd even put our names up on the wall in some paper balloon, memorializing our first condom run for the entire city of Baltimore.

Caleb's no is a lot more polite than my *are you kidding me* stare, but somehow we make it back outside, bag in hand. We hurry back to the hotel, my thoughts blaring—is he nervous? Was there anyone besides Margot—did he and Camile Santos, the mayor's daughter, ever fool around? How will this go once we reach the hotel room? Do we dive into bed movie style, or talk for a while?

Caleb waits in the lobby while I check in. Then we're in the elevator, too far apart to accidentally touch. My hands are in my pockets, and my eyes are staring ahead at the mirrored doors, and everything I've ever felt for him feels too big for my body—every emotion pressing against my skin from the inside—and even while I try to tell myself this isn't a big deal, people do it all the time, it *is* a big deal.

I jump at the ding of the elevator, and his head snaps in my direction, brows arched in a question I don't even know how to answer. I hurry out beneath the glass chandelier, making a wrong turn before I find room 623.

As I press the key card into the slot, he comes up behind me. His hands slide heavily down my sides to my hips, an anchor before my thoughts carry me away.

"Nothing has to happen tonight, you know. We can watch a movie if you want."

My mind goes blissfully silent.

He steps closer, pressing a kiss to the back of my head. "I just want to be with you."

I turn. The toes of our shoes touch. My chest is an inch away from his, heart pounding so hard I'm sure he must hear it.

His head lowers by fractions, until we're breathing the same air.

The door clicks locked again. I'd forgotten the key card was still in the lock.

I laugh a little and try the key card again. This time when the green light flashes, I push through into the room, gaping at the sight before us. It's the kind of hotel room you see in movies— plush gray carpet, a giant bed with a clean, white duvet and enough pillows to disappear into. The bar has two champagne glasses and an iced bucket of sparkling cider, and our luggage has been placed on the rack beside the bathroom.

"Adequate," I say.

"Leaves a little to be desired," he agrees.

Grinning, we race to the window; the curtains are drawn back to reveal the black water of the bay blending seamlessly with the night sky. Glimmering lights line the docks along the Inner Harbor. We follow the curve of the wall to the bathroom, where everything is white and pristine. Tiny bottles of shampoo and soap sit in a mirrored dish beside a vase of lilies, and the mirror catches the soft waves in my hair and the blush on my cheeks.

I slip off my shoes and my coat, and crawl into the bathtub. It's big enough for four adults and has little water jets like in a hot tub.

"You coming?" I ask.

He shrugs out of his coat and slides in beside me. Even with his long legs, there's still enough room for us to sit on opposite sides. My feet come up to his thigh, his press flat against my side of the tub. His socks don't match—one is white, the other blue. It's one of my new favorite things about him.

We sink down so the rim is over our heads and our knees are bent. It's like we're two kids in a fort. Like nothing bad can get us inside these porcelain walls. But it's ridiculous too—us in this giant bathtub, in a five-star hotel in Baltimore—and soon I'm giggling, and he's cracking up, and it feels strange and good just to laugh.

As the giggles fade away, my gaze traces the hard line of his jaw and the curve of his lips. His glasses are crooked again, and when he smirks, the flutter in my belly presses against my ribs.

Tomorrow we could end this. All this waiting, running, *hiding,* could be over. We could put our lives back together. We could make Dr. O pay for Raf, and Jimmy, and everyone else he's hurt.

Or the thin bindings holding everything together might finally snap, and this night could be all we have left.

A reckless bravery takes hold of me.

"Is there a reason we aren't kissing right now?" I ask.

He rakes his fingers through his hair absently, like he has no idea how sexy that single move is. "Not that I can think of."

He reaches beneath my knees and drags me across the tub to his side. I'm still grinning when he leans in and kisses me, but it's seared away as his hands frame my face and draw me closer.

My fingers slide up his chest, over his sweatshirt to his shoulders, then around his neck, finding the heat of his skin. His hair tickles my palms, and as our kiss deepens, I rise to my knees, and his grip slides to my hips to pull me onto his lap.

Heat explodes in my chest like a firework, and suddenly this isn't enough. I want more kisses. I want his hands beneath my clothes. I want to feel his skin on mine. I want *closer,* and *more,* and *now.*

He feels it too, and our mouths become urgent. His lips find my throat and elicit a sharp gasp. He shifts, then helps me straddle his hips, and when I lower we're pressed together in all the right places. A soft groan tears from my throat.

I hate every stitch of clothes between us.

His sweatshirt comes off—his glasses with it. His T-shirt stretches across his chest. My hands find his skin, nails scraping the rise of his abs, and he growls against my collarbone, the vibrations echoing through me.

My shirt is next. Then his. Our chests press together, his skin burning and smooth and perfect. The smell of his shampoo invades my senses. He tugs at the strap of my bra—a question—and I answer by unhooking it for him. When he looks at me, there's reverence in his gaze—even his stare makes me feel beautiful.

His touch sets my whole body ablaze. My breath tumbles rapidly from my lips as I kiss the corner of his mouth and his jaw.

We shift together, a tangle of limbs that ends in laughter and his body over mine. The tub is cold against my back, and I arch into his chest with a gasp. For a moment we're frozen like that—chest to chest, his weight hovering above me. His jaw is tight as he blindly swipes for a shirt to stuff under my back.

"Sorry," he says.

I taste the end of his apology, dragging him closer, longing for the weight of him over me. Then he's there, settled between my legs, and it feels so right it's almost familiar. My knees rise up to bracket his hips. His forehead presses against my shoulder as he sucks in a harsh breath.

I want him. I want to give this part of me to him. I want him now, and I want him months from now, and I want him forever.

The realization shakes through me.

"Okay?" he whispers.

I nod.

His fingers skate down my stomach to the top button of my jeans, skimming back and forth beneath the waistband. "Still okay?"

"Yes," I breathe, sparks igniting beneath his touch.

He unbuttons my jeans. I tremble, and he trembles, and we both smile and inch closer. I've only ever been with Marcus, but this is different. Caleb's touch is slow and careful and intense. He is mapping my body. He's learning what I like. And when his eyes ask again, I trace a *Y, E, S,* into the palm of his hand.

The lines between us blur and blend. I feel his heart beating against the palm of my hand. He asks if I want to go to the bed, and I nod. He leads me into the bedroom, and we crawl over the white sheets, kissing and touching, everything slow and warm. The rest of our clothes come off, and when it's time, he gets the box of condoms we bought and opens a wrapper with shaking hands.

It makes me think of his uncertainty at the store, and I wonder if I was wrong about how far he and Margot had gone.

"Have you done this before?" I ask.

His furrowing brow is confirmation enough. "Does that bother you?"

No. A million times no.

I shake my head. "Does it bother you that I have?"

"No."

I give a small smile, and tell him what Marcus was once kind enough to tell me.

"It's okay if you aren't ready. I can wait."

His laugh is dry, and instant. "Just tell me what you like, all right?"

And I do.

CHAPTER 19

It's late when Geri texts to tell us she and Marcus are going to a movie and not to wait up. We order room service and crash— after a while—and when I wake it's to the slow glide of Caleb's fingers along my calf.

I sit up, blinking in the low light of the lamp, reveling in the softness of his T-shirt against my skin. He's lying on his stomach in his boxers, drawing a small city along the length of my calf with a ballpoint pen.

It tickles, just like the brush of his fingertips beneath my knee, and brings a rush of heat to my skin.

"Sorry," he tells me, with a grin that says otherwise.

I don't mind. I wish we didn't have to sleep at all.

"Why aren't you drawing anymore?" I ask.

He glances up, one eye hidden by a curtain of raven hair.

"I am right now."

"You know what I mean. You used to do it so much you had ink stains on your fingers."

He focuses more diligently on my leg, and to be fair, I don't really mind.

"I lost my inspiration," he says quietly.

My heart throbs.

"And now?"

The point of the pen curves around an arching rooftop. "Now it's back." His brows knit together in concentration. "My dad's awake. Damien's going to help us. And I'm probably in love with you."

He doesn't look up.

I'm pretty sure the entire world has been put on pause.

"Probably?" My voice is tight.

His gaze finally lifts to mine. It's thoughtful, hopeful, though the pen in his hand now tapping against the comforter tells a different story.

"Damien's *probably* going to help us," he says.

"No, *probably* the other part."

"Probably my dad woke up?"

I kick at the elbow he's propped his head upon. "You know what I'm talking about."

"No idea. Maybe you should just say it."

He's smiling now, though I feel like I'm perched on the edge of a high-rise, ready to jump.

"You're probably in love with me." The words come out in a rush, bringing a flush to my cheeks.

"Did I say *probably*?" He runs the back of the pen up my calf, sending warm shivers straight to my belly. "I meant *definitely*."

"Well." My throat is in knots. I stare at my leg. I wish it were a tattoo that would never wash away. "That's a pretty big development."

He leans forward and presses a kiss to my ankle.

My breath catches.

"It's okay if you aren't ready to say it back," he says against my skin, a wicked smirk curving his lips. "I can wait."

He kisses the top of my shin.

"I . . ."

His mouth moves to my knee. His fingers slide up my calf, softly tracing the tendons beneath. My breath comes faster. I had no idea the back of my knee could feel like this.

"You what?" he prompts.

The bed creaks a tiny bit as he moves to my thigh.

"I love you," I whisper. It's easier to say than I thought. It's easier than lying, and for me, nothing is easier than that.

His gaze meets mine. "Yeah?"

I nod. "I love you." And because it feels right, I say it again. I nearly shout it.

Then the lock clicks, and I jolt up as the door pushes inward, and I'm blinking at Geri, flipping on the lights in the entryway.

Her arms are crossed over her chest. The curve of her smile looks like mine must when I've just nailed a con.

"Well, isn't this sweet?" she says.

My whole body heats until I'm certain every inch of skin is cherry red.

"Geri," Caleb groans, dragging a sheet over us. "Maybe you can give us a minute."

I stifle a giggle into the pillow, only now noticing that Geri's normally perfect hair is ruffled, and she isn't wearing a speck of lipstick.

My gaze shoots to the clock. It's 5:12 a.m.

The last text I got from her was just after two, when she said they were heading to a diner to "discuss the film."

"How was your night?" I ask, and now it's her cheeks that blossom. A dreamy, dopey kind of smile lights her face, and when I gape, she snaps at me to "shut up," and makes a straight line for the bathroom, adding, "By the way, we need to be at the airport in twenty minutes," on her way by.

Caleb and I turn to each other and swear.

In five, we're dressed and running out the door.

AT THE AIRPORT, we convince the security guards to push us to the front of the line, then run through the terminal, catching the gate attendant just as he's closing the door to the jet bridge. With a stern look, he lets us through, and as we collapse into our seats, Geri and I start to laugh.

"Too close!" she manages between gasps.

"Thanks to your all-nighter," I say.

I expect her to turn the blame on me, but she only laughs.

"I've got a missed call from Margot." Caleb's scowling down at his phone as a woman in a trim blue suit begins pointing to our exits.

"Margot?" Geri's posture grows rigid beside me. "Why is she calling you? Is she all right?"

"I don't know." Caleb's already pressed the button to call her back, though the flight attendant is now motioning for him to put his phone away.

"Margot?" he says when she picks up. "What's going on?"

I lean closer as Geri practically crawls over me to hear.

Caleb turns the phone so we can both listen. "You're *what*?"

"I'm ending it." Margot's voice is fast, and muffled, as though she's on the move.

"What does that mean?" I ask. Geri's gaze tightens as she meets my eyes.

"Brynn," Margot says, recognizing my voice. "How was your trip? Did you have a nice time? I'm sure Dr. O put you up in a nice hotel."

"Margot," Caleb says firmly. "We're on our way home. We got Damien. He's going to help us."

"He'll never help," she says with a dry laugh. "He's got everything he wants. I'm sure he's already reported you to Dr. O."

Icy doubt trickles over my resolve. Ahead, the flight attendant's face pinches as she points to the phone.

We sink lower in the seat.

"He wouldn't do that," I say. "He said he's with us. I believe him."

She laughs. "Didn't you learn anything at that school? The only person you can trust is yourself."

I think of June, eavesdropping in the hallway outside Geri's room. Grayson, outside on the park bench. I've definitely had my concerns about Geri.

But this is what Dr. O wants—us not to trust each other. To trust only him.

"What's she saying?" Geri's practically on my lap. "I can't hear!"

"Damien's scared," I tell Margot. "He's scared like us."

"I'm not scared. Not anymore. I realized that last night. If you're scared, it means you still have something to lose, but I've already lost everything."

"Margot, stop." Caleb's heels begin to tap. "We'll be home in two hours. Let's meet at HQ. We'll talk about this."

"I'll be gone by then," she says.

Perspiration dews on my hairline. "What are you going to do?"

"I'm going to make him pay for Jimmy." She doesn't sound angry, she sounds resigned, and that terrifies me even more.

"How?" I press.

"You don't need details," she says. "That was my mistake before.

I never should have put this on you. This was my fight. The less you know the better."

"Don't do this!" My pulse is racing now. I glance to Caleb. Should we get off the plane? It will take four times as long to get home if we do. "Margot, *think*. He's beaten us one at a time before. You go up against him, he's going to win. We're stronger together."

She laughs coldly. "You and Caleb really are perfect for each other, you know that? I'm going to let you in on a little secret, Brynn, from one hustler to another. When it comes down to it, people like us are better alone. We don't get family. We don't deserve it."

Cold streaks through me.

"That's not true—" Caleb's interrupted by the flight attendant, standing expectantly beside him.

"Put your phone away, sir." She's done being polite.

He gives her a desperate smile. "I'm sorry. My parents mixed up their work schedules and now my sister's home alone. I'm talking to a neighbor right now to see if they can check in on her."

"I understand, sir, but the entire flight is waiting . . ."

Her words fade into the hum of the jet engine as Margot says goodbye.

"Margot?" I grab the phone from Caleb, holding it to my ear.

The line is dead. She's gone.

"Give it to me," Geri says, voice trembling. "I'll call her back. She's always listened to me."

"You can make as many calls as you'd like from the terminal," says the flight attendant, her brows arched in challenge. "Or you can continue talking, and the air marshal can escort you to security. Your choice."

I lean forward in my seat, queasy.

"We're fine," Caleb says. "We need to get home."

"That's the spirit," she says flatly.

As soon as she's out of view, we call Margot back, but there's no answer. We risk calling her from Geri's school phone, but it goes straight to a generic voicemail. I try Henry next, but even he doesn't answer.

Neither does Charlotte.

Neither does Sam.

I send my mom message after message, but there's no response.

"Something's wrong," I say, as the plane takes off. My stomach churns as the bile climbs up my throat. I can't close my eyes without seeing Raf, without seeing my mom and friends in his place. "Something's happened."

Caleb's mouth is set in a grim line. He grabs my hand, his palm slick with cold sweat. Geri links her arm in mine.

The next two hours are the longest of my life.

CHAPTER 20

As soon as the flight attendant rings the button to stand, we bolt into the aisle, and despite her disapproving glare, we are the first off the plane. The terminal is crowded with people—some running to catch their planes, some searching the TV monitors for direction where to go. We shove through them without apology, racing for the nearest exit.

"I tried Margot again," Geri shouts from the back of the line. "No answer!"

"Henry and Moore aren't picking up either!" Paz, Bea, Joel. None of them are answering. I didn't even get their voicemails—just a generic message that I'd been disconnected.

"The Jeep's parked in lot four!" I shout to Caleb, and he veers left under a sign pointing to the garages. Breath searing my chest, I jump as my phone vibrates in my hand.

The screen lights up with a number I don't recognize.

"Hello?" I answer between breaths.

Caleb glances back over his shoulder, brows furrowed.

"Where are you?" a male voice snaps.

"Grayson?" I ask, tension drawing my shoulder blades tighter. "I'm at the airport. Geri and I have been trying to get in touch with Vale Hall all morning. What's going on?"

"Is Henry with you?"

Fear clenches my chest. "I don't know where Henry is. His phone's—"

"Ms. Maddox did some kind of security sweep. Everyone's phones have been wiped clean. All unknown numbers are blocked," Grayson interrupts. He's in a car, I think. I can hear the blare of a horn as it whips past. "Belk said it was some new safety protocol before Dr. O's swearing-in ceremony."

I can tell by the sound of his voice he's not buying this, but I don't know if his disbelief is an act—if Dr. O has told him more than he's letting on.

"Unknown numbers? Geri and I aren't unknown." I glance down at the screen. "Where are you calling from?"

"You think you're the only one with a secret phone?"

My teeth press together. He knows I have a burner. Has he been in my room? Traced my calls to Caleb? Given that information to Dr. O?

This number could be his direct line to the director.

Dread cools my blood as I remember the last time our phones were wiped clean—when the two detectives came to Vale Hall, looking for Grayson. Moore keyed some kind of code into the front gate, and by the time we got back to the residence, Ms. Maddox had gotten rid of every shred of evidence that we weren't a normal boarding school. Our phones were blank. Our online messages were deleted. Whatever incriminating evidence that had been on paper had magically disappeared.

Why is this happening again now?

My thoughts jolt to the other students—to all the things they don't know about Dr. O, about what they're truly doing all these assignments for, and my stomach sinks. "When did she clear the phones?"

"Last night."

"When? Late?" After our visit to the *Kings of Rochester* set? Is it possible Damien called Dr. O after we'd been there and ratted us out?

Are we the security breach? If so, Charlotte's in danger. Sam. *Henry.*

"I don't know, sometime after dinner."

Caleb holds open a swinging door and Geri and I burst through onto a cold, cement sky bridge. Lot four is only twenty feet away.

"Where's Dr. O?" I ask. "Why did you ask about Henry?"

I dig the keys out of my pocket, tossing them to Caleb as the Jeep comes into view at the end of the lot. He snags them midair while I run to the passenger side. Geri's right behind me, though her feet are silent thanks to the boots she's now carrying in one hand.

"Because they're both gone!" Grayson's composure breaks, the sound of his strained voice driving a spear through my focus. "I found Henry earlier hiding in one of the classrooms talking on some old phone. He said something about this being too dangerous, and that he was going to some headquarters to talk. That was the last I saw him."

Was Henry talking to Margot? Was he meeting her at the train yard to stop her from whatever she planned to do to Dr. O?

Doubt slides in over my panic. This could be a trap. Dr. O could have orchestrated this through Grayson, the way he has other games.

But if Henry's in danger . . .

"Grayson, if you're lying—"

"I'm not," he says, his voice still strained. "And if I ever have to you, I swear it was for your own protection."

His words trip the thundering roll of my heart, and slow my steps.

He's telling the truth. I'm sure of it.

But I've been sure before.

"What happened after you found Henry on the phone?" I pull open the passenger side door.

"I tried to talk to him, but he wouldn't listen. Then he and Charlotte and Sam tore out of the garage like the house was on fire. Belk saw them."

My heart pumps faster. I slide into the car, slapping my hand against the dash for Caleb to drive.

"I tried to distract him, but he jumped in the SUV and followed."

A new dose of panic grips my throat as I imagine Belk hunting down my friends. I can't even get in touch with them with my phone number blocked. "Grayson, I need you to call Charlotte or Sam. Tell them they all have to go somewhere public. Somewhere with a lot of people." My voice is shaking. Caleb's started the car now, and is waving a hand toward Geri, whose questions of what is going on keep getting higher in pitch.

"I can't!" Grayson says, a squeal of tires cutting through his words. "I left my Vale Hall phone at school. This number will be blocked."

Which means he can't even call Moore for help.

"Where are you?"

"Right behind Belk. We're in Sycamore somewhere. Thistle Street. What's going on, Brynn?"

The road where the old library sits isn't far from the train tracks.

"We're coming to you. Hang on," I say.

"Too late," Grayson says. "Belk's stopped at some train station. I've got to go."

"Grayson, be careful," I warn. "Belk is dangerous."

"So am I," he says, and hangs up.

"What was that?" Caleb stops the car and shoves the ticket into the automated teller so we can leave the garage.

"Forget Vale Hall," I say. "We need to get to HQ. *Now*."

CALEB PARKS ON the back side of the tracks, where he and the others once hid their cars to host the recruitment rally. No one else is parked here now, though, and that sends another bolt of worry through me. Did Charlotte, Belk, and Grayson all park at the street entrance? Anyone could have seen them.

"This is where you meet?" Geri asks. "You couldn't go to a coffee shop?"

I ignore her, eyes narrowing through the tattered chain-link fence and down the tracks, to where a white billow of smoke rises in the air.

"Fire." Caleb's eyes are bright with fear as they glance my way.

Heart in my throat, I race to the twisted section of fence. Caleb scrambles over, and Geri and I aren't far behind. Gravel sprays out from under our shoes as we follow the path between the tracks, now slick with patches of dirty snow and frozen puddles. Before us, the smoke has doubled in size, a white-gray cloud coughing into the overcast sky.

Henry. Charlotte. Sam.

What has Belk done to my friends?

Where is Grayson?

I glance over my shoulder, but Geri, wearing her high-heeled boots, has fallen behind. She's keeping to high ground, jumping from one rail tie to the next on the track beside us.

From ahead comes an ear-splitting crack of wood, followed by a high-pitched scream. *Charlotte*. I race harder toward the collection of train cars, now only a hundred yards ahead. As we hurl over a steep incline, Caleb grabs the shoulder of my coat, forcing me down. I know he's looking for Belk, but over the rise of gravel, I only see Charlotte and Sam, and someone kneeling on the ground between them. I squint, and register Grayson's dark hair. He falls forward on his hands and knees, as if he's not strong enough to stand.

A groan of old wood, and the flames appear. Whips of orange and red, striking through the darkening plume of smoke above. Gripping my heart like a scalding fist.

I don't see Belk.

I don't see Henry.

Caleb and I scramble over the embankment together, careening toward the others.

"Sam!" Caleb shouts. "Where's Henry?"

Sam spins toward us, Charlotte gripping his arm. Tears streak down her face, now dirty with soot.

"He went in there!" Sam points toward the maze of train cars, now misty with smoke.

A tremor rakes through my bones, weakening my legs until I have to focus to keep standing. The sharp scent of burning wood fills my nostrils and coats my throat. I can feel the heat, even twenty feet away. It's like standing beside an open oven.

"He was calling for someone." Grayson gives a hacking cough, then forces himself up. Soot is smeared across his forehead and jaw, and sweat has soaked through his button-down shirt. "I could hear him when I went in."

"Margot," Charlotte says. "She called him at school. She—"

Charlotte stops as Caleb launches toward the inferno. I've snagged the back of his jacket, but he tears free. When he looks back, his jaw is set, his eyes clear.

He's going in after Henry.

"I'm going with you," I tell him.

He grasps my hand, pumping my fingers hard within his fist.

"Look for Belk," he says.

Everything in me screams *no*. I can't let him go in there alone.

I can't lose him or Henry. I don't even want anything to happen to Margot.

But if Belk's still here, the fire isn't our only danger.

"I've already searched the train cars on the left," Grayson says quickly, stepping beside him. He wouldn't know where to find the car with the painted wolf.

Caleb's hand rips out of mine.

I watch their backs as they disappear into the smoke between two cars, feeling as if my lungs have just been ripped from my chest.

When they're gone, I lunge at Charlotte, whose wild, orange hair looks dull against the fire behind her.

"Where's Belk?"

She shakes her head rapidly. "I don't know."

"We saw him running when we smelled the smoke," Sam says, his face contorted. "He started the fire, I'm sure of it!"

The punch of fury is sharp and swift, but it's overridden by a greater panic. I stare at the flames, now crackling and roaring like a monster that's come to life.

Belk waited until four people were trapped in a maze of train cars, then lit it on fire.

"He followed you," I say, shaking. I run up another embankment, climbing to the top of a track where I can see the cars parked against the road. Two small black sedans. No SUV.

He's already gone.

Rage churns with the bile in my stomach. Where did he go? Is he telling Dr. O that Henry, Margot, Sam, and Charlotte are dead? Did Dr. O order it?

Over the roar of the flames comes a siren.

"The fire department's coming," Sam says, now beside me. "Maybe they can help."

"They'll think we started it!" Charlotte screeches.

I stare toward the flames, jumping when another resounding crack fills the air. Throwing reason aside, I slide back down the gravel slope, nearing the entrance where Caleb and Grayson disappeared.

"Come on," I mutter, wiping the sweat from my brow as I edge closer to the wall of smoke. "Come on, come on."

The sirens grow louder.

"Caleb!" I shout, then cough on the smoke. My bones are shuddering. I feel as if I might break apart. "Henry! *Grayson!*"

Sam's hand grips my shoulder, pulling me back.

"You can't go in there!" he yells.

But if they're trapped . . .

If they need my help . . .

I'm just about to tell Sam and Charlotte to run when I hear a hacking cough ahead. I jerk out of Sam's grasp and run into the smoke. A shadowed figure stumbles toward me, moving too slowly to escape the flames now catching on the cars on either side. I rush toward him, the air searing my throat as I pull my shirt collar up over my mouth and nose. Tears stream from the corners of my eyes as they lock on Caleb.

I charge toward him, stumbling when I see the small figure cradled in his arms.

"Margot?" I gasp.

She isn't moving. Her head rests against his chest, her skin black with soot. Terror fills the gaps between my ribs as I help prop her between Caleb's shoulder and mine.

She can't be dead.

Not after Raf, and Jimmy, and all the rest.

Caleb blinks, dazed, as another coughing fit takes him.

"Move!" A voice behind Caleb cuts through the flames. Grayson, with Henry hoisted against his side. The five of us run toward the exit, tripping over each other, falling in a heap on the ground just outside the wall of smoke.

Caleb gags as I lean over Margot, feeling for a pulse on her flushed skin.

"Margot? Margot!" Geri's beside me now, hands on Margot's cheeks. "Is she breathing?"

I lean down, listening for breath, and hear a faint sip of air.

"I think so!"

Beside me, Grayson's fallen onto his back. Henry's on his knees beside him, coughing, his yellow hair stained black with soot.

"Next time . . ." Grayson heaves between breaths. "You want . . . to be dramatic . . . wear some eyeliner . . ."

Henry laughs. Chokes a little. Then leans down and kisses Grayson right on the mouth.

I gape at them, a sob building in my chest as Grayson's hands reach around Henry's jaw to pull him closer.

"You *do* have it bad for me," Grayson mutters.

I sputter a laugh.

Then Charlotte's tackled Henry, squeezing so hard it induces another coughing fit, and Sam's hugging Caleb, and Caleb's kissing me while Henry's arms wrap around Grayson's waist, and we're all crying and coated with soot and dirty snow but alive.

"She needs help," Geri says, snapping my focus back to Margot. Her eyes are still closed, and she's not breathing any deeper. "I think maybe she took in too much smoke. I don't know!"

Over the rush in my ears comes the sirens.

"We have to get out of here," Sam says.

He picks up Margot, and I grab Caleb's hand. Charlotte helps Henry and Grayson up, though as soon as she does, she draws back, as if remembering who Grayson is.

He's going to explain what's going on. But first, we need to move.

"Fire trucks have us blocked in," Grayson mutters as he peers over the edge of the gravel embankment toward his car. "We have to go another way."

"The Jeep."

Caleb points ahead toward the edge of the property where we entered, and we run away from the burning cars, toward the Jeep. As soon as we're all over the fence, Geri says, "Where will we go? We can't take her to a hospital."

We can't go home.

It hits me then. Belk tried to kill us. All the things we were fighting for have been ripped away. I'm not even sure I have an identity still.

"My mom," I realize. "She'll be next. I need to—"

"Moore will take care of it," Caleb says, but I can tell he's worried too.

"Dr. O's got eyes on Moore," Charlotte responds.

My breath comes out in a huff. He can't protect Mom or Caleb's family if he's with Dr. O, but maybe he'll be better able to monitor what the director's plans are.

It seems a weak thing to hope for, but if I go to her, someone may follow. Someone might be watching *me* right now.

I rip my school phone out of my back pocket and drop it on the ground, then crush it beneath my heel. Even if everyone else's phones have changed, I'll bet Dr. O still has a way to track this one.

Charlotte's phone follows. Sam's. Henry's.

Grayson's.

The only ones we have left are burners.

All I have left are the clothes on my back and a bag in the back seat of the Jeep.

"Are there any other ways to track us?" I ask.

"The files in headquarters are gone," Henry wheezes, prodding a deep gash on his forehead with his fingertips. "Margot was destroying everything we had when I found her. Not that it matters now."

Flames have now consumed the train yard, the burning wood snapping and groaning as it takes car after car. The far gate, where Grayson and the others have parked, falls with a clang of metal as a red fire engine rolls through it.

"I'll call my dad," Geri says.

"*No,*" Caleb and I say together.

"If you're with me, he won't hurt you!" she argues. But there's doubt in her voice, and I can tell she's not certain.

"I know a place," Grayson says, his slate-blue eyes flicking to mine. "We'll be safe there."

I stand on the edge of a cliff, doubt holding me back. I still don't know what role Grayson plays in all this—if he's Dr. O's spy, or if this is just another favor for the director to get close to us.

"He saved my life," Henry says, grabbing Grayson's hand.

Grayson's Adam's apple moves as he swallows. His gaze never leaves mine.

Cold realization spears through my suspicion. It doesn't matter if he sold us out, or if it was something I did by accident, or if Charlotte or Sam or Henry or Geri or even Caleb are responsible. We're all on our own now, which means all we have is each other.

"Okay," I say.

Grayson reaches for the keys in Caleb's hand, but Caleb jerks away.

"You can tell me where to go," he says. "But you're not driving."

"Fine," Grayson answers.

We pile in the car, and speed away from the burning train yard.

Grayson directs us to the highway, which takes us north, out of the city. After we stop at a highway restaurant to exchange the plates on the Jeep with another in the lot, Grayson tells us where we're going. A cabin near Lake Winnebago—a private place his father bought under a different name to avoid the public finding out—almost two hours away.

"Sounds like the perfect place to get murdered," Charlotte mutters as thick white flakes begin to fall from the gray sky. She's crammed on top of Sam's lap in the back seat, Margot's feet draped over her lap. The rest of her is laid over me and Geri, smashed together against the window.

My legs keep falling asleep, but I don't complain. None of us do. We're alive.

"He wouldn't try anything," Sam says, loud enough for Grayson to hear. "There's too many of us."

"He can hear you," says Henry, half sitting on Grayson's lap in the passenger seat. They seem to have reached a tentative truce— saving Henry's life was big, but it doesn't erase all the other things Grayson has done.

"Then he should know that it's poor form to deceive a pregnant woman." Charlotte's voice grows edgy.

"Pregnant, huh?" Grayson's brows are quirked as he looks over the seat, but his tone bears no surprise. "Mazel tov."

"Thank you," she says begrudgingly.

Margot's leg twitches, and a quick glance down at her face pelts me with another wave of concern. Her eyes are open, her breath steady. She woke up an hour ago, but all she's said is "Let me out."

That's not happening.

There's something different about her, a quietness, an *absence*, that terrifies me. It's as if the fire burned the fight out of her. She needs medical care, but we can't risk taking her to a hospital. People will ask questions we can't afford to answer, and in her current state, I'm not entirely convinced she wouldn't talk.

We still don't even know if she did whatever she was planning to do before we arrived. Every time we've asked, it's always the same answer.

I got her.

Not *him*. Not Dr. O. *Her*. We ask who she means, but Margot doesn't say any more than that.

A shiver rakes down my back as Grayson points Caleb toward an exit. I crane my head to watch Grayson as we take the off-ramp past a cluster of fast-food restaurants and gas stations, down a two-lane road that cuts into the woods. His mouth is set in a grim line, his eyes focused ahead. The only sign of anxiety is a bulge in the vein along his throat. I wonder what that means—if he's worried about this cabin, or if he's plotting something, or if this worry is simply about Henry, smashed into the seat beside him against the passenger side door.

Around us, the trees grow denser, their naked branches reaching out over the road and scraping at the sides of the car. Frost coats the asphalt, turning it a shimmering gray.

This road is not often driven.

"There." Grayson motions Caleb to a turn on the left. At first, there's no road apparent at all—ahead is a cluster of brush and fallen branches. But Grayson and Henry get out, and a few moments later they're clearing away the debris to reveal a metal gate.

"Definitely not creepy," Charlotte says.

Sam hums his agreement.

"He wouldn't save Henry just to sell us out now," Caleb says, gripping the steering wheel with his right hand. My gaze drops to his left, which has been fisted on his thigh since we left the train yard, and another knot tightens at the base of my neck.

Grayson motions us through, and the dead branches and old snow crunch under the slow roll of the tires. Caleb stops after we've cleared the gate, and after Grayson and Henry have replaced the blockade, they hurry back to the car.

"It's freezing out," Henry says. His nose and ears are pink, even through the soot he's managed to wipe away, and he rubs his hands together rapidly to bring feeling back.

No one answers.

"Just down this road," Grayson says, voice tight.

Charlotte's hand finds mine and squeezes. Wariness prickles through the air.

The road grows bumpy, and Caleb is forced to steer around large drifts of snow that block the path. In the back seat, we brace ourselves against the seat and the ceiling and each other, jostling with every movement of the Jeep.

Finally, a cabin comes into view.

It's small—like a gingerbread house built of graham crackers, with two square windows beside the door and a sloped roof.

My pulse settles minimally.

At least there really is a cabin.

Caleb parks in front, and we begin to unload, Sam and Charlotte practically falling out the side. Margot remains limp as I slide out from under her, and as soon as we're gone, she curls into a ball, hugging her knees against her chest. She makes a sound I mistake as pain, but when I lean closer, I hear her soft laughter. It spreads icy tendrils through my chest. This isn't her. This isn't okay. Is she hurt? Is this from the fire, or did something happen before?

Whatever she might have done affects us all now.

Grayson steps in front of me.

"I'm sorry," he says. "For everything I said. For all of it, actually."

A fist squeezes around my heart. Why is he apologizing now? What has he done?

I don't ask, though, because at that moment, the cabin door pushes outward with a squeal, and a woman appears on the snowy wooden deck.

Immediately, Grayson throws up his hand. "We didn't have a choice!" he calls. "We weren't followed."

I take in the woman in pieces. The shotgun lifted at her shoulder. The crutch under her left arm. The belt around her jeans that shows her narrow waist, and the thick sweater with the hole in one shoulder.

Her hair is white blond, and pulled back into a tight ponytail. Her face is familiar, as if from a dream.

Or a painting.

I stumble back, nearly falling before Grayson snags my arm. At once, my heart is racing, beating so hard I'm sure it will break my ribs.

It's her.

She's here.

She's *alive*.

The woman's rifle lowers slightly. Her pinched gaze moves from one of us to the next, finally landing on me.

"Everyone," Grayson says, "this is Susan Griffin."

CHAPTER 21

Whispers rise from our beat-up group like steam from a hot bath—Charlotte recognizes Susan from the portrait in the director's office now, as does Geri. Sam is skeptical. Caleb slowly approaches for a closer look.

Beside me, Grayson scratches his head, looking, for once, uncertain.

"Not to be rude," Henry says. "But isn't Susan Griffin supposed to be dead?"

"Yes," says Caleb.

"Okay," says Henry. "Just checking."

"How is this possible?" I blurt. "Does Dr. O know?" I can't think of what that might mean—if Dr. O is somehow behind this, if it really is a trap Grayson's led us into.

Forget not knowing who to trust—I don't know what's *true* anymore.

At her brother's name, Susan hisses, as if she's just stuck her hand on a hot stove.

"No," Grayson says sharply, looking to Susan. "No one knows but me and my dad."

I can't make sense of this. "Grayson, your dad is in jail for her *murder*. You said you ran her off the road!"

"Who cares?" Geri screeches. "Can she help us or not?"

With a flash of guilt, I remember Margot in the back seat, but am unable to move.

Susan Griffin is alive. The woman Grayson killed at Dr. O's orders is here, standing in front of me. Everything I've known about him, and Dr. O, and my role at Vale Hall, is crumbling.

"We ran into trouble in the city," Grayson explains to Susan. "There was a fire. Margot's hurt."

"Margot Patel?" Susan's voice snaps my spine straight. It's lower than I imagined. Harder. Not soft or delicate, like the woman in the white dress from the painting.

The recognition in her voice strikes me a moment later. She knows Margot—or at least *of* Margot.

Does she know all of us?

"All of you. All at once." Susan's squinting gaze lifts to the road behind us, then a sigh presses through her clenched teeth. "He's outdone himself this time." She lowers the rifle completely and motions us closer with her other hand. "Hurry inside. It's cold."

Grayson cuts in front of me when my feet stay planted in the frozen, snowy ground.

"It's fine," he says. "She's one of us."

I balk. "Who are *us*?"

His jaw darkens. He avoids my eyes.

"The ones who keep the secrets," he says.

He helps Caleb gently pull Margot, no longer laughing but wincing in pain, from the back seat. Once she's secure in Caleb's arms, I stumble after them, up the creaky wooden steps to the deck where Susan is standing. Grayson thanks her, and she lays a hand on his shoulder, then hurries him through the door.

As Caleb approaches, Susan's brows knit with worry. Margot's gaze stays lifted on the sky. She doesn't even acknowledge Susan's presence.

"Inside," Susan orders, pulling at a small key on a chain around her neck. "On the bed."

I don't have to wonder which bed she means—there's only one inside. Against the back wall is a twin mattress, a red and white quilt pulled neatly to the top. The rest of the cabin is sparse, but warm. A small kitchen to the right boasts a stove and a small metal sink. The shelves above are filled with cans and boxes. Beside the bed is a bathroom, and through the open door I see a tiny shower. The wall to my left has two leather couches, a lamp on a wooden end table, and a half-finished painting of the woods on a coffee table easel.

There are books on the shelf above it, stacked against the walls and on the kitchen table, and the warm air smells like old paper.

Caleb rushes forward and lays Margot on the bed. Her black hair sticks to the soot on her face. Caleb's shoulder is now stained with the same blood on Geri's left thigh—from a gash on the back of Margot's head.

My breath trips ahead, all the fear and worry from the fire and car ride now catching up to me. A buzzing fills my ears as Susan begins snapping out orders for water and rags and the medical kit she keeps under the sink in the bathroom.

"Is she okay?" Geri keeps asking. "I think she has a concussion."

Susan leans heavily on the crutch as she walks, and when she sits on the side of the bed, her left leg barely bends at all. While we hover over her, she turns Margot's face to check her pupils.

"What happened back here?" Susan's frown tightens as she cleans the wound on the back of Margot's head.

Margot inches closer to the wall. "Go away," she whispers.

Susan pauses.

Fear tightens its hold on my lungs. *Broken*, it whispers.

"The roof of the train car collapsed on us," Henry says, his voice trembling. "I think she got the worst of it."

"You don't look much better." Susan's green eyes flash to him. "Take care of that cut on your head before it gets infected." With a wave of her hand, she dismisses us. "That goes for all of you. There are blankets and towels in the bathroom. Take any clothes you need."

My gaze flicks to our group, our shoes now dripping on the hardwood floor. We've seen better days. Ash and grime cover our faces and clothes in varying degrees. Grayson's shirt is ripped around the collar. Henry's gash has now raised into a purple and yellow welt. Even those who weren't near the fire—Sam, Charlotte, and Geri—are covered in grime and half soaked with mud and melted snow. Half of us are visibly shivering.

But those of us standing are ready, anxiously perched on the balls of our feet, as if we may still have to run or fight.

"I want to know what's going on," I say.

Susan stiffens, but doesn't look away from Margot.

"I assure you, you don't," Susan says, without turning my way.

Fury heats my cold skin. She doesn't get to shove me off after everything I've been through—after everything we've survived today alone.

"You're right." My voice is sharp as a knife. "Maybe if I hide in this cabin for a while, all my problems will magically go away."

Her sigh rounds her back, and I see the woman from the portrait then, thin and fragile.

"Let's clean up," Grayson says. "Then we'll talk."

My teeth press together, but I nod.

"Come on." Grayson takes Henry's hand and leads him to the kitchen sink. I watch them only a moment, then turn toward Caleb.

I meet his eyes and tilt my head toward the bathroom.

He follows, an unspoken conversation passing between him and Sam about keeping an eye on Henry.

In the mirror, I catch my reflection—my eyes are red, my cheeks pale and streaked with black. My hair looks like a flock of birds have made their nest in it. As I wash my hands, he closes the bathroom door. Then he comes behind me, his arms around my waist, his forehead resting on the back of my shoulder.

At once, my walls fall away. My breath comes in a silent shudder. He holds me tighter, until my back is flush against his chest and I can feel his chin on the side of my neck.

I don't say a word. I don't close my eyes, because I know I'm going to see him running into that fire again. I don't ask if he thinks we can trust Susan, because I know he doesn't know either.

We're alive, and together, and that's all we have right now.

"Let me see your hand," I rasp.

He lifts his half-closed fist in front of my waist, and I stare down at his long fingers, blackened by ash. Gently, I try to unfurl his hand, but he flinches and bites off a hiss.

"Margot was under a board," he says tightly.

I imagine him lifting it off her. He probably didn't even think twice.

Carefully, I rinse his fingers, then lather them with soap. His other hand finds my side, sliding beneath the hem of my shirt, holding on.

I clean away the soot to reveal an angry pink welt that stretches from his thumb to his pinky, already blistering around the edges. It needs a bandage, and those are in the main room with Susan and Margot.

"Ready?" I ask when we're done cleaning up.

He presses his lips to my neck in answer.

The others have gathered on the couch. Henry's face is clean now, the gash on his head closed with butterfly bandages and glossy with antiseptic ointment. He's wearing a flannel bathrobe. Beside him, Grayson sits on the edge of the couch cushion in jeans and a white undershirt. A blanket is thrown over his shoulders.

Charlotte and Sam sit on the opposite couch, a full cushion between them and Susan.

Geri is still in the back of the room, sitting on the foot of the bed. Margot is curled up, facing the wall, as far away from Geri as possible.

"She'll talk when she's ready," Susan says, again pulling at the tiny silver key on her necklace. "She needs time."

I nod, willing that time to hurry up as I take a seat next to Henry. Caleb sits on the floor beside me. Someone's started a fire in the old iron stove near the wall, and the crackling of the wood within sets my teeth on edge.

"Brynn," Susan says tentatively, as if trying out my name. "I know you deserve an explanation. You all do. But the more you know, the more you're at risk. It's imperative you consider that."

"We're already at risk," Charlotte says, one hand on her belly. I glance to Grayson, whose jaw is working back and forth.

"I'm sorry for that," Susan says, the weight in her tone like a wet blanket on my shoulders. "It was never supposed to be that way."

The pop of wood in the old stove makes me jump.

"Well. Start talking," I tell Grayson.

Grayson leans forward, hands on his knees. The muscles in his forearms flex into hard lines.

"David—Dr. O—and Susan were friends of my family," he starts. "They'd been around as long as I can remember. Birthday parties. Fundraisers. David basically sponsored my dad's first run for local office. I came to the opening of Vale Hall, ten years ago. David told me I'd have a place there when I was older. He was kind of like an uncle, I guess you could say."

I glance to Caleb, finding his brows furrowed. It's unsettling hearing Grayson refer to Dr. O as *David*, as a family friend, even now.

"He was very opinionated when it came to my dad's career," Grayson continues. "I think because he'd donated so much money, he thought he could have a say when it came to his politics."

"How so?" asks Sam.

"He wanted Matthew to vote certain ways. *In the best interests of the city,*" Susan quotes with a growl in her voice. "Of course that meant protecting his precious Wednesday Pharmaceuticals."

I remember what Dylan said during the Wolves party—that Dr. O had that company only because he'd blackmailed the previous majority shareholder to disappear.

"Of course it comes down to money," Charlotte says.

"How do you think Vale Hall is funded?" Susan asks. "Our father despised him. He left David nothing. When my brother said he wanted to start a school, I gave him the estate. I thought it might clear some of the resentment he held toward me from our childhood." She sighs, and I'm thrown back into Dr. O's office, when he told me about how his father abandoned his mother, then walked her into suicide.

"I thought it did for a while," Susan says, "but I was naive about many things."

From the kitchen comes the shrill whistle of a teapot.

Susan stands, using her crutch to cross the room. She turns off the stove as the kettle quiets, and removes a series of mugs from one of the shelves.

Grayson's fingers begin to drum on his knees. "My dad did what David wanted at first—I think he figured he owed him for all the campaign donations—but once he became a senator, all that stopped. He couldn't do it anymore. He told my sister and I we weren't allowed to talk to David—they'd had some kind of fight. He thought David might try to contact me, get me to guilt my dad into getting back in line. My dad . . ." Grayson rakes his hair forward. "You don't know him. Not really. He's a good person. He'd never hurt anyone. Bending his values to make David rich . . . it just wasn't something he could do."

I try to wrap my mind around this new version of the senator, but it's like sticking a round peg into a square hole.

Still, I remember that moment in the stairway outside Matthew's campaign office last summer. He'd been so desperate to find Grayson. I'd almost believed he was really scared for his son's welfare.

Maybe he really was.

Susan loads the steaming mugs onto a tray, but carrying them proves difficult with her crutch. Grayson pops up before she can ask for help and brings it over to the coffee table for her.

"I knew my brother was upset," she says, motioning for us to take the tea she's made. "I didn't think he would really hurt anyone. He was always righteous with his causes. Even with Wednesday, it was all for the purpose of feeding the school, raising savvy young people to fight corruption. We wanted this city to be cleaner, *better*. He saw Sikawa as a family, and its leaders as parents. He didn't want anyone like our father in control." She takes a mug for herself, scowling as she blows away the steam. "When Matthew refused to comply with his wishes, he became, to David, a man just like our father. A neglectful hypocrite. An obstacle to justice."

Grayson has collapsed back into his seat, and he laughs dryly, though he looks slightly ill. "David doesn't like hearing the word *no*."

I once thought the same of Grayson.

Now, as I look at him, I'm not sure I know him at all.

Susan grasps the mug, but doesn't sip her tea. "After their falling-out, David and I grew apart. He assumed I was the enemy, just like everyone else in his life. We talked little in those days. I distanced myself from the school, hoping it would protect the students. Then Margot Patel showed up at my art studio."

I glance back to the bed to Margot—Caleb's once girlfriend, Geri's once best friend, the con who'd occupied my room before me. She lost everything thanks to Dr. O, just like Susan, and even as I'm worried about what she's done, I'm sick at the sight of her lying still in that bed.

"She was sent by a friend, someone I trusted." Susan's brows pinch together, then relax with a forced blink. "She was a mess— with good reason. She told me that she'd been assigned to gather critical information on Matthew Sterling from a young intern working in his campaign office." At this, Susan glances back to where Margot is laid out on the bed, her limp hand in Geri's grasp.

"Jimmy Balder," I say, thinking of the intern I was sent to dig up information on in Sterling's campaign office. I watch Susan carefully, curious about this trusted friend. Who else knew about what Margot had done? Did they have to run from Dr. O as well?

Susan nods. "She'd fallen in love with him while they were working in Matthew's campaign office together—the job my brother had sent her to do to earn her place at Vale Hall—and in the process she broke the school's cardinal rule of secrecy. Jimmy knew who Margot really was, and that she had been assigned to gather blackmail information on Matthew. David, unfortunately, had already figured this out."

"Because I told him what she'd done." Caleb's voice is empty, his hands clenched into fists. "I didn't think he'd . . . I didn't think."

Because Dr. O had put him in an impossible position—spying on his own girlfriend. Losing his continued enrollment at the school, and his father's health care, if he didn't tell the director the truth. It hadn't mattered if he'd wanted to cover for Margot, the cost was too high for his family.

In the end, he was forced out of Vale Hall anyway. Because of me.

I shudder, remembering that conversation with Dr. O after the fight between Caleb and Grayson in the pit. I'd been trying to protect them both. Dr. O had promised he'd take care of Caleb.

I should have known he'd play us against each other.

I won't make that mistake again.

Susan's stare warps with pity. "It's not your fault. My brother will always be the desperate boy he was after his mother died. He will do anything to protect himself. To *survive*." She leans closer and pats Caleb's knee. "This wasn't about you. It wasn't about Margot either. It was always only about David."

I know this, but to hear someone else—his own sister—say it warms the cold hollows inside me.

I take Caleb's unburned fist and pull it over my thigh. His fingers stretch open, warmth pooling beneath his touch as he lets out a tight sigh.

Susan sets down her mug. "I tried to reason with David, but he was impossible to deter. He attacked me. He threatened to kill me, and Margot, and the boy she'd worked with." With a scowl, Susan clears her throat. "I didn't know where to go. David was watching me—his wolf, Min Belk, was on my heels all the time. I couldn't go to the police, David had already told me what would happen if I did that. I knew I had to warn Matthew so that he could protect his intern, but I couldn't get near his house, so I offered up a painting I'd done to one of his upcoming fundraising auctions at a gallery in Uptown—something for homeless children, I think."

Family First. I see the campaign banner hanging in Matthew's office, as clearly as I did my first day on the job.

My head is pounding as I absorb what she's telling me. The threats. The attack. Mark Stitz—the internship supervisor at Sterling's office—told me that he'd seen Susan and Matthew talking to Jimmy the night of a fundraiser. He'd overheard them offer him money to get out of town—a bribe I later learned was for Jimmy's protection.

Silence has stunned our group. No one knows what to say. Henry's biting his thumbnail. Charlotte and Sam are staring at Susan. Geri, listening from the bed, looks grim.

"I didn't know Margot," Grayson says. "I didn't know any of this was happening. But I trusted David, even though my dad had said to keep my distance. When he came to me and said my dad was having an affair with Susan, I believed him."

His eyes lower to the floor.

Susan gives a bitter laugh. "Another lie. Matthew was a friend, nothing more."

"My dad and I were close," Grayson says. "We did everything together. He loved my mom. They were always . . . I don't know, on the same page. They got each other. I wanted to be like them."

"That's sweet," says Henry.

Grayson's scowl deflects the compliment. "David got in my head. He said they'd been caught together at some bed-and-breakfast outside the city. There was proof—the hotel in Susan's name, paid for by Matthew's credit card and signed by him." Grayson laughs dryly. "I checked, of course."

Beside him, Henry frowns. His heel taps against the floor, and I feel his tension spike across the couch to me.

I remember a story on *Pop Store* about that—I saw it when I first started researching for my assignment to befriend Grayson, and learn what I could about his family. Anything was fair game. Potential blackmail to feed to Dr. O.

"It was a story for the news—Matthew may have gone to that B and B, but it certainly wasn't with me," Susan says. "I couldn't get anywhere close to Matthew without Min Belk knowing."

She pulls at her necklace again, and I can't help wondering where Moore was in all of this. Did he follow her as well? I can't see him co-signing any efforts to attack a woman.

I wish he were here with us now.

"I believed him," Grayson says, defeated. "He asked me to call him if I ever saw Susan with my dad, and I did—the night of that fundraiser. I saw them leaving together. I didn't know David had threatened to kill Susan or the rest of them. I just thought he was going to confront them." He sends a bitter stare Caleb's way. "Bet you don't feel too bad about what you did now, do you?"

Caleb's gaze turns to pity, then understanding.

"You didn't know," he says.

Henry, his cheeks now blotchy and pink, touches Grayson's shoulder. The small gesture makes Grayson shudder, then warily, tentatively, lean into him.

"David showed up at the fundraiser." Grayson stares at the floor, as if holding it down with his gaze alone.

"Gray," Susan says softly. "You don't—"

Grayson shakes his head. When he continues, his voice is thin enough to snap. "I went to his car, and told him that Susan and my dad had gone to the campaign office. It was just a few blocks away."

A tear trickles down Grayson's cheek, and I feel my own throat swell as I picture the dark city streets. Part of me still wants to question the truth in this story, but I can see it. Grayson's struggle to understand what his father was doing. The way Dr. O must have clouded his judgement and filled him with doubt. Grayson had needed someone to trust, and Dr. O had filled that gap, just as he'd done with me when I'd come to Vale Hall.

"I shouldn't have followed him. I wanted to see it, I guess. I wanted him to call her out for sleeping with my dad. I thought if I did, maybe I'd have the courage to call my dad out too."

Tears are streaming freely from his eyes now, and he swipes at them with the back of his hand. Henry moves closer, so that they're sitting thigh to thigh. His arm wraps around Grayson's shoulders.

"Susan didn't see either of us when she came out of the building. She got in her car, and David followed, and I followed him, all the way to Route Thirty-nine. It's so dark out there at night. There weren't any other cars on the road. I started getting sick about the whole thing—I thought he was going to talk to her, but they just kept driving. I tried calling him, but he didn't answer. He just kept going faster, and faster, until she started swerving to get away from him." Grayson blows out a quaking breath. "They came around the turn, and he hit the side of her car. She went straight into a tree."

The story I've been over so many times in my head shatters, and pieces back together in a different way. It brings a throbbing between my temples.

Grayson wasn't driving the car.

Dr. O ran his own sister off the road.

Beside me, Grayson is barely holding it together.

"I pulled over behind him, I guess. Everything kind of jumbled together after that. The next thing I know, I'm outside Susan's busted-up car, yelling at David to tell me why he did that. He told me that sometimes you have to do terrible things to do great things. He said if I ever talked, my dad and mom and sister were next." Grayson closes his eyes. "He thanked me for calling him."

I think of all the anger and shame I've seen reflected in Grayson's gaze since I've met him. He's blamed himself for this. Even when he told Henry and me that Dr. O ordered him to do it, he blamed himself.

My hate for Dr. O is potent, and cold as ice.

Grayson shifts. "He started to leave. I said we needed to help her . . . she might still be alive. He told me to go check. As soon as I did, he took off. I didn't realize then that he expected me to take the fall."

"Of course he did," mutters Charlotte.

"I didn't know if she was alive," Grayson continues, faster now. "She wasn't moving. I couldn't tell if she was breathing. I didn't know what to do. I was too scared David would kill my family if I called the police." His body clenches in a sob, and he hides his face behind his hands. "I thought he was already on the way to my house to hurt them."

"Okay," says Susan. "That's enough. We don't have to—"

But Grayson barrels on.

"This phone started ringing—Susan's phone. It was on the floor by her feet. I grabbed it, and saw my dad's name on the screen."

"He was calling to make sure I'd gotten home all right," says Susan weakly. "He'd known Min Belk was following me."

"He asked where Susan was, and what had happened, and I panicked," says Grayson. "I told him she'd been in an accident. That it was my fault. I knew about the affair, and couldn't stand what he'd done to my mom, and I'd tried to scare Susan and run her off the road. He told me not to go anywhere. He'd be right there. When he showed up, Susan was starting to come around. We pulled Susan out of the car. Her leg . . . was broken."

The way he says it makes it seem like it was not a clean break. I glance to the crutch, now leaning against the side of the couch.

"I told him I'd made a stupid mistake. I didn't want to go to prison," Grayson says. "I begged him to call his contacts in the police and cover it up—make it look like a hit-and-run."

"You were trying to save his life," I say, my voice raw.

Grayson's red, swollen eyes turn my way, and the breath locks in my throat. "A doctor my dad knows fixed Susan up as best he could outside the hospital, and my dad agreed to move her to the cabin, all to protect *me* from the fallout."

"Your dad knew I was in danger," Susan says to Grayson. "It made sense for me to disappear."

The word strikes me like an out of tune key on a piano. Does everyone Dr. O come in contact with *disappear*?

"Let me get this straight," says Sam. "You all faked her death to protect her from Dr. O?"

Grayson nods. Henry hugs him tighter.

Sam blows out a stiff breath.

"And your dad still went to prison?" I ask. "Doesn't he know the truth? This happened two years ago!"

Susan's face turns grave.

"He still thinks I did it," says Grayson, the shame making him look years older than eighteen. "The only piece of evidence that Susan wasn't alone that night were my fingerprints on her phone. I gave it to you to give to David, remember?"

I nod, remembering too well the phone in the plastic bag, hidden in the old tree at the site of the crash.

"I thought if I gave him that, he'd let my family off the hook. He had enough to pin me for her death. I hoped that was enough."

"You gave up?" I ask. I can't believe this. Susan's alive. She can testify that Dr. O tried to kill her—that she's been in hiding for two years because of him. She could have gone to the press. Ended this.

"Yeah, I gave up," Grayson says, his voice sharp and familiar now. "He sent you after me, remember? You came into my house to spy on me. You talked to my sister and dad. You don't think that was a threat?"

I slouch into the sofa, realizing how this must look from his side. There were times I felt bad for conning Grayson, but I never thought of myself as a threat to him.

Now that I know what Dr. O's capable of, I see how I must have looked.

"But you took the phone back," I say. "You got Henry to plant it on your dad. Why would you do that?"

Henry's arm slides off Grayson's back. Again, all eyes turn to the senator's son.

"Because my dad's detectives had gotten another warrant to come back to search Vale Hall. You remember when they came the first time? They were there for me. My dad was convinced Dr. O was holding me there against my will."

"And he was right." A wave of unsteadiness crashes through me as I finally realize the angle I was sure Grayson was hiding behind.

He's been blackmailed, and the life-or-death game he's played has gone on for *two years*.

"Of course he was right," Grayson says. "You think I chose to live with him after what he did? What he made me do? My dad thinks I *killed* someone." He shakes his head. "It was just a matter of time before his detectives figured out I was a prisoner there. If and when they found me, how was I supposed to explain what had happened? David made it one hundred percent clear what would happen if I talked."

"You had your dad arrested to *protect* him?" Henry asks.

"It's safer in prison than at home. And with all of the press around my mom and sister right now, there's no way David would try to hurt them." Grayson swipes at his eyes. "I call Susan once a week to check in. If she doesn't answer, it means Dr. O's found her."

"It means you run like you should have a long time ago," Susan says in a firm voice, as I remember Grayson outside June's window on the bench, phone in hand.

"And what would that accomplish?" I ask.

Every face turns in my direction.

"I'm sorry," I say. "But you're hiding in the woods. Grayson's dad's on trial for murder so he *won't* get murdered. We all could have been killed in a fire just a few hours ago. How does running make any of us safer? Dr. O's proved he can track us down if he wants!"

"She's right," Caleb says, leaning forward. "Susan, if you come forward, you can prove he's a sociopath."

"Yes!" My knee bumps Caleb's shoulder as I slide to the edge of the couch. "And you're on the school board! If Damien votes for you to take over, it wouldn't matter that Tim Loki's already voted for Belk to be director!"

"Belk's going to be director?" Charlotte screeches.

"This is my nightmare," groans Henry.

Susan holds up her hands and silence reigns. "What's this about Tim Loki?"

"He's another board member," Caleb says. "Don't you know him? Damien said the three of you were executive members. Tim had already voted for Belk, and Damien . . ."

He pauses when Susan snorts a laugh.

"I'm sorry," she says. "Tim Loki was the name my brother used when he blackmailed our father. He doesn't exist."

"Hold on," I say. "Tim Loki *is* David Odin?"

"It makes sense, doesn't it?" she says bitterly. "A school board oversees a director's activities. What better way to keep your illegal pursuits quiet than to assign a dead woman, an actor with much to lose, and yourself to the governing body? That's my brother for you."

"But Damien said Tim was rich. He had all those businesses overseas." Was that a lie, fed to him by Dr. O? I feel stupid. It makes sense now why Damien's never seen the third board member in person.

"I'm sure on paper *Tim Loki* does," Susan says. "David will always protect himself. He was poor as a child, and he won't be poor again. Those companies Damien mentioned are likely shells—ways to funnel the money from Wednesday Pharmaceuticals into different accounts to avoid taxes and keep his options open in case he has to cut bait and run. He did the same thing when I . . . was alive." She frowns, a tight crease beside her mouth. "A single account with modest funds for the public eye, several others feeding into it when needed."

It's a perfect fit for him. A public image of dignity and service. A private alias doing the dirty work behind the scenes.

Susan flattens her hands on her knees. "I've been through this, believe me. If I come forward, it puts Gray in danger. Margot too. All of you—anyone connected to me—will be punished. It's too dangerous."

"*He's* too dangerous," I argue, hands open and pleading. "Do you know what's happened to the other students? Rafael Fuentes is dead. Dylan Prescott told me Jack Hauser and Sonya Hallsburg are too. He doesn't even give us scholarships, or set us up with internships! Yeah," I say, when Charlotte's mouth drops open. "Damien let us in on that little fact while we were in Baltimore. He's using us, then throwing us out with the trash."

"And how do you propose we make it stop?" I wither as Grayson meets my gaze. I misjudged him from the beginning, and all I see now in his blue eyes is the threat I was to him, the fear I must have made him feel.

I was never a con artist. I was a weapon.

He was never a killer. He was a hero.

"Blackmail," I say, but the word falls flat.

Grayson scowls. Susan sits forward, her cheeks pale.

"The other students don't know he's not really planning on sending us to college," I say. "When they find out, they'll be furious. With everything we've got on him, we can break him."

Or he can break us with everything *he's* got on *us*.

"You don't blackmail my brother and come out alive," Susan says. "And now, with this Senate position . . . the public eye is on him. He's expected places—to attend events. If he doesn't show up, there will be an investigation. Once he's sworn in, he'll have extra security. People following him everywhere. You'd have better luck asking him to resign then forcing him out of the picture."

"Then what do we do? How are we supposed to stop him?" I'm standing now, fury and desperation raging through me. It's too much—Grayson and Raf and Margot and Caleb. We can't lose anymore. If we bend any more, we will be broken completely.

"Margot and Henry could have died today!" Geri's risen and is walking toward the group. Her cheeks are wet with tears. "Belk and Dr. O need to pay for that!"

"What about your dad?" Charlotte snaps. "He doesn't need to pay? Isn't he the one who killed Margot's boyfriend?"

"He didn't have a choice!" Geri argues.

"Sure he did," Sam throws back. "Say no. It's that easy."

"And how many times have you said no to the director?" Grayson's tone is biting.

"That's different." Caleb stands.

Grayson stands.

"Stop fighting!" Henry shouts.

My head is pounding. Dr. O has pushed us to this, but we can't fall apart now. This is what he wants. To single us out. To make us believe we have no other choice but to follow him.

"We need a plan," I say, but I don't know what to do. Sam, Charlotte, Henry, and Grayson were all supposed to be in that fire. Dr. O will know when Geri and I don't come back from the airport that something's off. We don't even know if Margot actually did something to Dr. O today.

"It's time for us to disappear," says Sam, glancing at Charlotte.

"I don't even have a toothbrush!" Charlotte snaps.

Sam rips up the front of his shirt to reveal a strange belt on his chest—the kind people carry passports in. He unzips it and tears out a flash drive and a bunch of folded papers. "Forget your toothbrush. I've been stashing go bags hidden all over the city with money and clothes. I've got train tickets and plane vouchers and fake IDs for us both. And, if we somehow manage to graduate, I've got applications for family housing at different schools with law programs, and financial aid packets." He shoves two ID cards with their faces on them in Charlotte's direction.

Her eyes well up with tears. "Did you make spreadsheets?"

He kisses her knuckles. "Flow charts. This isn't a spreadsheet kind of activity."

"Dad of the year," says Henry.

"You're pregnant?" Susan's voice pitches with anxiety. "No. My brother can't know about this. He'll see this as a liability. Hugh can only do so much. He can't protect you from David!"

Hugh Moore? No one ever calls our security guard by his first name. The mention drags something he said from my memories— from the day he attacked Grayson. *I promised to protect them. But every time I look at him, I think about what he did . . .*

Surely Moore knew Susan—they would have met prior to Dr. O's falling-out with Grayson's dad. But he can't know that Grayson didn't kill Susan, otherwise he wouldn't have been so on edge around him, and so furious about Grayson coming near the other students.

Susan said earlier that when Margot had gotten into trouble, she'd been sent to Susan by someone she trusted. Was that Moore's doing too?

Was he working with Susan against Dr. O before he thought she died?

"David already suspects you're having a baby," Grayson says, tired and beaten.

Terror laces through me. "What?"

"He's got his own spies, Brynn. Surely you know that."

People are starting to notice.

An image of Raf on the floor of his apartment, surrounded by Wednesday pills, lights up the back of my mind.

"Who?" Henry wrings his hands together. "Please don't say you."

"June," I whisper, remembering how she'd waited outside Geri's room, and asked me about Margot. How she notices things, like Charlotte's pregnancy, and Grayson's phone calls.

"Try Maddox," Grayson says, bringing an image of our old silent housekeeper to mind. "June's clean that I know of."

My jaw tightens.

"That lady hears everything." Henry wrings his hands together.

"I tried to warn you," Grayson says to me. "She's been following you around for weeks. She got Paz a fancy new phone and Bea new earrings in exchange for what they know about you. She has access to everyone's messages and emails through that program she uses to wipe all our devices clean. Every day you're in class with the Shrew, she's meeting with Dr. O."

I deflate. I remember the shine of Bea's new silver earrings. Paz ignoring my driver's license because of her new phone.

"How did she find out about Raf?" I ask.

"She intercepted a message on Moore's phone," he says. "Something about a rent check. I heard David telling Frank Allen to go check it out."

I think of Grayson's face when he saw Geri's dad at Vale Hall.

"Did you know . . ." I can't finish the question.

"I knew it wasn't good," he says grimly. "But I didn't know who or what or when."

Behind him, Geri's gripping her waist, her face pale.

Ms. Maddox has access to our messages. She got Raf killed. It could have been Caleb—Moore paid his rent too.

I knew she was a spy—we all knew—but we weren't careful enough, and now more people are dead.

The walls draw in again, or maybe it's just my ribs, pressing against my lungs.

Everyone is looking to me, just like they did when I got the files from Dr. O's office. When I told them we couldn't be like him, that we were stronger together, that blackmail would be enough.

They listened to me, and we've lost everything.

"It's going to be okay," I say, because I have to. Because we can't let him win.

Because I don't know how to quit.

"I believe you." Henry steps beside me, chin lifted. "If Brynn says it's going to be fine, it's going to be fine. We've trusted her this far."

My back bows with the weight of his faith. I'm not in charge of this operation. I never asked to be.

"I'm with you," Geri says to me.

"Did hell freeze over?" Charlotte says, one brow quirked in her direction. She folds her arms over her chest as she looks back at me. "If you say we've got a shot, I'm still in the game."

Sam sighs through his teeth. "Then I am too."

"You know where I stand." Caleb's fingers thread through mine, warm and steady. For a flash, I wish I was back in Baltimore, in that hotel room, locked away from the rest of the world.

Grayson nods. "So what's our next play, then, fearless leader?"

I wish he wouldn't call me that.

Their gazes all point my way. Even Susan, now frowning with reserved curiosity, waits for me to speak.

"I don't know," I say. "I need a second to think."

I pull out of Caleb's grasp. Worry fills his gaze, then Sam's, then Charlotte's, spreading like a virus around our circle. I push through them toward the door.

"Let her go," I hear Charlotte say behind me as Caleb tries to follow.

I shove outside, gulping down the frigid air. I skip down the steps, past the Jeep.

I can still fix this.

I can fix anything.

But my hair and clothes smell like smoke, and I can still feel the searing heat of the flames on my skin.

CHAPTER 22

Night has fallen, black and still. Glassy beads of ice line the frail branches of the trees on either side of the drive, lit by the screen of my burner phone. My footsteps on the fresh snow make a crunching sound as I walk. Puffs of breath cloud in front of my face.

There isn't any cell phone reception at the house, but it might be better closer to the main road. I need to call Mom—make sure she's okay. I'd ask Moore to check on her, but since the security wipe, I can't get in touch with him.

I walk faster, checking the bars for reception. Still nothing.

The darkness around me takes on life; the moon, made hazy by clouds, stretching the shadows of the trees across my path. Sounds begin to filter through the woods—breaking branches, the scurry of small animals.

Wrapping my arms tightly around me, I hurry on, thinking of all the things Grayson told us in the cabin about his father, and Susan, and Dr. O. I remember the first night I met Grayson at the party. I'd thought he was aloof and spoiled, playing with his money, ignoring his friends. Had he known then that I was planted to spy on him?

A bar lights up on the phone, and I quickly dial Mom's number. The phone rings once. Twice. I walk farther as the signal glitches.

"Hi, honey," she says.

My breath comes on a sob. She's alive. I didn't realize how afraid I was until this moment.

There's noise in the background. Voices. The clatter of dishes. For a moment, I think she must be at work, but then I remember she doesn't waitress at Gridiron Sports Bar anymore. She's got an office job now.

"Mom?" My voice breaks, and I cover my mouth with one hand.

I need to get it together. I need to make sure she listens when I tell her she has to hide.

There's a muffled male voice in the background, and then Mom says, "Just a minute. It's my daughter."

"Who is that?" I ask, pulse quickening.

"No one," she says quickly. "What's wrong?"

Everything. Tears make cold tracks down my cheeks.

"I don't know what I'm doing," I say.

"What do you mean? With school? Oh, honey, is it finals?"

A strained laugh escapes my throat. I wish finals were my biggest concern.

"Look," she says. "You're the smartest person I know. You got into that school. I could never do anything like that."

You need to run. I've put you in danger. People are getting killed.

I almost watched my friends die this morning.

They are looking to me to fix this.

"It's not finals. I got in some trouble, Mom, and—"

"Honey?" The line goes fuzzy, and I hurry farther down the road to get the signal back. ". . . trouble hearing you," she finishes.

"Mom?"

I walk in a circle, back to where the signal was stronger, but the connection weakens again. Ahead, a looming shadow blocks the path and sends a bolt of fear down my spine.

Just the gate, covered by brush and branches.

The road is close.

". . . but I can barely hear her," Mom says to someone else.

"Mom, where are you?" I practically yell. "Who is that?"

Her sigh crackles over the line. ". . . with a friend. You remember Frank, right? I met him at Family . . ."

Static.

My pulse quickens.

"Family what?" I press, hoping this isn't what I think it is.

"Day," her voice is a crackling whisper. "Family *Day!* His daughter Geri is a junior at your school. I ran into him earlier at work, and he asked me out to dinner. Isn't that nice?"

My feet stop. My heart is a hammer, striking my ribs.

"Mom. He's not who you think. You need to leave, right now. You need to get away from him."

Static.

"Mom? *Mom!*"

Static.

". . . hear me. . . . talk later. . . . love you more than blueberry muffins!"

The line goes dead.

I drop the phone in the snow. Pick it up. Dial her number again with shaking hands.

No service, the screen says.

"No, no, no," I chant, sprinting toward the gate.

A sound to my right steals my breath. I slide to a stop, falling forward onto my knees. My eyes search the woods, but there's no movement. I shine the cell phone screen into the dark, but see only the stretching finger-like shadows of the trees.

"Hello?" My voice wavers.

Just an animal. A frozen branch, breaking.

Another shuffle, this time by the gate.

I open my mouth to scream, but it's too late. A dark figure rushes from the gloom and slams into me. I'm thrown backward onto the cold ground, snow and gravel biting the bare skin on my back as my sweater hikes up my waist. Something heavy lands on my chest, forcing the air from my chest. The moon is blotted out by a black knit cap, pulled low over my attacker's face.

On instinct, I swing hard, my fist colliding with soft neck flesh. A male grunt punctuates the darkness. My knee thrusts up into his groin. I open my mouth to scream, but a leather glove slams over my mouth, hard enough to knock the back of my head against the ground.

I scream through it, but the sound is muffled, and weak. Fear seizes me. Caleb is back at the house. Henry. My friends. They'll come, I just have to be louder.

I struggle again, but his weight increases on my chest and I can barely breathe.

"Come quietly, or this ends now."

Terror crystallizes in my blood. I go still.

Belk.

Belk has found me. Belk has found all of us. Is he going to kill me? If I do what he says, will he kill them next?

The faces of my friends flash before my vision. Charlotte. Henry. Sam and Susan and Geri and Grayson and Margot.

Caleb.

The frame pauses on him—brows knotted in worry, glasses the slightest bit crooked, just like his smile. I want to scream his name. I never should have come out here alone.

Please don't let this be the last time I see him.

When Belk hauls me up, I shove back, but I don't run. Partly because I believe his threat. Partly because of the gun he's now pointing directly at my chest.

The silver barrel gleams, lethal and steady.

He tips his head toward the gate.

Caleb.

Get them out. Get them far away from here.

I don't have the phone. I can't call him and warn him. Without glancing back at the cabin, I walk. Belk follows, close enough that I can't get away.

The gate is open—I see now that I'm closer. It's cracked the slightest bit.

"How did you find me?" *It doesn't matter,* I think absently. *He did. And now he's going to kill me.*

"I installed a tracking device in the Jeep after your little fast food expedition at the mall the other night," he says.

Dylan and the Wolves' party flashes through my head. Belk knew I was up to something when I wasn't with Charlotte and Henry.

He's worse than Dr. O, you know. He does whatever his master wants. No questions.

The black SUV waits just down the empty road, and as we make our way toward it, I consider running one last time. Screaming my warning through the night. But I don't do either, because he will shoot me before I complete my task.

"What do you want?" I ask.

"Get in."

He opens the back door, like he has dozens of times for any of us at school. I shouldn't get in the car. Isn't that what people always say? If you get in the car, you're dead.

"Come in, Brynn."

My stomach bottoms out.

Across the middle seat, Dr. O sits beside the far window, faintly illuminated by the moonlight. He's wearing a black wool coat over his shirt and tie, and his slacks are as neatly pressed as always.

Has he come here for me? Or his sister?

Does he even know she's here?

"A little faster, please," Dr. O says. "You're letting in the cold."

Terror shudders through me, tinged with rage. He sent Geri's dad—Frank Allen—after my mom. She's with him right now. My friends are a half mile down the road. They don't know what's coming for them.

I have to figure out a way to stop this.

I get in the car.

Belk closes the door and waits outside. My gaze bounces from Dr. O to our traitorous security guard. I'm ready to bolt out of the car and tackle him should he make a move toward the cabin.

"How was your campus visit?" Dr. O asks, his voice as lethal as Belk's gun.

"What do you want?"

Dr. O sighs.

"Have I not been fair to you, Brynn?"

I don't answer. My hands are fisted and ready. I perch on the edge of the seat.

"Have I not given you everything I've promised? A home. An education. A future?"

There is no future. It's all a lie, that's what Damien said.

"Where's my mom?"

He shifts in his seat. "Enjoying a date in the city, last I heard. She was taken to an Italian restaurant called Vincenzo's in Uptown. It's a lovely location. Excellent beef brasato."

I can't handle this fake small talk. "What do you want?"

"The same thing I've always wanted," he says. "Useful information."

My lips curl back from my teeth. "You mean compliance."

He shrugs. "Compliance is mandatory at Vale Hall; you agreed to this when you came on."

"Get to the point. If you're going to kill me—"

"Oh, Brynn," he says, voice heavy with exhaustion. "I don't want to kill you. I need you. Now, it seems, more than ever."

I stare at him. "You tried to murder me today."

"Not true," he says, the shadows on his face cut deep as he scowls. "Mr. Belk was merely trying to eliminate some dangerous information. Files that had been stolen from my safe." His head turns slowly toward me, his cool gaze meeting mine for the first time. "You wouldn't know about those, would you?"

A shiver works down my spine as I bite the inside of my cheek.

"They are dangerous weapons in the hands of someone like Margot Patel. Did you know she showed up at a meeting I had at the mayor's office this morning? She managed to steal Mr. Belk's firearm. If not for Mayor Santos's daughter, Camille, recognizing her, I might be dead now."

My stomach twists. Margot tried to kill Dr. O. She brought a gun to the mayor's office. I picture Camille Santos—Caleb's old mark—standing beside her mother in the press conference announcing Dr. O's position. She could have been killed.

"Margot ran before I could speak to her. Mr. Belk tracked her to an abandoned train station in Sycamore Township," Dr. O says, facing forward again. "Security assumed it was an attack on the mayor, of course. She has many enemies since her public dismissal of the Wolves of Hellsgate."

I got her.

Was Margot trying to attack Mayor Santos? Blame the attack on Dr. O? My thoughts fly through explanations, but don't land on an answer that makes sense. I can't even say for certain that Dr. O is telling the truth.

If he is, if Margot tried to murder him in front of all those people, then she's farther gone than I thought. She's a danger to all of us.

My gaze switches back to Belk, who hasn't moved. Questions

fly through my head, too slick to grasp on to. Why didn't Margot shoot? What did she do with the gun? Did anyone else see her?

"You have nothing to say on the matter?" he asks.

I don't.

"I become a U.S. senator in twelve days," Dr. O says, folding his hands on his laps. "Finally, I'll have a chance to rid the system of corruption from the inside—not just on a local level, but on a much larger scale."

Susan's warning about extra security flashes through my mind. I swipe at the sweat on my temple, hot against the cool interior of the car.

"This should have been an exciting time for all of us. I thought we were on the same page. I thought you wanted what I did, a world without glass walls and ceilings."

My hands turn clammy as he cites the essay I once wrote for a scholarship—the same essay he claimed had gained his attention to bring me to Vale Hall. It was a lie of course. He recruited me because he'd caught Pete stealing from the Wednesday Pharmaceuticals warehouse.

"Damien Fontego called before this mess with Margot. Apparently, he'd been trying to get in touch with you, Mr. Belk, for some time." He sends a cold look to the front of the car.

"Lost my phone," Belk mutters.

"No matter," Dr. O continues. "He reached me."

My blood turns to ice.

No, I think. *Don't say it.*

Damien wouldn't.

"At least he recognizes the value of loyalty."

My eyes pinched closed. I want to wipe Damien's kiss off my cheek. His dimples out of my head. A new wave of fear hits me. If Damien told Dr. O about what happened, he must have mentioned Marcus. Is Marcus in danger?

I never should have told him we were coming.

"I'm disappointed," Dr. O says, as if this will trigger my shame.

"Me, too." The truth cuts too close to my nerves. "This wasn't exactly what I signed up for."

He grunts. "I told you the rules when you came to me—before you ever agreed to come to Vale Hall. There are consequences for exposure."

"Disappearing, you mean. That's quite a magic trick."

"Dissolving my students' identities is a kinder sentence than those who put my students and faculty at risk deserve."

My eyes flick to the door handle. This is it. This is the end. He's going to kill me, or have Belk do it. I'm done, just like Jimmy Balder, and Raf, and the others that Dylan mentioned.

But we're still sitting here. Why keep talking if he just plans on having Belk shoot me?

"I've decided to give you one chance to make this right, Brynn. I need you to tell me the truth. If you do, we'll return to Vale Hall, your mother will return home, and everything will go back as it should be."

I balk. "The truth about what?"

He inhales with a flare of his nostrils. "How exactly you came to be in contact with my sister."

The breath squeezes from my lungs. He knows about Susan. Belk must have been spying on us from outside the cabin while we were talking.

That will mean he knows Caleb is here too. And Margot. And Grayson, who already fears for his life.

There is no denying it now. He knows too much.

"And if I tell you, what will you do with that information?"

He sighs. "That's for me to worry about."

"You'll kill her."

"She's already dead."

His blunt tone sends a stab of terror through my ribs. He could murder her, really do it this time, and no one would know because she doesn't exist.

A panicked sob rises in my throat. I try to swallow it down. I can't fall apart now. I need to think. I need to change his path.

"And if I don't?"

"You're going to find the future very difficult, I'm afraid," Dr. O says. "New light will be shed on your mother's boyfriend's case—Pete

Walsh will accuse you of collaborating with drug sales by the Wolves of Hellsgate, and you'll be arrested and charged for distribution and intent to sell. They'll find your fingerprints at the apartment of Rafael Fuentes, where a witness, Renee Gibson, will step forward to say you threatened him into an overdose."

He has Renee.

I'm in a free fall, unable to catch myself. He has one of us. He's going to pin me for a murder. He's going to say I was selling *his* pills with Pete and send me to jail. He's not going to kill me, he's going to destroy me.

"Your mother may succumb to similar causes," he says clinically.

I'm across the car in a shot, my hand fisted in his jacket, the other around his throat. "You stay away from her. You—"

"The wheels are set in motion." A slight sneer pulls at his lips. "And I am the only one who can stop them."

I release him as if he's burned my hands. His warning is clear: I can't hurt him without hurting my mom.

"There was a bill I stole from one of the interns in Matthew Sterling's campaign," I lie quickly. "Something I found when you sent me to work at The Loft. Sterling was paying for power to some cabin off the books, and the bill accidentally got sent to the office. I didn't know what it was at first. I asked Grayson, but he hadn't heard about it." Is this enough to save him? In the dark of the car, I can't even see Dr. O's face to tell if he's buying this. "I've never been here before today. I didn't know she was here. I just thought . . . I don't know, we needed a place to hide."

My tears aren't part of the act. They're 100 percent real.

Please believe me.

"There," he says. "That wasn't difficult." He retrieves a phone from his pocket, and presses a few quick numbers, then lifts it to his ear. "Yes," he says. "Please see Ms. Hilder home safely. No, that won't be necessary. Thank you, Frank."

I want to throw up.

"What happens now?" I whisper.

"Now you go back to school," he says. "And my sister and I have a little talk."

Is he serious? I'm supposed to put on my seat belt and let Belk drive me back to Vale Hall? What happens to Susan? What happens to my friends?

"What about the others?" I whisper. Have they begun to worry about how long I've been gone? Has anyone come looking for me?

"It grieves me to say they have become problematic. I thought they'd be more careful. Charlotte, at least, with a baby on the way. And Caleb, now that his father's rallied."

His words hang between us like knives ready to drop.

He knows Charlotte's pregnant. Does he know where Caleb's family is hidden?

"They're not a problem," I say. "They got the point at the train yards. They won't be any trouble for you anymore."

"I believed Margot Patel wouldn't cause me trouble, and look what happened."

"I gave you what you wanted!" Desperation takes control of my voice. "I'll talk to them, okay? They listen to me. I'm convincing. You taught me to be convincing, remember?"

He rubs his forehead absently with two fingers, as if he sees no choice but eliminating his students.

An idea takes hold, charred and flaking with defeat. I grasp it with both hands.

"I'll bring them back to Vale Hall," I say, before I've fully considered what this means. "You'll be able to watch them there. No one has to get hurt. It looks bad for you if all of your senior class goes missing right before you're sworn in, right?"

His fingers drum on his knees. I'll take that as agreement.

"You can have us all there for the ceremony, cheering for you." I'll beg if that's what it takes.

"How will you convince them?"

"I'll tell them they don't have a choice. If they don't get in line, they're dead."

"Just the kind of sentiment that breeds more resistance." His fingers still. "You need to find their pressure point, Brynn. That's the way things like this are done."

I don't know what he's talking about, only that this is the first real conversation we've ever had, and I regret every second of it.

I search for anything I can say to make him come around, but I can only think of Susan in that cabin, and what will happen when Dr. O sees her, and Henry's last words before I left. *If Brynn says it's going to be fine, it's going to be fine.*

I realize then what I have to do. I don't have to find their pressure point, like Dr. O says, because I already know what it is.

It's me.

I need to convince my friends our fight is over. I can't shout for them to run; Belk will hurt someone. If I warn them Dr. O has threatened us, they could rally and take Dr. O and Belk out—there are enough of us to do it. But Geri's dad has already made contact with my mom, and Dr. O told me only he can stop her from getting hurt.

Which means I can't let him get hurt.

We have to go back to Vale Hall, and to get them to do that, I need to sever their hope. I need to break their trust. There are no other ways to keep everyone safe.

"They'll come," I say as confidently as I can. "I'll tell you everything I know once everyone is safe. Susan and my mom included."

A faint smirk tilts his mouth. "You're not in a position to make that deal."

"You're not in a position to kill your sister twice and get away with it," I shoot back. "She's not stupid. You think she doesn't have a plan? That people won't come look for her if she doesn't check in? They're going to leak the truth if she goes missing."

Grayson was the only one checking in on her that I know of, but I'm not telling Dr. O that.

"Is that what she said? My sister is a liar, Brynn. She always has been."

"You want to test her?" I ask. "Because if she's not, this will go south for you, fast."

His eyes narrow—he's trying to tell if I'm bluffing. But this game I know well, and even if my insides are quaking, I hold his gaze.

"Are you so eager to take responsibility for the lives of your friends?"

"Yes," I answer without delay.

Because they're not just friends. They're family.

"Then it's a deal. Their futures depend on you."

He holds out a hand for me to shake. I want to spit into his palm. I want to break his wrist.

"I'll go talk to them," I say. "You wait here."

But he smiles. His hand lowers to his lap. "I don't think so. We'll go together. I look forward to hearing you rally the troops."

He pats my knee, and it's in that moment that the disgust and terror give way to despair, and I know we've finally lost.

CHAPTER 23

I enter the house first. This is Dr. O's idea, just like it was his idea to leave the car around the bend of the drive, just out of sight, so no one sees or hears it and tries to run. As I push through the door, a part of me hopes my friends have already scattered, but I am not so lucky.

Caleb is standing just inside the door, and I nearly collide with him as I step through the threshold. He's in the process of zipping up his coat, and his face is drawn in worry.

"There you are," he says, leaning down to kiss my cheek. "I was just about to come looking . . ."

His gaze lifts to the two men behind me, standing on the deck, and like a shot, he's grabbed my arm and whipped me around his side, away from them.

My stomach twists so hard I can barely stand upright.

I'm sorry. I'm so sorry.

There is a split second of frozen confusion, then everyone is moving at once. Susan is yelling at us to get back. Sam is shouting for Charlotte to get behind a couch. Geri's hand is in mine, and she's pulling me away as Caleb tries to slam Dr. O and his henchman outside.

Grayson goes for the rifle beneath the window.

Belk stops the door from slamming with his shoulder, and he roars as Caleb throws his weight against the wood. Belk's arm swings wildly, knocking down a standing coatrack with a clatter.

"Stop!" I shout, but no one listens. "*Stop.* They're not going to hurt us!"

I don't know how Henry got in front of me, but he's beside Caleb, blocking me from the door. My protectors, until the end.

They grow still as my words sink in.

Grayson's stare slides to mine, pinched with doubt.

"I . . ." My gaze darts around the room, glancing off the people I trust—who trust me.

They will die if I don't do what Dr. O wants.

They will never do what he wants if I don't convince them it's the only way.

I can't convince them without crushing them. Otherwise they will fight—maybe not right now, but as soon as they land back on their feet. They will fight, or they will run, and Dr. O will chase them to the very end.

"I called Dr. O and Belk," I tell my friends. I look at Caleb, and it takes everything I have to hold his gaze. "They're with me."

Caleb's chin pulls inward. He blinks in confusion, and then his eyes grow guarded, and I'm reminded of how he can turn on the con at the snap of his fingers.

You know I wouldn't do this, I think, just as I will him to follow my lead.

Even if none of them believe me, even if they know I'd *never* betray them, they have to make Dr. O believe that I've broken their trust. Otherwise we're never going to get out of this alive.

"You what?" Geri is the first to speak.

There can be no room for doubt. Their lives are depending on me. My mom is depending on me.

I inhale truth, and exhale lies.

"It's over," I say calmly. "Open the door, Caleb."

It hurts even to say his name.

Henry releases the door. He looks at Caleb. Caleb looks at me.

I hang my head, trying to look repentant but not destroyed. That's what they would expect of someone who just betrayed them. That's what *Dr. O* would expect.

"Do not open that door," Susan snaps, and any dream I had of publicly confronting Dr. O with the truth of her survival burns to ashes. Her voice is wobbling, as is her stance. She's dropped the crutch on the floor, and doesn't seem to trust herself to move without it.

Dr. O walks slowly through the threshold, jaw flexed, a vein rising on the corner of his forehead. His gaze travels across the room, narrowing on Geri—someone he clearly thought was in his pocket—then stopping on his sister. His head tilts as he stares at her, examining her as if she might not be real. As the shock gives way to acceptance, his lips part slightly, and he siphons in a quick breath.

"Susan," he whispers, and for however much a monster he is, I can see her presence hurts him.

I hope that pain lasts the rest of his life.

Belk shoves in after him. I can't see his gun, but I know it's hidden somewhere in his waistband beneath his coat.

"Get out," Susan orders, teeth bared. "Get. Out."

Dr. O shakes his head quickly, as if waking from a daze. "You're alive."

"No thanks to you," she replies.

"What's going on?" Charlotte asks, voice low.

"What do you mean you called him?" Sam says.

Their doubt, even if it's an act, shreds me. "It's time to go home."

"Home? What are you talking about?" Henry asks.

"Yeah," says Grayson, hands clenched at his sides. "What are you talking about, Brynn?" He says my name like people curse when they're angry.

Dr. O's stare moves from Susan to Caleb, and his lips thin into a flat line. "Mr. Matsuki. I didn't think we'd cross paths again."

Caleb says nothing.

Belk waits for Dr. O's orders.

"Don't make this harder than it has to be," I say. "You all had your fun with your little resistance operation, but it's over now. It's time to go back to the real world."

"Am I dreaming right now? *Brynn*." Henry steps closer to me, but Caleb snags his arm.

Good, I think. *Make it look real.*

"You're a rat," Grayson says, catching on to my intent. He chuckles coldly, then swipes back his hair. "I guess I should have seen that coming."

"She's not a rat," snaps Charlotte. Someone's got to side with me for this to be believable, but part of me is crushed by the thought that she doesn't know I'm acting. I wait for Caleb to object too, but he doesn't. He's looking at me like we're strangers—like last night my heart wasn't in the palm of his hand in that hotel room.

Show or not, it hurts.

"It's just a job," I say. "He wanted to know what you were up to, who he could trust. I delivered. It's not personal."

"It's not *personal*?" Geri repeats with a manic laugh.

"Easy," I tell her. "If I recall, you were working me when I first got to school."

She crosses her arms around her waist, like I just punched her. I wonder if she's thinking about Baltimore. About us agreeing to be friends. About her night with Marcus, my ex.

I know I am.

"He wanted to find the lost students before the senator gig. We found them," I say.

"And what?" asks Grayson. "You get a scholarship now? A trip to Paris?"

His anger focuses me.

I shrug. "Maybe."

"You sold us out?" Henry's eyes are as wide as saucers.

Dr. O's gaze jerks to mine, challenge blending with anger.

Their futures depend on you.

"Technically Damien sold you out," I say with a wince. "Sorry. We needed to see how far you'd take this."

"Damien?" Geri whispers, as I watch Caleb's shoulders hunch in defeat.

His last hope—our last hope—is gone.

"I just did my job," I say.

"Just as all of you have," adds Dr. O. "And she'll be rewarded, just like I promised each of you. Regardless of what you choose to think of me, I am a man of my word."

"You're a murderer!" Charlotte's voice cracks off the ceiling.

"Is that any way to talk to the man who kept you out of juvenile detention after a fit of arson?" Dr. O asks calmly.

Sam moves in front of Charlotte, blocking her from Dr. O's gaze.

"My sister has clearly put ideas in your head," says Dr. O with a scowl as he motions to Susan. "I hope you are not so naive as to believe a stranger over someone who has taken you in, fed you, *cared* for you."

"We have different definitions of *care*," says Sam.

"Says the boy whose mother went to prison for neglecting her son," says Belk, and I almost falter when Sam hunches forward.

"I didn't need Susan to tell me what you did," Grayson says, diverting the focus away from Sam. "I was there, remember? I saw what you did."

"And yet you still sent your father to prison for it," Dr. O answers.

"To protect him from *you*," Grayson says.

"Can you prove that?" Dr. O sighs. "The truth is a complicated matter. I know you all are confused. If you come back to Vale Hall, we can reach an understanding. I'm certain of it."

"They're not going anywhere," Susan says.

Dr. O hums quietly, and if she says another word, I'm certain he will break the deal and kill her on the spot.

"Susan, don't make a scene. You're going to be fine," I say, willing it to be so. "I already told him someone's checking on you to make sure you're alive—that if you go missing, there's going to be trouble. We can't risk that right before Dr. O becomes senator."

Grayson flinches, questions flashing through his eyes. Susan's chin lifts. She's clearly believing she misjudged me.

Dr. O exhales in a hiss, like the air from a tire. *You can't kill her,* I think. *Not now.*

But she's on limited time.

"Let's go," says Belk. "Grayson, Caleb, Henry, Sam, Geri, and Charlotte, get in the SUV. The director will drive Ms. Griffin, Brynn, and Margot in the Jeep."

They're separating me from Caleb. Me from my friends.

"Brynn." Charlotte takes a step toward me. "This isn't you talking."

"I'm sorry, Charlotte," I say with a forced shrug. "It's probably better you just go. Don't want to hurt the baby, you know?"

Her cheeks go blotchy with shock. Sam's glare is hot enough to burn through me.

I've gone too far.

I have to, otherwise it won't look real.

Belk grabs Henry's shoulder.

Grayson shoves Belk back, teeth bared. "Get your hands off of him."

"Stop," I warn him. "No fighting. I promised none of you would fight."

"And if we, say, decide we don't care what you want?" he throws back.

"Then there are consequences," I say. *Please. Do not push this.* "With your dad. And your sister and your mom. I'd think of them if I were you, Grayson."

His jaw flexes. For a moment I think he might launch himself at me, but his shoulders bunch, and then fall in defeat.

You need to find their pressure point, Brynn. That's the way things like this are done.

Dr. O's gaze narrows. "I don't want more trouble. We can discuss it more when we get back to school, but now, it's time to go."

"You heard him."

We all turn to Margot, now standing beside the bed. I think of what Dr. O said about Belk's gun, about the attack in City Hall. I don't know her half as well as I thought I did.

But then again, I never really knew her at all.

Her eyes are open now, and there's a light of anger burning in them that scares me.

She walks straight past me. "Should have known," she says quietly as she heads out the door.

The others take more time. More convincing. I don't remember what else I say, but in the end it's only Dr. O, me, and Caleb standing in the cabin. He's still said nothing, and his silence is breaking me.

It's the acknowledgment of defeat. It's the uncertainty about what will happen to his family. It's a goodbye to everything we might have had.

"At least you're going to graduate," I tell him.

He looks at me for a long time. Then his head lowers, and he walks to the car.

CHAPTER 24

When we return to school, Vale Hall feels like a tomb.

Twinkle lights and garlands line every arch of the roof, and inside, dozens of small Christmas trees and wreaths with gaudy gold bows fill each open space. But despite Ms. Maddox's dedication, the house is cold and unwelcoming. Paz and Bea erupt in a flurry of whispers as Caleb enters, but barely acknowledge my presence. Joel and some of the others gathered in the kitchen avert their gazes from Margot, as if they know she's trouble. None of them were here when she was a student before.

June's the only one who looks at her as she trudges by. With wide eyes, she asks me what's going on. I tell her nothing.

We go to our respective rooms, which have all been tossed in a security search, and I don't come out to see if it gets better by dinner, because I know it can't possibly. Susan didn't even come back with the rest of us. I can only hope she's all right, that I made the right decision by exposing her.

I am terrified Dr. O decided to kill her anyway.

The next morning, Belk, who's spent at least half the night roaming the halls, summons me to final exams with a reminder of my promise to the director. But I'm not sure how I'm supposed to report any suspicious activity when everyone else at school has begun avoiding me like the plague.

Charlotte and Henry won't look at me.

Caleb keeps a careful distance.

Paz and Bea whisper about me whenever I pass.

I feel like an outsider. And even though it hurts, I pretend I don't care, because that's what is expected of me.

I have one role to play now: Dr. O's pet.

Shrew allows Caleb to sit for finals after he says he's been keeping up with our coursework, and just like that, he's back in the mix. When our first test is done, I have lunch with June and some of the underclassmen. I smile at the right times and eat, though I can hardly taste anything, and at the first opportunity, I excuse myself to my bedroom to have a panic attack in the shower and call Mom, for the tenth time, to check in.

The next two days get worse. June tells me Ms. Maddox has given Geri an envelope of pictures of her father at the scenes of various crimes—evidence the police could use to send him to prison. Caleb and Henry are emailed shots of their moms on their way to work. Charlotte and Sam find a copy of their last ultrasound slipped under their doors.

Margot is locked in her room, and doesn't come out.

I feel like I'm walking on eggshells, waiting for some threat about Mom, or word about another date she had with Geri's dad, but it doesn't happen. Somehow that's worse.

The morning before Christmas Eve, Sam fights through a strong closing speech for Model UN and we're formally awarded Petal the platinum pig, which Shrew has been keeping since Henry tried to give her to Grayson. Charlotte tosses it into my lap as if it's no more than plastic and spray paint, but when her knowing gaze holds mine, I look away. It doesn't matter how this happened, or why. It doesn't change the outcome.

We lost.

I'm trudging back to the main house from the gym when a hand jets out from behind the pool's stone waterfall and snags my arm. With a gulp of surprise, I find myself hidden beneath the snowy boughs of an old evergreen, pressed up against the cold brick of the house's siding.

Caleb stands before me, so close I can feel the warmth of his breath on my face. His eyes are clear now—not distant like they've been all week—and his mouth is drawn in a tight, serious line.

"Finally," he says. "It's been impossible to get you alone. Ms. Maddox and her groupies are all over you."

Panic rises in my throat as I recall how I caught Paz rifling through my notebooks this morning when she "accidently" mistook it for hers. Caleb and I can't do this. We can't be seen hiding together—it will look like we're plotting something. Someone will see and report to Dr. O. He'll find the pressure points. Caleb's mom and dad. His brothers. My mom.

I shake out of his hold on my wrist, and his jaw clenches.

"Are you all right?" He takes my face in his cold hands, and maybe it's weak, but I don't pull away. I've missed his touch so much. I've missed his voice. I've missed everything.

"It's okay," he says quickly, pulling me close, and on a shuddering breath, I inhale the scent of his skin. "It's going to be okay. We're leaving tonight. All of us. We're—"

"What?" I jerk back. He glances out between the heavy snow-laden limbs of the tree, searching for watchful eyes. "You can't do that. You can't go. You have to stay here."

Pity fills his eyes. "It's all worked out. You, me, Sam and Charlotte, Henry, even Grayson. None of us have gotten to Geri yet—Belk's been all over her since we got back—but I'm sure she's in. And Margot's been in her room since Shrew put her on that independent study—"

"No!"

He flinches at my volume, eyes growing wide. "Quiet! Someone's going to hear you."

I put another foot between us.

"Be careful what you say right now," I tell him.

He lifts his brows, and when I force myself to meet his gaze, his chin lifts.

"Or what?" he asks.

My heart breaks.

He can't leave. None of them can leave. If they do, Dr. O will hurt Mom. He'll hurt everyone.

Their futures depend on you. Your mother depends on you.

Everything I knew Dr. O was capable of is now coming to pass. He sent Mom out on a date with a hitman. He killed Raf and other students, and sent Belk to burn Margot up in a fire. I always knew what he could do, but since the cabin it feels like all our efforts to fight him have fallen on my shoulders. He's picked me as the champion of the resistance, and if I don't do what he wants, my friends will all suffer.

I can't do this on my own.

I can't watch Caleb—any of them—die. Not when I had a chance to follow Dr. O's rule, however crushing it may be, and keep them alive.

I siphon in a frigid breath. "Or I'll tell the director."

Caleb's brows pinch together as he shakes his head. "This isn't you."

"It doesn't matter," I say. "It was stupid of me to think we could beat him. You know what he'll do if we don't fall in line."

"You know what he'll do if we do!" He steps closer again, one hand gripping my shoulder. "More people will end up missing. We won't be the only ones threatened, or left empty-handed. We don't even have a future here—you remember what Damien said about the money."

That there isn't any. It's all a con to lure us in.

I can't do this. I can't think of anything beyond right now— beyond my mom going out with Frank Allen, and Caleb and Henry's families, and Charlotte and Sam's baby. I try to walk away, but he blocks me with a straight arm. I swipe it away.

"We can figure this out," he says, hands open now. Pleading.

"I've already figured it out," I tell him. "I'm not letting you leave, Caleb. I won't walk into some apartment and find you, or any one else, on the floor like Raf."

Because I love you.

Because I love all of you.

I will myself to feel nothing, but shattering hurts, and I can barely breathe.

He falls back a step, his shoulder knocking into a branch that drops snow onto his old Converse shoes. In the cabin, he knew something had happened. He was doing what I said to protect me—to protect all of us.

But now, he thinks I might actually betray him.

He's right.

I hate him for trying to save me. I hate him for loving me. I hate his crooked glasses and his unquestioning loyalty and the perfect city on my calf I retrace in ink over and over so it won't wash off.

I hate until I feel nothing, and finally, I'm numb.

Don't feel, don't fail. That's how I save him. That's how we all get through this alive.

"What's going on in there?"

At Moore's voice, I jump, and then shove out into the cold sunlight. His jaw is clenched as he peers past me to find Caleb leaning against the stone waterfall.

I try to push past him, but he grabs my arm.

"You can't do this," he says, pulling down his sunglasses so I can see his eyes—as if this will somehow make me realize how serious he is. "Both of you need to stop. Things have changed."

I step away from Moore, frozen straight through. "Stop protecting me."

One brow lifts.

"What's going on with you?" When I don't answer, he lowers his face to mine. "What's Min Belk up to? I haven't seen him since you brought Caleb and Margot back."

Susan. He must be with her somewhere. I can't think of what else Dr. O might be keeping secret.

If Moore's asking me this, it means he might not know that Dr. O's sister is still alive—or at least that she was when we left the cabin.

Why wouldn't Dr. O tell him that?

Because he's being watched like the rest of us.

Any relief that Moore still has my back is crushed by a sudden, drenching fatigue. I'm so tired of these games we never win.

"Ask Dr. O," I say, just as Ms. Maddox steps outside to wave us in for lunch.

CHRISTMAS EVE, I show up at Mom's second-floor apartment, half asleep from restless nights, half wired from finals I'm sure I barely passed, a dozen college applications in the messenger bag over my shoulder.

Visit your mother, Dr. O told me earlier today, after I finished my last test. *I'll see you after Christmas.*

He isn't afraid I'll run, and it's not like I have anywhere else to be.

Caleb and the others didn't try to leave without me, and since Caleb and I talked, they've kept even more distance. Without regular classes, I barely see them at all.

I've become invisible.

My arm is heavy as I lift my fist to knock.

"Door's open, sweetheart!" Mom calls from inside. Irritation scalds my numb heart as I turn the knob and am greeted by a blast of heat. I drop my bag on the floor beside my shoes, then hang my coat on the rack next to hers.

"Mom, you have to lock the door."

She's in the kitchen making bacon from the smell of it. When I called to say I was on my way over, she shouted, "Breakfast for dinner!" told me she had to go wrap my presents, and hung up.

"Why? This isn't Devon Park," she calls back over the sound of *Pop Store,* her favorite celebrity gossip show, blaring on the television. "Besides, who's going to mess with me?"

She leans around the kitchen partition, a knife raised in one fist. She's trying to look tough, but her teeth are bared only for a second. In the next, her too-long bangs fall over her eyes, and she blows them aside.

"You're right," I say flatly, as some of the tension releases from my shoulders. "You're terrifying."

"Told you." With a happy squeal, she sets down the knife and runs around the corner, wrapping me up in a giant hug. I slouch into her, trying to push down the sharp bite of pain before it takes over again.

"I'm so glad you're here. I wasn't sure if you'd be able to come home." She pulls back, and her smile falls a little. "You're looking rough, sweetheart. Were finals that bad?"

"Brutal," I lie.

I crane my head down the short hallway to glance into her messy bedroom. It's empty, as is the bathroom beside it. The living room/kitchen combo stretches before me, small but new, and nice. She's put up some art on the walls since the last time I was here. A framed poster from an Aerosmith concert she went to when I was a baby. A picture of me and her at the lake when I was about ten. I'm holding a blue balloon and have a stupid look on my face. I don't know why she likes that picture so much.

She hurries back into the kitchen as the smell of burning pancakes fills the air.

"Need help?"

"Nope." Waving a towel, she dispels the smoke as I take a seat at one of the stools at the counter. "Talk to me. How's life? How's Charlotte and Henry and that cute Grayson Sterling?"

I swallow. "Fine." I don't want to get into it, otherwise I'll fall apart. "What about you? How's Geri's dad?" My stomach clenches.

"Frank?" she asks, with a small smirk. "Fine, I guess. Kind of boring. We were supposed to go to dinner tonight, but he cancelled right before you called. I'm not brokenhearted, in case you're wondering."

I'm sickened by the fact that Dr. O arranged another date with Frank Allen, only to have it cancelled when he gave me the night off. Was that a threat? Did Dr. O know that Mom would tell me this?

The urge rises in me to tell her to run—a thought I banished a hundred times on the drive over. Dr. O knows I'm here. If she runs, he will find a way to punish me.

"You should break up with him," I say, arms wrapped around my waist. "I hear he's a jerk."

She glances up, brows quirked. She and I look alike, especially when she makes the sassy, is-that-so? face.

"I think after twenty-nine years I can fend for myself, don't you think?"

Which is why she was with Pete-the-drug-dealer for so many years, I'm sure.

A tense sigh slips out of my lips. I can't force the issue without risking her saying something to Geri's dad, or something to someone who might be listening at her job at Wednesday, and it getting back to Dr. O.

"Twenty-nine came and went a few years ago," I mumble.

She gasps, and takes a plate of bacon off the stove. "Guess that school didn't teach you manners."

I try to smile, but it deflates.

"You know what you need?" She points a spatula at me. "Presents!"

I grin as she races out of the kitchen to her bedroom. From inside comes the sound of crinkling paper, and I make my way to my messenger bag to pull out the small, unwrapped velvet box from the pocket. There are other gifts inside too, that I'd hidden in my room, and somehow couldn't leave behind at school. Stupid things I've collected over the past few months. A baby shirt that says *My Aunt Is My Favorite* for Charlotte, along with a bag of M&M's. A silly friendship bracelet for Henry with blue and silver stripes, the colors of his favorite hockey team. I even have our small, Australian flag for Sam to commemorate his hard work in Model UN. My fingers close around the slim side of a notepad, and my heart lurches.

Don't feel, don't fail.

I take the jewelry box and close the bag. By the time I'm back at the stool, Mom's carrying two small wrapped gifts my way.

"You first," she says, setting them on the counter. "And just so you know, I'm also taking you shopping. I've got a big, important job now."

My gut sinks. I wish she'd never taken that job with Wednesday Pharmaceuticals.

"Okay." I reach for the first gift, a rectangle wrapped in shiny red paper. The corner of a black frame reveals itself, and then an old photo comes into view. A man sits in a green vinyl chair holding a swaddled baby, not more than a few hours old, with blotchy pink cheeks and half-opened eyes. His smile is a sickle moon, and his eyes gleam like stars.

My throat locks up.

It's my dad and me.

"I found it when I moved," she says. "It was in a box in the attic with some of your baby stuff. Little onesies and *Bunny Boo*, that stuffy Ms. Malcom down the street got you. You remember *Bunny Boo*?"

I don't, nor do I remember my father's smile—it's faded in my memory, and most of the pictures disappeared when Pete came to live with us.

"I thought he had a beard," I manage. In the photos I did see, he always had one.

"Oh." She laughs. "He grew that when you were about two, I think." She pauses, her eyes growing worried. "You like it?"

I nod. She puts her arm around my shoulders.

"He loved you so much," she says. "When we brought you home, he sat outside on the front steps with you every day so the neighbors would see you as they walked by. *My girl's here!* he would shout. It was so embarrassing." She smiles and wipes a tear from her eye. "He used to speak only Spanish to you when you were a baby. He was convinced he'd take you to Colombia. His mom wanted to meet you. Meet both of us, I guess."

"What about his dad?" My grandfather? It's strange to think of family when my mom's estranged from her own parents.

"Died of cancer before you were born," she says. "And his mom went shortly after your dad did—some complication of the flu, I think. Your dad's sister still lives there, I think. I don't really know. I never met her."

A door I never knew was shut cracks open. I want to go to Colombia. I want to see where my dad grew up.

I want Caleb to come with me. To geek out over all the different buildings. To hold my hand when I meet my aunt.

My heart clenches.

How will we do any of that after what I told him I'd do if he ran?

"Did you love my dad?" I ask.

"More than applesauce." She sighs.

"Did you love Pete?"

Her brows draw together. She pushes her bangs aside. "In the good times I loved him a lot. In the rest . . . I was waiting for the next good time to show up."

I remember the fear in her voice when the tension filled his. She was waiting a lot when it came to Pete, and the payoff wasn't always worth it.

Maybe that's what happens when the wrong person unlocks the best and the worst in you.

My thoughts drift to Moore, and the last words I said to him.

I hope he's still protecting the others, even if he can't protect me. Still doing what Susan asked all those years ago.

"Here," Mom says, pushing Moore from my mind and the other package my way. It's the size of a fist, and when I unwrap the small box, my brows lift in surprise. "It's a rock."

She grins. "Really a top-notch education you're getting at Vale Hall, isn't it?"

I lift the small gray stone out of the box. It's no bigger than the tip of my thumb, and looks like any other piece of gravel you'd find on the street.

"Thanks so much," I say.

She laughs. "It's from the house. The spot out front, remember? Next to the stairs, where the weeds always grew."

I remember the patch of rocks. "Again, thanks?"

Her hand reaches around mine, and closes my fist. "It's a piece of our home, Brynn. Take it with you. You've got big things on the horizon, but you can't forget where you came from. That's the place that made you."

The stone grows warm in my hand. I try to think of something snarky to say. The house on Midgard was a heap—a dilapidated pile of bricks with weak plumbing and no central air, across from an abandoned factory where people went to do drugs.

But it was my home.

It was where Mom and I would make cupcakes on my birthday, and watch *Pop Store,* and eat wings late at night from Gridiron Sports Bar. Where my dad sat on the front steps and called out to the neighbors, *My girl's here!*

It makes me think of something Marcus said in Baltimore. *Devon Park's a place. You give it hate, you give it power.*

I gave it hate, but it made me who I am.

A cheat. A liar.

Unbreakable, even now.

I feel the tears well up in my eyes, but I bite the inside of my cheek until they subside. I can't fall apart now. I need to be strong, the way Devon Park made me. The way Mom taught me.

She squeezes me close, and my head rests on her shoulder.

"I love you more than chocolate fudge," she says.

"I love you more than anything," I reply.

She sniffles.

"Stop it," I tell her, shoving the rock into my pocket. "Your turn. Sorry I didn't wrap it. I've been a little busy."

Guilt swamps through me as I shove the jewelry box her way. I should have gotten her something thoughtful. Nothing is as good as what she gave me.

She waves a hand, and pulls back the lid of the box. Then screams like I've given her the keys to a new car.

She holds up the gold dangly earrings with the small red stones from the outlet mall in Mason. "I love them!"

Maybe Henry knows what he's doing after all.

I wish I knew what he was up to right now. What all of them were doing. They don't generally go home for breaks—Vale Hall, each other, it's all most of us have.

Dr. O chose us for that reason. Less chance for others to find out what we're really doing to earn our keep.

It's probably better I'm not at school with them.

"Good," I tell her.

A hard knock comes from the door, and immediately, I brace for a fight.

"Who is that?" I ask harshly. "Geri's dad?" *Belk? Dr. O?*

My heart is racing as she scowls and makes her way to the door. "I don't know. I didn't think anyone else was coming."

"Mom, wait . . ." I cut in front of her as she reaches the entryway. "Brynn!"

Was this Dr. O's plan? Get me away from school? Get us together, then finish us off? I am sick with myself. I shouldn't have fallen for this. There's not even another way out—we're on the second floor, and if we try to go out her bedroom window, it's a hard landing on the parking lot below.

Mouth dry, I peek through the peephole and see two shadowed figures standing on the front mat.

One steps closer as he knocks, and I can make out his blond hair shaved up sharply on one side and the collar of a worn, brown leather coat.

I rip back the door before his fist strikes the wood.

"Henry?"

He lowers his fist, a nervous half smile on his lips, tired bruises beneath his eyes. Beside him stands Grayson, looking as serious and severe as ever.

"Can we come in?" Grayson asks.

I don't know what to say. I glance behind him, but no one is there.

"What are you . . . what's going on? Why aren't you at school? Did something happen? Are you okay?" My pulse rages in my ears. "Is it Charlotte?" *Please don't let Charlotte be hurt.* My hand covers my mouth. "Is it Caleb?"

A knowing pity fills Henry's eyes.

"You really are a train wreck," says Grayson, his annoyance providing only minimal relief. Why are they here? *How* are they here? They're being watched.

They step inside.

"Grayson!" My mom rushes forward to hug him, and with only a second delay, he hugs her back.

"Merry Christmas, Ms. Hilder." He might as well be offering condolences at a funeral.

I shouldn't have left. They needed me there to stand between them and Dr. O.

Mom pulls in Henry next, clearly immune to their somber attitudes. "Brynn didn't tell me she invited her friends over. This is perfect! I made so much bacon!"

With that, she rushes toward the kitchen, leaving the three of us unsteady in the entryway. I still don't know why they're here, and my resolve to stay strong is holding on by a thread. I'm so scared, and I don't know how to keep this act up anymore.

"You look like you're going to cry," Henry says to me.

And I sort of hate him right then, because he's exactly right.

CHAPTER 25

I hold it together until Henry hugs me, and then it's all over.

I cry. Not just a few tears, but silent, racking sobs, and when I grip his leather jacket in my fists, he pulls me closer, until I'm sure I'm soaking the collar of his shirt.

"Dinner's read—oh." Mom's voice is close again; she must have come out of the kitchen. Her hand rests between my shoulder blades, but Henry doesn't let go, and I don't either. "Why don't you help yourselves to some food?" she says quietly. "I need to wrap some more presents in my bedroom."

She pats my back, and the next sound I hear is the door to her room scuffing closed over the carpet floor.

"The earrings look great on her," Henry whispers.

I hiccup a sob. "Thanks for that."

He shrugs, and I pull back a little to find Grayson glaring at me over Henry's shoulder.

Wiping my face on the back of the sleeve of my sweatshirt, I stand straighter. "So, what's going on?"

"You tell us." Grayson crosses his arms over his chest.

I cross mine too, mirroring his posture.

"There's nothing to tell."

"Don't do that," Grayson says. "I wrote that game. I patented it. If you want to play cold and indifferent, you owe me twenty percent royalties."

My mouth quirks.

His glare hardens.

"Can I eat bacon while you argue?" asks Henry. His fingers thread through mine, and he pulls me toward the kitchen. Grayson follows reluctantly.

"Did you know I started at Vale Hall my sophomore year?"

Henry says, using the tongs on the batter-splattered counter to load two half-burned pancakes and bacon onto a plate. "My mom had an episode and got in some trouble, and Dr. O showed up in court to vouch for her and agreed to take me to school while she got her meds figured out." He searches through the drawers until he finds the forks, then places one on the plate and passes it my way.

I glance at Grayson, but he's worrying the corner of his lip between his teeth, his focus on Henry.

"Things were great at first. Kind of overwhelming, but Caleb was . . . you know. Caleb. So things were good. I didn't have a big assignment like everyone else. I had tasks—*scavenger hunts,* Dr. O called them. I had to get someone's phone from a locker room, or plant a receipt in someone's wallet. It wasn't bad. Not like some of the rest of you. I didn't even know what he did with any of it." Without looking up at either of us, Henry fills another plate and passes it to Grayson. "Then he asked me to take this guy's credit card at some big fancy dinner in Uptown. He even got me a tux for it."

Henry pauses before filling another plate, and judging from the drumming of Grayson's fingers on the counter, I'm not the only one who's noticed the queasy look on his face.

"I got his wallet, and the card, and then I took it to this hotel outside the city. A . . . bed-and-breakfast."

Grayson's fingers stop drumming. Henry's face twists into the same pained expression he had at the cabin when Grayson said he'd been able to prove his dad's affair.

My heart aches for them both as another domino slides into place.

"I had to pay for a hotel room with it, and fake a signature, then get back before the party was over." Henry faces us, back straight as if braced for judgment. "The room was registered to someone with the initials S.G."

"Susan Griffin," says Grayson bitterly.

"I didn't know it was her, or who she was at the time. I just knew the setup was supposed to make them look like they were having an affair. I didn't know why until you told that story at the cabin." The shame bows Henry's shoulders as he faces Grayson. "I'm so sorry. I didn't think about things before. I was just happy . . . to be able to help someone. I could never help my mom. I tried, but . . . I wasn't enough."

"You were doing your job," I say, when Grayson stays quiet.

"That doesn't make it okay." Henry rakes his hands through his hair, messing it all up. "If I hadn't taken your dad's credit card that night, you wouldn't have believed Dr. O when he said your dad was having an affair. You wouldn't have called him that night, and he wouldn't have crashed into Susan, and you'd still be home with your family."

Another slice of truth punctures the images I have in my mind of the night of Susan's supposed death. We're all connected in this web of lies.

Grayson rises and walks around the counter to Henry. He stops just before him, a softness in his gaze I've never seen before.

"If you hadn't planted that phone in my dad's safe like I asked, he might be dead now. So maybe you saved his life too."

Henry heaves out a sigh when Grayson slowly lifts his hand and slides Henry's hair out of his eyes.

"The way I see it," Grayson says, "you're kind of my hero."

There's honesty in his voice. A humbled kind of honor. And I have the sudden feeling that I'm intruding on something private passing between them.

A blush lights up Henry's face. "So you'd forgive me for stashing pills in your house to keep Brynn out of trouble?"

Grayson's hand pauses. His brows arch as an image of Henry confessing he'd hidden a bunch of Wednesday pills in Grayson's air vent last summer slides out from my memories.

"*Anyway*," says Henry quickly. "I knew I screwed up when I got back and I saw your parents on the balcony at that party. They seemed so happy. I felt terrible. I tried to leave school, but Dr. O told me that if I did, the person I'd come to care about most would be punished."

Another game.

Grayson sneers. "Your mom?"

Henry shakes his head.

"Caleb," I realize, the name echoing through my bones.

Henry nods rapidly. "So I stayed. I snuck into his room at night to make sure he was okay. He thought I had nightmares, and I guess . . . I let him think that. It was better than him knowing the truth—that Dr. O was going to hurt him because of *me*. I thought I could protect him, but I couldn't, just like I couldn't protect Brynn by planting those pills in your house, Grayson. Just like you can't protect us now, Brynn."

I exhale roughly. Henry's words swirl around me. I see him taking Matthew Sterling's credit card. Sneaking into Caleb's room after curfew, just to watch the door.

He's held his own secrets, just like the rest of us.

"I . . ." My confession waits on the tip of my tongue, but before I can give it, another knock sounds at the door.

I glance from Grayson to Henry, who shrugs and smiles.

"Are we expecting someone else?" I ask on my way to the door.

"It's going to be fine, Brynn," Grayson calls flatly. "We're here because we care."

I'm not sure what this means until I open the door and find Charlotte standing on the mat, wearing a T-shirt that says in bold letters: *THIS IS MY INTERVENTION SHIRT.* Geri and Sam are in tow, both looking battle ready.

"Sorry we're late," Charlotte announces. "I had to stop twice to pee. This kid won't get off my bladder." She sniffs the air. "Is that bacon? I can't tell if I like it or I'm going to puke."

"She's going to puke," says Sam.

"Focus, people," Geri snaps.

"How did you all get here?" I ask, palms clammy. "I thought you were being watched."

"Told you to expect resistance," says Charlotte, raising one finger to give herself a point. "My girl is as stubborn as they get."

My girl. Maybe she doesn't hate me after all.

"Dr. O is at a party with the mayor," says Grayson from the living room. "Henry drugged Ms. Maddox with some of the sleeping pills Dr. O had prescribed for him. And Belk appeared out of thin air only to grab two plates of Christmas ham and then promptly disappeared again."

"Where did he go?" I ask.

"Somewhere he can walk," said Charlotte. "He didn't take a car."

A few days ago, Moore said that Belk had been missing as well, and I'd suspected he'd been with Susan since Moore didn't seem to know about her. If he was grabbing extra food, that could be proof that she's still alive.

But not at Vale Hall. Someone would have seen her.

"Dr. O's house," I realize. "That must be where he's keeping Susan." The mansion, situated below the garden at the base of Vale Hall's property, flashes through my mind. I saw it just the other day from June's window when I was watching Grayson on the park bench.

"That's what I'm thinking," says Sam.

"Ms. Maddox has been packing extra food for him all week," says Geri.

I sag in fleeting relief. "What about Moore?"

"He's making sure Ms. Maddox stays in dreamland," says Geri. "And diligently focusing his efforts on her and the other students for two and a half hours, *not a minute more*."

I get the sense he told them that before they ducked out.

"Kind of cold out here, Brynn," says Sam.

I step out of the way to let them in.

Henry locks the door behind me, then pats my shoulder as everyone moves to the living room. Grayson's muted the TV, but the voices from the evening edition of *Pop Store* playing in Mom's room still press through her door.

"It's nice to be together, right?" He smiles, but his eyes are sad, and my heart is heavy. We're not *all* together. Caleb's not here.

As I look around the faces of my friends, his absence feels like a great gaping hole.

Did he choose not to come?

Panic stirs at the base of my spine. I haven't let myself think too much about what I said to him after Model UN that day, or how he must have taken it, but I feel reality pulling on the edge of my control now, and I'm not sure I can hold it back.

Are Caleb and I over?

I follow Henry to the couch, where Charlotte is wafting the unavoidable smell of bacon away from her nose and Sam is hovering next to her, holding Mom's ceramic bowl where she puts her keys.

"Did you start without us?" Geri asks, fists on her hips.

"Start what?" I shift uncomfortably.

"The intervention, obviously," Charlotte says, pointing to her shirt, and the now undeniable baby bump. "You wouldn't tell Dr. O I was pregnant unless the end of the world had actually come, so let's hear it. What's going on?"

They all look to me expectantly. The way they did in the cabin when they asked what the next move was—just after we'd all almost been killed.

"I . . ."

Their futures depend on you.

Henry's arm links through mine. He rests his head on my shoulder, and his hair tickles my neck. "Maybe we should go around the circle and all say one thing we love about Brynn to start off."

"I love it when she tells her best friend the truth," says Charlotte, making me wince.

Henry's head snaps up. "That wasn't exactly what I had in mind."

"I love how Brynn used to say, *We're stronger together*," says Sam, still extending the bowl toward Charlotte.

"Still a little off the mark." Henry cringes.

"I love that time that Brynn went outside the cabin to call Dr. O, and somehow he managed to get to our exact location, two hours away from the city, in five minutes," says Geri with a self-righteous bat of her eyes.

"Maybe I called him earlier," I mumble.

"We were in the car with you earlier," says Grayson. "Nice try, though."

"Maybe they teleported," suggests Sam. "Research suggests we're not far from that kind of technology."

"Well, I love Brynn because she's so brave!" Henry announces.

And just like that, I buckle.

"All right!" I nearly shout, cringing as I realize Mom probably heard me. I lower my voice. "When I left the cabin, I tried to call

Mom to make sure she was okay. She was out on a date with Geri's dad."

Geri goes pale. Sam inhales sharply.

"I kept losing the signal, so I walked closer to the road. That's where Belk ambushed me. He'd put a tracker in the Jeep. Dr. O was waiting in the car. They'd already seen Susan—they'd seen all of us. If I didn't tell them how we'd found her, he was going to give the okay to Geri's dad to take care of Mom."

Geri slumps. Charlotte huffs, then puts an arm around her shoulders.

Now that I've started, I can't stop.

"I told Dr. O that I'd found the address to a cabin when I'd done an assignment spying on the interns in Sterling's office. I told him none of us—not even you, Grayson—knew Susan would be there. He seemed to buy it, but he had plans for the rest of you, so I made a deal that if I could bring you back to Vale Hall—if you all fell in line—then he'd let you off the hook. I know you didn't believe me—that you were still plotting our escape—so I told Caleb I'd rat you out to Dr. O if anyone tried to leave. Is that what you want to hear?"

The truth crushes me, and I tip forward, held upright only by Henry's arms, now circling my waist. Relief is doused by guilt. Have I condemned them? Are we all already dead?

"Did he know about the baby or did you tell him?" asks Sam, breaking the silence. He's sitting on the couch now, the bowl forgotten in his lap.

"He knew," I say weakly. "Ms. Maddox must have found out and told him."

"You owe me a twenty." Grayson holds a hand out to Sam. "I said Maddox told David. Sam said you told David to save Charlotte."

Sam snorts, and pulls his wallet out of his back pocket.

I gape at them.

"And you can go right ahead and pass that to me," says Geri, snatching the bill out of Grayson's hand as soon as Sam's handed it over. "I said Belk must have roughed you up. Your hair was all tangled in the back. I had a good view when you were facing the other way."

I don't know what to say.

"I abstained from betting on principle," Charlotte says. "Best friend rules."

"Enjoy your high horse while I buy myself some new lip gloss," Geri answers.

I don't know what to say. I knew they didn't believe me, but I thought after Caleb and I talked, they were genuinely upset. They had every reason to be.

"You don't hate me," I finally say.

"Of course we don't hate you," says Charlotte.

"Speak for yourself," says Geri. "I hate everyone."

"We had to pretend we were really mad," says Henry. "It was the worst."

"Henry nearly blew it ten times a day," Charlotte says.

"I didn't blow anything," Henry says, then winks at Grayson. "Yet."

Grayson's face turns scarlet as Sam whistles and cackles fill the room.

They know I've been trying to protect them. They care about me enough to risk their lives to come here to tell me so. And yet, as overjoyed as I am, there's something missing.

"If you knew," I say, "where are Margot and Caleb?"

I trip over his name.

The room quiets.

"Margot's been hard to get to," says Grayson, in a way that sounds an awful lot like, *She thinks you really are a rat.*

Heavy silence blankets the room.

"And Caleb?" I ask, steeling myself for the worst.

"He went to check on his family," Henry says, releasing me to slide his hands into his pockets. "He knew you were in trouble, he just . . . he thought you'd talk to him, I think."

We can figure this out. The certainty in his tone slices through me all over again.

I hurt him, and that's why he's not here now. Not because he didn't know me, but because I didn't trust him.

I didn't trust any of them. I thought I could handle it on my own. Be a lone wolf, like Margot said. But we can't do this alone. We can't survive Dr. O without each other. We need to stop him—I see that now more than ever. Damien's gone, and Margot's lost faith, and Susan's locked up in some house. We need to stop this before anything else happens.

And we need Caleb to do it.

I need Caleb.

I *miss* Caleb.

I should have trusted all of them the way they've trusted me.

Henry leans closer. "We can keep an eye on your mom if you want to go for a drive."

I'm already backing away toward the door, fighting the voice in my head that says I should stay so we should figure out our next move. We need to talk more about what happened. There are a dozen more things I should say.

But all I manage is "Thank you." First to Henry, then to the rest of them.

Charlotte smirks at me. "Good luck, tiger."

With the first real smile I've had in days, I grab my messenger bag and dart out the door.

CHAPTER 26

As I ride the train to Devon Park, I watch the dark shapes of the buildings fly by with a strange sense of peace. The intersecting streets I used to rush down once felt like spiderwebs, trapping me in place, but now I can see that they're just broken asphalt lines, leading to stores I used to visit, and a home where I was raised. I think of the stone Mom gave me from outside our old front door, and how that place shaped me, and instead of hate, I remember that not everything that happened here was bad.

Mom's apartment is near a station, and Moore's aunt's house is too. Still, the train takes twice the time it would have if I'd driven, and it's after seven by the time I'm standing outside the small, boxy house where Caleb's family is staying, and the sky is already black. The cold air bites at my face and neck as I pause at the end of the driveway. A green car I don't recognize sits on the asphalt, the roof covered with a thin layer of snow. People move inside the lit window beside the door, their identities masked by thin peach drapes.

Cold tickles my throat as I swallow a deep breath and hurry toward the front door. The truth has already waited too long.

Hand fisted, I knock twice, then wait.

I hear the creak of the floor inside as someone approaches, then a pause, and the slide of the dead bolt.

Caleb's face appears in the crack, a strip of light from a gas station on the corner lighting his scrunched brows.

All the *I'm sorry*'s I practiced on the train ride over are lost as my tongue ties in knots.

"Brynn?"

"Hi." I wave, because that's the perfect way to start a conversation. Maybe I can shake his hand next.

"Hi?" The door opens further. He searches the empty walkway behind me, his scowl growing deeper. "Everything all right?"

"Yeah. Yes. I just wanted to say . . . Merry Christmas."

Really bringing my A game tonight.

"Brynn's here!" Christopher, Caleb's seven-year-old brother, has shoved by his hip and is pointing at me. His lips tilt in a smile.

"Christopher, quiet voices, please!" Maiko hushes him from inside. I hear another set of footsteps approach, and the door is whipped back to reveal thirteen-year-old Jonathan. He's grown at least three inches since I saw him last, and his hair is doing a weird flip on the side I'm pretty sure is on purpose.

"I didn't know we could invite girlfriends." His voice cracks adorably.

My throat goes dry at the word, and I'm filled with too much hope as Caleb's gaze darts my way.

"That's because you don't have one," Caleb responds.

"Do too."

"Do not."

"Do—"

"Brynn!" Maiko shoves between them, beaming as she reaches forward to take my hands. "Come in! It's freezing."

Maiko pulls me into the living room, which is brightly lit by two standing lamps, but empty. Faded rectangles line the yellow walls from pictures that have been removed.

"I'm sorry we aren't at home," Maiko apologizes. "We had some unfortunate problems at the house. The city has moved us here until everything's resolved."

I think of Sam's forged note explaining the situation and wince.

"It's great," I tell her.

"At least we're together." Maiko's even more positive than usual. "That's what matters, right?"

I feel Caleb's gaze on my face and grow warm. "Yes," I say quietly.

Their shoes are neatly lined up in the tile foyer, and I toe mine off to add to the end. Caleb takes my coat and hangs it on the rack. Jonathan reaches for my bag, but I'm gripping the strap tightly against my chest.

"Are you hungry?" Maiko asks. "We have so much food. I made all the boys' favorites."

"She's been cooking for *days*," says Christopher, trudging farther down the hall into what I assume is the kitchen. The lights are brighter there, and the smell of something warm and salty makes my stomach grumble.

"That's because there's nothing else to do in this place," groans Jonathan.

"You could always name the mouse," Caleb answers.

"I already have," says Jonathan. "I call him Caleb. He craps everywhere."

Caleb's face cracks into a smile. "That does sound like me."

"Boys, *please*," says Maiko. "It's Christmas. Be polite."

"Be polite," Jonathan squeaks.

"I'm trying," Caleb squeaks back. His face grows serious again as he turns to his mom. "Can Brynn and I have a second?"

"Of course." Maiko nods. "Take your time."

"They need *privacy* to *kiss*!" shouts Christopher from the kitchen.

My neck grows warm.

Caleb's ears grow pink.

"I should have invited my girlfriend," Jonathan mutters as Maiko ushers him down the hall.

And just like that, we're alone again.

"Sorry," Caleb says, as if he has to apologize for his brothers to me.

"No," I say. "I'm sorry."

He waits, watching me carefully. His blue collared shirt is the slightest bit wrinkled; his black and white Chucks peek out below the ends of his jeans.

"I thought I could save everyone if I did what Dr. O wanted."

He leans against the wall beside the coatrack. "No one asked you to take him on alone."

"I know. I got scared." I swallow. "Because I love you."

He's still for a long moment. It reminds me of the way sponges take on water. Bit by bit, absorbing more with each passing second. Finally, he reaches a hand toward me—a question without words. I release the strap of my bag to weave my fingers through his.

"I told you," he says.

I hiccup a laugh. He pulls me closer until my socked feet are between his and our bodies line up. The thunder of his heart fills my ear. One muscle at a time, I melt into him. One breath after another, the tension eases from my jaw, my shoulders, my chest.

"So who won the bet, Sam or Grayson?"

"Geri, I think."

He smiles. "Sorry I missed the intervention."

I inch closer. "Does this mean you forgive me?"

"There's nothing to forgive." He sighs. "I might have done the same thing in your place."

I tilt my face up to look at him, and find warmth in his dark eyes. I reach to his jaw, my fingers grazing his smooth skin, and with a small grin he leans closer, his lips a breath away from mine.

"I knew it," Christopher says, standing in the hallway.

Caleb's forehead falls against mine as his body goes slack. "Get out of here, creeper."

Christopher giggles and disappears back into the kitchen, but though I can't see him, I'm pretty sure either he or Jonathan is spying.

"I have something for you," I say.

Worry scrunches his brows. "I didn't bring . . . I mean, I didn't know you'd be here . . ."

I shake my head. "I know."

I let go of his hand to open my bag and pull out the thin notebook. Excitement has me bouncing on the balls of my feet. I really hope he doesn't think this is stupid.

He takes the notebook, opening the front page, and he beams.

"It's graphing paper," he says.

"For designing buildings." A man at a shop in Uptown told me it was what all the pros used. I gauge Caleb's reaction by the brightness of his eyes, and soon I'm giggling like Christopher.

Caleb turns the page to find a numbered list of structures, scratched in my terrible handwriting.

"It's all my favorite buildings. The ones that remind me of you." I reach over him to turn the page. "Here are the ones we've seen together in the city."

"The Times Building," he says. "That's my favorite."

"I know." I turn the page. "This is a list of the best in the country. The Peabody Library in Baltimore is on there. What if we go see the rest one day? I left spaces so you can sketch them if you want."

He looks up at me, a short laugh bursting from him. "I would love that."

"Yeah?"

"Yes. This is incredible. *You're* incredible."

His fingers run over the pages, and when he smiles at me, the world slows and slips away.

"Thank you," he says.

I am shining brighter than the sun.

Closing the book, he takes my hand. "Come on. There's someone I want you to meet."

I follow him into the tiny shotgun kitchen, where the counters are filled with different kinds of food. Everything from pizza to a potato bar to small, gummy, bean-bag-looking things that Jonathan is popping into his mouth like candy.

"Mochi," he tells me, mouth full. "Have to eat them before Christopher takes over."

Christopher is currently reaching toward the box, while Jonathan, one hand on his little brother's head, straight-arms him back.

But I don't answer, because in the corner, Maiko is feeding soup to a man in a fancy wheelchair.

Caleb's father.

My heels dig into the worn linoleum. I didn't know he'd be here. But of course he is. This is Christmas Eve, maybe his first night home with his family.

I'm intruding.

Caleb pauses and glances back at me. I can't leave now, and I don't want him to think I'd be going because I didn't want to meet his father.

I do. I *really* do.

My worries fall silent as Caleb's dad lifts a quivering, emaciated hand an inch off the armrest of the chair and beckons me forward.

"He can't say much yet," Caleb warns me. "And we can't keep him up too late. Mom rented the car out front so we can bring him back to the rehab facility before eight."

I remember how he was the last time I saw him, tubes sticking out of his nose and mouth, his body completely motionless. I can't believe he's actually sitting upright, looking at me.

I step forward.

"Dad, this is Brynn, my girlfriend." He glances at me, as if to make sure this is all right.

It's more than all right. It's perfect.

"Hi, Mr. Matsuki." I take his hand carefully, feeling like I'm holding a baby bird. He doesn't look great, if I'm being honest. His skin is pale, and it hangs from his cheekbones and forearms. His brown eyes look too big for his thin face.

But they're Caleb's eyes, and the tilt of his mouth is Caleb's too.

Mr. Matsuki's hand barely squeezes mine. I take a foldout chair next to him, and Christopher leans against my side, the way kids do before they develop any notion of personal space.

"I'm glad to meet you," I say. "Caleb's told me a lot about you."

"Dad, look at this." Caleb opens the book and shows him the graphing paper. There's an anxious look in his eyes as he waits for his father's reaction—for recognition, I realize a moment later. No one is sure how Mr. Matsuki will recover, or how much he remembers from before his accident.

But Caleb's dad nods, a small move that grows bigger until his hand, still in mine, is shaking. Then his lips part, and he laughs.

Or croaks.

I think it's a laugh.

"Oh my." Tears fill Maiko's eyes as she sets the broth on the counter.

Caleb puts the book in his quilt-covered lap, and his father releases my hand to run his fingers over the smooth pages.

"He remembers," Caleb says, and then he makes a sound halfway between a choke and a sob, then starts to laugh.

Soon, we're all laughing. Maiko's hugging her husband, and Christopher's half lying on his lap, and Caleb's got his arm around Jonathan's lanky shoulders. Tears have made both of their eyes glassy, though Jonathan is quick to blink his away.

Thank you, Caleb mouths to me.

I feel like I've won a marathon, or rescued hostages, or discovered the cure to some rare disease. I think of the photo Mom gave me of my father, holding me in his arms right after I was born. Sam making flow charts for where he and Charlotte will go. Grayson carrying Henry from the fire. I think of Moore, telling me only a coward regrets loving the right person, and how I will never regret one moment with Caleb, because he's unlocked a joy inside me not even Dr. O can stamp out.

Something shifts inside me then. The last piece of a puzzle set in place. A key inside a lock that finally turns.

I stand up like a shot, drawing every eye in my direction.

"Um," I say. "I need to get going. I'm sorry. It was so nice meeting you, Mr. Matsuki."

His eyes smile.

Caleb's brows arch in curiosity.

"Okay," says Maiko. "Do you want to take some mochi?"

"Yes, please." I meet Caleb's eyes and tilt my head toward the hallway. He follows me there—it kills me a little to drag him away from this moment.

"I understand if you can't leave," I say. "I don't want to leave either, but—"

Caleb presses a finger to my lips. "Where are we going?"

I grin. "Back to school."

CHAPTER 27

An hour later, Caleb and I huddle together in the cold beside Barry Buddha in Vale Hall's garden. Our breath makes clouds, and my hands, even wrapped in his and shoved into the pockets of his coat, are numb. I long for the heater from the rental car we drove from the rehab facility after dropping off his dad, but we had to park it down the road and walk so we didn't alert anyone to our presence.

We did not go into school, but around it, along the perimeter fence.

"Henry said your mom's doing well. He told her you had a *romantic emergency*," says Caleb. They talked briefly in the car on the way over.

"He's right," I say.

Caleb gives me an incredulous look. "Pretty sure that's the sweetest thing you've ever said to me, Brynn."

I elbow him in the side, but freeze as the icy grass crackles beneath falling footsteps around the hedge. A moment later, a tall man in a long wool coat appears, his expression, as always, set to dead serious.

"Oh, good," Moore says as Caleb and I wrench apart. "This again."

"Thought you might like to take a field trip," I say. "Raven style."

Moore sighs heavily. "What does that mean?"

I move closer, keeping my voice low. "There's something we have to show you, but it's in Dr. O's house."

Moore turns. "I'm leaving."

"You'll want to see this," I say. "I promise."

"But we need to get rid of Belk for a little while. He's there keeping guard." Caleb stamps his feet against the cold.

"What do they have in there?" Moore's curiosity leaks through, tinged with concern. He's known something's been up with Belk.

"More like who," I say.

Moore turns quickly, his jaw set. "Renee Gibson?"

I flinch, thinking of how Dr. O got to her. Wherever she is, I hope she's okay.

"The power meter at Dr. O's house is probably outside by the garage," Caleb explains before I can answer. "If I can break that, and make it look like a fallen branch did the damage, it can sever the line. When the power goes out, Belk will check the circuit breaker first, but once he figures out that won't work, he'll walk the perimeter of the house. It should give us enough time—"

Moore pulls his phone out of his pocket and presses a few buttons.

"We're running low on supplies in the girls' hall. I need to run to the pharmacy before they mutiny. I'm taking some of the kids with me. Need you to come keep an eye on the rest of them." A pause, then, "Yes. Good."

He hangs up.

"Or we could do it your way," says Caleb.

"We've got twenty minutes." Moore's already striding deeper into the garden, down a path I've never been. It circles the pond, and then cuts straight into the back hedge. For a moment, I think he's about to run into the brush—it's dark, and it's possible he's lost his way—but a sharp turn reveals that the high hedge walls are staggered, and a path cuts out the back.

On the other side, the woods stretch out before us, stark and eerie, blackened by the heavy night. None of us chance turning on a phone for light, and as we keep to the narrow trail, brittle branches reach out to snag my shins and arms.

Soon, Dr. O's house comes into view, the outside lights dark, and only one window on the top floor lit.

"There," says Caleb, pointing to a bobbing flashlight moving along the back privacy fence. Squinting, I make out Belk's thick form hurrying toward Vale Hall.

"Twenty minutes." I hope Susan's here.

I hope it's enough time to get her out without Belk catching on.

Moore strides across the patch of snowy lawn to the back porch. Caleb and I jog after him, searching for any watching eyes or security cameras. At the double glass doors, Moore keys a security code into a small plastic box, and a light at the bottom turns from red to green.

"That's handy," mutters Caleb.

"I'm head of security," Moore reminds us as he opens the door.

The inside of the house is dark and quiet.

Nerves buzz in my ears.

"Well?" says Moore. I jump at the volume of his voice. He's not even trying to be covert.

It takes a minute for my eyes to adjust to the dark. We've entered a kitchen. The shiny counters are lit by the moonlight outside, but look to be the same dark marble as in the main house. There's an island in the center topped by a basket of fresh fruit. A small kitchen table with barstools sits before two couches, situated around a fireplace.

No one is here.

"The light was on upstairs," I say.

We scuff the snow off our shoes on the mat as Moore closes the door behind us.

"Stairs are by the front door," he says.

We hurry past the living room, down a hall with a bathroom. I bump into a basket on the floor with two umbrellas inside, but Caleb snags the handle before it tips.

We climb the carpeted stairs, Moore on our heels.

The hall curves around to the top of the steps, four closed doors stretching to the front of the house. The last door is framed by a thin line of light, and locked by a sliding bar from the outside. With a nod, we hurry toward it, but my hand falters on the doorknob. What if Susan isn't here? What if behind this door is something we do not want to see?

What if Dr. O never went to the party with the mayor, and this is his room?

I am moved aside by Moore, who unlocks the bolt, shoves open the door, and comes face-to-face with Susan Griffin.

My gaze darts from Susan's face, paling in shock, to the metal spoon extended before her like a shank. It falls from her hand and bounces silently on the carpeted floor beside her bare feet. She's wearing the same threadbare sweater and loose jeans I saw her in at the cabin.

Moore jerks back in surprise, bumping into Caleb. He grips the doorjamb for support, as if he might fall over.

"Hugh," she whispers. Both hands go to the key on the chain around her neck, gripping it like a lifeline.

The right person unlocks the best and worst in you.

"Susan," Moore breathes. "How is . . . How did you . . ."

When she says nothing, I move past him into the room. The decor is sparse. A bed with no blankets or sheets. No pictures on the wall. Atop a dresser sits a tray of untouched food—Christmas ham.

Susan does a double take of my face, then braces for the worst. "Brynn."

I raise my hands in surrender. "I'm not really a rat."

"Okay," she says slowly.

"Will someone please tell me what is going on," says Moore.

"She's been living in a cabin outside of town," Caleb tells him. "Grayson and his dad hid her there after the accident."

Moore turns sharply to Caleb. *"Grayson?"*

"Turns out he didn't drive her off the road," I say.

"Then who—"

"My brother," says Susan.

Moore's chin drops as he absorbs this information. His pain leeches across the gaps between us all. Confusion. Fury. Grief.

Love.

I didn't realize she was the one he lost until I was at Caleb's, but the signs had been there the whole time. The woman he shouldn't have been with. His promise to her to protect the students.

The way he didn't know who Belk was guarding, which made me realize that Dr. O didn't tell him that she'd been found.

"I thought you were dead," Moore whispers.

It is like watching a boat crash against dry land. He is breaking, and I don't know how to stop it.

Tears fill Susan's eyes. "I know."

"We don't have very long," says Caleb.

Moore nods curtly. "Right. We're leaving."

"We can't." Susan's hands drop to her waist. "I've been assured there will be consequences for the students if I do."

Another threat.

"I can handle the students," Moore says, pushing into the room. The muscles beside his neck are bulging. His anger is a physical force, filling the room. "I'm not leaving you here."

"Hugh." She takes a step closer, unsteady without her crutch. I don't see it in the room. Belk or Dr. O must have taken it from her.

Moore freezes, and stares at her leg with another clench of his jaw.

"Okay," he says, as if this is the only word stopping him from tearing down the walls. "You need help. That's fine. I'll carry you."

"*Wait*. I have an idea," I say.

"Me, too," says Moore. "I'm going to kill him."

I shiver at the cold, lethal bite of his tone.

"You can't," I tell him. "People will look for Dr. O, right? That's what you said, Susan. He's in the public eye now."

Her eyes flick to me, and narrow. "That's right."

"You said the best way to beat him was to get him to step down. To resign."

"Where are you going with this?" she asks.

"We need to hurry." Caleb passes me a look, then disappears down the hall to see if he can spot Belk returning.

"The first thing Moore taught me about conning was to figure out what someone wants," I say. "What does your brother want?"

"Get to the point," growls Moore.

"*Power*," I say, jabbing the air with one finger. "And the senator job is the best way to get it, but it's also the most public. People are looking at him now, the way they used to look at his father."

Susan limps to the bed and takes a seat on the edge of the mattress. Moore watches her like a hawk. He doesn't come closer, as if he's afraid to step inside her bubble.

"Dr. O hated your dad, but he didn't kill him. He destroyed him. He took away the thing that mattered most by blackmailing him with the truth about his mother's death. He took your father's power. *That's* how we take Dr. O down."

"Five minutes!" shouts Caleb from down the hall.

"Explain," says Susan quickly.

"I have a plan," I say. "But it means you'll need to stay here for a few more days."

"No," says Moore, hands slicing the air. "That's not happening."

Susan holds a hand out to quiet him, and he groans in frustration. "We're listening," she says.

As fast as I can, I tell them my plan for the party after Dr. O's been sworn in, one week from today. As I talk, their expressions grow grave, but I don't let up. I made the mistake of thinking I could do this alone before. I won't do that again.

"We cut off the legs he stands on," I say. "The people he trusts. His money. And his secrets."

Silence stretches between us, and I wait with bated breath, feeling each passing second flick against my raw nerves.

"When this is done, you leave my brother to me," says Susan.

Moore's gaze aligns with hers and holds steady.

Slowly, he nods.

"Deal," I say.

Caleb appears in the doorway. "We've got to go. I think I see a flashlight up at the house."

I charge toward the door, but hesitate when Moore doesn't follow. He's still standing there, staring at Susan as if his boots have taken root in the floor.

"Go," she says. "The students need you."

Still, he hesitates.

"Kiss her and come on already," I say, feeling more than a little like Christopher.

Susan grins. It's the first time I've seen her smile, and in that moment sparks light between them. The chemistry so bright and urgent I take a step back.

Moore leans in, his back to me as he takes Susan in his arms.

It's the kind of kiss that stops traffic.

The kind I really didn't ever want to witness Moore taking part in.

When they're done, Susan touches his cheek. "See you soon, baby."

I toss a *wow* look at Caleb, who's already sending one back my way. Then we jet down the stairs, out the back, and straight through the woods. We need to get the car back to Caleb's family and talk to the others. We need to plan the details of the greatest con I will ever pursue.

Tomorrow, we begin our take-back of Vale Hall.

CHAPTER 28

Because Dr. O expects it of me, I return to my mom's for Christmas. She's delighted, of course, and we repeat the breakfast-for-dinner thing for actual breakfast the next day. Three pancakes and four pieces of bacon later, I've hugged her goodbye and am taking the bus outside the city, in the opposite direction from Vale Hall.

There's one stop I need to make before I go back.

Mimir State Penitentiary is on the edge of White Bank. Everything about it, from the rolled wire atop the high chain-link fences to the cement-block buildings, screams *prison,* and as I exit the bus my stomach grows queasy.

This is not a place I ever imagined going, but one of the many things I learned from Vale Hall's Vocational Development class was the importance of research. There's someone here who knows more about conning than I do.

It's time to get in and get out.

The bus was overflowing with families today, and the waiting room is already packed when I go in. Kids are crying. Moms are giving them quarters for the snack machines to keep them busy. Guards in beige uniforms wait behind bulletproof glass with less-than-amused looks on their faces.

An hour after I check in, I'm called to the visitation room.

It's a long hall, lined with black phones and partitioned walls that give the illusion of privacy. Three guards stand behind the line of visitors as we find the number on the booth corresponding to the plastic card we've been given.

I lift my chin and keep my shoulders back as I sit on a cracked vinyl stool and pick up the phone.

"Merry Christmas, Brynn," says Pete.

My mom's ex looks like he's adjusted to prison well. His blue eyes are sharp as tacks. His face is clean-shaven. If he's leaner through the jaw and neck, it only adds to his ferocity. It's not the first time he's had a stay at this lovely place, but this will certainly be the longest—he's got a twenty-year sentence for selling pills to the Wolves of Hellsgate, thanks to me.

"Not the Hilder I expected to see," he goes on, flicking something off his bright orange shirt. "But not altogether disappointing."

"Mom's over you," I say. "I doubt she remembers your name."

His thin lips curl in amusement.

"So it's just my sweet daughter who's come to spread some holiday cheer. Isn't that nice?"

"Not your daughter," I say, conscious of the rising pitch in my voice. "I need a favor."

I glance over my shoulder, to a guard who's pacing toward a man who's started yelling at the opposite end of the room.

"A favor?" He chuckles. "Well, if it isn't a Christmas miracle! The girl who knows everything needs my help!" He stands, one hand to his heart, looking like he might burst into tears.

"Shut up!" I wince. This is an act, just like everything else with him.

"Sit down or you're done!" shouts a guard on the other side of the glass.

Pete sits, grinning again. "What do you want, Brynn? Some cigarettes? A cup of noodles? Commissary just got in some chocolate bars. Allie always loved—"

"I need to get into Wednesday," I say, interrupting any sentiment about my mom. "The way you used to do it. To do what you used to do." *Sell stolen pills.* I'm not sure if someone's listening in on these phones, or if a guard nearby can hear, and I don't want to take any chances.

He tilts his head.

"Why don't you ask your boss? Doesn't he own it?"

Mr. Wednesday—that's what Pete once called Dr. O. The only reason the director knew about me at all was because Pete had been stealing pills from his pharmaceuticals warehouse. That's why I'm here.

"He's a little busy," I say.

Pete chuckles, then full on laughs. "So the good life isn't all it was cracked up to be, huh? What, did you get tired of all that money? I'm glad to see you're embracing your true calling, Brynn."

I motion to his orange jumpsuit. "You too."

"You're more like me than you'll ever admit," he says, then sighs. "The answer's no, by the way, but thanks for the laugh. I needed it."

"Please," I say between my teeth.

"Least you've learned some manners since you left." He chuckles again. "Why would I tell you that? You're the reason I'm locked up, in case you forgot." His eyes narrow as he leans closer to the glass, and I can't help the shiver that traces down my spine. "Yeah, I know you called the cops to bust me that day. Got jealous that I was taking over your deal with the Wolves, and brought the house down over my head. Poor Brynn has a fit when things don't go her way, doesn't she?"

He still doesn't realize that the whole thing was set up. I was never trying to sell drugs, I was trying to get Pete to think I was, so he'd step in and get arrested.

I force my eyes to meet his. "Guess I am a little like you in that way."

His smug grin fades, and his gaze drops. After a moment, he leans back in his chair, rubbing his palms over his thighs. His ego seems to deflate, like air hissing out of a balloon. He doesn't even look angry, but given what he believes I did, he should be.

"I guess you are," he says.

I don't like this acceptance. I don't trust it.

"You're wrong, you know," I say. "I did it because I had orders. *Mr. Wednesday* is the reason you're in here, not me, and if you tell me how to get into the warehouse, I'll make sure he's put here with you so you can thank him personally."

Pete holds one hand out to the side, a disbelieving smirk on his face. "So this is *his* doing."

"He knew you'd been stealing from him. He wasn't exactly a big fan of yours."

Pete's hand drops to his side. He taps his bottom teeth against his top lip, sizing me up with his cold gaze.

This is part of the act as well. We both know he wants revenge, and I've just served it up on a plate before him.

"You know when I met you, you couldn't even spot a pigeon."

I swallow, remembering how he taught me to read a crowd, and figure out who would make a good mark. A woman with an open purse. A man who'd had too much to drink. Anyone who looked lonely, in need of a friend. They weren't hard to see once you were looking.

"You thought a shell game was something you did with turtles."

I look away, not wanting this stroll down memory lane.

He chuckles quietly. "The first time I set you up to do a color grab, you remember what you asked me?"

"'Won't they be sad?'" I say quietly, thinking of how he taught me to snatch items off unsuspecting tourists by the lake.

"Won't they be sad," he repeats. "You never had a doubt in your mind you could get the job done. Even at eight years old, you had quick hands."

His voice is light with something that sounds close to pride.

"Yeah," I say. "Well. You learn fast when you need to."

"Yes, you do," he says. "And now, look how far you've come."

A long moment of silence stretches between us. I don't want his fatherly sentiment. I don't want to share the same space with him longer than I have to. But I think of what Mom said about home, and how it made me, and even if I hate Pete, I wouldn't be here now without him.

"You really think you can pull this off behind Mr. Wednesday's back?" he asks quietly.

I nod, and his lips turn up in a smile.

"If I help you, that doesn't make us even."

"I have no interest in being even with you," I tell him.

He laughs, and for once, it isn't filled with spite or manipulation or hate.

Twenty minutes later, I have the location of Wednesday Pharmaceuticals warehouse's security cameras, what the boxes I'm searching for look like, and the security code to the loading dock where the trucks make their deliveries.

I'M BACK AT school before dusk on Christmas Day. A few of the underclassmen who have families they still speak to are out on a pass. Geri's with her father. Sam's on a pass to see his mother at Bennington Max. They weren't supposed to leave, but Dr. O thought it might raise more suspicion if they didn't.

The rest of the seniors are all unofficially grounded, and abiding by their sentences now that the director's back in his office at Vale Hall. As I make my way across the kitchen, I can hear the sounds of a *Road Rules* tournament stretching up from the pit. With a pang, I remember my seventeenth birthday party there. How, for the first time, I felt at home in this strange, enormous house.

Now the walls have ears, and suspicion has me walking on eggshells.

I'm not heading to the pit now, but to the dining room table, where a girl sits alone with a book. Her eyes are down, but I don't get the impression she's reading. Since I walked into the kitchen, she hasn't turned a single page.

"Hi, Margot," I say, sliding around the table beside her.

She doesn't look up.

"How are you feeling?"

No answer. I grip the back of one of the dining room chairs, bracing it before me like a shield. I'd be lying if I said she didn't make me more nervous than she ever has before.

I knew she was a top-level liar. I knew she wanted to bring Dr. O down more than anything.

But I didn't expect her to walk into City Hall and grab a gun.

Even now, being near her feels like standing beside a loaded grenade. Her face has been on the news since the day of the attack—security footage got a grainy, black-and-white image of her profile, but being the ghost that she was meant there were no pictures online to match it. Still, it's enough that Dr. O is keeping her housebound until further notice.

Despite it all, I can't help feeling sorry for her—this girl who's lost everything.

In fresh clothes, and without the soot stains on her skin, she looks better. I heard the MRI Belk took her in for came back normal, and a doctor stitched up the back of her head. Still, she looks tired and disconnected.

From the basement, I hear the pad of footsteps, and Ms. Maddox appears. She's wearing a new shade of lipstick—dark enough to match her soul—and her red plaid dress is festive. Once, that would have comforted me, but now her efforts to make herself and everything here homey grind my patience.

Her watchful gaze glances off mine before she grabs a plate of decorated sugar cookies off the kitchen island and carries them down the stairs.

"Do you need anything?" I ask Margot. "I could get you something to eat. I know Ms. Maddox made a pie for last night." My voice tightens over her name, and my mind flashes to Raf, and how he might be alive now if not for her reading Moore's messages.

Margot says nothing.

The basement stairs groan again, though no one comes up the shadowed steps.

"You can't ignore me forever," I say.

"I can try," she whispers.

I pull back the chair and sit down, the gap between us large enough to fit two more people.

My throat is tight, the words thick on my tongue. "I did what I had to do."

"You ratted us out," she says, still staring out the window. "You gave your friends up to a monster."

"I didn't have a choice."

"Sure you did," she says. "You chose wrong."

I lean closer. "So I should have stolen a gun and tried to shoot him in City Hall?"

Her lips tilt in a grim smile. "Who says I tried to shoot him?"

Cheers erupt from the pit, and from the front of the house, I hear the garage door open with a steady hum. The stairs creak as someone descends, but no one enters the kitchen.

There is no privacy in this house. Not today. Not anymore.

My gaze narrows on hers, trying to decipher what this means. Dr. O said she attacked him—not that I can take his word. But she's not denying that she stole Belk's gun, just what she did with it.

I got her.

Got who?

Even if it was safe to ask right now, which it's not, I don't have time to, because she's leaning closer, holding my stare with her cold, brown eyes. "Does it feel good? Selling out the people who counted on you?"

I flinch. "At least you're all still alive."

A sour expression curls back her lips. "You call this alive? Living in this house, without being able to go outside? You know, I did what he wanted too once, and look at me. I'm a prisoner, and Jimmy . . . Jimmy's *gone.*"

I flinch at Jimmy's name, her grief a cold knife in my side.

She swipes her forearm over her eyes to clear away the tears, then closes her book and stands.

"He'll get rid of all of us. It's just a matter of time. And if you trust Dr. O when he says you're safe, you're stupider than I thought." She's louder than before. Angrier.

My back straightens. "Who said anything about trusting him?"

She was turning away, but pauses.

The floor outside the kitchen groans quietly. I need to hurry. I don't want the wrong people hearing this.

"I've got a plan, Margot." I grasp her cold hand, willing her to remember that beneath all of the lies, we were friends once. "I'm going to get him back. For you. For Jimmy. For all of them. Dr. O's got accounts overseas, did you know that? Places he dumps his money into . . ."

The creak in the basement stairs makes me pause, but when I look, no one is there.

"You don't need to worry," I finish quietly.

A glimmer of surprise rises and fades in her eyes.

"Better be careful talking like that," she says. "You never can be sure who's listening."

She rounds the other side of the table, taking care not to come anywhere near me. As she passes the stairway to the pit, I think I catch a flash of red plaid, but it's gone before I can say for sure.

As the garage door closes, I stride through the kitchen, passing Paz and June as they make their way toward the pit. They don't look at me as they pass—they're too busy staring at Margot as she rushes by on her way toward the stairs.

I meet Sam just as he comes through the garage door.

"Everything all right?" he asks.

"Fine," I tell him. "How was the visit with your mom?"

His slow grin says it all.

CHAPTER 29

New Year's Eve

By noon, the foyer of Vale Hall is filled with boxes. "Congratulations Dr. O" signs and banners lean against the walls. Bags of uninflated silver and black balloons sit beside a rented helium tank, and white New Year's paper horns and cardboard bowler hats have pushed aside the Christmas decorations on the entryway tables.

The doorbell's been ringing all week with deliveries Geri has purchased on the Vale Hall account for tonight's congratulations party. The house has been a frenzy of activity. News reporters have been in the house interviewing Dr. O and the students in preparation for his swearing-in ceremony today at three o'clock. Security has been at an all-time high.

Every word spoken to the press is a beautiful lie, accented with a hustler's smile.

"Dresses are here!" screams Paz as another beige-uniformed deliveryman sets the third of four enormous boxes on the front steps. In an instant, half the girls at school have flocked toward the door. Charlotte hurries by as I make a slow descent down the stairs, the weight of today's tasks looming over my shoulders.

Today Dr. O becomes a senator.

Today, we cut him down.

Covertly, I slide my hand over Caleb's burner phone, concealed in my back jeans pocket, beneath the bottom of my baggy sweater. I've been carrying it all week, but it has yet to ring.

"Oh, no." Bea's voice rises above the rest. "This is all wrong. Pink? I don't do pink!"

"You'll do pink, and you'll do it with a smile." Geri strides in from the kitchen, a tie fastened around the collar of her crisp white shirt. She's all business today—has been all week. This party tonight is her doing.

"It's not all pink," says Paz. "It's got some black. Wait . . . Is this a jumpsuit? The names must have gotten mixed up. These calves don't hide behind wide-leg pants."

"It's a travesty," says Bea.

"You think?" asks Paz, a little shyly.

"You both are incredibly subtle," says June, who grins at the simple black frock she's been assigned.

The boxes have been dragged into the foyer and half shredded in the attempt to pull the dresses free. Each one is wrapped in white paper and sealed with a sticker and the name of the recipient.

Geri picked them all, like a bride choosing the attire of the world's most dangerous wedding party. She informed us at a party planning meeting earlier this week that we would be wearing shades of black, with accents of fuchsia and silver to go with the decor. Apparently Bea didn't think her dress, a knee-length sheath of black lace over a pink slip, would be quite so *accented*.

"Here it is." Geri, digging through one of the boxes, stands, holding a neatly wrapped package. "These would have been here last week if not for your special order, Charlotte."

"How come she gets a special order?" whines Bea as Geri hands it off to Charlotte at the bottom of the stairs.

"Because it came with a matching bib," grumbles Paz.

With a condescending smirk, Charlotte tears back the paper. Now that we know Dr. O knows about the baby, she's stopped bothering to hide it around the house. Everyone's been supportive for the most part. Joel even made her a cake.

"Really?" Charlotte asks as I find my package, considerably larger than the rest, tossed out of a box and on the floor. "You decided *this* was the best way to go?"

Pinching the shoulder straps, she releases the black, floor-length gown that rises to a high, choking collar. It won't disguise her baby bump in the slightest, which is fine here since the cat's out of the bag, but is an interesting choice for tonight's very public event.

"You'll look conservative and repentant," says Geri dryly, eliciting a burning glare from our local redhead.

"I'm neither," says Charlotte.

"Then the good news is you'll have a dress to wear to Geri's funeral," I add.

Charlotte hides a smirk against her shoulder. Rumors about what went on at the cabin have mostly died down since finals, but we're still laying low and keeping our distance from each other in order to hold off any potential gossip. Dr. O's threats may have stopped, but he can still hurt us if he thinks we've stepped out of line.

"The director wants you to stand near him during the toasts." We all jump to find Moore standing on the stairs behind us.

There you are. Since I talked to Margot on Christmas about my plan to make things right, Moore's made himself more visibly present. Most of the time, he's close enough to make everyone uncomfortable. The rest, he's half-heartedly sorting through my room for contraband.

I have a tail, mandated by Dr. O, thanks to information supplied by the real rat in this house, Ms. Maddox. I can only assume this has something to do with his learning of our attempts to sabotage him, though he must doubt the information because he has yet to expel me. While I'm glad the tail is on my side, it's not the result I was hoping for.

We need to get Belk away from Susan.

We need to get Belk out of the picture completely.

As Moore strides toward us, I grip the package to my chest, giving him a wary stare I'm sure Paz and Bea notice. We have a limited window to get him into Dr. O's house unnoticed, and one shot to make it work.

"It'll show the director's progressive and in touch with the tough issues current teens face," Moore continues, his tone void of all emotion.

"So glad I can help the cause," says Charlotte between her teeth.

As Moore makes his way to the kitchen, she chances a look of disgust in my direction.

I open the package, my stomach sinking even as my brows hike high. My chosen dress's fitted halter top is deceiving—it looks normal enough, but the waist gives way to an explosion of tulle, like a ballerina's tutu got into some insta-grow and rolled around in coal.

"Are you kidding me?" I mutter.

"Ouch," says June with a cringe.

"Oh, yes," says Geri, crossing her arms with a cruel smile. "I picked that one out special for you."

Paz hides a snicker in her forearm. Bea laughs out loud. Even Charlotte winces, then cracks up.

It's the worst dress I've ever seen—a prank I'm sure my new friend Geri finds very amusing. It even has a hole in the hip where the skirt has pulled free from the bodice.

"Thanks so much," I say flatly.

"Least no one will be looking at me," says Charlotte.

I groan.

The doorbell rings. Geri, glancing through one of the narrow windows beside the door, gives a shriek of annoyance and rips back the door. There are already four wooden crates sitting on the front mat, and two workers in black ball caps are delivering more out of the back of a truck.

"This isn't right!" Geri's waving her hands at the crates. "These were supposed to be delivered to the Rosalind! I told the man on the phone no less than six times . . ."

The girls in the foyer inch closer for a view of the drama, and they aren't the only ones. Soon Sam and Henry have abandoned their lunch to see what's going on, and Caleb and Joel aren't far behind. The attention even brings Dr. O out of his office, and the sight of him, already in his suit and red tie for the swearing-in ceremony in a few hours, sends a wave of hate through me.

Be patient, I tell myself, even as my hands curl into fists. Even as I fight the urge to call my mom and make sure she's alive. *Be patient. Be smart. Be steady.*

Again, I will the phone in my back pocket to ring. We are running out of time.

Behind him, in the shadows of the twin black marble ravens atop their thick stone pillars on either side of the office door, stands Grayson. His shoulders are hunched, his expression grave.

"What is the meaning of this?" Dr. O bellows. As he joins Geri at the door, I raise a brow in Grayson's direction.

"He wants me to stay here tonight," Grayson whispers. "Doesn't think it's a good idea for Matthew Sterling's son to be at the party."

His bitterness reflects in the grind of my jaw.

Grayson's out for tonight. I can't think about what that means now. We've got bigger issues on our hands.

One of the deliverymen, flipping through the screens on his tablet, shakes his head with an apology and hurries back to the cab of the truck. He's clearly scared of Geri, and I don't blame him.

"We can put the crates in the back of one of the SUVs," Dr. O tells Geri when they're back inside.

"It's packed with supplies already!" Geri flashes me a look of panic. "We can fit one or two in, but not all of them!"

I peek out the window at the ten crates. "Each of the cars is already making two trips, right, Geri?"

"Someone can take the Jeep," Moore offers.

"I can drive—" I start, but I'm cut off by the wave of Dr. O's hand.

"Sam will take the Jeep. Does that work for you, Sam?"

My shoulders sag. I glance at Sam, who's straightened in surprise.

"Me?" Sam nods quickly, recovering. "Of course. Sure. I'll get some people to help me load it up."

"Good," says Dr. O. He looks to Geri. "Good?"

Her hands deliberately unfist at her sides. "That's . . . fine."

A town car has pulled around the fountain, following on the bumper of the delivery truck. It's black and unremarkable, and aside from the tinted windows, it's like the cars in the garage. But it's not one of ours.

Two men step out of it, both wearing black suits and sunglasses. Both making little effort to hide the leather shoulder holsters beneath their coats, or the guns tucked within.

The sight of them sets my teeth on edge, and in seconds my heart is kicking against my ribs.

"Ah," says Dr. O, walking outside to greet them.

"Looks likes Dr. O just leveled up," says Grayson grimly when the director's out of earshot. "Government-issued security at its finest."

These men are Dr. O's bodyguards, hired to protect him as senator. They must clock in for duty today.

Susan said this would be coming, but seeing them here adds another unwanted layer of complication.

"I'm still in charge of the students," Moore answers. "And I believe you're supposed to be in your room reading."

Grayson sighs, annoyed, then, with a wary glance at Henry, stalks up the stairs.

"Come on." Sam tags Caleb and a few of the others to help him load the Jeep.

A buzz in my back pocket makes me jump.

The burner phone. *Finally.*

I shove the dress Geri's way. "There's a hole in the side."

"Good thing I can sew."

"Great," I say between my teeth. "Patch it up and you can put it with the others to take to the hotel."

She gives me a mock salute. "Will do, sunshine."

I'm already rushing down the hall into one of the empty classrooms. The chairs and couches are vacant, the television on the far wall dark. Gray light from outside slices through the gaps between the curtains as I quickly, quietly close the door behind me.

I press the button to answer.

"Dylan."

"I told you not to call me that," a low, male voice growls from the end of the line.

"Was that before or after you pulled a knife on me? I can't remember."

He snorts. "An inmate at Bennington Max told one of our old ladies you had an offer. Something you'd make worth my while."

My lips curl into a slow smile as I melt into the back of the door. Sam's message to his mom finally worked its way through the pipeline.

"I want to talk about your old friend, Min Belk."

Dylan hesitates only a moment. "You've got my attention."

CHAPTER 30

At three o'clock on the dot, the students of Vale Hall line up against the back wall of a public meeting room at the Sikawa City courthouse. The press has been invited—everyone from Channel 7 to *Pop Store* has a reporter in attendance. They crowd in front of us, turning back to snap pictures every few minutes as we wait for Dr. O to enter the room.

"Keep smiling," says Geri between her teeth.

My cheeks hurt from holding this pose so long, but we have to play the part. Happy, supportive students, dedicated to Dr. O and his new opportunity.

"If she says that again, I'm going to punch her," says Charlotte, on my right.

I roll back my shoulders, the slim black sweater bearing the school's Raven seal on my right breast heavy on my skin. We're all wearing Vale Hall attire today. It's like the pep rally for the Apocalypse.

Beside me, June shifts, uncomfortable in her blazer and skirt, even though they meet the prerequisite black. Ms. Maddox tried, silently, to get her to lighten up on the dark lipstick and mascara, but was clearly unsuccessful. June's dark-eyed glare at the reporters almost makes me proud.

Standing beside her, her arm jerking every time it brushes mine, I can't help but feel sorry for her. Does Dr. O have something on her? What happens to her—to everyone at Vale Hall, Paz and Bea included—if we fail tonight?

No student left behind. Margot—stuck back at Vale Hall with Grayson and Ms. Maddox—once accused me of trying to save everyone, but I never gave June the chance to join us. I didn't tell Paz or Bea what they were getting into when they aligned themselves with Dr. O. Maybe they knew. Maybe they didn't have a choice. But I can't help feeling like I should have tried harder to get to them.

I lean close to June, keeping my voice low.

"Can you get to Paz and Bea?"

June's head snaps my way.

"I know you see everything," I tell her. "I know you know they've been watching me."

She faces forward again, the only acknowledgment of my words a subtle lift of her chin.

"He isn't who they think he is. At the end of the day, he'll try to break them, just like the rest of us."

"What do I do?" she whispers.

"Just . . ." I smile broadly when another photog turns around to snap a picture. "Just tell them to be careful, all right?"

She sucks her top lip into her mouth.

"All rise for Judge Salvatore."

We're already standing, but the press in front of us, as well as those in attendance at the front of the room, rise from their chairs. I can see the mayor's red skirt suit through the crowd, and her daughter, Camille, standing at her side.

I glance a few people down to my left, to Caleb, and see his jaw working back and forth as he stares at Camille's back. I'm sure this is the first time he's seen her in person since he was conning her, and considering how she contracted the Wolves to punish him, she's still likely harboring some resentments.

Let's hope she can move past them.

The back door of the room opens, and a woman in black robes enters. She nods to the bailiff and then picks up a thick Bible from the table at the front of the room.

Dr. O follows after her.

His tie is cinched tight, his gaze serious. He stands where he must have been told to—behind the table. A man and a woman in suits stand behind him—representatives from D.C., Moore told us earlier. Dr. O's new security lurks near the door they just exited, hands low and folded.

My pulse skips faster, until my chest is rising and falling with each breath.

Stop, I want to scream. *You don't know who he is!*

"Dr. David Odin, please place your hand on the Bible."

He does.

It takes less than a minute for the most dangerous man I've ever met to become a U.S. senator.

THE ROSALIND HOTEL looks like it belongs in a black-and-white movie—gorgeous arrangements of flowers pour from giant glass vases. Ornate rugs, thinned to timeless classics, cover the marble floors. Intricate glass chandeliers hang from the ceilings.

Security stands outside the lobby, by the elevators, and at every stairway.

Some of them belong to the hotel, some of them to the two other senators who've been invited to tonight's party. The two assigned to Dr. O I've lovingly named Big Mac and T-Bone. Big Mac looks like he's never eaten carbs in his life. T-Bone's set expression drives a trench so deep between and above his brows that it looks like a capital *T.*

They stick to Dr. O like he's made of Velcro.

Our group splits inside the lobby. The boys commandeer the restroom to change. Dr. O, Big Mac, and T-Bone go upstairs to meet the mayor and Camille, and the other senators in from out of town. The girls are directed to a powder room on the second floor where we're assured our dresses have already been transferred via a movable rack.

Before we part ways, Caleb's hand slips into mine, the slide of his fingers as intimate as any kiss. I look down, just for a moment, to the gray smudges of ink on his thumb, and I make a silent promise to see him on the other side of this night.

If I don't, this will be the only goodbye we have.

The inside of the powder room is warm and smells like lilacs. Large mirrors reflect smiling faces—everyone loves dressing up for a party. Alice and Beth take over the outlet, plugging in flatirons and curlers. Paz's makeup bag slaps against the counter, and music fills the room from a speaker Bea brought. For a moment, I wish I could stay. I wish this were real. It reminds me of Charlotte's birthday party, when we all got dressed up and took a picture in the hall.

"Where's Charlotte?" asks Geri, standing beside the rack, her hand on a gown covered in a plastic sheath.

"Helping Sam with the last delivery of champagne and cider, I think," I respond.

"I thought Henry was doing that." Paz uses the mirror to line her eyes with a black pencil.

Bea, standing behind her, meets my gaze in the reflection, then quickly turns away.

"I don't know." I dig into my zip-up dress bag, which is substantially larger than the rest. There's no dress within. Instead, threaded through the hanger is Henry's lucky leather coat and Caleb's old ball cap. Careful to keep the contents hidden, I remove both, stuffing them under my arm, then covertly drop my Vale Hall–issued phone in the bottom so I won't be tracked. "They should be downstairs by now. I'll go check."

"Paz, here's your dress." June shoves the plastic-wrapped gown in Paz's direction, knocking her makeup to the floor.

"Oops," June says, as Bea kneels to help her clean it up. I send June a silent *thanks*.

They're so distracted they don't even see me leave.

Outside the powder room, I slip on the hat and turn in the opposite direction, along a hall that runs on the exterior of the ballroom. At the end is a door that will lead down a back stairway to the side street between the Rosalind and the parking garage.

Before I reach it, a man steps out of one of the ballroom exits.

Moore's hand reaches into his pocket and retrieves a set of keys. Without slowing, I snag them, glancing down at my palm to find a folded knife among the glinting metal.

My stomach gives a sharp twist.

"I need you to wrap up whatever you've got going on," he snaps into his phone. "Brynn's off the grid. Odin wants you to take care of it."

I hesitate at the back door and slip on Henry's coat, placing the knife in the pocket. The cool leather collar brushes against my neck. It smells like Henry's cologne.

"No, he's in a meeting. If he wanted to talk to you, you'd be talking to him. He told me to call."

Moore turns away, and I shove through into the cold cement stairwell. My heart is pounding as I run down the steps toward the parking garage behind the pool. Memories of a different day flood through me. Grayson's Porsche. His confession about killing Susan by accident.

I shove them aside. There's only room for tonight now.

The black sedan is parked on the first level, spot 18A, which Moore reserved when we booked the room. Keeping my head low, I jog toward it, and am inside with the engine growling a moment later.

I check my mirrors, just like Moore taught me. Then I pull out of the spot, out of the garage, out of the safe reach of my friends.

There's no turning back now.

CHAPTER 31

The entrance to the Wednesday Pharmaceuticals warehouse is closed at night, raised spikes across the driveway promising to pop any car's tires that dare to pass. A high, chain-link fence stretches around the property's circumference. The back gate, where the trucks pull in to make deliveries, is guarded by a security officer, two well-aimed cameras, and motion sensor lights.

But on the south side, there's a drainage ditch with a cement tube wide enough for a man like Pete to crawl through and cut a permanent gap in the interior grate.

This is my entry point.

Hugging Henry's coat tight to my body, I run from the safety of the car, parked at the apartment complex across the street, to the ditch. It's dark already, but my path falls under the dull glow of Wednesday's floodlights, positioned on the top corners of the building. I keep the hat pulled low over my eyes, slowing once I reach the weeds that consume the land up to the parking lot on the opposite side of the fence.

My blood is pumping as I pause to catch my breath.

Why didn't you pay off the gate guard?

Can't erase the video footage, Pete had said with a grimy smirk. *This isn't the movies.*

I stare into the dark at the cement tube ahead, probably filled with black widow spiders and rats and who knows what else.

One more breath, and I run for it.

I'm aware of every crunch my shoes make over the snow and frozen weeds. Of the growing darkness as the ditch deepens. The cement circle rises before me, and I'm struck by a sudden, suffocating claustrophobia.

Don't feel. Don't fail.

I chant this in my head as my steps drive me forward, and I have to crouch through the tight space.

Don't feel. Don't fail.

I feel down the cold cement wall, one hand stretched before me. I bump the grate hard enough to bruise my knuckles and feel for the gap.

Be here. Be here. Be here.

The rough edge of the metal dips beneath my palm. It's lower than I thought. I squeeze through. How did Pete, short, but thicker than me, manage this with bags full of pills?

Once I've cleared the grate, I'm running toward the light. With a huge gasp, I erupt from the other side, nearly colliding with a dumpster. Sneaking around it, I take a moment to get my bearings.

Front entrance to my left. Loading dock to the right.

Hunching low, I make for the loading dock, running alongside the brick exterior. My thoughts turn to Caleb, and Geri, and Moore. The party will be beginning soon. Geri can only cover for me for so long before Paz and Bea get suspicious.

They're already suspicious.

I can't worry about that now.

At the edge of the building, I pause, peering around the corner to the cement lot, and the line of pull-down doors, all shut for the night.

The second garage is the one you want. It's between two video feeds.

Keeping my burner phone, the one I save to contact Caleb, tucked close against my side, I check the time. 6:17 P.M. Guests will be entering the party now—officials from all over the city. Lawmakers, wealthy business owners, unsuspecting friends of the master con himself. The students will be escorting them to their tables. Camille Santos would have seen Caleb at the swearing-in ceremony. Will she try to confront him? Blow his cover?

He knows to keep off the radar.

My fingers drum a pattern against my thigh.

6:20.

6:21.

"Come on," I whisper.

On cue, one of the motion sensor lights far down the fence, beside the back exit, snaps on. My breath catches. I wait.

A guard in a blue uniform exits the back door on the opposite side of the docks, fifty feet away. In his hand is a black walkie-talkie. His bald head is illuminated by the floodlight directly overhead.

It's time.

As he makes his way toward the light on the fence, I stride quickly through the shadows toward the second dock. The door is sealed with an electronic lockbox. I type in the code: 1111.

They always keep it the same, Pete said. *Changing guards can never remember what it is otherwise. That's what my buddy always said.*

Pete's buddy—an old guard here that's since been fired.

Let's hope the current staff can stay distracted until I get inside.

The numbers light up red.

Teeth grinding together, I try it again: 1111.

Red.

"No." Pete did not get me this far just to screw me over.

I try it again, but nothing.

Sweat breaks out on my hairline, dripping down the back of my neck. 2222, I try. 3333. I keep going, checking every few seconds for the guard.

"Work," I demand. *"Work."*

9999.

The box clicks. I can hear the guard talking. The hiss of a radio, too close for comfort. I yank open the garage door with all my might, cringing at the metallic groan it makes, and roll into the warehouse. The door settles with what must be a deafening thud behind me. I'm bathed in darkness.

Up. Get up!

I jolt to a crouch, Pete's directions roaring through my mind.

Straight shot to the first row. Don't step off the line on the floor. You'll be between two camera feeds.

The door on the opposite side of the dock clicks. I don't have time to whip out the burner phone for light—I can't risk drawing the attention anyway. I race down the pale line on the floor into the black void ahead, hands outstretched, until I collide with a metal shelf.

As the lights turn on, I cut to the side and dive into an aisle.

The harsh overheads bring spots to my vision. I force my eyes open, cramming myself into the smallest compartment at the bottom shelf. Frantically, I take in the sights around me. Shelves, twenty feet high. Boxes—some small enough to carry, others packed in wooden planked crates. A forklift sits to my left.

A *W* for Wednesday is stamped onto every cardboard surface.

Footsteps squeak across the cement ground. I hold my breath.

Static hisses from a radio. *"You see anything?"* comes a voice from the other end of the line.

The boots stop.

My chest feels like it's about to explode.

"Nah. Must have just been animals out by light thirty-seven. I didn't see anyone."

Another hiss of static.

"Roger that."

The boots roll away.

I wait until a door squeaks open, and shut, and the lights overhead go dark again. And then I exhale hard.

On shaky legs, I stand, the blood pounding in my ears as I strain to hear anyone coming. I can't believe Pete did this so many times. He had help—someone to turn off the cameras. He was arrogant enough to think he couldn't still get caught.

I am not so delusional.

Using the light from my phone, I crawl from my hiding place and begin searching the boxes.

Blue label, Pete said. *Those are the narcotics. Aisle four.*

Red labels. Yellow labels. More white than anything. I run around the end of the shelf to the next aisle. Panic brings the bile up my throat.

Finally, blue.

My phone begins to buzz in my pocket. I'm out of time. I need to get out.

I jerk back the line of tape over the top and peel back the cardboard. Inside, heavy plastic surrounds thick bags of pills.

I just need one, but I grab the whole box, just to be sure.

Without delay, I run toward the second garage door, the heavy box clutched to my chest. I'm careful to keep to the line on the floor that the forklifts follow when they load the trucks, the line between the camera feeds, but my phone is buzzing again. Two calls is urgent. Two calls means there's trouble.

When I'm pressed against the garage door, I hit the button to open it.

This time, I don't bother waiting, or closing it after me.

I jump down from the loading dock and run toward the nearest gate—the back gate, now open, a black car parked halfway through. Its lights are bright, making silhouettes of the two men striding toward me.

One is a guard.

The other is Min Belk.

"There she is!" Belk shouts, and begins sprinting toward me.

Panicking, I drop the box and run in the opposite direction, toward the dumpster and the drainage ditch. My legs pump beneath me. A yellow flashlight cuts across the ground, across my eyes as I turn back.

With a cry, I trip on the embankment of weeds and go sprawling forward. The cold graveled ground bites into my palms. My knees crack against the dirt, sending bolts of pain up my legs.

Belk is on me in seconds.

"Get up," he growls. His giant hands grip me roughly around the shoulder and the side of my waist.

This is too soon. I needed more time. How long was I inside the warehouse? How did he get here so fast? He must have left Vale Hall as soon as Moore called him and told him I was missing.

Frantic thoughts beat against my skull. *Get away*, they scream. *Fight. Run.* I have the knife. I feel it in my pocket. *Not yet. Not yet.*

I go limp in his hold. I make him carry me like a rag doll.

It takes time. A few more precious minutes. I hope it's enough.

The guard is yelling at him. Another is outside running toward us. Belk is explaining it's not their problem. He tells them not to call the police. He says he's private security for the company's owner.

He throws me into the front seat of the car and before he closes the door, whispers, "Run. I dare you."

I don't run.

The two guards look at each other blankly. They don't even look at the open garage behind them.

They don't realize how long they've left the back gate unattended.

"Did you think I wouldn't find you here?" He berates me as we back out of the entrance to the warehouse and onto the dark street. "I told you before. I tracked that Jeep. Teenagers never lis—"

As he turns the car, the movement ahead cuts his tirade short. The Jeep is parked on the road facing the opposite direction. Sam is standing by the headlights, a box with a blue *W* stamped on the cardboard siding, clear as day.

"Where did they—"

"Get in!" Charlotte's shriek cuts through the windows of Belk's car.

Sam throws the box into the back, slams the door, and jumps into the open passenger side.

"Did you think I was stupid enough to come here alone?" I ask as the Jeep speeds away.

Belk doesn't answer. His teeth flash in the dark as his lips curl back in a tight grimace.

My head smashes against the back of the seat as he slams his foot down on the gas, and we race after my friends.

CHAPTER 32

I'm supposed to be in that car, I think as Charlotte's red lights swing around the bend in the road. *We were supposed to be together.*

Plans have changed.

I glance at Belk, finding glistening beads of sweat now clinging to the stray hairs of his blunt ponytail and the wisp of his mustache.

I slide my hand into my hip pocket, my fingers closing around the folded knife Moore passed me in the Rosalind hallway. My heart is tripping in my chest. I'm not going to die tonight. I'm not. I refuse.

The Jeep swerves around another turn, and a small cry bursts from my throat. Charlotte's driving recklessly. We're close enough that I can see the boxes in the back of the Jeep slide to the opposite side.

"Where is she going?" Belk demands.

"How am I supposed to know?"

He's going too fast for me to jump out—not that I would now. I won't leave my friends behind.

Each second measures my pulse. Shops with barred windows flash by—a quick cash lender, a pawnshop, a gas station. People on the sidewalk stare at us without surprise. A car chase is just another night in White Bank.

"Slow down! You're going to run them over!" I press back against the seat as if that will put more distance between the Jeep and Belk's car.

Belk ignores me, his eyes trained on the road.

The road Charlotte takes tears away into the dead area of town. Abandoned warehouses tagged with graffiti give way to glassy black river and patches of dirty snow, dull in the moonlight.

Just a little farther. We can make it.

My eyes dart to the clock on the dash: 6:48 P.M. At the party, appetizers are being served. Mayor Santos will be preparing her welcome remarks.

A little farther.

An upside-down speed limit sign on the right side of the road flashes white as Charlotte's lights hit it. The Jeep jerks left, then barrels off the asphalt, as if she's trying to avoid something in the street. Gravel sprays behind the tires as she slams to a halt.

"Something's wrong," I say as Belk pulls off behind her.

"Yes, it is." He pulls the keys from the ignition. A gun flashes in his waistband as he opens his door, turning my blood cold. "Get out."

Frantically, I search for movement through the window, but there is no one around. No people. No lights. This area is deserted.

If Belk kills us, no one will know.

I reach for the handle, cold beneath my clammy hand. The clock on the dash says 6:54. Is this the last minute of my life?

I force myself to exit the car. Ahead, Sam gets out of the passenger side, closest to us. His hands are raised above his head.

"We just want to talk," he says.

"Everyone in the car, get out!" barks Belk.

The frigid air scrapes against my face, my neck. I grip the knife in my pocket, sliding it down to my side. I open it, feeling the cold, thin blade against my palm. Ten feet stand between me and Belk. I edge closer.

Out of view, the driver's side door clicks open.

"Stay in the car!" Sam shouts at Charlotte.

"That's not what I said." Belk opens his coat. Flashes his gun.

I step closer.

"Go, Charlotte," Sam pleads, quietly enough to make my hair stand on end.

From the distance comes a rumble, like thunder.

Belk removes the weapon, aiming it toward the ground as casually as if he were holding a cooking spoon. Sam's hands stretch higher.

"If she goes anywhere, it's on you," Belk says. "You ready for that, Sam?"

The rumble grows louder. From behind Belk's car comes a pin-prick of light.

"Are you?" I ask Belk, as the dot of light broadens, then doubles. "How are you going to explain what's happening here to witnesses?"

Belk glances back, a sneer pulling at his lips. The roar is deafening now. I can barely hear myself think.

The two lights aren't headlights; they're too widely spaced. Behind them, more single lights brighten the gloom. A dozen, at least, with others adding to the pack.

Belk quickly tucks the gun away as the lead motorcycle slows. His arm waves in a wide circle as he ushers the rider forward.

The rider pulls off.

"Car trouble?" a man asks. His face is obscured by the bright light as he props his bike onto a kickstand.

"Nothing to concern yourself with," Belk calls back. "Just dealing with some troublesome teenagers."

One by one, the bikes stop. They don't bother pulling off the road. They block the street, the pop and grumble of their engines filling the night.

I raise a hand to deflect the glare as the front rider steps forward.

"Nothing worse than troublesome teenagers," he says. As he moves around the bike, a dangerous smirk carves into the shadows across his face.

"Hi, Charlie," I say. Sam approaches beside me, blowing out a hard sigh.

"A little close, don't you think?" he mutters.

We're all ahead of schedule. I don't find this necessary to mention to Charlie.

"Brynn," says Charlie, his hair windblown and wild. His black leather cut bears his name on the right corner. I don't have to see the back to know the wolf will be there, howling at the moon. "Mr. Belk. It's been a while."

"Dylan Prescott?" Belk asks incredulously.

"He has a gun," I inform Charlie.

"So do I," says Charlie. He tilts his head. "So do they. I'd say he's outnumbered."

"What is this?" Belk says. "What do you want, Dylan?"

"It's Charlie now," I offer.

"I'll start with that weapon," says Charlie. "And your phone. I know how you like keeping track of folks with it."

The security guard's eyes bulge. He glances at me. I shrug.

"The Wolves?" he says to Charlie. "You joined a gang?"

Charlie smiles as laughter erupts behind him. "It's not like I wasn't in one before."

Belk goes stone still.

"I'm not going to ask again," Charlie says.

Another moment's hesitation, and Belk lays his gun on the ground. The new phone he got this week follows. He's flustered now, his hands up in surrender, his breath coming in heaves.

"We ended in a rough way," Belk says. "I understand that. I had a job to do. Surely you understand."

"Oh, I understand," says Charlie, retrieving the items off the ground. He passes them to a shadowed figure behind them.

"I can fix this," Belk says. "What do you want? Money?" He reaches for his wallet in his back pocket.

From the darkness comes the telltale click of at least three guns.

Sam and I ease farther off the road, putting more distance between us and Belk.

"Easy," Charlie warns. "No sudden movements."

"It's just my wallet. I can pay you whatever you want!"

"I don't want your money," Charlie says.

"Then what . . . Drugs! *Pills!*" Belk's nodding rapidly now. He points to the Jeep. "The back's filled with Wednesday narcotics. Use them. Sell them. Whatever you want."

My teeth clench tighter.

"Really?" says Charlie. "Let's go see."

They stride toward the back of the Jeep. Charlotte jumps out the front, circling around to Sam and me. As her hands grip her stomach protectively, angry whispers rise from the dark.

"You all right, sweetheart?" a man calls.

Charlotte nods.

Belk pops open the back trunk of the car. Four boxes are stacked there, all with blue *W*'s on the side.

"Ah. This just got interesting." Charlie reaches for the top box and pulls open the lid. He scoffs. "Is this a joke? You always did have a terrible sense of humor, Belk."

"What? There's no joke!" Belk scrambles for the box, pulling open the flaps so hard the cardboard rips. "No. This isn't right . . . this was . . . I saw . . ."

A dark smile pulls at my lips.

For Caleb, I think. *For Margot. For Jimmy.*

For all of us.

Charlie pulls a sleek olive-colored bottle from inside. "Champagne?"

As Belk tips the box to the ground and opens another, Charlie pops the cork with a knife from his belt. It makes a resounding crack in the air, and brings a slew of cheers.

"No," Belk is chanting. "No!" He turns on us, standing near the car. "You did this on purpose!"

"I don't know what you're talking about," says Charlotte, though I distinctly remember her being the one to paint the boxes blue, exactly as Pete had relayed to me, before Sam transferred the bottles Geri needed delivered to the Rosalind into them.

Charlie takes a long swig straight from the bottle.

"They set me up," Belk explains.

"Preaching to the wrong choir," Charlie tells him. He tosses the bottle toward the river, where it shatters against the rocks with a satisfying crash.

He steps closer to Belk.

"Since we're old friends, I'm going to make you a deal," says Charlie, his words hard and scary, like they were in that back room at his party. "Get in your car. I'll give you ten seconds head start."

Belk makes a sound like he's choking.

I close the passenger side door. "Better hurry."

"Clock's ticking!" calls Charlie.

Belk doesn't hesitate another moment. He hurls himself toward the car, slipping on the ground on his way to the door. By the time Charlie's started counting down, Belk's tearing out of the spot, tires squealing as he hits the asphalt.

"Pleasure doing business with you, Brynn," says Charlie, returning to his bike. "You need a favor, you know where to find me."

A favor from a Wolf? I'm not sure what to think of that.

Charlie's bike growls, and in moments, he's leading the pack to the road, gunning it after Belk.

How are you going to save the world, Brynn Hilder? Caleb whispers in the back of my mind.

I have a three-step plan.

Step one, remove those Dr. O trusts from the picture.

CHAPTER 33

Charlotte drives us back to White Bank, but instead of returning to Wednesday's back gate, she circles the property, finding the apartment complex and Moore's black car parked in the back row of the lot.

As we approach, she flashes her brights twice, and the driver's side door opens.

Henry appears a moment later, looking very Bond in his black tuxedo and gelled hair.

"How'd it go?" he asks as we park beside him.

"Oh, you know," Charlotte says as I jog around to the rear of Moore's car. "Brynn got abducted by Belk. Wolves were early. Sam was nearly executed. Just another night in the big city."

Henry cringes. "He's gone, though?"

"Belk?" I nod. "He's gone. When we set this up, Charlie told me that they wouldn't kill him, but he wouldn't be coming back to Sikawa City anytime soon."

I open the trunk, where a full plastic bag of narcotics sits beside three neatly folded garment bags and two crates of sparkling cider.

"Everything go all right on your end?" I ask Henry.

"I tripped the lights on the fence, just like you said." Henry reaches into the back to remove Charlotte's bag as I take the largest one, marked with a capitol *B*. "Then I ran over here to the ditch. It's farther than you cared to mention, by the way. I nearly died. I think I should take up jogging. Get in shape."

"Good plan," says Sam, taking his bag.

"Anyway," I prompt.

"Anyway," Henry continues. "I grabbed the pills you dropped while everyone was distracted at the gate. In and out, easy peasy. Coat looks great on you, by the way."

"It's lucky," I tell him.

"Told you." He winks.

We pile into Moore's car, leaving the Jeep behind. Sam drives. Henry sits shotgun. Charlotte and I take the back seat and furiously strip down to our underwear.

Tulle explodes all around us as I unzip my garment bag.

"Geri thinks she's so funny," I grumble as Charlotte helps me bat it down so I can stuff myself inside. At least she fixed the hole in the side—and added some alterations of her own.

"Really?" Charlotte asks as I slip my feet back into my worn Chuck Taylors.

I grin.

As we drive back into town, Charlotte fixes my hair. When she's got it up in a messy-but-sophisticated knot, she works on hers, and I dig through her makeup bag.

"Coal eyes, dark pink tips on the shadow," she orders. I try to do what she says, but in the end, she takes over, brushing the splash of color across my closed lids.

We pull back into spot 18A at the Rosalind parking garage exactly two hours after we left. Dinner is just ending, and the program will be moving forward into speeches and toasts.

Geri will be keeping everyone to a rigid schedule.

We pile out of the car. The boys grab the crates and hurry toward the front doors, while I grab my silver and black skirts and follow with Charlotte. Inside, the lobby is alive with people moving in and out. A line has formed for the restaurant on the right. We veer the opposite way, to the wide wooden staircase on the left. At the bottom, beside a grandfather clock, Caleb is waiting, and the sight of him sends renewed hope surging through my veins.

As he strides toward us, that hope swells into something warmer. Slim black pants brush over the lean muscles of his thighs. The black jacket hugs his broad shoulders and narrow waist. The crisp white collar and knotted tie draw my eyes to his neck and the hard lines of his jaw.

I bite my lip as his gaze narrows down my body.

"You look like an angry ballerina." His lips quirk. His hand twitches at his side.

Maybe it's just adrenaline raising the temperature in my veins, but I'm pretty sure the sparks between us could start fires.

"So *that's* how babies are made," says Henry.

"Just about," mutters Charlotte.

Sam's already climbing the steps.

"We good?" asks Caleb. He knows I'll fill him in on the details later.

"We're good."

But at the top of the stairs, we're stopped by T-Bone, who's got the gall to wear his sunglasses even though we're inside. My breath catches as he blocks our path. I grip my skirts tighter in my fists and set my expression to surprise.

"Floor's closed for a private party. Take the elevator, please."

"We *are* the party," Charlotte says. "We go to Vale Hall."

T-Bone's mouth twitches. He points to the crates. "What are those?"

"Champagne and cider for the toasts," Sam says. "We're running behind. Got stuck in traffic."

"I'll have to take a look." He taps an earpiece. "We've got five students here. Say they're from Vale—"

"Finally!" From the ballroom's double doors bursts Geri, her classy A-line dress swinging around the straps of her spiked heels. "The staff's about to start pouring for the toasts. Come on! What are you waiting for?"

T-Bone steps back, hands folded in front of him. Clearly, Geri's already established dominance.

I exchange a *that was close* look with Caleb as we're ushered around the corner of the ballroom, toward a door marked "Employees Only."

"Is he ready?" I ask Geri quietly.

"He's got some notes on the 'script,'" she air quotes, "but I think he'll manage."

If anyone can, it's an Emmy Award–winning actor.

Geri shoves through the door without hesitation, making room for Charlotte, Sam, and Henry behind her. Inside the bright lights and silver countertops are a stark contrast to the classy, deep colors of the hall, and the music from the ballroom thumps over the clatter of dishes and shouted orders of the staff. In the back of the room, a woman in a pink suit is dimming the lights in the ballroom beyond, at a set of switches the size of a circuit breaker board.

"Good luck," Geri says quickly, and the door swings closed behind them.

Taking my hand, Caleb pulls me across the hall. A few quick turns, and we've reached the emergency exit—a concrete stairway that smells vaguely of pine cleaner, and is marked by red signs pointing to the ground floor. I start to climb up the steps, but he grabs my hand and whips me toward him. The momentum makes me crash against his chest, and in an instant, his lips are on mine, urgent and hungry. One hand finds the small of my back, dragging me closer, while the other skims my bare shoulder.

I'm burning up.

His touch sears my skin. Heat spills through my chest. I kiss him back hard, lips and teeth and tongues. Need shatters fear. Desire burns away doubt.

Then I bite the corner of his mouth and draw back.

His breath is rough, his eyes dark.

He smiles.

"Now that that's out of the way," he says, straightening his jacket.

I wipe away the lipstick on his mouth with my thumb. A small growl slips from his throat.

It tells me this is far from over.

"Right," I say. "Upstairs?"

"Upstairs."

We go upstairs.

On the landing to the second floor, our pace slows. One hand on the door, he rolls back his shoulders, a soldier preparing for battle. I rest my palm between his shoulder blades—enough pressure to remind him I'm here. That he's got this.

He pushes into the hall.

This corridor is not unlike those downstairs. Long, worn rugs stretch down wooden floors. Small sconces cast dim lighting over the classic art on the walls. Doors to each room sit on either side of the hall. A man in a black suit waits outside one, staring blankly toward the elevator bank in front of him.

Quietly, Caleb and I slip around the corner. Retrieving his phone from his pocket, he sends a quick text, and less than a minute later, the guarded door opens and a girl's high voice calls, "Angelo? Can you crack the window for me? It's a little stuffy in here, and I can't reach the latch."

We peek around the corner just as the security guard goes into the room.

Moving fast, we stride down the hall. Caleb slides a room key from his breast pocket, stopping in front of the door beside the one the guard was just outside. He slides it into the lock, which clicks, and we enter.

It's quaint, but classy, with a gray comforter on a giant bed and a cherry-stained desk topped with old books.

"Remind you of anything?" I ask, my fingertips dancing over the comforter.

His jaw tightens, and I know he's thinking of Baltimore too.

In the hall, a door nearby opens, and we both freeze. The security guard is back in the hall.

Our room has a door that connects the adjacent suite—the one he is guarding. It opens inward, and a girl in a white dress, fastened around the waist with a silver ribbon, steps toward us.

"Hi, Camille," Caleb says, a little stiffly.

Nerves prickle along my arms. I remind myself Camille Santos is a survivor of Dr. O's games too—her mother would never have been investigated for taking bribes from the Wolves if Dr. O hadn't wanted it—but all I can think of is Caleb's face, bloodied and bruised, from the retaliation Camille ordered on him.

"Ryan." Her skin is flawless, her heart-shaped lips painted pink to match her shoes and her rose necklace. Her dark hair is twisted into a perfect knot on the base of her neck.

There is a dark, unhealed anger in her eyes.

I blink. *Ryan* was Caleb's alias when he was working her. *Ryan Ikeda.*

"I'm Brynn," I say. There's no point in giving her a different name now. We're too far in.

"Great," she says flatly, then turns back to Caleb. "You have it?"

I nod, having forgotten that all these skirts are bunched in my hands for a reason. Geri may have gone overkill when I told her I'd need something loose, but it's served the purpose.

I reach beneath the splash of black, into the pocket against my thigh that Geri's sewn in, and remove the full bag of Wednesday pills. I've already cleaned off any fingerprints in the car, and am careful to keep the fabric between my hand and the plastic.

Camille's eyes widen. She wipes her palms on her hips.

"You know what to do?" I ask.

She nods. Steps forward. Takes the bag. It's heavier than she must think, because her hands bob under the weight.

Caleb moves closer, hands now in his pockets. He fixes his glasses. "Are you sure you're all right with this?"

"Of course," she says harshly. "I'm not delicate, as you well know."

Caleb nods slowly.

"I'm sorry," he says. "I never meant for it to come to this."

For a moment, her hard exterior thins, and her posture slumps the tiniest bit. "I just want it to be over. I want David gone."

"Me, too," I say. I feel for her then. She doesn't deserve to be punished for her mother's mistakes. Now Dr. O is blackmailing their family again—making the Wolves bribery situation disappear in exchange for her mother appointing him as senator. I'm sure both Mayor Santos and her daughter are wondering where it will end.

I know where it ends. I saw it in a run-down apartment in Bakerstown.

That's why we have to stop him, *tonight*.

Camille straightens. "Goodbye, Ryan."

"Thank you," Caleb says.

She leaves the room, closing the door softly behind her. In somber silence, we wait, finally hearing the ding of an elevator down the hall.

Quick, light footsteps sound beyond the hallway door. Angelo mutters a curt "Ma'am."

The main entrance of mayor's suite opens. Caleb and I move to the door between the rooms, our ears pressed against the wood.

"What's wrong, *mi amor*?" Mayor Santos rushes across the room, the quiet creak of the floor beneath her feet.

Camille's harsh sob is followed by a flood of confession.

"He put these in my purse at the party. He said someone would be coming to get them!" Her voice hitches. "What is this? Are you on drugs, Mama?"

"No!" Mayor Santos says. "Who did this? Who was this man?"

"I don't know! He had a ponytail! He was mean-looking. I don't know!"

I glance at Caleb, impressed at her casual description of Belk. Camille wouldn't make a half-bad hustler.

"David Odin is behind this, I know it!" Mayor Santos lets loose a growl that would rival a bear's. "It's okay, *mi amor*. This ends tonight. No more extortion. I'm calling that man at the FBI back."

The FBI? My eyes widen. Caleb's teeth flash beside me.

"But, Mama—"

"No," Mayor Santos says sharply. "Odin sends someone to my daughter? He has messed with the wrong woman. *Angelo!* Angelo, get in here!"

The outside door to their room clicks, and without a word, Caleb and I race to the stairway exit.

CHAPTER 34

Caleb and I enter the ballroom through the kitchen doors, smoothly snagging glasses of sparkling cider from a nearby server. Circular tables fill the room, covered with draping white cloths and crystal vases filled with roses. Three hundred people were invited tonight—I know, because Geri made Bea and Paz handwrite the invitations—and at least fifty of them have press passes dangling around their necks. Attire ranges from business to ball gown, and the room reeks of wealth.

On a stage erected in the back of the room, I spot Dr. O. He's talking to a young man in a white tux, which somehow doesn't look ridiculous with all the swagger oozing off him. T-Bone and Big Mac stand off to the side. Below, a dozen photographers are snapping candid pictures of the two laughing.

My stomach tightens.

I take a sip of cider, starting as the bubbles glide over my tongue. Not cider. Champagne.

"Don't drink it," I tell Caleb as I take another sip. "Little-known fact. Some Japanese people lack the enzyme to process alcohol."

He smirks at me and sets the glass down on a nearby table. When he steps behind me and his hands find my waist, my thoughts return to the stairway, and the promise in his eyes.

I take another sip.

"Ladies and gentlemen." Geri's voice, amplified by a microphone, fills the room. Gradually, conversation begins to break off, until all attention is pointed at the pixie standing behind the podium. She smiles broadly, brushing her dark, side-swept bangs out of her eyes.

"Our next speaker is someone a few of you may know from a little show called *Kings of*—" Before she can even finish, cheers have erupted across the room. The response is so deafening, Damien breaks out laughing, and runs up beside Geri to sling an arm around her shoulders.

"Oh, so you've heard of him?" Geri gives a cute smile, Damien's white tux even brighter against her black dress. "Well, what you may not know is that Damien Fontego is actually a Vale Hall alum. Dr. Odin—I mean, *Senator* Odin—"

This gets a few cheap laughs and leads me to take another sip of champagne.

"—was one of Damien's first champions. He recognized Damien's talent immediately, and helped him to refine the skills that would lead him to Broadway, and the silver screen. Damien now serves on the board for Vale Hall, and helps current students whenever he's able, isn't that right, Damien?"

She flashes him a grin.

His arm lowers from her shoulders. His dimples do not falter.

Behind him, Dr. O's arms cross over his chest.

"Always," Damien says.

Maybe it's wishful thinking, but I swear his gaze meets mine across the room.

"Damien's here to make an announcement as part of our celebration, so without further ado, I present to you *Damien Fontego!*"

"I think we should find better seats, don't you?" Caleb whispers in my ear. His lips press a chaste kiss against my bare shoulder.

"Absolutely," I say.

We wind through the crowd, heading toward the front tables, where the Vale Hall students are seated. June's sitting opposite Bea, biting her thumbnail. Standing behind a row of reporters, Charlotte, Henry, and Sam are sipping cider from their glass flutes. Margot's at home with Grayson and Ms. Maddox tonight. Apparently she couldn't be trusted in a public forum after the whole trying-to-shoot-the-director thing.

"Welcome back," says Charlotte.

I give her a winning smile.

Upstairs, I imagine Camille and her mother plotting their own takedown of Dr. O.

As the applause subsides, Damien stands before the mic. His hands rest easily on the sides of the podium, and he tilts forward the slightest bit. He seems more comfortable in front of all these people than he was with just a few of us, alone in his trailer.

"Thank you," he says. "Thank you very much. Yes, Senator O and I go way back. When I applied to Vale Hall, I was just another kid getting tossed around the foster care system. No steady home. No future. Vale Hall was just another application I filled out on my quest to find another job in food service, or demolition—anything that would take me." Damien pauses, head drooping, the pain in his tone pushing even me to the balls of my feet. "But when Dr. O brought me in, my life changed. He took a poor kid from the system and gave him a home, a *family*. A shot at being something more."

My mind slips to three days ago, when Damien made a surprise visit to Vale Hall. Geri had invited him to speak, and as he told the other fawning students, he didn't turn down an opportunity to help the man who gave him everything.

It was later, after dinner, that I found the note in my pocket to meet in the garden.

He promised if I helped you I'd end up with a trailer full of pills and a stint in rehab.

So what are you doing here? I'd asked, still unsure if I could trust him.

His smile was all dimples.

Making sure that doesn't happen.

"David Odin is a man who believes in people's futures, which is why his parting gift to Vale Hall is a scholarship fund, dedicated to the students he's believed so much in."

He pauses for applause, tilting his head to Dr. O, behind him, who's grinning through his own confusion.

Damien waits for the crowd to quiet. "The Jimmy Balder fund was created to honor a young intern who died before his political dreams could be achieved."

Dr. O's face pales. His body goes rigid, and in the dim light I can see the bulge of a vein in his neck.

The clicking of cameras and the flashes of light remind him to smile, but his hands stay bunched at his sides.

When he looks down at us, standing in the front row to cheer him on, I give a small, slow wave.

His eyes go cold as an Arctic winter.

Damien doesn't look at the script I wrote—he's probably already memorized the lines. "Jimmy Balder was a hard worker, and a dedicated public servant. And for that, the first presentation of the scholarship in his name—the Jimmy Balder Memorial Fund—will be awarded to a senior who has shown exemplary fortitude in academics, and a strong interest in serving the young people of her community. She's going to be a lawyer, ladies and gentleman. I give you Charlotte Murphy!"

Charlotte's hands, raised to clap, drop to her sides. Her face goes scarlet. She looks to Sam, and then to me and Caleb, confusion giving way to well-acted shock.

"Go!" I prompt her, because Geri's now delivered Damien a comically large check for two hundred thousand dollars made out in Charlotte's name.

She runs to the stage to collect the check as everyone cheers, and if she hears the rise of whispers as her hand rests on her belly, she doesn't falter.

Even if it's part of the act, I love her more for that.

Dr. O's face has turned a dangerous shade of scarlet. His smile is razor thin, his jaw is tight enough to crack teeth. *The whole room knows Jimmy's name now,* I think, and I wish Margot was here to see this.

Their futures depend on you, Dr. O told me.

I haven't forgotten.

"You ready?" Caleb whispers in my ear.

Nerves thrum through my body like electrical currents. I have never been so ready for anything in my life.

I head toward the stage, keeping my eyes on Dr. O, who is watching me with a vindictive heat in his glare.

He's still smug, even now.

He has so much more to lose.

"Now, to announce tonight's guest of honor, I give you another of Vale Hall's most likely to succeed, Brynn Hilder!" Damien holds out a hand to help me up the steps. I'm careful with my gown, not wanting to trip and make a fool of myself.

As I reach the top of the stairs, I glance to a clock on the back wall.

8:27 P.M.

On the podium, my blue note cards are sitting in a pile under a sticky note that says *BRYNN*. I move it aside and glance over my own handwriting, nerves fluttering through me.

"Good even—" The sound of my own voice echoing off the walls makes me startle. I pull back a little from the microphone as my friends snicker in the front row.

All except Caleb, who's not taking his eyes off the director.

"Sorry," I say. "I'm not as good at this whole public speaking thing as Damien."

Chuckles erupt from the dark room. I give my best smile, but it falters as I catch movement in the audience. A girl in a black dress, her dark hair swept into a braid over her shoulder. She meets my gaze for only a moment before she disappears into the crowd.

Margot.

My mouth goes dry. Margot isn't part of the plan. She's supposed to be at school now, locked in her room like Grayson. What is she doing here? We can't chance a replay of what went down during Dr. O's meeting downtown with the mayor.

I search for her again, but see no one who resembles her. Did I make it up? My gaze lands on Caleb's, and when I nod to the audience, he turns, searching for anything off.

There's no pressing *pause* now.

"Good evening," I begin again, my voice unsteady. *Get it together, Brynn.* "When I met Dr. O I thought I had it all figured out. I was going to make some money. Go to college. Get out of Sikawa City and never look back." I pause. The room is too quiet. The photographers keep snapping pictures. As Dr. O comes beside me, my palms go damp with sweat.

Charlotte's gaze finds mine. She gives an encouraging nod.

"The only problem," I continue, my voice stronger, "is those dreams aren't a reality for everyone. At least they weren't for me until I met Dr. O."

Dr. O moves closer, until our arms are almost brushing. Caleb's facing me again, his brows drawn in confusion. When I look back through the crowd, I don't see Margot. I don't see anyone moving, or trying to hide.

She isn't here. I must have mistaken someone else for her.

I blow out a tense breath.

"He promised me a future. The same future he promises everyone. A scholarship if I worked hard. He said I was special—that I was wanted at Vale Hall. No one had ever told me anything like that."

I look to Dr. O, standing straighter at my side.

The muscles around one of his eyes twitch.

"He changed my life. Like Damien, he made me part of a family. He taught me to believe in things I never really thought were possible."

An involuntary grief pangs through my chest. I don't feel stupid anymore for believing him. Instead I'm sad for the girl who put so much faith in someone else to solve her problems.

In the back of the room, I catch sight of Moore, standing near the exit. He lifts his hand in a small wave—a show of support to anyone watching.

I refocus on my note cards, flipping to the next to find my place.

"A friend recently told me that if you give something hate, you give it power." I picture Marcus, and stand tall. "I didn't understand that at first, but I think I do now, thanks to Dr. O. I hated Sikawa City for holding me back, but I realize now that it was only me standing in my own way." I swallow, looking up for Moore again, but finding him missing. The crowd before me is shifting, and my eye catches a reporter, standing near Caleb, who elbows the photographer beside him. They point into the sea of people, then hurriedly check their phones.

I lift my chin. "This is my home, and it's worth fighting for. It's worth making better, and defending at any cost. Dr. O taught me to never give up, and for that, I can't thank him enough. So before I give you our esteemed senator, I'd like to present him with a gift on behalf of all the students he's saved over the years."

I glance to Dr. O. Geri suggested a hug, but I can't manage it.

Instead, I hold out my hand, and he takes it, just as he did the first day I met him in his office.

"A gift," he says quietly. "You shouldn't have."

He has no idea.

I lean back toward the microphone.

"If you've ever been in Dr. O's office, you'll know he keeps a beautiful painting over the fireplace—of a woman he talks rarely about, but who is known by many of us as his sister."

Dr. O's hand clenches mine so hard I wince. It takes effort to pull away smoothly, to keep my composure for the audience. I want this part over with as much as I want it to last as slowly and painfully as possible.

"Susan Griffin," I continue, a dark thrill running through me at the sight of Dr. O's paling face, and the sweat that is now running down his temples. "Our director's confidante and friend. His only surviving family."

Another reporter before us is talking to the first, and vying for a better position—not to see me, but to see who is parting the crowd.

"As some of you may know," I continue, my words faster now, keeping pace with the tempo of my racing heart, "she died in a car accident a few years ago—one many people believe to have been caused by Dr. O's predecessor, Senator Matthew Sterling."

"What are you—" Dr. O starts, but his growl is stopped short as a woman in a pale pink gown appears below the stage, her hair tied in a sleek knot at the base of her neck. She's assisted by people standing on either side of her. An older woman in a matronly eggplant dress on her left, a large bag clutched to her side. A girl in a sleek black halter top and skirt on her right.

Ms. Maddox and Margot.

I flinch, expecting one of them but not the others. Ms. Maddox is a spy. She's in Dr. O's pocket. She was supposed to be at Vale Hall with Margot.

But Ms. Maddox is scowling at the director, her lips set in a disapproving frown I've never seen. And as my worried gaze meets Margot's, she nods, as if to tell me this is all part of the plan.

Her lips mouth three words. *I got her.*

Ms. Maddox. How this is possible, I don't know, but it doesn't matter now. If Ms. Maddox has been turned, she poses an insurmountable threat to the director. She knows things that would bury him.

As I watch, she opens the bag at her side, revealing a stack of file folders.

Our student files. My name is on one. Caleb's is on another. Margot's. Charlie's. Raf. All the people we've lost. All the people he's blackmailed.

She had access to the safe in case there was a security breach.

She's holding the evidence we exist, even after Dr. O erases us, in her hands.

I press my shaking fists to my sides.

I got her.

Now, we've got him.

Ms. Maddox isn't just holding our identities. Those files contain our secrets. Pressure points the director has used to blackmail us. If she takes those to the police, it won't take long to find a path of missing people.

Dr. O's stare shoots from his sister to our housekeeper. A muscle twitches in his neck as he realizes his old secret-keeper may not have been as secure as he thought. She doesn't have to say a word. The files are enough to show him he's lost his oldest ally.

It was Grayson's idea to convince Dr. O it wouldn't be suitable for him to be present at tonight's event. He was home alone with Margot and Ms. Maddox when Belk took the call to chase me down at the Wednesday Pharmaceuticals warehouse. Grayson was supposed to slip the housekeeper another sweet-dreams sedative, then use the security code from Moore to break into Dr. O's house to get Susan, so she could appear at our gala, alive, ready to uncover one of the biggest scandals in Sikawa City history. But clearly something changed, because Susan's entourage is more than I expected.

"I am happy to say," I go on, over the voices now rising in the room, "that Susan survived that night, and that we found her for you, so that you could be reunited, and heal the way we have under your care at Vale Hall."

I give my brightest smile as the crowd erupts with questions and accusations. Margot is grinning in my direction, making my chest fill with pride. I consider a bow, but think that might be too much.

Beside me, Dr. O is frozen, locked in place by Susan and Ms. Maddox's punishing glares. I motion him forward to give a speech, but he doesn't move—not until the photographers start taking his picture. The burst of flashes send a shudder through him.

"Are you really Susan Griffin?" a reporter calls out.

Susan's gaze finds mine, and I get the sense she's ready for whatever they're about to throw her way.

"I'm Susan Griffin," she says. "And there are a few things you should know about my brother before you place your trust in him." She steps closer to the podium. "Including how far he will go to make those who threaten him, disappear."

Whispers spark like flames on dry leaves.

Again, my eyes turn to our silent housekeeper. This feels too good to be true.

"I . . ." Dr. O springs to life, jumping to the microphone. "This is . . . unexpected, to say the least. Susan? Is it really you?" He turns to T-Bone, who immediately exits the stage and makes a beeline toward one of the reporters.

The press begin to pepper him with questions, and soon they're shouting above the people behind them, who are talking over each other trying to get answers.

"Is she really your sister, Senator?"

"Dr. Odin, was Matthew Sterling involved with your sister's accident?"

"Susan, why have you been hiding since the accident?"

The last question hangs in the air, and the silence stretching across the room seems to go on for miles.

"She . . ." Dr. O's stare flies across the room, over the reporters. Then it returns, to land on me.

Step two, take away his secrets.

"Thanks for teaching me the importance of family," I tell him.

Without another word, he shoves past me off the stage, and begins to run toward the kitchen exit.

CHAPTER 35

The reporters follow him like an angry mob. Their questions burst over the confusion of the crowd: "Did you have something to do with your sister's disappearance? Have you spoken to Matthew Sterling?" Dishes clatter as people bump into servers. The lit screens of phones wink from a hundred different positions across the room, and in seconds, Susan's statement is being recorded by a dozen different news sources.

"I'm only sorry I didn't come forward sooner. I was afraid, you see. Afraid of what my brother might do . . ."

I race through the reporters after the director while Damien's voice comes through on the microphone. "I'm sorry for the confusion. If everyone could please sit down, I'm sure Susan would be happy to come up to the stage . . ."

I lose the rest as I collide with Caleb, cutting through the crowd toward me. Margot is behind him, having left Susan with Ms. Maddox.

"You see him?" I shout. Above the crowd I catch sight of T-Bone's buzzed head. "There!"

"He'll get out through the kitchen!" Caleb ducks between two photographers with bulky cameras, more mobile in his suit than I am in this stupid dress. Behind him, I catch Henry following close on his heels.

"I'll go around, head him off at the stairs!" shouts Margot, before she disappears toward the ballroom's main entrance.

When it's clear the kitchen door is bottlenecked ahead, I skid to a stop, and turn to the main ballroom entrance where I saw Moore minutes ago. If he's there now, I can't tell. The way is blocked by party attendees in gowns and suits, half of them on their phones.

"Move!" I shout as I push through a group and erupt into the hallway. Across from me is the wide staircase to the first floor. We came up this way earlier—Geri led us around the corner to the kitchen entrance.

I throw myself toward that door, hoping I'm not too late to block him. In case Dr. O bolted, Moore was guarding the front doors, but the kitchen exit was left unattended.

A host of screams comes from the ballroom behind me, and my steps falter. Glancing back, I find a long shadow protruding across the floor from the room, where there was light only seconds before.

He's turned out the ballroom lights from the kitchen switchboard.

He wants to use the cover of darkness to escape.

Or maybe he only wants us to *think* that's what he's doing.

Making a split-second decision, I race toward the kitchen exit, where half a dozen waitstaff in white jackets are spilling into the hall. Am I wrong? Has Dr. O gone the other way? Fear tearing through me, I stall again to spin back, but catch sight of one of the waiters quickly crossing the hall to the stairway Caleb and I took earlier to Camille's room.

His hair is thin, his head down. His pressed pants, fancier than those of the other waiters, end in glossy black shoes.

Dr. O.

I tear after him, jolting sideways just as Big Mac shoves through the waiters and crosses the hall. My teeth clench as I push harder. Will he help Dr. O escape? I can't let that happen.

"Hey!" I shout, trying to get his attention. "Hey, hold on a second!"

He pauses. Looks over his shoulder. I don't know what I'm going to say.

It doesn't matter.

Just then, a girl in a black jumper bursts out the kitchen door. Stumbling over her wide-leg pants, she collides with Big Mac, the flash of her makeup bringing a new wave of fear. The girl in the pink dress behind her trips over them, and the three of them fall in a heap, smashing into one of the waiters.

"*Go,*" Paz shouts as my gait falters. She is on top of the others, clumsily struggling to stand, slowing Big Mac's own attempts to rise.

June appears behind them. She's lifted Big Mac's weapon, and with a grim grin my way is hurrying in the opposite direction.

A nod of thanks is all I can offer. I shove shoulder-first through the hall door, into the stairway, just in time to see a white jacket disappear out the ground-floor exit on the floor below.

He's going out the back of the hotel.

He's getting away.

Hitching up my skirts, I grab the bannister with one hand and launch myself down the last few steps. I stumble, bouncing off the wall, shoving myself around the turn to the last steps.

He's already outside.

Where is Caleb? Henry? Moore? Are they combing through the ballroom, looking for Dr. O? Have they blocked the front entrance of the hotel? I ditched my phone in the powder room so I wouldn't be traced, but now I wish I had something to call my friends.

Yanking down the door handle, I burst outside, the cold air striking my bare shoulders and neck like a cloud of needles. I glance left. Right. My pulse is firing like a machine gun. *Where are you?*

"Pick up," I hear a male voice say near the pool, and veer toward that direction. "Pick up, Belk!"

Dr. O. He must have taken the path toward the parking garage. As I turn the corner, I hear another quiet order to *answer*. He's somewhere behind the lifeguard station—I can't see him in the dark.

"Guess he's busy," I say, hoping I'll startle Dr. O into making enough noise to give away his location. The scuff of shoes against concrete to my left draws my focus, but I've only taken two steps in that direction when someone jumps out from behind the small utility shed beside the stairwell door and grabs me by the hair.

My back slams against Dr. O's side. His forearm closes around my throat, kills the scream before it can leave my lips. He smells like sweat, and fury, and expensive aftershave.

Panic roars between my temples. Its claws dig into my muscles.

I swing my elbow against his side, connecting to the soft flesh below his ribs, and he squeezes tighter.

He drags me forward, down the path. My feet can't find bearing. I scrape at his arm, but it only tightens. Soon, white frames my vision.

The knife is tucked in the bodice of my dress. I reach for it, but his elbow is blocking my way. I'm gagging, sipping each breath through a closing funnel.

"Let go," I manage.

"What did you do with Mr. Belk?" he asks quietly.

Any triumph I'd felt at dismantling Dr. O's regime has come to a slamming halt. Now, all I want is someone to find us.

I suck in a breath to scream, but before I can, he slaps a hand over my mouth.

"I don't think so," he responds. "Come with me. You and I have much to discuss."

Dread scrapes down my spine.

"How did you think this would end?" he hisses as we round the edge of the pool, emptied for winter. My feet scrape off the brick siding. *Shout for help*, I will myself. I can't even suck in enough oxygen to breathe. Police sirens have filled the night. They're coming closer.

I struggle for the knife.

"You ruin me publicly, and then what? I disappear? I fade into the darkness? No, I don't think so, Brynn. I do not break so easily."

His voice is so raw, so warped by fury, it's nearly unrecognizable.

We reach the edge of the pool, hulking close to the ground. Behind us, the emergency exit has opened again, and heavy footsteps are clattering in our direction.

"Here," Dr. O calls quietly.

From the shadows, I see T-Bone approach. From his stiff, low arms the silver barrel of a gun emerges.

I freeze.

"We need to get to the car. Quickly. *Quickly!*" Dr. O orders.

T-Bone rushes toward us. His glasses are gone now, and his dead eyes stare down at me with an emptiness that fills me with terror. He presses one finger to his lips, and quietly says, "Shh."

Dr. O loosens his grip on my throat.

I swallow huge gulps of breath, nearly crashing to my knees.

"He will kill you if I say so. Is that clear?" Dr. O asks, implying that these may not just be the government-issued security guards Grayson suggested.

He doesn't wait for my response.

We're moving again. Dr. O doesn't have to drag me, not with T-Bone's weapon trained at my side. Still, the director's arm stays tight around my shoulders as we walk.

He's going to kill me.

I have to run.

I have to get away.

I'm the only one who can stop him.

We're nearing the parking garage. He'll have a car there, and even though the police sound close, they aren't here yet.

Fighting my fear, I turn toward Dr. O, secretly sliding my hand into the pouch of the dress to pull free the folding knife. I hide it tight in my fist, blood pumping in my ears.

I'm not going to die tonight.

I'm not going to let him win.

"Where are we going?" Even my whisper trembles.

"Nowhere you need to concern yourself with," he says.

"You won't get far."

He scoffs at this. Mist rises on the air as we come to the concrete corner of the parking garage. I know this entrance. It was where I met Grayson just before he took me to Susan's crash site.

"What makes you think that?" he asks, as T-Bone opens the metal door, and does a quick scan of the area. The light over the stoop buzzes in the cold dark, its yellow glow deepening the shadows of Dr. O's grimace.

"You have nothing left," I tell him, my confidence the only delaying tactic I have left. Once I use the knife in my hand, I'll have only seconds before T-Bone tries to shoot me.

I need to make those seconds count.

"Your friends are gone—everyone sees who you really are now. You can't blackmail us anymore after what you've done. You don't even have any money."

His teeth flash in a thin smile as T-Bone motions us across the open alley between the rows of cars. I recognize the black town car with the tinted windows from when it arrived at Vale Hall earlier.

We're getting too close. If I get in that car, it's game over.

"You think just because you know about some extra accounts, I don't have any money? Do you really think I'm that stupid?" His hand clenches painfully around my shoulder. "I knew you found out about that. I have ears everywhere. If you try to steal from me, I think you're going to be disappointed."

"I'm not trying to steal from you," I say, amused, even now, that he thinks Ms. Maddox overhearing my conversation with Margot was all he needed to guess my true intentions. "I already have," I say.

Dr. O goes still.

"All Tim Loki's overseas accounts closed once you realized we were on to you. But that money had to go somewhere, didn't it? Right into his private U.S. account. I mean . . . *your* private U.S. account, right?"

Those companies Damien mentioned are likely shells—ways to funnel the money from Wednesday Pharmaceuticals into different accounts to avoid taxes and keep his options open in case he has to cut bait and run.

It's what he used to do when I . . . was alive.

I meet Dr. O's glare, watching the doubt dig trenches between his brows, and his lips curl in fury.

"You don't know what you're talking about. You don't have access to that account."

"Senator." T-Bone's voice is cold, but laced with urgency. He's got the back door to the car open.

"Sure I do," I say. "Tim Loki made it public earlier this week. Turns out, it isn't that hard to turn a private account into a trust for the students of Vale Hall. The Jimmy Balder Memorial Fund has been writing checks all week long. You had a lot of alumni who were owed some big money."

Is there a program for hustling bank managers? Because it turns out I'm pretty good at that.

Caleb turning his father's trust into an account to pay their medical bills gave me the idea of how to handle Tim Loki's funds. After that, it was just a matter of signing the papers.

"No," says Dr. O, jerking me to face him. He's shaking his head so hard his jowls wobble. "That's impossible. I would have had to be there in person to sign the transfer."

"We didn't need you," I say, a slick, greedy vengeance now clawing to the surface of my fear. "We had an Emmy-winning actor play the role. He was better than the real thing, so I hear."

Step three, we take his money.

I see the moment it clicks in his brain. The panic that tightens his grim expression. The rage that chases it from sight.

I want him to feel it all.

I want him afraid. I want him *furious*.

I want him to know that we cut him down, one lie at a time, until there was nothing left but an empty shell.

"Let her go."

A male voice booms off the low cement ceiling, making me jump. I turn to find Moore striding through the entrance of the parking garage in his black suit. His head is lowered, a cat ready to pounce. He's holding a gun in his hands, and isn't slowing.

He doesn't see T-Bone.

The next seconds happen in freeze-frames.

Dr. O shields himself with my body.

Moore lowers his weapon, drops his shoulders.

Charges toward us.

My hands are raised to stop him.

The shot reverberates off the ceiling.

Crack!

My ears ring in the aftermath.

Moore spins and falls to his side, clutching the side of his chest. Then his arm flops to the ground, and he is still.

CHAPTER 36

N o!" I'm screaming. I unlatch the knife and drive it behind me blindly. It sinks into the flesh of Dr. O's thigh.

He shouts in pain and shoves me down. My knees hit the pavement. The blade is still lodged in his leg as he takes two hobbling steps toward the car, then stops, and pulls the metal free with a sickening *slurp*.

"Get in!" T-Bone is shouting. But I can't look at him, because Dr. O is staring down at me with wrath in his beady eyes. He's got the knife in his hand, and I'm unarmed.

I scramble back on my hands and heels, crabwalking, flipping in a tangle of tulle onto my side.

"I underestimated you." Spit sprays from his mouth. "I see that—"

Crack!

With a scream, I flatten against the ground, but Dr. O doesn't fall. It's T-Bone. He caves forward on his knees, the gun sliding across the ground toward me.

I spin to see Moore, half kneeling, his weapon now aimed at Dr. O.

"Brynn, run!" he shouts to me, his collar now stained red from the shot to his shoulder.

He doesn't need to tell me twice.

I jump up, grab T-Bone's gun, and race behind Moore. Other people are coming now—I see their shadows in the mouth of the garage, but my gaze darts too quickly to latch on to anyone. Moore shoots again, but Dr. O dives into the car, surprisingly nimble. I hear the door open and slam shut.

He's inside. He's going to get away.

Moore rises, his left arm dangling at his side.

"Get out of here," he growls.

I grip T-Bone's gun, slightly behind him. I'm not leaving. I'm not letting Dr. O escape.

Footsteps race toward us. Henry. Grayson. Margot. *Caleb.*

They block the exit of the parking garage, standing shoulder to shoulder with me. No questions. No hesitation.

"He's in the car!" Through the windows, I can see Dr. O in the driver's seat. Does he have the keys?

"He's not going anywhere," Grayson says. I don't know how he's so confident.

From behind us come more footsteps and shouts. *Stand down!* Someone yells. *Sikawa City Police!* The sirens are deafening now.

"Put down the gun," Moore tells me.

I wait for him to lower his first, and he does. The police swarm around us in seconds, a sea of black uniforms, blocking my view of the car, cutting me off from my friends. The gun now feels like it's twenty pounds. I nearly drop it before Moore snags it out of my hands.

"My student . . ." I hear him growl. "She's no threat." His arm is around my shoulders, pinning me to his side. I can see the blood soaking through the shoulder of his coat.

"He needs a doctor!" I shout.

Up the garage's incline, T-Bone is being loaded onto a stretcher. His car is surrounded by cops aiming their weapons at the driver's seat.

Dr. O is still inside.

Rage shoots through me, hotter than adrenaline.

Get out, I will him, through the wall of black uniforms. *Get out!*

A woman's voice, pitched in fear, breaks through the noise.

"Leave those students alone! They are not the problem here! Hugh! *Hugh!*" Susan shoves through the crowd to our side, leaning heavily on a cane. Ms. Maddox is close behind her. "You've been . . ." Susan nods quickly, jaw flexed. "We need a paramedic!" She's tossing out orders like a drill sergeant, and people fall in line right and left.

"Where is he?" Susan demands. Her path through the crowd has opened a lane for Caleb, Henry, and Grayson to rejoin the group. I lunge toward Caleb, my arms around his waist, his hands in my hair.

"Still in the car," Grayson says. "I unhooked the battery. Didn't want him to try to get behind the wheel again."

"I wondered where you ran off to," Margot says.

"How did you know which car was his?" asks Caleb.

"Did I say *his* battery? I meant *every* battery on this floor," says Grayson.

Beside him, Henry grins. "He's nothing if not dedicated."

Grayson blushes.

"Hands up!" shouts a cop as the car door opens. Caleb grips me tighter, but I don't turn away. I want to watch this. Dr. O needs to see that we're still standing.

He steps out of the car, and brushes off his white waiter's jacket. His chin lifts, just as proud as it was the first day I met him at Vale Hall. Blue lights from the nearby cop cars flash across the side of his face. He limps out, his pants stuck to his thigh with blood.

"Please," he says, hands rising. "There's been a huge misunderstanding. I'm sure once we talk this through with my lawyer—Ms. Maddox!" he shouts, when he sees her. One last attempt to pull at old loyalty. "Ms. Maddox, call my lawyer!"

Ms. Maddox stands straighter than I've ever seen, and shakes her head in a firm no.

Dr. O bares his teeth. "They've gotten to her. They're working against me. You'll all see—"

One of the officers grabs him and throws him against the side of the car.

"David Odin, you're under arrest for the attempted murder of Susan Griffin. You have the right to remain silent. You have the right . . ." He continues to spout off the Miranda rights, but I'm too busy watching the silver glint of the handcuffs close around Dr. O's wrists.

Maybe he'll stay in prison. Maybe he'll meet Pete there.

Maybe he'll be out before the end of the year.

It doesn't matter. We've taken his power. He has nothing left to come home to.

Moore grunts in pain as a paramedic forces him to sit on a gurney they've wheeled up behind us. He tells them he doesn't need to lie down. He's fine.

Susan points to the bed, and with another grunt, he does exactly as the paramedic asks.

"Is he going to be okay?" I ask.

"Of course I'm going to be okay. He barely clipped me," Moore says irritably.

"He'll be fine once I give him a sedative," the paramedic deadpans.

"There he is. There!" Marching through the crowd comes Mayor Santos, still wearing her red gown, cinched tight across the waist. She's pointing a condemning finger at Dr. O, and leading a giant of a man in a gray, ankle-length coat.

At the sight of him, my mouth goes dry.

"Officers, thank you for your diligent efforts here tonight," Mayor Santos says, "but I believe this is the FBI's jurisdiction, isn't that right?"

"Yes, ma'am," says Geri's father, flashing what looks like a legitimate silver badge at his belt. The crowd moves around him as he walks—not just because of his proclaimed title, but the sheer volume of his shoulders.

Dr. O gives a quick huff of relief, then drops his head.

Geri's dad is the FBI agent the mayor was talking about? My stomach plummets as I envision Dr. O setting this up, but he couldn't have. He wouldn't have known we'd go to Camille Santos and her mother.

Fury trills through my veins. This can't happen. I need to stop this. He's not getting away like this.

Where is Geri? She was supposed to keep her dad clear of this event tonight! She said he'd promised he wouldn't come. Desperation, hot and slick, slides down my spine.

I glance at Caleb, but his jaw is set.

Grayson and Henry don't seem to have any clue what's going on either.

Beside them, Margot looks like she's seen a ghost. I don't blame her—the last time she saw Frank Allen, he was driving Jimmy

Balder away. Henry, standing closest to her, puts a steadying arm around her waist, but she doesn't seem to notice.

"Finally, I have the proof to end this," Mayor Santos spits at Dr. O. "Those pills you had your henchman give my daughter? Nice try. We'll be adding extortion to your long list of crimes, David."

Dr. O's face warps to confusion, but he doesn't say a word.

I jolt forward, but Caleb's gripping my hand. When I look back, he gives a quick shake of his head. He's right, and it kills me. We can't say anything. We can't make it look like we had anything to do with this.

The path clears as Geri's father takes Dr. O roughly by the handcuffs and leads him toward a car parked across the exit of the garage. He shoves Dr. O in the back seat, and after a few short words with one of the policemen, gets inside the car.

I don't know what to do. We ruined him, but this still feels like a loss.

"Don't look so worried." Geri's strides up from behind us, her arms crossed. "This ride won't be as comfortable as Dr. O thinks."

"What are you talking about?" I ask.

Her mouth turns up at the corner; she's a vengeful pixie to the end. "Let's just say my dad's working for the new director of Vale Hall."

My gaze shoots to the ambulance. The back is open, and Susan stands in the bright lights from inside. Her hand is still in Moore's, but her hard gaze cuts through the windshield of Frank Allen's car.

Her chin dips in a nod.

My throat goes dry.

When this is done, you leave my brother to me.

"Oh," says Henry weakly. "I suppose it's safe to assume we won't be seeing Dr. O again."

"That would be a safe assumption," says Geri, giving Margot a small smile as she wipes at the tears gathering in her eyes. "Though Susan didn't want him dead. Just roughed up a bit and taken somewhere outside the country. It should be hard getting back with no money and no identification."

A smile tips the corners of my mouth. The knots between my shoulders begin to untie, one by one. Even Margot seems to think this is an acceptable solution.

"So we did it," I say. It feels too good to be true. My eyes turn to Ms. Maddox, taking notes on a small pad as Susan dictates a list of orders. I'm not sure where that pile of folders ended up, but with Susan in charge, I'm not worried. She'll protect us, like her brother always promised. "How'd you turn Ms. Maddox?"

Margot tucks a stray hair behind her ear. "Same way I tried to get you. By pretending to be someone else."

My brow quirks.

"Maddox has access to everyone's messages—it's part of her security clearance so that if there's a breach, she can wipe everyone's devices clean."

I think of Raf—of the message she intercepted on Moore's phone with his address—and my heart pangs.

"So I knew she'd see a message from Belk to Dr. O, especially if it came right before a security breach," Margot continues.

"We just had one of those," says Henry. "Ms. Maddox cleared all our phones."

"You don't say." She grins.

"You did that," I realize. "You caused the security breach."

"I wasn't going to that meeting to get Belk's gun," she says. "I was there to get his phone. The gun—that was just for show to trigger the security protocol."

Belk told me he'd lost his phone when he grabbed me in the woods outside Susan's cabin. I didn't even think that Margot might have taken it.

"When I was running from town hall to the train yards, I sent a message from Belk's phone to Dr. O's that he would take care of Maddox. Two minutes after I sent it, the phone went blank. I burned it in the fire Belk was so kind to start for us."

"So she thought Dr. O wanted her dead," says Caleb. "That Belk was coming for her."

Margot nodded. "She's thought she was safe for too long."

"You could have let me know," I say. "I only gave you that message about Dr. O's accounts because I knew Ms. Maddox was listening." A lot hinged on that interaction—if that information hadn't been relayed to Dr. O, we wouldn't have been able to get to his money.

Margot laughs. "Of course she was listening. Which is why I gave her my own message."

Lines crease the space between my brows as I think back to our conversation in the dining room. *He'll get rid of all of us. It's just a matter of time. And if you trust Dr. O when he says you're safe, you're stupider than I thought.*

I'd thought she was angry with me when she'd said this. I'd worried that her raised voice would attract the wrong attention. But it didn't. The message went exactly where she'd wanted it to.

"You didn't need to worry. I saw Paz eavesdropping on the other side of the kitchen and knew she'd take your message to Dr. O just like you wanted, even if Ms. Maddox was having a change of heart." She makes a show of examining her nails. "Tonight, all I had to do was tell Ms. Maddox it was our only chance to save ourselves. She was more than happy to join the party."

I stare at Margot, then laugh. She's gotten me again. I didn't even see this coming.

She smiles, and for the first time since I thought she was Myra, I think we might actually make pretty good friends.

"This is a fun game of who's the better con," interrupts Geri, "but don't you have a plane to catch?"

She's talking to Margot, whose grin widens. With a nod, she turns, only to stop, spin back, and wrap Geri in a tight hug.

"Thanks," she says quietly.

"No problem," says Geri, blushing.

As Margot hurries away, cutting in the line of gala attendees trying to catch a cab, I turn my questioning gaze to Geri.

"Where's she off to?"

"To find Jimmy, I guess," says Geri, beaming now.

Caleb looks to me, his eyes wide with concern.

"Did I say my dad didn't tell me everything?" Geri shrugs. "Maybe that's not entirely true."

"Wait. He's alive?" Caleb asks.

"In Malaysia. Which is where Margot's heading tonight."

I blink at her, too impressed to be angry. Jimmy Balder, the intern I once conned my way through Sterling's staff for information on, Margot's lost love, is still out there. I can't believe it, but Geri's face is 100 percent smug, and I know she's telling the truth.

Apparently she wins the best con prize.

Beside me, Caleb and Henry are laughing in disbelief.

"I couldn't tell anyone until we were sure Dr. O wouldn't find out," she says. "I guess it doesn't matter if he knows now."

"You are the best liar in the world," says Henry.

"Hi," says Grayson. "I did a pretty decent job."

"Yeah." Henry pets his shoulder. "Better than Brynn pretending to be a snitch, anyway."

"Hey," I say, as Caleb's hands circle my waist. I feel his low, rumbling laugh as he pulls me against his chest.

In the flashing blue lights, I watch Geri's dad drive Dr. O away from the Rosalind Hotel. As the ambulance doors close behind Moore and Susan, I think of Margot and Jimmy Balder. Dylan—Charlie now—and Renee, and Raf. All the things we've lost, all the things we've fought for.

Then I look up at Grayson, his arm over Henry's shoulders, and a peaceful smile on his face, and I lean back against Caleb's chest, and squeeze Geri's hand beside me.

We're going to be all right, because we've got each other. This family is the home I've been looking for all my life.

"What happens now?" I ask as Charlotte and Sam find their way through the crowd to our sides.

"Susan said she'll call with an update on Moore," says Geri. "She'll meet us back at school."

"Which means there's time for an after party," Charlotte says, and when we gape her way, she throws up her hands. "What? There's at least five unopened crates of sparkling cider and a check with my name on it in the ballroom. I'd say that's cause for a celebration, wouldn't you?"

"Works for me," says Sam.

"I'm in," says Grayson.

Henry grins. "Will there be dancing?"

I think of Henry and Grayson sliding gracefully across the floor in our ballroom dance PE class and grin.

"I hope not," says Caleb with a wince. He was never a very good dancer.

"Excuse me! Over here!"

"Ugh," says Geri, turning her back away from the news reporters now charging toward us.

"What do we tell them?" asks Henry.

"To get lost," says Grayson flatly. "I hate the press."

They shout their names and news stations, begging us for a comment as the flashes go blinding. We ignore them, striding quickly back to the hotel, but I pause when one woman's voice rises over the rest.

"Brynn Hilder! R. G. Rock with *Pop Store*! Can any of you tell us anything? *Anything*, please!"

I turn to face the reporter with an apple-shaped face and red-framed glasses.

Anything?

My friends grin as I lift my hand and wave. "Hi, Mom." I know she's watching.

And then, a giddy laugh bubbling up my throat, I slide under Caleb's arm, and we head inside for the after party.

EPILOGUE

One year later

O ne final question, Ms. Hilder. What do you hope to get out of your time at Prosedda College?"

I sit before six scholarship committee members in a classroom with wide windows and long wood tables. The speaker, a man with kind eyes, a full beard, and patches on the elbows of his tweed jacket, leans over his forgotten notepad. Beside him, a woman with a white streak in her black hair is nodding, though I've yet to answer.

I've got them hooked, I just need to reel them in.

"That's easy," I say. "I want the skills to change the world."

One of the committee members—a man with a German shepherd lying calmly at his side—chuckles at this. "How will you know when you have them?"

"I don't know," I answer, smiling. "I don't know what I want to be. I don't know what I'm going to do. All I know is that there are holes in this city that need patching. There are kids like me slipping through the cracks every day, and people who would try to exploit them instead of help them." I take a slow breath.

Think about who you are. What makes you, you, right now. And if that's not the person you want to be, use the next few years as a vehicle to get you there.

What happened to you're fine just the way you are?

Then I suppose you, like me, have found your place in this world.

"I don't have the answers. All I can tell you is that I know how to fix things, and if you give me the chance, I'll be able to do more. I've found where I'm supposed to be, now I want to make it better."

The committee members are smiling. A woman in a black suit claps her hands and says, "Well said!"

"Thank you, Ms. Hilder," says the man who asked the question. "You'll be hearing back from us soon, I think."

"Thank you," I tell him. "And thank you all for agreeing to meet me so soon before the semester starts."

I rise to shake their hands. The man with the dog holds mine tight and says, "I enjoyed the stories of your travels immensely. You're going to do great things, Brynn."

I appreciate him saying so, but I don't need this validation anymore. I know I'm going to.

I've already started.

I applied to three colleges after Susan Griffin took over as director of Vale Hall—all of them in Sikawa City—but Shrew convinced me I had a little soul searching to do before I settled down. It didn't take much to convince Caleb to join me, and we spent the summer traveling through Colombia, looking for my aunt Daniela, whom we finally connected with at the end of July. She brought us into her home, and for two weeks fattened us up on *arepas de queso* and fried empanadas and showed us all the places where my father grew up.

And then we found Rise Up—an international program dedicated to building houses in impoverished areas, and the sweltering days of August stretched into the greatest four months of my life.

Caleb and I lived with host families in each of the towns we went to. We made friends with the women who worked the *tiendas*, and drank sodas out of glass bottles in their air-conditioned shops, and stayed up late watching stars with ranchers and their herds of cattle. We fell in love with the people, and made things to help them. We built strong, beautiful things that wouldn't break, and it healed the parts that had been scraped raw inside us.

When fall came, we decided not to wait another semester to go to college. Caleb missed his father, and I missed Mom.

It was time to come home.

Outside the humanities building, I wrap my scarf, a present from Tia Daniela, tighter around my neck, and zip up my coat to fend off the cold. It hasn't snowed in days, but the ground is still covered in white, and the spindly tree branches gleam with icy tips.

On the bottom of the steps, a boy leans against the railing, the collar of his jacket pulled up around his neck, his black hair gleaming in the afternoon sun. His glasses are slightly crooked as he smirks down at his phone, and, as always, my heart does a slow roll in my chest at the sight of him.

When he hears the door close, he looks up and holds out his arms.

"How'd it go?"

I jog down the steps, launching into his embrace. My cheek finds the perfect place on his shoulder. His chin rests on my head. I keep my eyes open, looking at the snowy quad where I've seen pictures of students in Prosedda College Valkyrie shirts playing Frisbee when the weather's nice, and the stone building behind me that Caleb was sure to mention was built in 1827.

In three weeks, I'm starting here.

I have a feeling I'm going to love it.

"Good, I think. What were you smiling about?"

"We got new pictures."

"Oh, gimme!" I grab at his phone, realizing mine's been off since my interview began, and scan through the newest text from Charlotte and Sam of baby Chloe. At eight months old, she still doesn't have much hair, but she drools like a champ, and her smile is all Charlotte's.

She's wearing a onesie that says *My aunt is better than yours.*

"Are they still good for tonight?"

Caleb nods. Charlotte and Sam live in Southern California now. He's taking long-distance courses at NYU, and she's going to UCLA and spending a few days a week at a law internship. Money's a little tight, but the Jimmy Balder Memorial Fund covers child care and their apartment.

I miss them like crazy, but we video chat once a week. They're coming home for a visit in February. It'll be Chloe's first plane ride, and our first time seeing them since we got home from Colombia.

I have a daily countdown in my room at Mom's, where I'll be staying until I move into the dorms in two weeks.

"I have more good news," Caleb says. "Unless you want to be surprised."

"I hate surprises. Better to know everything up front, that way I can manipulate what I need to in order to get what I want."

Caleb grins. "Spoken like a true Raven."

I laugh. Susan sends messages to check in on us from time to time, but Dr. O still hasn't surfaced. I know he's out there somewhere, maybe plotting revenge, but the power he wielded over us is gone. He's alone, somewhere far away, and we're moving on with the futures he promised.

"Waiting," I remind Caleb as we begin walking toward the edge of campus and the SCTA station, where a train will take us into Uptown for tonight's festivities.

"It's not just going to be Henry and Grayson at dinner."

I side-eye him, wondering if Henry's still dragging Grayson around the city looking for decorations for Henry and Caleb's dorm room. They'll be six rooms away from mine in the new building Mayor Santos just had renovated over the summer. A lot of schools have social work majors, but not a lot have top-rated architecture programs and a best friend to bunk with.

Grayson, much to the frustration of his parents, is going to Sikawa State instead of a fancy private school, where he's planning to major in psychology. He'll be a twenty-minute train ride away, and, as Henry's informed me on multiple occasions, he'll have a private room.

"Go on," I prompt.

"Geri's coming," he says. And as if that's not good enough, he adds, "She's bringing a date."

"Marcus?" I practically squeal. "I thought he wasn't coming back until the wedding!"

Caleb laughs.

Geri and Marcus continued their relationship over the phone after our visit to Baltimore, and over the summer, she spent two weeks at a theater camp at University of Maryland. Needless to say, things got a little steamy, and they've been flying back and forth ever since.

Geri's already returned the plus-one response to Moore and Susan's wedding, happening over spring break in March.

"Best night ever." I pull him down for a kiss hot enough to make my jacket seem no longer necessary, and to have me wondering if we can make it to Mom's apartment before she gets off work.

Caleb's ink-stained fingers link through mine, reminding me we have time.

We have all the time in the world.

As we walk toward the train station, I can hear the birds in the trees, and the rush of the cars on the faraway highway, and laughter from some people gathered outside the library. I can hear that laughter in Devon Park now when we drive through, though I don't remember hearing it when I lived there. It's still not exactly a destination resort, but I don't think of it with the same resentment I always did.

It's a part of the city that made me, and the girl I turned out to be isn't half bad.

"You think they'll give you a full ride?" Caleb asks as we cross beneath a stone archway bearing the words *Prosedda College*. Warmth laces up my arm as his thumb traces along the inside of my wrist.

The Jimmy Balder fund went to every student Dr. O had ever promised a future to—from Renee, now sucessfully hiding somewhere out west, all the way to Charlie. Those who we lost along the way had funds delivered to their families. I deferred my scholarship, as did Henry and Grayson. We gave it all to Caleb, to take care of his father. It was hard for him to accept such a big gift, but the truth was, we didn't want Dr. O's money, and someone needed it more.

The rest of the account was set up by Susan to feed into Vale Hall, to help the students there get the best education they could in order to be eligible for scholarships and awards.

I think they're all doing pretty well on their tracks to greatness.

"I don't know," I say. "If they don't, I'm sure I'll think of something."

He laughs, and as we climb the platform to our train, a gust of wind plays with the ends of my long hair. Full ride or not, I'm going to be okay. Because here's the truth: some people get lucky, and some don't.

The rest of us? We make our own luck.

ACKNOWLEDGMENTS

I am not ready for this journey to be over! Can we please all stay at Vale Hall forever?

I have so much to be grateful for with this series. First, thank you, reader, for joining the flock and becoming a Raven. From the beginning, I knew this series would be special. I felt it in my bones. At night, when I lay in bed, I dreamed of Brynn and her crew. I giggled wickedly at the twists and turns this story would take. At no point during the writing of it, did I ever suffer through the process. Some books sing to you. From *The Deceivers* to *Payback*, I heard nothing but music.

So thank you for being a part of it.

Thank you to my editor, Melissa Frain, for making these books the best they could be, and for loving these characters as much as I did. Thank you for swooning and laughing at all the right parts, for pushing me when we needed to go deeper, and for all your "!!!" when I threw twists your way. You are forever my reader. Vale Hall will always be as much yours as it is mine.

Thank you to my agent, Joanna MacKenzie, for taking my hand and leading me in this direction. Before Vale Hall, I was at a point in my career where I was starting to wonder if I still had it. Enter Joanna, who compiled a physical list of all my strengths and joys in writing, and helped me find the road to Brynn and her crew. I wish every writer had an agent in their corner like you.

Thank you to my editor, Ali Fisher, for swooping in and helping with logistics, and your thoughtful feedback along the way. Thank you to Saraciea for being an amazing publicist always, but especially during these crazy Covid times. Thank you to Anthony and Isa for your great marketing ideas and implementation, and your support along this journey. Thank you to Michael Frost Photography for these truly excellent covers, and to Hania, Nate, and Jacques—you are truly the embodiments of Brynn, Caleb, and Grayson.

Thank you to Kathleen Doherty for beginning this road and Devi Pillai for finishing it.

I'm so grateful for my writing friends who've been there for me along the way: Katie McGarry, where would I be without you? Mindee Arnett, my voice of reason. Sara, the other half of my brain. I would be nowhere without my mom friends, and my workout friends, and of course, my family. Mom and Dad, Steve and Elizabeth, Lisa, Lindsay, and Deanna and Craig. I love you. Thank you for loving me back!

And last but not least, thank you to Jason, for making me believe in love, and to Ren, for being my everything.